Elizabeth Wren is an Australian author with a passion for the Victorian era, especially the might-have-been and never-was Victorian world of steampunk. She enjoys writing men with feelings, women with brains, and couples with happily-ever-afters. Elizabeth lives in Sydney with her husband and daughter.

ELIZABETH WREN

The Scotland Steampunk COLLECTION

TEA DREAMS

FLYING HIGH

HIDDEN DEPTHS

PAC BOOKS

First published by PAC Books in 2024

www.pacbooks.com.au

A catalogue record for this book is available from the National Library of Australia

ISBN-13: 978-0-6489825-5-5

CONTENTS

TEA DREAMS
Chapter 1

The muggy Hong Kong air hit Genevieve Conlon like a bucket of water to the face. She wondered how the locals could stand it; even at five o'clock in the morning it was overpowering. She felt a very long way from home. She'd had plenty of time on the airship from London to get used to the idea, but now she'd been here for twenty-four hours, her mission was about to start, and she was still completely overwhelmed by the noise, smells and utter foreignness of the place. Somehow, she had to pull herself together before she met her target. It was vital that he didn't realise she was a blow-in.

She'd barely had time to get her bearings in the city after her airship had docked at the cruiser terminal the previous morning. She'd spent the night at an unremarkable hotel, and now she was trying to find the commercial airfield. It seemed ridiculous to travel all this way by one method only to head straight back home again by another, but such was the nature of the job. Her governor, Inspector Thomas Flint, had made it clear there'd be no time for sightseeing.

"We've had a tip-off about a major smuggling operation out of Hong Kong," he'd said when he'd called her into his office a month earlier. "Intercepting it will be our best chance of bringing down the Eismans." His walrus moustache twitched, as it always did when he was agitated.

Gen raised her eyebrows. The Eismans were the most powerful crime family in Scotland, and until now they'd been all but untouchable. Everyone knew what they got up to—mostly smuggling and trading stolen goods—but pinning it on them was another matter.

"What are they smuggling, sir?"

"Tea," Flint said. Gen knew better than to be surprised. With import duties on tea at 110 per cent, four-fifths of the tea drunk in Britain was smuggled, and Scotland was a particularly lucrative market.

"We've tried to catch them at it before," Flint said, "but we're always too late. They change their plans at the last minute and move the cargo before we can inspect them at the airfield. Our intelligence doesn't seem able to keep up."

"So why do you need me, sir?" She'd worked these kinds of operations back in London, but that had been a long time ago, before everything had gone belly-up and she'd been demoted and packed off to Edinburgh in disgrace.

"You served in the Aerofleet, correct?"

"Yes sir, for five years before I joined the force."

"So you know your way around an airship, then?"

"Well ... yes, sir."

"Good. Turns out you're the only one around here who does. We want to put an operative undercover on the Eisman airship, to confirm that the cargo is there on departure from

Hong Kong and help make arrests when it reaches port in Edinburgh—and, more to the point, to keep us appraised of any changes to the schedule on the way."

"Undercover as what, sir?"

"You'll be serving as crew. Rumour has it the Eismans run these missions very light—usually only the captain and one crew member—so there's fewer people to talk. So there'll be nowhere to hide. Can you handle that?"

Gen swallowed.

"I ... I don't know, sir."

Memories of her last undercover operation assailed her. Thanks to her, her partner—and best friend—had paid the ultimate price. Ever since, she'd burned through a series of partners, not wanting to let them trust her; she didn't want to let someone down again. And she knew Flint had noticed.

Her boss crossed his arms and stared balefully at her.

"I won't lie to you, Genevieve," he said. "Your performance to date has been...suboptimal. I've had to go out on a limb just to keep you on. You weren't our first choice for this—but unfortunately you were our only choice. And if you don't perform on this mission, or if indeed you choose not to go, then I'm afraid I'll have no option but to dismiss you."

Gen stared at him for a moment. She knew things had been bad, but she hadn't realised just how dire they'd got. And she was nothing without her job. She took a deep breath, then squared her shoulders. This was the chance she'd been waiting for—the chance to show everyone, including herself, that she was still a good cop. The chance for redemption.

"Yes, sir."

Flint frowned. "Good."

NOW THAT SHE WAS FINALLY here, after four days meandering across most of Europe and half of Asia on the cruiser, she wasn't so sure. The airfield gates loomed before her in the half-light, and she patted her pocket containing the all-important letter of introduction. She hoped it would be enough.

The gate was manned by a standard service automaton, its domed brass head gleaming in the dawn light. It looked at Gen and then said something in Cantonese that she didn't understand. She shook her head.

"English?" she asked.

"Name?" the automaton said.

"Genevieve Morrison." They'd agreed it was less risky to keep her real first name, so only the surname was false. She handed over her papers, hoping the police forgers had done their work well.

"Ship?"

"The *Blue Diamond*." The automaton whirred for a moment, and Gen wondered if it was running through a list of ships in its head. Then its eyes clicked back into focus. It handed back her papers.

"Proceed. Berth thirty-two."

"Thank you," she said, but the automaton had already moved on to the next person.

The airfield was laid out in neat rows of berths, each marked with a wooden number. As she neared her destination, Gen's nerves increased. She took a deep breath, trying to calm the churning in her stomach, but she couldn't shake the feeling that she was making a terrible mistake. Her last undercover operation had been a disaster—what was to stop this one going the same way? But it was too late to back out now—if nothing else, she wanted to keep her job.

She swallowed, hitching her haversack higher up her shoulder, and continued along the row until she reached berth 32. The *Blue Diamond* was smaller than she'd expected—a trim little freighter designed for speed. She supposed its size helped it not to stand out, and it could be flown with minimal crew. Its gondola looked more like a regular sailing ship than the sleek, fully enclosed ones she'd served on in the Aerofleet, with an open deck and a substantial hold below. She wondered if the contraband tea had already been loaded.

A man who looked to be a couple of years older than her was on the deck, coiling ropes and generally making the place shipshape. Gen squared her shoulders, adopted what she hoped was an expression of casual confidence, and hailed him.

"Hello there! I'm looking for Captain William Eisman."

He paused in his work and stood looking down at her. His fair hair was cropped short, and there was two days' worth of stubble on his chin. He was tall, and his rough white shirt was unable to hide his well-muscled arms.

"That's me."

"I'm your crew."

Will Eisman frowned. "You're not Matthias."

"No, sir. I'm his cousin. My name's Genevieve Morrison. Most people call me Gen." She dug in her pocket and fished out the letter. "He asked me to give you this."

She approached the ship, and Will walked down the gangway. He took the letter from her and scanned it.

"This seems to be in order," he said at last.

I should hope so, Gen thought. Matthias Cole was a small-time crook who hired out his services to the likes of the Eismans, as well as dabbling in his own various shady ventures. It had been an easy job to pick him up and squeeze the letter out of him as the price of his freedom. As a further incentive, Flint had strategically arrested some of Matthias's competitors. If Matthias kept quiet, he'd get a clear run at his business. But if word of the sting got back to the Eismans, Flint would let all the crooks go and tell them it was Matthias who'd turned them in. Matthias was a coward by nature and not that bright—Gen was confident he wouldn't talk.

Even so, she was surprised it had all happened so easily. Either Will Eisman was far too trusting, or he was planning to try and catch her out some other way. Close up, she could see the fierce intelligence in his brown eyes—he wouldn't be that easily fooled. She'd have to watch her back.

WILL EVALUATED THIS strange new arrival as she boarded the ship. Matthias had never mentioned a cousin, but that was hardly surprising. They'd always had a somewhat uneasy relationship—Matthias was one of his brother's men, and Will had long suspected that his true role was to spy on him. But the letter certainly looked authentic enough—Matthias's chicken-scratchings were unmistakable—and, when it came down to it, he needed a crew. The *Blue Diamond* was an easy ship to fly, but she had her quirks and he couldn't handle her alone. And this woman, Genevieve, knew what she was doing. There was a look that true aeronauts had, and as he watched her appraise the ship he could see it in her. He'd never flown with a female aeronaut before, but as a rule they were highly competent, mostly because they'd had to fight so much harder to earn their place. Now the trading companies were starting to recognise it, and there were more and more female captains appearing, much to the chagrin of the types of fliers—like his brother John—who spent more time in the portside bars than at the wheel of an airship. Personally, Will knew whom he'd rather trust his life to.

Still, he couldn't discount the fact that she could easily be a plant by his family to keep tabs on him. This was his first big solo mission—ridiculous really, considering his age and experience, but he knew it had nothing to do with his skill as a flier. John had chafed when their father had entrusted this job to Will, and had called him all the usual names, but for once the old man had held firm. Absentmindedly he rubbed his left thumb against the inside of his right wrist. This was the only chance he had to prove he was more than they all thought, and if Genevieve was indeed a family spy, then he'd just have to show her too.

"Come aboard and stow your dunnage," he said. "We leave in an hour."

"AN HOUR?" GEN GASPED. "So soon?"

Will raised an eyebrow. "The cargo was loaded earlier than expected," he said. "Time is money and all that. I trust there's no problem?"

Gen composed herself and shook her head.

"No, sir."

In actual fact, there was a problem—quite a large one. The original flight plan, around which the whole operation was based, had the *Blue Diamond* departing at dawn the following morning. If they kept the standard flight time and didn't delay during their stopover in Aden, they'd arrive a day early and the whole sting would be ruined. Gen took a deep breath. There were all sorts of things that could delay an airship *en route*. If they were still running early once they'd crossed the Arabian Sea, she'd just have to wire Flint from Aden. How she'd get away for long enough to do it was a problem she'd deal with when they got there.

Chapter 2

It was unusual to find a poorly patronised pub in Edinburgh, but the proprietor of the *Maiden's Arms* catered to a very specific clientele, who preferred a place where numbers were limited and there was less chance of being overheard. A dingy dive in one of the rougher parts of town, it was a favourite of those who frequented the city's underworld, and the landlord knew better than to ask any questions.

The two men who met there one drizzly evening weren't regulars; as part of Edinburgh's criminal elite, they considered themselves above the riffraff who patronised the *Maiden's Arms*. But they were making an exception, because they needed to talk somewhere where they would be neither overheard nor recognised.

The first man to arrive was young—around his late twenties—and good-looking, with smouldering dark eyes and an easy charisma evident even in the way he walked. He ordered a drink at the bar then took it to a booth in a dark, secluded corner of the pub. By the time his companion arrived, he'd been there long enough for people to forget that the booth was even occupied.

The second man was a good decade older than the first, with none of his friend's good looks or charm. He looked slightly rumpled, as if his clothes didn't quite fit, and his mousy brown hair was thinning on top, which he tried unsuccessfully to hide by growing one side long and combing it over. When drunk, he was given to boorishness; when sober, to a grandiosity of ambition disproportionate to his talents. He nodded at his younger companion as he sat down, but by prior arrangement neither of them used names.

"How's things?" he asked. "I could murder a pint."

The younger man signalled to the waitress, then waited until she returned with the drink before speaking.

"I heard the Eismans are planning a tea shipment out of Hong Kong. I don't suppose you know anything about that?"

The older man shrugged.

"Might do. What's your interest?"

"Well, I've been thinking. This Eisman–Haverford rivalry is getting ridiculous. It's bad for the market. What we need is a third party to inject a bit of...competition...into things."

"What did you have in mind?"

"A partnership."

"Like in London?"

The younger man's lips thinned.

"London was ... messy. This will be different. You've got the information we need, and I can get the men. We'll do a quick, clean interception of the shipment once it makes port here and sell the cargo fast. The money can finance future operations—once we've taken our cut, of course."

The older man frowned.

"You're asking a lot of me, you know. What sort of cut are we talking about? Sixty–forty?"

"Come now, that's hardly realistic. You've got to think beyond the money—think of the opportunity. I'm giving you the chance to finally run your own show. Isn't that what you've been banging on about for years now?"

"Well, yes, but…"

"But what? You'll never get a chance like this again. I'll tell you what, we'll split it three ways. A third for you, a third for me, and a third to go towards financing the ongoing operations. You can't ask fairer than that."

"They'll know the information came from me."

The younger man rolled his eyes, as if frustrated at having to do all the thinking.

"Not if it's plausibly deniable. There must be someone else it could be."

"You mean…frame someone?"

"Old Ralph Eisman runs a tight ship, but it can't possibly be that tight. There's always someone."

"Well, now that you mention it…"

The younger man held out his hand.

"So we have a deal, then?"

The older man nodded, and they shook.

"Excellent." The younger man stood. "I'll be in touch about the specifics. I suggest you start figuring out how to cover your tracks." He threw some coins on the table. "Buy yourself another drink on me."

After he left, the older man sat for some time, his mind twisting itself in knots. The shipment was leaving Hong

Kong even now, and unbeknownst to Will Eisman, the police were hot on its tail thanks to his timely tip-off. This vendetta was personal; he wanted more than anything to see Will squirm, particularly once his parents, Ralph and Shirley, realised what had happened. With any luck, Will would also be arrested. But this new development presented another opportunity. He could play the Haverfords, the police and the Eismans all off against each other: The police would arrive to intercept the Eisman shipment and would end up arresting the Haverfords, and he, with some loyal helpers, would be able to get his hands on the cargo in the meantime. Then he could either drop Ralph and Shirley in it with the law or use the whole episode as leverage to increase his influence with them—whatever took his fancy at the time. Either way, Will would be *persona non grata* with his family and, hopefully, would end up rotting in gaol.

The man smiled to himself over his pint, congratulating himself on his own genius. Now he just needed a suitable foil to implicate Will in tipping off the police and the Haverfords. Three beers later, one thing was clear—he would have to pay a visit to Matthias.

Chapter 3

Will led Gen down below and showed her to the first mate's cabin, located forward of the hold. It was small, but clean and comfortable—certainly better than the crew hammocks she'd bunked in during her time in the Aerofleet. In any case, she knew she'd really only be in there to sleep between watches; the rest of the time she'd be up on deck or in the galley.

"I'll give you a quick tour," Will said as she dropped her haversack at the end of the bed, "then we just need to do the final departure checklist and we're good to go."

"I'm sorry I wasn't here earlier, sir," Gen said. "Matthias told me you weren't leaving until tomorrow."

Will shrugged. "Last-minute change of plans," he said. "It happens. You're here now, and that's the main thing."

The ship was small enough that the tour didn't take long. She saw the hold, packed with wooden crates, their sides stamped with Chinese characters and the words 'Finest-Quality Tea'; she was a little surprised that they hadn't even bothered to try and disguise the smuggled contents. The galley was simple but functional, and she sighed with relief, because she knew one of her roles would be to cook the ship's meals. The engine room was aft of the hold, and the captain's cabin was up on the main forward deck.

"Now, come and meet the rest of the crew," Will said when the tour was complete and they were again standing topside.

"The rest?" Gen said, trying to hide her alarm as Will led her to the poop deck. Flint had told her it would be just the two of them—her job would be that much harder with more people watching.

"This is Alexander," Will said, gesturing to a figure at the wheel. It took a moment for Gen to realise that Alexander was an automaton—he was dressed in breeches and a shirt like an ordinary aeronaut, and his brass facial features were so exquisitely crafted that from a distance it was easy to mistake him for a real person.

"Pleased to meet you," Alexander said, offering his hand.

"Likewise," Gen said, tentatively shaking it.

"Alexander is our helmsman," Will said. "He flies the ship during the cruise phase, unless there's bad weather or other issues."

"Extraordinary," Gen breathed. She'd seen other service automatons in the Aerofleet, but they'd been clunky, boxy things designed to do one or two simple tasks—nothing as complex as piloting the ship. Alexander, on the other hand, was as close to human as it was possible for a creature made of brass to be.

"Right," Will said, glancing at his watch. "Time for final checks. Gen, take the mooring ropes and cast off on my signal. Alexander, man the throttle." He took the wheel and worked through the checklist, while Gen stowed the gangway then stationed herself at the mooring rope. She was surprised how good it felt to be back on board a working airship; it was as if she'd never left. Being a passenger on a cruiser didn't count.

Will picked up the thaumaturgical radio and spoke into it. "Hong Kong departure, *Blue Diamond* requesting clearance for launch."

There was a silence, then a voice crackled a response. "*Blue Diamond,* cleared for launch."

"Roger that." Will turned to Alexander. "Engines to full." He leaned over the railing and called to Gen, "Cast off!"

She loosened the mooring rope and attempted to haul it in, but it caught on the mooring mast. Too late, she realised she'd undone the wrong end—a basic mistake, and the first thing that new Aerofleet recruits were taught not to do. The airship rose, buoyed by the gasbag floating above the deck, and thrust forward with the momentum from the two powerful engines. If she didn't act quickly, the tangled rope would rip the mooring mast clean out of its socket, and she hated to think what would happen after that. She reached into her boot for the knife she always carried there—standard issue from her Aerofleet days for just such an emergency—and sawed frantically at the mooring rope. Will saw the danger and called to Alexander, and she felt the engines throttle back, but she knew they couldn't afford to lose too much power or they wouldn't get off the ground. She hacked away until, just as all seemed lost, the rope snapped and fell away, and the *Blue Diamond* was clear and free. Gen slumped on the deck rail in relief as Will and

Alexander piloted them out of the busy Hong Kong airfield and away over the harbour. It wasn't until they were out above the ocean and free of the city air traffic that Will handed control to the automaton and came down to the forward deck. His lips were thin and there was fury in his eyes.

"What the hell happened back there?" he asked. Gen had expected him to rant and rave as she'd known other captains to do, but this quiet, measured anger was somehow worse.

"I'm sorry, sir," she said, finding it hard to meet his eyes.

"Look at me when I'm talking to you, please, sailor."

She lifted her gaze. "It was my fault," she said. "I undid the wrong part of the rope and it got tangled. It was a silly mistake and I apologise. It won't happen again." Mentally she kicked herself—what a terrible way to start. She needed to earn Will Eisman's trust, not dazzle him with her incompetence. She was meant to be a working aeronaut, not an ex-Aerofleet sailor who hadn't flown for seven years.

Will stared at her gravely, but some of his fury seemed to have abated.

"I appreciate you taking responsibility," he said. "But we don't have room for mistakes. You risked our lives back there. Do that again and I'll put you off at the next port, do you understand?"

"Yes, sir."

"Fine. There's some spare rope in the hold. Can I trust you to tie on a new mooring line?"

"Of course, sir."

"Good. Get to it, then."

AS GEN HURRIED BELOW, Will rubbed his face in frustration. His immediate anger had fizzled out, leaving him wondering. Who was this woman, really? He could tell she knew her way around an airship, but to make such a simple mistake straight out was alarming. *Experienced, but rusty,* was his eventual conclusion. He briefly considered returning to Hong Kong—they had a long flight across the ocean ahead of them, and he was nervous about doing it with someone he didn't have complete faith in. But then he thought of what his parents would say, and immediately decided against it. This was his first solo job and he was on a deadline; he needed to get to Aden and then to Edinburgh on schedule. He needed to prove to them he could do it. He'd just have to take a risk and hope this mysterious Genevieve cleaned up her act, and quickly.

THE REST OF THE DAY passed uneventfully, but Gen could feel Will watching her whenever she was on deck, and she got the feeling he was just waiting for her to make another mistake. At lunchtime she did a quick inventory of the stores and was able to rustle up a passable meal in the galley, which seemed to earn her a little redemption, but she knew there was a long way to go. She tried to make it up by following Will's orders as quickly as possible and doing the thousand little tidying jobs that always needed to be done on a ship in flight, but she couldn't shake his gaze. She didn't like being thought incompetent; since the morning's incident, proving her worth had become less about maintaining her cover and more about showing him that she was indeed a capable aeronaut. She wasn't quite sure why she wanted Will Eisman to think well of her, but there it was.

In the late afternoon, the clouds began to build and the sky to darken in a way that Gen knew from experience didn't bode well. They ate an early dinner together on the deck, looking out with some apprehension at the clouds rearing up ahead of them, purplish-gold like an old bruise.

"I think we're going to be in for a bit of weather," Will said in what Gen thought would prove to be a massive understatement. "I'll take first watch—try to get some sleep if you can."

"Are you sure?"

"Of course. I'll call you if I need you."

It was much earlier than she'd usually go to bed, but one of the skills she'd developed in the Aerofleet was the ability to nap anywhere at any time. So, not long after crawling into her narrow bunk, she was sound asleep.

SHE WAS WOKEN SOMETIME later by the pitching and rolling of the airship. A glance at her watch showed she'd slept some three hours or so, and it was fully dark. She climbed up the ladder from belowdecks but, upon emerging through the hatch, she was immediately assailed by a violent gust of wind and driving rain. She hurried back to her cabin for her oilskin coat and sou'wester hat, then clambered back up onto the deck. Will was at the helm, fighting to keep the *Blue Diamond* on course. She'd wondered why he hadn't woken her, but it was clear there was no way he could leave the wheel, and Alexander wasn't built for climbing up and down ladders. She was just thankful she'd woken up when she had. Without waiting for orders, she began adjusting the guy ropes that attached the envelope to the gondola, and which had grown taught with the rain and were pinging like violin strings. The airship rolled as the wind caught it, then dropped with a stomach-churning thud as it hit an air pocket. Gen had flown through plenty of storms before, and she wasn't a nervous flier, but her heart began to race. This was one of the worst she'd seen, and with just the two of them it was going to be a fight to get through it.

"Where are we?" she asked as she clambered up to the poop deck, yelling against the gale.

"Over the Arabian Sea," Will bellowed back. "We're still a fair way from Aden, but we're getting a shove along with the wind."

Gen held onto the deck rail and tried to get her bearings. The wind was violent and gusty, and seemed to mainly be coming from behind them. But she could feel it beginning to change; after a few minutes, she was certain.

"The wind's turning," she said.

"What?"

"The wind's turning. We're going to get it broadside soon if we're not careful. You need to adjust the course."

Will looked at the compass and shook his head. "We're on course for Aden. If we adjust too much, who knows where we'll end up."

"It doesn't matter if we're a bit out. We can correct it once the storm's over. But you really don't want it broadside. Keep it at our back and we'll be out of it faster."

The wind had turned now, striking her right cheek rather than the back of her neck. The airship rolled violently as a gust hit it, sending Gen careering into Will.

"*Change course!*" she implored as they disentangled themselves. "Please! Trust me!"

He glanced at the compass again, then did as she said. As the wind moved aft, the ride became marginally smoother and they began to pick up speed. Gen sighed with relief, but almost immediately braced herself for the next impact. It was going to be a long night.

Chapter 4

It took several more hours for the storm to blow itself out, but eventually the wind began to drop, and the stars winked out between the raggedy clouds. Gen exhaled, feeling like she'd been holding her breath the whole time.

"I think we're out of the worst of it now," she said. She looked at the compass and the chart, trying to work out where they were. "We've come a bit too far south," she said, pointing to their position, "but we've made good time with the tailwind. I actually think we'll still get into Aden pretty much on schedule."

Will ran a hand over his face; he looked exhausted. "I owe you an apology," he said.

"What for?"

"For questioning your competence. You saved me from making what could have been a critical mistake. I'm sorry."

She shrugged. "It happens to the best of us. That's why you fly with a team."

"Well, I'm very glad you're on mine. When we get to Aden, I'll take you out for a proper meal to celebrate being back on solid ground."

Gen smiled. "I'd like that." She stretched, trying to loosen the tension in her shoulders. "Why don't you get some sleep? I'll wake you when we're on final approach."

As if to make her point, Will gave an enormous yawn. "Thanks." As he crossed the deck he turned, looking at her with something like respect. "You did well tonight."

"We both did. Sleep well." Gen watched him go into his cabin. She wondered what lay ahead in Aden, and why the prospect of dinner with Will Eisman in an exotic port city felt far more enticing than it should.

THE REST OF THE NIGHT passed uneventfully, and as they descended into Aden Gen's heart began to race with excitement. It was still quite early, but the port was bustling with activity. The airfield was at Steamer Point, near the main shipping port, and they landed to a scene of vigorous morning trade. Airships were arriving and departing, and the airfield was swarming with workers busily loading and unloading cargo. The air was warm, although not quite as muggy as Hong Kong, and redolent with spices and the smell of the sea. Gen breathed it in deeply as the *Blue Diamond* docked. She loved new places, but since leaving the Aerofleet she hadn't had much opportunity to travel.

"How long will we be here?" she asked, trying to sound casual.

"We'll leave tomorrow," Will said. "It'll probably take most of the day to get refuelled—you can see how busy it is. Why?"

"I've never been to Aden before. I'd like to have a look around—and telegraph my landlady. I want her to check on my cat." She hoped the lie would give her enough time to get a message to Flint.

"You know what, I'll come with you," Will said. "It's been a while since I did any sightseeing myself."

Gen's heart sank. "Oh no, that won't be necessary."

"It's no trouble. The post office is a bit difficult to find. I'm happy to show you where it is."

While he made the necessary arrangements to replenish their fuel and water, and paid a guard to keep anyone too interested away, Gen stood on the deck, thinking furiously. As long as he didn't actually read her message, she should be fine. He was just being kind, offering to show her around—it didn't necessarily mean he suspected anything.

At first, Gen was concerned about Will's presence, but as they ventured deeper into the old city's maze of twisting streets, she began to be thankful to have someone who knew where they were going. She had no doubt that without him she would have been hopelessly lost.

Will didn't rush her, and she was glad, for there were so many interesting things to look at. She was fascinated by the tiny shops, with their exotic goods and foods, and more than once she had to remind herself that she was there on business, not pleasure, and that there was too little money in her purse to go splashing it around on every trinket that took her fancy.

Out of the corner of her eye, she watched Will as they walked, trying to figure him out. There was an ease to his manner that suggested he'd been to Aden many times before and was incapable of being charmed by its wonders. But he was also alert, subtly scanning for threats as they went, just as she'd learned to do in her police training. She wondered if he was concerned about anything specific, but she could hardly ask him. Although he'd been polite, even kind to her since they'd left Hong Kong, there was a wall of reserve in him that seemed to be beyond her reach. Gen speculated on what she might find if she could ever convince him to lower his defences, then chided herself for it. Will was a smuggler and her target—developing any sort of emotional attachment to him would be a terrible idea.

WILL NOTICED HER WATCHING him but said nothing. He couldn't lie—he enjoyed seeing her experience Aden for the first time, and the look of childlike wonder on her face. She radiated a joy of discovery that he hadn't felt for a long time, and which cracked her facade of what, up till now, had been a rather cool professionalism. If he was honest with himself, he wanted her to turn that smile on him. But long experience had also taught him not to give in too readily to hope. When she found out what he really was—as she inevitably would, sooner or later—he knew there'd probably be precious little left from which to salvage even a friendship, let alone anything deeper. He sighed and went back to watching the street.

The post office was an elegant stone building that left visitors in no doubt as to the Settlement's colonial masters. Many traders and money changers had set up outside, and the square was bustling.

"I'll wait out here," Will said. "Take your time."

She smiled at him and pushed open the big, brass-handled door. Will stood to the side, leaning back against the cool stone wall, watching the traders in the square. Presently his eye was drawn to a young beggar boy sitting on a dirty mat, a battered tin in front of him. He was shirtless, and Will could see a long scar on his chest, but more striking was the blue cog tattoo on his right cheek. He pushed his tin forward, trying to attract the attention of passers-by, and Will saw that in place of his left hand was an intricate brass prosthesis. The boy was a brasscore—someone who, due to injury or infirmity, had been augmented with sophisticated clockwork technology. In many cases it saved their lives, but they ended up both more and less than what they had been. Many people saw brasscores as unnatural and less than human, and a large number were reduced to begging, like this poor lad.

As Will watched, a gang of young Englishmen surrounded the boy. Their clothes and general air spoke of an upper-class upbringing—men who were used to lording it over all they surveyed.

"What's this, then?" one sneered. "What's a mangy brasscore like you doing taking money from decent, law-abiding folk?"

The boy scrambled to his feet, gathering up his mat and tin. "Sorry, sirs," he muttered, head bowed, as he tried to step around them. But the bully wasn't finished yet.

"Where do you think you're going? Look at me when I'm talking to you." He prodded the boy under the chin with his cane until the lad was forced to meet his eyes. Then he took his gloves and backhanded the boy hard across the face. Will could hear his own heart thundering in his ears. He knew there was no way he could just stand by and do nothing.

SENDING THE TELEGRAM had been quicker and easier than Gen had hoped. Now, much to her relief, Flint would be aware that they were a day ahead of schedule and could adjust the operation accordingly. Walking out, she felt happier than she had since they'd left Hong Kong.

Stepping from the cool of the post office into the heat of the morning, she glanced around for Will. Immediately, her police instincts began to tingle, and she spotted the trouble within a few seconds. Will had apparently leapt to the aid of a young brasscore boy, and was currently locked in a pitched battle with three well-dressed young men. She was surprised at how well he was holding his own. Quickly, she assessed his opponents. She'd encountered men like them before, many times: with more money than sense, they had an overinflated sense of entitlement and would ride roughshod over anyone they considered beneath them, which was just about everybody. It was the easiest decision in the world to go to Will's aid.

Gen had topped her class at the academy in hand-to-hand combat, and her years patrolling the streets of London and Edinburgh had only sharpened her skills. The young men, typically of their sort, had had plenty of fencing lessons at school but no real street brawling experience. She took one by surprise from behind, kicking his legs out from under him. Will turned, his eyes widening as he saw her, then he quickly knocked down the ringleader. Gen's man struggled up painfully and, along with his friend, pulled the dazed and bleeding bully to his feet.

"Come on!" he whispered loudly.

"How dare you...you—peasant!" The ringleader spat at Will's feet. "I'll make you pay for this! You see if I don't!"

Will raised an eyebrow and tipped his hat. "I look forward to it," he said sardonically. Gen caught his eye and gave him a surreptitious grin.

As the bullies limped off, Will turned back to the young beggar. "Here," he said, handing him a gold piece—more than the boy would make in a month. "Probably best to stay away from here for a while."

"Thank you, sir," the boy said, bowing.

"Run along, then." But beneath the gruff tone, Gen could hear his voice tremble.

The crowd that had gathered to watch the fight began to disperse.

"I think we should go," Gen said. "We don't want any more trouble." She noticed that Will's cheek was cut. "You're bleeding."

He swiped at his face. "It's nothing."

"Come on," she said, impulsively taking his arm. "Let's get that seen to."

They hurried back towards the airfield, neither of them speaking. Gen could feel the anger practically radiating off Will, and she wondered what was behind it. From what she'd seen of him, he was usually calm and mild-mannered; it must have taken something particularly personal to set him off like that. It was clear he there was something he wasn't telling her, but for the life of her Gen couldn't fathom what.

Chapter 5

Matthias Cole was one of the *Maiden's Arms*'s best customers, a fact that he didn't bother to hide. He could be found there most nights propping up the bar, so it was naturally the first place the man thought to look, and he wasn't disappointed.

Even he knew better than to confront the old aeronaut in a public place, so he took a seat in a quiet corner and waited...and waited. Matthias showed no inclination to leave before last drinks were called, and even then he lingered over his final pint. By the time he finally staggered to the door, the man's patience had worn very thin.

He had no idea where Matthias lived and no discreet way of finding out, which was why this charade had to occur in the first place. He grumbled to himself as he followed the old drunkard home through the darkened streets. It had rained earlier, and the cobbles were slick with damp. More than once the man stumbled and almost turned his ankle, which only soured his mood further. He wasn't a keen walker at the best of times, and traipsing through Edinburgh on an overcast night wasn't his idea of fun.

By the time they arrived at Matthias's dingy flat, the man was thoroughly annoyed. In some ways, he welcomed it—it would make what came next easier. It took several attempts for Matthias to successfully insert the key into the lock, but he managed it eventually, and pushed the door open without a backward glance. It wasn't until they were inside and he turned to close it that it became clear he wasn't alone.

"Who're you?" he slurred, blinking owlishly at the man. Then something seemed to click. "You!" he exclaimed. "What are you doing here?"

The man sighed. He'd wavered for a moment, but there was no way he could leave Matthias alive now.

"I need something from you," he said. He reached into his bag and pulled out a piece of paper, a pencil—and a knife. "I suggest we do this the easy way, but it's really up to you."

SOME TIME LATER, THE door to Matthias's flat opened and the man emerged, peering carefully into the street. Confident he wasn't being observed, he stepped outside, gently closing the door behind him. Someone would find the aeronaut eventually—perhaps his landlady or an acquaintance from the pub wondering why he didn't show up—and they'd also find the apparent suicide note he'd left, detailing how, in league with Will, he'd tipped off the police about the Eisman tea shipment, and how they'd also been secretly spying for the Haverfords. It was out of character for Matthias to have a crisis of conscience, but there was no mistaking his handwriting—the note was, in that regard at least, genuine.

It was the first time the man had ever had to get involved in matters in such a hands-on way—usually he had people to do this sort of work for him—but he didn't feel as bad about it as he'd expected. On the contrary, he congratulated himself on a job well done and a plan that was quickly coming to fruition. All that was left to do now was to intercept the shipment—and there was no way anyone would be able to pin it on him. The clouds had blown away while he was inside, and the rain-slicked streets now glistened in the moonlight. The man headed home, whistling as he walked.

GEN AND WILL RETURNED to the *Blue Diamond* just as their stores—mostly jars of fresh water—were being delivered.

"Go and fix yourself up," Gen said as they climbed the gangway. "I'll take care of these." Will nodded gratefully.

In his cabin, he gazed at his face in the small mirror on the washstand. Apart from the cut cheek, he'd come out of the fight remarkably well—mostly thanks to Gen, he acknowledged. He wondered where she'd learned to fight like that.

He was dabbing a damp cloth on his bloodied face when there was a knock at the door, and he opened it to find her there.

"I've stowed all the stores," she said. "Do you mind if I go and do a bit more sightseeing?"

Will nodded. "Of course. Will you be all right on your own?" As much as he wanted to go with her, he couldn't quite face the streets of Aden right now.

She smiled. "I can take care of myself."

"I know. Of course you can. Enjoy yourself."

After she left, he sat down on the bed and put his head in his hands. The incident with the beggar boy had shaken him up more than he cared to admit. He'd seen brasscore beggars before, of course—you were just as likely to find them on the streets of London or Edinburgh as Aden—but not for a while, and since starting the voyage with Gen he'd been able to forget that on his right wrist he carried a blue cog tattoo identical to that on the beggar boy's cheek. Britain had stopped mandating the use of face tattoos just five years before he'd become a brasscore, for which Will was deeply grateful, but even though he could cover it up, he was never really allowed to forget what he was. It was what had made the preceding days so magical—up there in the sky with someone who didn't even guess the truth, and who took him as he was, he was free to be just Will Eisman, aeronaut.

His status was an open secret among Edinburgh's criminal underclass, but his family was rich and powerful enough that no-one dared to mention it to his face. But in every crew that he'd ever served with, he could tell that they knew. Some of them didn't care, but most of them, he knew, had feelings of quiet revulsion. Aeronauts were a superstitious bunch, and brasscores were often the target of all sorts of wild theories, or blamed for every type of misfortune. Some aeronauts even refused to fly with them, believing they brought bad luck.

Will couldn't fathom how Gen hadn't heard the rumours—not least from Matthias—but it was clear that she had no idea; Will had become familiar through long experience with the strained look people got around him when they were trying to pretend that everything was fine. He wasn't sure if he could bear to tell her, but equally he didn't think he could bear her not knowing. He rubbed his eyes, feeling suddenly exhausted. Kicking off his boots, he lay down on the bed. After the stressful, broken night he'd had, maybe all he needed was a good sleep.

When Will woke, the warm golden light of late afternoon was drifting in through the window. He checked his watch and found he'd been asleep for nearly three hours—and, surprisingly, he did feel better. The incident with the brasscore boy still gnawed at him, but some of his despondency had lifted.

He pulled on his boots and went out onto the deck, where he busied himself with making sure everything was shipshape for their departure the next day. He was just finishing the last of his chores when he saw Gen crossing the airfield. He waited for her at the top of the gangway.

"Had a good day?" he asked, reaching out a hand to help her up. Her cheeks were glowing and her eyes shining, and Will's stomach fluttered.

"It was wonderful," she said, smiling. "What an extraordinary city."

"I almost expected you to come back loaded down with keepsakes," Will said with a grin. "I was wondering if we'd need to repurpose part of the cargo hold."

She stuck out her tongue. "I was sorely tempted, but I restrained myself. I only got this." She pulled a small bottle from her bag, made of exquisitely carved glass and intricate brass filigree. Will recognised the golden liquid inside as rose attar, a perfumed oil sold in the markets.

"Good choice," he said.

"What have you been up to?"

"Not much, just pottering around." He took a deep breath, feeling suddenly nervous. "Would you still like to have dinner? I know a good place and I thought it might be nice to celebrate getting to Aden in one piece." In the moment it took her to answer, Will had convinced himself that asking had been a terrible idea—then she smiled.

"That'd be lovely. Just let me wash and get changed." She went below, and Will returned to his own cabin to shave and smarten himself up, glad he'd thought to pack a decent set of clothes. As he polished his boots, he wondered again whether this was a good idea. He was honest enough with himself to admit that it wasn't an entirely impartial invitation—he knew he wouldn't have made the same offer to Matthias, for example. But the more time he spent with Gen, the more she intrigued him, and he wanted to get to know her better. It had been a long time since he'd felt that way about anyone. *But what will she think once she knows more about you?* a nasty little voice niggled in the back of his mind. *What will happen once she knows what you really are?*

Maybe she won't care, Will thought, but he couldn't really believe it. To calm his nerves, he went back out onto the deck and paced, watching the sun sink over the city in a blaze of molten glory.

He turned at a sound behind him and saw Gen emerging onto the deck. His jaw dropped, and he quickly tried to look nonchalant. Instead of her usual rough flying breeches and shirt she was wearing a long, full skirt of deep forest green and a simple white high-necked blouse, with a brass brooch glittering at her throat. Her dark hair, which was usually pulled back in a functional bun, was pinned softly at the nape of her neck. As she came over, Will caught the faint scent of rose.

"You scrub up well," he said, trying to sound casual.

She gave him an appraising look, smiling. "You're not so bad yourself."

Will automatically offered her his arm, a gesture that would have felt strange and unnatural in their normal aeronaut roles, but now seemed perfectly reasonable. Gen took it and together they set off into the city.

The restaurant he'd chosen was called Ahmet's, a hole-in-the-wall place in the old town. It was easy to overlook, but Will had discovered on a previous trip that it served some of the best food in the city. The waiter showed them to a small table at the back of the restaurant, in an enclosed courtyard hung with sparkling golden lanterns and wispy greenery. In one corner, three musicians were tuning their instruments, and above the tables the stars were glittering in the darkening sky. It certainly wasn't the usual aeronauts' haunt.

"Like it?" Will asked as they sat down, smiling at the look of wonder on her face.

"It's enchanting," she said. "I would never have guessed this was here."

"Wait till you try the food."

"Why don't you order for both of us?" she suggested. "I wouldn't even know where to start."

Will signalled to the waiter and reeled off a list of dishes that Gen had never heard of.

"You must get to see some amazing places, travelling as much as you do," she said as the waiter returned with steaming cups of mint tea.

"You don't?"

Gen shrugged. "Lately I've been doing more domestic jobs. This is the first time I've been abroad for a while."

"You didn't learn to fly as well as you do by being stuck in Scotland, though," Will said. "Where did you learn to do that?"

She smiled. "Five years in the Aerofleet."

Will raised his eyebrows. "Really? I never had you picked for a military type."

She shrugged again. "My parents were killed in a steam-carriage accident when I was sixteen, and the only way I could support myself was to join the military or go into service. And I'm definitely not cut out to be a maid."

"Oh, I'm sorry. About your parents, I mean."

"It's all right." She looked wistful for a moment. "That's just life, isn't it?"

"So why did you leave the Aerofleet?"

"I don't know—I guess it wasn't what I thought it would be. I had all these romantic ideas, and it turned out to be just routine patrols over the Channel most of the time. Their unofficial motto was 'hurry up and wait.' I wanted something where I had more control over my life."

"And here you are."

"Here I am." She fidgeted with the edge of the tablecloth. "But enough about me. What about you—how did you get into this line of work?"

"Well, it's the family business, so it was where I was destined to end up, really. Both my parents were aeronauts in their young adulthood, before they settled down. They didn't really want that for me, but I eventually convinced them."

"Why didn't they want you to fly?"

Will bit his lip. This was the perfect opportunity to tell her the truth, but now that he was faced with it, he didn't think he could. She would be revolted, and he was enjoying their conversation so much—why destroy a good thing?

"I was ill as a child," he said. "Afterwards, they were convinced I was permanently weakened. They thought most things were beyond me." It *was* the truth, he reflected, just not quite the *whole* truth. "To be honest, they still do." He glanced at her; he hadn't meant that to slip out.

"Oh, Will," she said, a small frown creasing her brow. "That's awful. Not to believe in you...especially when you've got so much potential."

"You think I've got potential?"

Gen blushed. "No ... I ... sorry, I didn't mean to patronise you. What I mean is ... "

"It's all right," Will said, laughing. "I'm flattered." *More than you know*, he thought. "Anyway, my brother John has always been the golden child. It used to bother me, but now I just let him do his thing and we stay out of each other's way."

"You don't get on?"

He gave a short, barking laugh. "You could say that."

"You know, it's funny," Gen said. "I've always had this idealised vision of sibling relationships, because for as long as

I can remember I wanted a brother or sister. It was just me and my parents...but now I don't have anyone."

The words hung in the air between them for a moment, and she laughed self-consciously. "Ugh, that sounds morose. I'm doing well tonight, aren't I? I must be such great company." She took a sip of tea, the flush returning to her cheeks.

"I wouldn't want any other company," he said. He wished he could take her hand and reassure her, but he didn't dare to be so forward.

Thankfully, at that moment the musicians began to play, and all around them diners took to the makeshift dance floor in the middle of the courtyard. Will took a deep breath and screwed up his courage.

"Shall we dance?" he asked, offering his hand. For a second, he thought she might refuse, then she met his eyes with a smile that made his heart skip a beat.

"I'd like that."

He led her to the floor, and when he took her lightly in his arms it was as if the world around them stopped. There was nothing but the two of them, the glitter of candlelight, and the faint scent of rose.

AT A TABLE IN THE FAR corner, a man sat alone, sipping thick, sweet coffee from a small cup. Every now and then he glanced towards Will Eisman and his mysterious companion, but they were too engrossed in each other to notice him. His brief had said nothing about a lady, and his curiosity was piqued. He would have to find out who she was, he decided—it was information that could come in useful. Because if the look on Will Eisman's face was any indication, he was already falling hard, and that made him vulnerable. The boss would undoubtedly be interested in that. The man smiled to himself, finished his coffee and rose to leave. He didn't need to see any more.

Chapter 6

Gen sat back with a contented sigh. "I couldn't possibly eat another thing. That was delicious." The delectable main course had been followed by a dessert of sweet flaky pastry filled with crushed pistachios and drizzled with honey, which was unlike anything she'd ever tried before.

"I'm glad you enjoyed it," Will said, giving her a slightly crooked smile that made her heart beat faster. "Let me get the bill." He signalled to the waiter.

"Thank you," she said as they left the restaurant. "I had a lovely time." She took his proffered arm—a courtesy she wasn't really accustomed to, but quite enjoyed nonetheless—and together they walked back towards the airfield. The streets were still bustling with late-night traders, their stalls glowing with coloured lamps. Neither of them spoke, but it was a soft, companionable silence. Gen was remembering how it had felt to dance with Will, and she was acutely conscious of his arm tucked against her side.

They had just reached the airfield gates when they were approached by a brasscore girl with a begging bowl. She couldn't have been more than about six or seven, but both her legs were brass from the knee down. Gen felt Will's arm tense, and she squeezed it in what she hoped was a reassuring manner. She took a couple of coins from her purse and handed them to the girl, just as the airfield guard burst out of his hut, brandishing a cudgel and shouting loudly in Arabic. The girl turned and fled, hobbling away on her brass legs.

"So sorry, ma'am," the guard said. "Filthy scum they are."

Gen glanced at Will, expecting him to be angry, but instead she saw a strange mix of pain and fear flash across his face. She frowned to herself, wondering again what he wasn't telling her.

They returned to the *Blue Diamond* without further incident and found all as they had left it. Gen chatted idly, trying to regain the previous mood, but Will seemed deflated, sad even.

"I'll make some tea," she said at last, and went down to the galley, leaving him on the deck. As she boiled the kettle on the thermocrystal stove, she thought back to the morning's incident outside the post office. She was beginning to get an inkling of what might be troubling Will, but there was only one way to know for sure.

Loading the two steaming cups onto a tray, she climbed back up to the deck. Will was leaning on the railing, gazing down at the lights glittering across the airfield and the city beyond. He wore a small frown, as if he were grappling with serious thoughts.

She put the tray down and stood beside him, leaning on the railing, their shoulders not quite touching. He was so lost in his thoughts that he jumped when he saw her there.

"Sorry." She smiled. "I didn't mean to scare you."

"It's all right. I was miles away."

"Thinking about brasscores?"

He gave her a piercing look, as if debating whether to deflect her question. Then he shrugged.

"How did you know?"

"A lucky guess." She wished she could ease his pain, but again she got the feeling that he was holding something back.

"Defending that boy was an honourable thing to do," she said. She would never have expected a career criminal to stand up for a brasscore, of all people. But then, Will Eisman was confounding her expectations in all sorts of ways.

He shrugged again, his lips twisting. "It won't make a difference, not really. Those kids are usually part of gangs—they snatch them away from their parents and mutilate them, then pay for their treatment, because they know brasscore beggars bring in more money."

"Really?" The thought of children being deliberately harmed like that filled her with horror.

He nodded. "It will keep happening, and on the other side of it those bullies will still pick on the next unfortunate brasscore they see. Nothing I do will change that."

"Maybe not. But it made a difference to him."

They stood in silence for a moment.

"It made a difference to me," she said at last. Will said nothing, but looked at her, inviting her to go on.

Gen took a deep breath. "My best friend was a brasscore," she said. She'd never spoken of this to anyone, and she wasn't sure why she was now, except that she desperately wanted him to know that she understood some of what he was feeling. "She got a clockwork lung after a childhood illness. Until I met her ... well, I didn't really understand how hard life could be. How cruel people could be." In fact, she'd met Becca in the aftermath of an awful incident at the police academy, but she couldn't tell Will that.

"What do you mean she *was* a brasscore?" he asked. Brasscores had permanent modifications; it wasn't something you could grow out of or change later.

Gen swallowed.

"She died. Two years ago."

"I'm so sorry. What happened?"

"We worked together. There was an...accident...on the job."

"You were there?"

She nodded, then gazed out across the city.

"Anyway," she said, "I just wanted you to know that even if you don't think it was much, what you did meant a lot to me. Becca would have been proud." She gave him a watery smile. Their eyes met, and suddenly the distance between them seemed both a chasm and much, much smaller.

WILL COULD SENSE HER moving closer, and he felt himself falling into the dark depths of her eyes, drawn to her by the force of his own desire. But still a small voice in the back of his mind—one borne of long experience—urged caution. Just before their lips met, he pulled away.

"Wait," he said, registering the shock and hurt in her eyes as he did so. "It's just ... I have to tell you something." He'd hoped he could avoid this conversation, but he realised now that he liked her too much to lie to her. He knew how this would play out, but he'd learned the hard way that it was for the best. Once upon a time he would have tried to hide it, but the truth always came out eventually, and then they wanted nothing to do with him. It was better to get the rejection out of the way upfront, before he got too invested.

"What?" she asked, bewildered. Will undid the cuff of his right sleeve and rolled it up to his elbow. The light was dim, but there was no mistaking the blue cog tattoo on the inside of his wrist. He held it out to her, searching her face for the telltale signs of revulsion.

"It's my heart," he said, to fill the silence. "I had a condition as a child, and a clockwork one was the only thing that saved me. I was twelve when I got it." The story wouldn't make a difference, he knew. They never much cared *why* he was a brasscore. All that mattered was that he wasn't truly human.

Gen said nothing, and he couldn't guess her thoughts. Then she took his hand and slowly ran her lips across the tattoo. It was so gentle yet so intimate that he gasped.

She met his eyes and smiled, unleashing in him a wave of relief that was swiftly followed by a resurgence of desire so urgent it was almost painful. Then they were in each other's arms, and as his mouth closed on hers, Will couldn't remember ever wanting something so much.

They were broken apart by a chorus of wolf-whistles and friendly jeers from a group of airfield labourers, and Gen realised that up on the deck they were in full view of anyone below. She felt the heat rise in her cheeks and laughed with embarrassment. She leaned into Will.

"Perhaps we should go somewhere more private?"

He grinned back at her and nodded.

As they crossed the deck to his cabin, Gen wondered if she was making an enormous mistake. She was a police officer and he was her target; there was no way this could end well. But there was also nothing wrong with having a bit of fun—after all, it wasn't as if they were going to fall in love. She could see in Will's eyes that he was lonely, and it was a feeling she knew all too well. He clearly wanted her as much as she did him, so why shouldn't they assuage some of that loneliness together on the long flight north?

At the cabin door he graciously ushered her in before him and lit the lamp. She removed her boots as etiquette demanded, then looked around. It was quite spacious, considering the size of the *Blue Diamond*, and sparkling clean. The bed was neatly made, covered with a patchwork quilt, and on shelves around the walls, in between stacks of books and charts, gleamed small clockwork figures of animals and birds.

Gen turned back to Will, meaning to ask about them, but he smiled at her and it was like opening a floodgate. Whatever lingering doubts she'd had were crushed under a wave of desire as he pulled her to him and kissed her passionately. As he kissed her neck, she ran her hands through his hair, laughing as they stumbled clumsily towards the bed, but the laugh turned into a moan of longing as he undid the top buttons of her blouse and kissed between her breasts. She pulled him up to her and kissed him hard on the mouth again, then sank back onto the bed, Will following. She smiled as he leaned over her, arching her neck as his hands explored her body, gently caressing her breasts before moving down and finding their way under her long skirt. It was so hot in Aden that she'd neglected to wear pantaloons or even stockings—all that was under her petticoat was a thin pair of silk underwear.

Will gazed at her with a desire in his eyes that made her catch her breath. She couldn't recall a man ever looking at her like that before—as if she was the most exquisite thing he'd ever seen. Her skin tingled where he touched it. Slowly he lifted her skirt and began gently kissing the inside of her thigh. Gen gasped at the sensation.

"Is that all right?" he asked softly, looking up at her.

"Oh, yes," she murmured. "It's just ... no one has ever kissed me like that before."

"If you want me to stop, just say the word."

"No—don't stop." She lay back as he returned to his task, then groaned with pleasure as he pulled aside her underwear and caressed her with his tongue. "Please don't stop."

ON WILL'S SIXTEENTH birthday, his brother John's present, despite all Will's objections, had been a visit to Edinburgh's best brothel.

"You're a man now," John had said as he'd all but shoved Will into the room. "Time to make it official."

The young woman waiting for him would have been around twenty-two years old. She had long blonde hair and a face that was pretty without being striking. Her scanty outfit was designed to show off her figure to best effect, and it worked. Will felt very young and inexperienced, and wished fervently that he was anywhere else.

"Hello there," she said, coming over and laying a hand on his chest. "I'm Candice. I'm under special instructions to give you a night you won't forget."

"I ... I'm Will ... " Will stammered. Involuntarily, he backed away until his back was against the door. He wasn't prepared for this. Candice looked at him keenly, clearly noticing it too.

"You don't want to be here, do you?" she said, dropping all pretence at seduction.

Will shook his head.

"It's nothing personal. It's just ... I'm not ready."

She sighed.

"Let me guess—it was your father who put you up to it? Time to become a man and all that?"

"My brother, actually."

"And I assume he's waiting outside for you?"

Will nodded.

"All right. You'd better stay the full hour, then. Don't worry," she added, seeing his face. "I'm not going to make you do anything you don't want to do. We can just talk." She sat on the edge of the bed and patted the space next to her. Reluctantly, Will sat.

"Have you...been doing this long?" He cringed as he said it, for it was hard to think of a worse conversation-starter. But Candice just smiled.

"Long enough," she said. "Long enough to learn a few things, that's for sure." She turned to face him. "Can I suggest something?"

"Of course."

"They tell me you're a brasscore—" Will started at this— "not that it worries me. But it's going to make life harder for you where women are concerned. That and the fact that you're obviously a virgin. So if and when you fancy a girl, you're going to have to work extra hard.

"Now, take it from me," she continued, "most men have no idea what they're doing when it comes to women. They just climb on and rut around till they're done. But—if you like—I can teach you some things that will make her beg for more. We can just talk if you like...but there's also a practical option, if you want to try them out for yourself." She grinned. "What do you say?"

Will smiled, beginning to relax now that the pressure was off.

"Sure."

CANDICE'S ADVICE HAD stood him in good stead, and over the years he'd come to realise two things—first, that what she'd said about most men was true, and second, that he really enjoyed giving pleasure to women, almost as much as he liked receiving it himself. With a woman like Gen, who had clearly never had any man put her first before, it was even better.

He caressed her expertly with tongue and fingers, smiling as her moans increased in intensity and her body responded to his touch. He guided her right to the edge of the precipice, then stopped, letting her float back down. Again he brought her close to the edge, and again he paused.

"Will!" she begged. "Don't stop!"

This time he took her all the way, until her body arched and pulsed around him, and she cried out his name in ecstasy.

GEN HAD BEEN WITH MEN before, but not for a long time, and never like this. It was as if fireworks had gone off behind her eyes, the pleasure intensified by the slow build-up. Will lay beside her and kissed her, and she cuddled into him, momentarily speechless. He held her, smiling to himself, while she floated away on a cloud of bliss.

Time slowed and blurred, but at last she was sufficiently recovered, and was surprised to find a rush of desire returning. She propped herself up on one elbow and looked at him.

"That was...I don't even know what to say," she said.

"My pleasure."

"And there I was thinking the pleasure was all mine."

Idly she let her fingers trace his jawline, then slowly began to unbutton his shirt.

"You're wearing far too many clothes, Captain Eisman."

"I guess you'll just have to help me out of them, then."

"I guess I will."

As she continued to undo his shirt, he leaned up and kissed her, and suddenly neither of them could bear a long, slow seduction. They laughed as they fumbled with hooks and buttons, fingers made clumsy with urgency, until their clothes were strewn haphazardly across the room, then held each other close, revelling in the touch of skin on skin. Looking into Will's deep blue eyes, Gen felt weak with desire. She pushed him gently back on the bed and straddled him, running first her fingers and then her lips down the long white scar on his chest. Will groaned as she took him in her hand and slipped him inside her, then they were moving together, transported in mutual pleasure and release. Afterwards, they lay curled together, drifting into sleep, as the stars wheeled above them.

Chapter 7

When Gen woke, for a moment she couldn't work out where she was. Then the memory of the previous night came rushing back, and she smiled. She rolled over, stretching out her arm—only to find that the other side of the bed was empty. She sat up, her heart beginning to race. Had Will had second thoughts? In the cold light of day, did he regret it all? Did she?

No, she thought. There were many things she regretted, but this wasn't one of them.

Her clothes were laid neatly over the back of the chair—Will must have put them there when he got up, because she clearly remembered them being tossed across the room in the heat of passion. She clambered out of bed and dressed, running her fingers through her hair, which was tumbling around her shoulders in messy waves.

Out on the deck she found Will giving orders to Alexander. He noticed her approaching, caught her eye and smiled. She smiled back, her heart lurching with relief; he didn't look like a man who regretted his decision.

"Good timing," he said. "We're taking off in half an hour."

Gen gaped at him.

"You should have woken me!"

"I was going to, but you looked so peaceful that I couldn't bear to," he said with a shrug. "You were smiling, like you were having a nice dream."

Gen thought back. It *had* been a nice dream—very different from her usual recurring nightmares. She gestured to her skirt.

"Just let me get changed and I'll be right with you," she said. She hurried down to her cabin, changed into her work breeches and shirt, and splashed some water on her face. Then she fought her hair back out of her eyes and into its usual bun. It had been nice to dress up a bit, she admitted, but long skirts weren't exactly practical for an aeronaut. Feeling a bit more like her old self, she rejoined Will on the deck.

"There's not much to do," he said. "We're just waiting for clearance to go. Would you like some breakfast?" He ducked down to the galley and returned with some delicious-smelling pastries and a pot of coffee, still warm.

"No tea?" Gen said with a smile, as they perched on the steps leading up to the poop deck.

"We can't be drinking the cargo, now, can we?" he said, grinning, and she laughed.

Another man wouldn't have heard the joke in that, she thought. She knew her sense of humour could be a bit hard to gauge sometimes. Becca had understood it, but she'd been one of the few.

They munched the pastries and gazed out over the airfield, which was busy with departing traffic. Mornings always were—aeronauts liked to get going before the wind got too strong. By the time they'd finished their breakfast it was almost time to leave. Will took up his captain's position next to Alexander at the helm, and Gen got ready to cast off. The thaumaturgical radio on the poop deck crackled and a plum British voice cut through: "*Blue Diamond*, cleared for launch."

Will lifted the handset.

"Roger," he said, "launching." Then, turning to Alexander: "Engines to full."

The engines, which had been idling, thrummed to life.

"Cast off!" Will called down to Gen.

She untied the mooring ropes, hauling them in hand over hand, and the *Blue Diamond*, free from the shackles of the mooring mast, drifted up into the clear blue sky. Will set a course out over the sea, and they rose higher and higher until the city was just a rapidly receding dot. Gen expertly coiled and stowed the mooring ropes, ready for their next stop—Edinburgh. She didn't want to think too much about that.

AS THE *Blue Diamond* ascended into the sunrise, a lone man paused at the edge of the airfield and watched her go. He'd been there when she arrived two days ago and had been discreetly following her crew ever since. He'd almost been tempted to intervene during the fight at the post office, because it would have upset the plans mightily to have Will Eisman languishing in an Aden gaol, but then that mysterious woman had saved the day and had allowed him to preserve his anonymity. When he'd later followed them to dinner—in a much more romantic spot than he would have expected for a meal between a captain and his mate—his curiosity had been even further aroused. He'd left them to it and returned to the airfield, where he had leaned on a contact who owed him a favour to get access to the flight manifest, and he'd seen her listed as Genevieve Morrison, first mate. He'd been doing this job a long time, and he knew the regular Eisman employees—and she wasn't one of them. The boss didn't like speculation—it had been made very clear before that he wasn't being paid to think—but if he was right, and his intuition told him he was, then it could be quite a useful piece of leverage to have. So once the *Blue Diamond* set sail, his telegram noted her time of departure and the presence of an unexpected and unexplained crew member, and two simple phrases: *Possibly police. Suspect romantic involvement.* It would be enough.

He smiled to himself. Will Eisman was about to get a homecoming he wouldn't forget in a hurry.

ONCE THEY REACHED THEIR cruising height, Will handed control over to Alexander and came down to the main deck.

"Looks like it should be a smooth flight," he said. "There doesn't seem to be much weather around." Indeed, there was hardly a cloud to be seen, and the landmarks on the coast below them, though distant, stood out clearly. They leaned on the railing, admiring the view. Gen was acutely conscious of their closeness; memories of the previous night flashed before her, and she blushed. Will turned and smiled at her, and she felt a surge of hot desire.

"About last night…" he said at last.

"Yes?" Gen suddenly worried that he regretted it all and was going to confess he'd made a terrible mistake. Her heart began to thunder in her ears.

"I just wanted to check you're all right. I know it all happened rather quickly."

She smiled in relief. "I'm fine. More than fine. It was…wonderful."

Will looked like a weight had lifted from his shoulders. "I'm glad. I thought so too."

"Also…thank you for telling me about being a brasscore. I know that couldn't have been easy."

Will nodded mutely.

Gen nudged him. "I'd already guessed, you know."

He gaped at her. "You knew?"

"Well…no…but I had my suspicions. After what happened at the post office, I figured it was either you or someone you cared about."

"You never let on."

She shrugged. "I knew you'd tell me if you wanted to. And if you didn't—well, it didn't change my opinion of you either way."

Will rubbed a hand across his face, looking stunned. "I don't know what to say."

Gen laid a hand against his cheek. "You don't have to say anything." Their eyes met, and as he pulled her into a passionate embrace, she reflected that it was just as well they had an airship to fly, or they might never leave his cabin again.

"If you could travel anywhere in the world, where would you go?" Will asked when they finally broke apart.

"Paris," she said without hesitation. That was easy.

"The City of Light, eh? Interesting."

Gen shrugged. "I stopped there briefly on a tour with the Aerofleet, and I've always wanted to go back. It just seemed so magical—like anything was possible." She glanced at him. "You?"

Will shrugged. "I think I've done enough travel for now. But I could make an exception to take you to one of the most romantic cities on earth." He gave her a suggestive glance and she laughed.

"I suppose you've seen a lot, what with being a dashing airship captain and all."

"Seen a lot—yes. But as a ship's boy, and as an ordinary sailor, and then eventually as a mate. This is my first trip as a captain."

"Really?" Flint's file hadn't mentioned that.

"And probably my last, too."

"Why do you say that?" She nudged him playfully. "You're not *that* old."

He smiled at her, but there was a wistfulness to it, and she wondered if she'd touched a nerve.

"I had to fight so hard to get this," he said. "When I became a brasscore, my parents got the idea that most 'normal' things would be beyond me. Suddenly I was something less than human, and if they had their way, I'd never leave the house. But over the years I managed to convince them to let me try some new things, and eventually I talked them into letting me become a cabin boy on one of their airships. I had to work twice as hard as an ordinary man, and I did: many of the crew didn't want me there, but after a while they started to respect me. But now I've finally made it to captain, and I've realised...well...it doesn't matter how hard I work. Nothing I do will ever be good enough for my parents." He shrugged. "Going into this voyage, I wasn't entirely sure, but I am now. I've decided to leave the family business for good. I'd be happy with a little cottage somewhere, my own shop...and a family."

Gen took his hand and squeezed it. "That sounds wonderful." Her own dreams held similar visions, but they'd always been flat and faceless. Now, she saw Will in an armchair in that cottage, bouncing a child on his knee. It was profoundly pleasing, but it also shook her to her core. This was meant to be just a bit of fun. Love wasn't part of the plan. She was just caught up in the romance of it, that was all. She wasn't thinking straight.

"What would you sell?" she asked, trying to distract herself.

"I make clockwork automata," he said.

"Like the ones in your cabin? They're beautiful."

"Thanks. I do more-functional ones too—they're not so pretty but they're bigger and they get stuff done. I built Alexander, you know."

"*You* built Alexander?" She was genuinely shocked; Alexander was the most sophisticated steering automaton she'd ever seen, even in the Aerofleet, and she realised she'd been underestimating Will.

"You wouldn't think it, would you?"

"I'm impressed."

He shrugged again. "I've always liked tinkering with things. I tried to show my parents when I built Alexander—having more like him could revolutionise their business—but they didn't have time. But I think there'd be a market for this sort of thing."

"I'm pretty sure there would be. And you know, I think you can achieve anything you put your mind to."

"Really?"

"Of course. You've clearly got grit—and talent. I believe in you."

He blushed. "We'll see."

Will stared out to sea for a moment, then turned to face her, his dark eyes serious. "I know we haven't known each other very long, but once we get to Edinburgh...well, I'd really like to see more of you."

"You've seen quite a lot of me already."

His face fell. "I understand."

"No, no, that's not what I meant! That sounds lovely. Why don't we get the voyage over with first and then take it from there?"

He nodded but gave her a look that said he wasn't entirely convinced. "Is everything all right?"

"Of course! Everything's fine."

They stood in silence for a long moment.

"You know, the thing about being a brasscore," Will said at last, "is that you get really good at telling when people are lying to you to make you feel better."

Gen felt as if all the breath had been knocked out of her. "Oh, Will," she said. "It's not about that. I need to figure a few things out, but I promise it's got nothing whatsoever to do with you being a brasscore."

"If you say so," he said, in a tone that told her he didn't believe a word of it.

"I do," she said. "Please believe me." But she could still see doubt in his eyes, so she kissed him.

Lying in bed that night, Gen mentally kicked herself. She should have been sleeping—she had to relieve Will at the helm in just a few short hours—but she kept replaying their conversation. Had circumstances been different, she would have jumped at his request for an ongoing courtship, but the telegram she'd sent to Flint from Aden would now make that all but impossible. Will would know she had betrayed him, and there could be no going back from that. And quite unexpectedly, the thought of hurting him broke her heart. In less than a day, that beautiful, impossible dream she'd built with him at the centre of it would all come crashing down.

Chapter 8

It was late afternoon when Edinburgh Castle appeared on the horizon. The sight hit Gen with a wave of apprehension. Over the last few days, she'd been able to avoid thinking too hard about the inevitable conclusion to their journey, but now there was no getting away from it. Her one hope was that she could approach Flint as soon as they landed, and they could all have a calm conversation that would spare Will from the worst of the police operation's repercussions. After all, he'd said himself that he was just a bit player in the family business, and he wanted out. There must be a way she could prevail upon Flint to make it happen. And maybe, just maybe, all wouldn't be lost between her and Will. Because, although it had just been a bit of fun at first, she was able to admit now that it was far more than that. More than anything, she wanted Will in her life.

The airfield was in view, and they descended slowly towards it. Suddenly, Will swore.

"What's wrong?" Gen asked, alarmed at his vehemence.

"See that ship down there? The black one?"

Gen looked and could see a large airship, painted black from hull to envelope. "Yes?"

"That's the *Black Mamba*. She's the Haverford family's flagship."

Gen gulped. Although the Eismans ruled Scotland, the Haverfords were arguably the most powerful crime family in Britain. The operation that had killed Becca had been a sting against them. It had gone so catastrophically wrong that the police hadn't been able to get near them since. And if any of them recognised her ...

"That could just be a coincidence, couldn't it?"

Will frowned. "I doubt it. My family is in debt to them. The proceeds of this cargo will be enough to clear it and then some, which is why we wanted to move it as quietly as possible. But it looks like somebody tipped them off."

"So they're going to take the cargo?"

"That way they get the debt money plus profit," Will said, "as well as the satisfaction of thwarting us. I tried to raise this possibility with my father before I left, but he wouldn't countenance it, because what would I know?" His mouth twisted bitterly.

"What are we going to do?"

"What *can* we do? We don't have the fuel to land anywhere further afield, and it's just the two of us. There's nothing to be done." He raised his hands helplessly.

Gen peered over the side as they drifted closer, looking for any sign of Flint and his men. Eventually she spotted them, but they were miles away, right back by the airfield gates. She hoped they could make it to the berth in time, before whatever was brewing between the Eismans and the Haverfords boiled over.

The descent took only a few minutes, but it felt much longer. Gen could see around ten black-coated figures waiting for them as they pulled into their berth, and her heart sank as she recognised a familiar face: Marcus Haverford, scion of the family and the target of the botched London raid.

"Will!" she said urgently. "I have to tell you something."

"Can it wait?" His lips were pressed together as he focused on steering the *Blue Diamond* down the final few feet.

"It's important."

He glanced at her. "It's really not a good time, Gen. When this is all over, I promise I'll listen to whatever it is you need to tell me. But when we land, stay behind me and don't say anything, all right?"

Gen nodded, cursing herself for leaving it too late.

Will stayed at his post at the helm as the docking workers tied down the *Blue Diamond*'s mooring ropes and set the gangway. As soon as it was in place, the Haverfords swarmed up it, fanning out across the deck and making for the hold. Marcus Haverford, who was clearly in charge, sauntered up last and approached the poop deck. His eyebrows shot up when he saw Gen, and any hope she had of his failing to recognise her evaporated.

"Well, well, *Captain* Eisman," he said, lip curling in a sneer. "It turns out pigs *can* fly. Who knew?"

Will stared at him balefully.

"What are you talking about, Marcus?"

Marcus Haverford threw his head back and laughed.

"You mean she hasn't told you?" He gestured at Gen. "Your mate here is one of London's finest. Tried to disrupt a business meeting of mine a couple of years ago. As I recall, her partner ended up on the wrong end of a bullet. Isn't that right, love?"

Gen clenched her jaw and said nothing.

"Is that true?" Will said, turning to her. "Surely he's mistaken. You're not police—are you?"

Gen looked down, unable to handle the hurt in his eyes. Then she nodded. "It's true."

"Get off my ship," he said quietly.

"Will, wait...let me explain..."

"No," he said. "There's nothing to say. I can't *believe* I trusted you. Just get your things and go."

"You should be thanking me," Gen heard Marcus say as she descended from the poop deck. "Imagine what your father would have said if you'd let the pigs disrupt your deal... Dammit!"

Gen turned, trying to find the reason for his exclamation, and saw Flint and his men running up the gangway. But there was also a third group, some of whom bore such a strong physical resemblance to Will that they could only be family. Gen backed hurriedly into an out-of-the-way part of the deck as all hell broke loose around her. From what she could tell, the police had quickly gained the upper hand, and Haverfords and Eismans alike were either making a mad dash for the gangway or being escorted off by Flint's officers. She was so caught up in the unfolding drama that she didn't hear someone approaching her from behind. Then a gloved hand clamped over her mouth, and a voice hissed in her ear.

"Right, officer, you're coming with me. Don't scream if you know what's good for you." She felt something hard press into the small of her back. "Nod if you understand."

She nodded. The man, whoever he was, hurried her off the deck, dodging the worst of the melee. As they reached the bottom of the gangway, Gen turned back towards the airship, sinking her teeth into the hand that held her as she did so.

"*Will!*" she screamed, with no hope that he'd hear her. Her captor cuffed her so hard about the head that she saw stars, but just before he bundled her into the back of a waiting steam wagon, she saw Will's shocked face staring at her over the side of the *Blue Diamond*.

Will raced towards the gangway, Gen's panicked cry ringing in his ears. Shoving two Haverfords and a policeman out of the way, he scrambled to the ground, but he was too late—the steam wagon was barrelling out of the airfield gates in a cloud of dust. Will sank to his knees in the dirt, staring after it.

Suddenly a hand was extended towards him, and he looked up into the face of Inspector Thomas Flint.

"I might have known you'd be behind this," Will said as Flint hauled him to his feet. "Whatever happened to the Code?"

"Nice to see you too, William," Flint said. "As for the Code, your family broke it first—although, come to think of it, you probably don't know about that. But 'live and let live' was off the table once they started interfering with my officers."

"Interfering with your officers? What do you mean?"

Flint waved the question away. "There's no time for that now; I'll explain later. Now, tell me, what exactly is your brother playing at?"

Will sighed. "I have no idea."

"No," said Flint, "I don't suppose you do." He ran a hand through his greying hair. "Look," he said at last, "I know you're not anywhere near as stupid as your family thinks you are. And to be honest, you're not the one I really want. Help me get Genevieve back safely and I'll make sure none of this—" he gestured to the airship behind them, where the police were rounding up the last of the Haverfords— "gets pinned on you. What do you say?"

Will hesitated for a moment. The shock of Gen's betrayal still stung, but he also knew what might happen to her if he didn't do something, and he couldn't have that on his conscience.

"All right," he said, sighing.

"Good lad. Now, do you know where he's taken her?"

"No. But I can guess."

"Excellent." Flint strode over to an unmarked police steam wagon and opened the door. "Get in."

Chapter 9

There were no windows in the back of the steam wagon, and Gen quickly lost her sense of time and direction. After what could have been fifteen minutes or an hour, the wagon shuddered to a stop. She blinked and threw a hand up to shield her eyes as the door was flung open and a lantern thrust in. Hands grabbed her roughly and hauled her out. She briefly glimpsed the outside of a nondescript warehouse, somewhere around the docks, she guessed, before she was shoved through a small door. She tripped, falling to her knees, hearing her captor come in behind her and the final thud of the door closing.

When she looked up, it took her a moment to adjust to her surroundings. She'd expected something dingy and industrial, but the inside of the warehouse was done up like a house, with overstuffed armchairs, a sofa, and a thermocrystal stove for heating—she felt like she'd fallen into someone's lounge room. The back of the warehouse seemed to have been sectioned off for bedrooms. *Is this a safe house?* she wondered.

Gen felt like her brain was spinning as she tried to take stock of the situation. She'd assumed she'd been kidnapped by a Haverford for some reason—perhaps to use as leverage against the Eismans. But whichever way she turned it, the situation didn't seem to make sense.

An older man and woman were seated in front of the fire, their feet resting comfortably on embroidered footstools. The man who'd seized her from the *Blue Diamond* hauled her roughly to her feet and dragged her over to them.

"The mission was compromised," he snapped, shoving her forward. "This pig was on board the whole time."

The older man raised an eyebrow. "Nice to see you too, son," he said. "Now, greet us properly and we'll try again."

Gen could have sworn she heard her captor growling with frustration. "Apologies—good evening, Mother, Father," he said. His words were a whisker away from sarcasm. "It appears the police got wind of the mission, and they sent this...officer...to intercept it."

"And you've brought her here with what purpose?" the lady asked. If she was shocked at the news about the smuggling mission, she didn't show it.

"They've seized the cargo," the younger man said. "I thought she'd be useful...leverage."

He stepped forward, and for the first time Gen got a good look at him. She was hit with a double wave of shock, first because he looked so like an older, jowlier version of Will, but mostly because *she recognised him.* He'd been one of Marcus Haverford's associates at that terrible meeting that had ended in Becca's death. The more she looked, the more certain she became that he was Will's older brother, John. That would make the couple in the armchairs Will's parents. It made a bizarre sort of sense that the Eismans would kidnap her to try to ensure the return of their cargo in exchange. But she couldn't explain why John Eisman would have been at a secret meeting with Marcus Haverford, when the two families were supposed to be mortal enemies. Were they putting aside their differences and forming an alliance? Everything she'd seen when the *Blue Diamond* docked, and everything Will had told her, suggested this was unlikely. So was John Eisman consorting with the Haverfords without his parents' knowledge or consent? It seemed possible, probable even. She held the knowledge tightly, hoping it might come in useful.

"Now," Mr Eisman said, addressing her for the first time, "you're going to tell me who you are and how you found out about our little...importation."

"Constable Genevieve Conlon," she said. There didn't seem to be any point using her alias.

"And how did the police find out about the operation?"

"I don't know." It was true—she knew it wasn't Matthias, because he'd been clueless about what they were smuggling until Flint had filled him in. He just turned up and flew the ship—he knew it was safer not to ask.

"Not good enough, I'm afraid," Mr Eisman said affably.

"Shall I try to loosen her tongue?" John asked with relish, and Gen shuddered. But Mr Eisman just rolled his eyes.

"There's no need for that," he said. "Not yet." He turned back to Gen. "You just sit and think for a while. Maybe something will come to you. You'd better hope that it does."

He waved her to the sofa, and she sat obediently. How was she going to get out of this mess? Presumably Flint knew she was here, or would shortly, as they intended to use her for ransom. But would he be able to protect her? She doubted it—she had to figure things out for herself.

She could see instinctively that John was the weak link. She'd read the briefing files, and she knew the Eismans had risen to prominence thanks to the efforts of John and Will's parents, who by all accounts were masterful diplomats, skilled in the act of both engendering loyalty and punishing transgressors. John, it seemed, was much more of a loose cannon. From what she'd heard, he had little patience with the subtleties of his parents' methods and was much more inclined to violence in the first instance. People were terrified of John, but they respected his mother and father, however grudgingly. While the elder Eismans had never shied away from violence, the consensus on the street was that their use of it was always proportional and as a last resort. But if you crossed them you wouldn't forget it in a hurry.

It was clear that John had captured her without his father or mother's approval—she very much doubted they would have used kidnapping as the opening gambit in negotiations with the police. And although Will had believed that John was very much his parents' favourite, watching them together, Gen wondered how solid the relationship really was. John obviously chafed under his parents' authority, and she doubted their patience with him would last forever. How long before one of them cracked? And would pushing the situation be in her interests or not?

Her head was spinning with all the possibilities, and she took some deep breaths to try to calm the churning in her stomach. She was snapped out of her thoughts by a knock at the warehouse door, an elaborate series of taps that was clearly a code. Mr Eisman gestured to John, and the latter unbolted it. Gen's heart lurched when Will stepped through into the light. He glanced around the room, his eyes alighting briefly on her, before he looked away as if she was of no more interest to him than the furniture. She knew it was imperative that they give no hint of their relationship, but she wondered if the coldness was real or pretend. After her betrayal, she couldn't blame him if he viewed her with contempt.

"Mother, Father," Will said respectfully. "Good evening."

His father nodded.

"William. Quite a mess we've got here."

"Yes, sir."

"You let a police spy infiltrate one of our most important missions."

Will hung his head. "Yes, sir."

"And how do you plan to fix it?"

"I believe the Inspector is a reasonable man who is capable of being negotiated with." Gen swallowed a snort of hysterical laughter; she'd never heard Flint described as 'reasonable' before.

Mr Eisman chewed this over for a moment. "Very well," he said at last. "Go and bring him here."

"I'm glad you said that, sir."

Will went back through the door and returned a moment later with Flint. Gen's jaw dropped when she realised he was blindfolded and his hands were bound.

"He consented to this," Will said. "I knew you wouldn't want him to know our location. It was a condition of the negotiation."

Mr Eisman inclined his head; his expression gave nothing away.

"Good evening, Inspector," he said as Will unbound Flint's hands and removed the blindfold.

"Ralph," Flint said. "It's been a while."

Gen couldn't keep the shock off her face, and Ralph Eisman noticed. "Thomas and I go way back," he said. "We're old adversaries. Isn't that right?"

"Indeed. I never thought you'd stoop to snatching one of my people, though."

"And I never took you for a spymaster," Ralph said. "But here we are."

"So you want to trade Genevieve in exchange for your cargo?" Flint asked.

"Almost. I'll trade her in exchange for our cargo—and the name of the person who tipped you off. I don't like having moles in my organisation, you know."

"Ah," Flint said. "In that case, we may have a problem. You see, our informant was anonymous. The only thing I can tell you is it was a man with access to a telephone." He shrugged.

Ralph Eisman frowned. "Don't lie to me, Thomas."

"I'm sure I know better than that," Flint said.

Will's gaze switched between his father and Flint as if he were watching an electric lacrosse match, but Gen looked instead at John. He seemed tense, staring intently at Flint as if waiting for some blow to fall. And as she watched him, her suspicion hardened into certainty.

"I'd strongly encourage you to think harder," Ralph said, and there was a new steel to his voice that chilled Gen to the bone. But Flint just shrugged again.

"Father..." Will broke in, but Ralph silenced him with a look.

"At the moment, William, my best source tells me it was you," he said. "I suggest you hold your tongue and hope the Inspector recalls otherwise."

"*Me?* That's absurd! I would never..."

"Silence!" Ralph bellowed, and Will said nothing further.

"I don't know what more I can say," Flint said. "It was an anonymous telephone call to police headquarters. The caller told us that the Eisman family was planning a large illegal importation of tea, the name of the ship and when it would be leaving Hong Kong, and that Matthias Cole was the only crew—in short, he gave us everything we needed. I agree that you definitely have a mole, but I'm afraid I can't help you find out who it is."

The two men stared at each other balefully; it was clear they had reached an impasse.

"You've got something to say, don't you?"

It was Mrs Eisman. Gen looked up and saw her watching her. She had a strong impression of strength and power, and she realised that although Mr Eisman fronted the family and the organisation, it was Mrs Eisman who really held everything together.

Gen took a deep breath—it was now or never. If she was right, it might just save both her and Will. If she was wrong...she didn't want to think too hard about what might happen.

"Yes, ma'am," she said. "I...I think I might know who the caller was."

"Go on, then."

"If I tell you, I want your word that you'll let me go. And please don't blame Will for this—he had no idea who I was." She briefly met his eyes, but he looked away.

Mrs Eisman thought for a moment, then nodded. "You have my word," she said. "If we can confirm who the mole is, you'll be free to go. We'll...continue negotiations...about the cargo." She looked pointedly at Flint.

Gen turned to John. "It was you," she said. Out of the corner of her eye, she saw Will's mouth fall open.

John raised an eyebrow. "Honestly," he said, "is that the best you can do?" He looked at his parents. "We already know who tipped off the police—it was William, in league with Matthias Cole. Matthias said as much in his note: *They promised us a reward, but I realise now that no reward was worth betraying my friends. Please forgive me.*"

Ralph narrowed his eyes. "I've known Matthias a very long time," he said slowly, "and I don't believe for a second that he hanged himself." Gen saw Will visibly start at this, and her stomach lurched—Matthias was dead?

"And in any case," Ralph continued, "how did you know what the note said? Nobody has set eyes on it except your mother and me—not even the poor sod who found him."

John looked momentarily taken aback, but he rallied.

"What reason do I have to lie?" he asked, seemingly the picture of innocence. "Why would I turn in my own family?"

For a moment Gen wavered, worried she'd got it horribly wrong. Then she saw John lick his lips nervously, and she knew she was right, no matter how much he tried to bluster his way out of it.

"Because you're working with the Haverfords," she said.

This time there was an audible gasp, although she couldn't tell from whom. Mrs Eisman looked at her with granite in her gaze.

"That's quite an accusation," she said. "I hope you have proof."

Gen swallowed. Her mouth was dry.

"Two years ago I was part of an operation in London," she said. "We were trying to disrupt a deal between Marcus Haverford and some of his associates. Marcus arrived at the meeting with another man, whom I didn't know. The police operation went very badly, and the other man started shooting. My colleague was killed. When I saw John here tonight, I immediately recognised him. He was the man with Marcus Haverford. I'll never forget that face."

Mrs Eisman turned to her son. "What do you say to that, John?"

"Really, Mother," John spat, barely able to keep the sneer out of his voice. "You'd believe the word of this pig over your own son?"

"You *were* in London two years ago, though," Will said. "You went down there for the season. And that was when we started having all that trouble with the Haverfords." He turned to his parents. "Don't you remember? I didn't connect the two things at the time, but maybe it wasn't a coincidence."

"Well, what do you have to say for yourself, John?" his mother asked again. Her gaze hardened. "And don't you even *think* about lying to me."

There was something in her tone that caused John to blanch. He licked his lips again nervously. "You know I was in London," he said. "So what?"

"Were you consorting with Marcus Haverford?"

John scowled. "This rivalry you have with the Haverfords is utterly ridiculous," he said, evidently deciding that attack was the best form of defence. "Think what we could achieve if we worked together."

"So you took it upon yourself to pursue an alliance, did you?"

"I'm trying to safeguard this family for the future. Heaven knows you can't trust Will to do it. You really want to leave your legacy in the hands of a *brasscore*? It's not like he's got the ticker for it."

Gen's heart ached for Will, but his expression was impassive. "Nothing wrong with my brain, though," he said. "You, on the other hand—you really aren't that bright, are you? Did you even think of what it would mean when you broke the Code? Or was it just easier to shoot first?"

"The Code is just a cover for weakness," John snapped. "You're a fool if you can't see that."

"No." The voice of Mr Eisman broke through, silencing both of them. "The Code is strength. We don't interfere with the police, and they don't interfere with us. And we all live and let live. Isn't that right, Thomas?"

Flint inclined his head but said nothing.

"And if I'm not mistaken," Mr Eisman continued, "our current problems with the police began not long after you returned from London. But I never once thought it was because one of our own—my son and heir, no less—wilfully and knowingly broke the Code. The Code protected us; it helped us do business. And it kept us human. It was the thing that made us different from the Haverfords and all the rest of them. And for decades, it worked. Do you have any idea what you've done?"

John finally seemed to wilt under his father's evisceration. He hung his head.

"Arrest him, Thomas," Mrs Eisman said. "Do whatever you need to do. Someone who would betray our family like that is no son of mine."

Gen finally got up the courage to meet Will's eyes, but his face was stony and gave nothing away.

Chapter 10

Gen initially expected John to resist arrest, but in the face of his parents' scorn he gave no opposition. Perhaps, she thought, he'd realised the game was finally up. Either way, it was quite a peaceful little party that trooped down to the police station in a convoy of steam wagons. At Flint's insistence, Gen drove while he rode in the back with John. Will went with them, and the elder Eismans followed behind. As she drove, Gen was acutely conscious of Will sitting next to her, but she concentrated fiercely on the road to avoid meeting his eyes. *Get the job done first*, she thought. *Everything else will have to wait.* She gritted her teeth, focusing only on guiding the steam wagon over the rough cobbles until they pulled up outside the police station.

After that, everything was a blur. Even though it was late evening, John was whisked away by the duty sergeant to an interview room, and Flint followed. Gen had half-expected to be called in as one of the interviewing officers, but Flint quickly put paid to that.

"You'll be on the other side for a bit, I'm afraid," he said. "We'll need to debrief you properly. I'm sure you understand."

"Yes, sir."

He nodded curtly and departed, leaving Gen alone with Will and his parents. The duty sergeant directed them to a set of wooden chairs, which proved to be even more uncomfortable than they looked, then went back to his paperwork. The silence dragged out.

"Well now," Ralph Eisman said at last. "This is a pretty mess. What do you have to say for yourself, William?"

Will hung his head. "I'm sorry, Father," he said. "I failed."

"Indeed."

"Don't be too hard on the boy," Mrs Eisman said. "We always knew it was a lot to ask, given his condition."

Gen bristled on Will's behalf but bit her tongue. Will said nothing; he seemed to be used to it.

"I won't lie, William—I'm disappointed," Mr Eisman said. "I'd really hoped to see better from you. But as your mother says, it's not entirely unexpected." He sighed. "We're going to have to rethink what happens to the business now, especially given this palaver with John. And I just don't know if there'll be room for you in it."

If Mr Eisman expected his son to be downcast at this news, he was mistaken; on the contrary, Will brightened. "Actually, Father, I've been wanting to talk to you about that," he said. "I agree that the business isn't the best place for me."

Mr Eisman looked startled. "You do?"

"Completely. It needs to be run by someone you trust. And I know that's not me," he added with just a trace of bitterness.

There was a silence.

"But what will you do, sweetheart?" his mother asked at last.

"I've thought about that. I want to go out on my own—nothing in competition with you, of course. Just a small shop where I can sell my brasswork."

"Those little figurines you make? I think that's charming." She glanced at her husband. "Don't you think so, Ralph?"

Mr Eisman shrugged. "So what you're saying is, if we set you up in this little shop of yours, you'll walk away from the business and not lay any claim to it?"

"I'm not asking for your help, Father, just your blessing. I can do it on my own."

"Hmm," Mr Eisman said with evident scepticism. "It's fine. We can afford to give you a start. I think this will be best for everyone, don't you?"

Will nodded. "Thank you, Father."

Gen marvelled at his grace in responding to his parents' clear insinuation that he was incompetent, when she knew he was nothing of the sort. She thought about what he'd said on the airship, about how he'd never be good enough for them, and now she truly understood what he meant.

As quickly as it had begun, the conversation seemed to be over. Mrs Eisman reached into her bag and withdrew what looked like a half-finished jumper, and for some time the only sound was the click-click of her knitting needles. Gen jiggled her knee in frustration. She knew how long interviews took, but it was painful being stuck here with these people. She couldn't bear to even look at Will for fear of what she'd see in his face.

After several hours, Flint re-emerged, looking surprisingly fresh for the time of night. Ralph Eisman immediately sprang to his feet.

"I say, Thomas," he said before Flint could even open his mouth, "is it really necessary for us to be hanging around in this interminable manner? You know where to find us—surely we can go home and get some rest."

Flint thought for a moment, then nodded. "All right. I'll send someone round to take your statements in the morning. I do need to talk to William tonight, though. And you," he added, with a quick glance at Gen.

"Very well."

The Eismans gathered their things, and Mrs Eisman kissed Will's cheek. "We'll catch up with you soon, son." If they were concerned about his impending interview, neither of them showed it. "Good evening, Constable Conlon."

"Good evening, sir, ma'am."

Flint gestured to Will. "This way, if you please."

The doors closed and Gen suddenly found herself alone. Even the desk sergeant had retreated to the back office. With nothing to do, she drifted into a half-doze, until she gradually lost track of time. She was only brought back to reality when the door opened and Will emerged, with Flint right behind him. Neither of them gave any hint of what had transpired.

"Your turn," Flint said.

Gen sighed and got up. As she brushed past Will in the doorway their arms briefly touched and she felt a jolt of electricity run through her, but if he felt the same, he gave no indication.

Gen had been in the interview rooms many times before, but never on this side of the table. A young officer was waiting, stifling a yawn, with a pen and paper on the table before her.

"How are you feeling, Genevieve?" Flint asked as he settled himself in his chair.

Gen shrugged. "Fine, sir."

"This shouldn't take long. It's just a quick debrief."

"Yes, sir." Gen knew better than to believe him.

"The good news is John Eisman is singing like a bird. We brought Marcus Haverford in too, although it's proving harder to pin anything on him."

Gen said nothing.

"Now, I'd like you to tell me what happened on that airship from the moment you boarded in Hong Kong. Don't leave anything out."

"Yes, sir."

She told him about the voyage, including the storm over the Arabian Sea and the fight in Aden—although she left out the details of the dinner and its aftermath, because there were some things he really didn't need to know. She finished with their landing in Edinburgh and her kidnapping.

"And that's when you and Will came in, sir."

Flint nodded. "Quite. Now, about Will. You became romantically involved with him, yes?"

Gen felt like she'd been punched in the stomach. She flushed.

"Did he tell you that, sir?" He must have been even angrier than she'd thought, to drop her in it with her boss.

But Flint shook his head. "Actually, no," he said. "He never mentioned it. Marcus Haverford had an associate tailing you in Aden. He sent a telegram when you departed, saying—among other things—that he suspected an attachment. And I can see from your face that he was right, wasn't he?"

Gen sighed. There was no getting out of it now. "Yes, sir."

"It's certainly not the first time an undercover officer has succumbed to temptation," he said. "But you have a particularly poor record with undercover operations. I would have expected more from you. I thought you valued your job more than this."

"I do, sir. I live for the job. You know that."

Flint rubbed a hand across his face. He looked suddenly tired. "I do know that, Genevieve, and I'm beginning to think that's part of the problem. It's not healthy to live for the job. And you're not performing at the level we need. You jeopardised this mission—what would you have done if it hadn't gone the way it had? Would you have confessed all to Will Eisman?"

Gen bit her lip, unsure of how to answer, but Flint barrelled on.

"You need to live for something other than the job," he said, "which is why I've decided it's in everyone's best interests to let you go."

"You're...sacking me?" Gen could hardly believe it. "Even after I delivered John Eisman to you? That's ridiculous."

Flint sighed. "You are of course free to dispute it through the appropriate channels, should you wish to," he said. "But I'd encourage you to think of this as a kindness, not a punishment. You can't go on the way you are. I've seen too many good men drink themselves to death after starting out like you."

There was a silence.

"Do you have any questions?"

"Are you charging Will?"

"No," Flint said. "We've struck a deal with Mr Eisman to not pursue charges in exchange for his cooperation with the investigation against his brother. He seemed happy with that arrangement. Anything further?"

"No, sir."

"Very well. You're free to go."

"Thank you, sir."

Gen rose and stumbled from the interview room. She marvelled at how her world could come crashing down so spectacularly over the course of just a single day. Now the man she cared about—no, she realised with a lurch, the man she loved—was gone, and her job too. Work had been the only constant in her life since she was sixteen years old. She didn't know who she was if she wasn't a police officer. Maybe Flint was right, and it would all be for the best, but she couldn't see it that way now. She pushed through the doors to the reception area for the last time, wanting nothing more than to go home, crawl under the covers and have a good cry.

Chapter 11

When she emerged into the reception area, she found with some surprise that Will was still there. Did he have further business with Flint? Or...was he waiting for her?

"I thought you'd be gone," she said.

"I should be. I don't even know why I'm still here. But I figured we had...things to say." He stared at her for a long minute. "You look awful."

"I lost my job."

"*What?*"

"Flint fired me." She shrugged, pushing past him towards the outer door.

"Here," he said, "let me walk you home."

Gen wanted to protest, but she couldn't find the energy, and having to cross the city alone late at night was more than she could bear.

"Thank you," she said. She felt weary down to her bones.

The night air was crisp and cool, and it went some way to reviving her spirits. They walked in silence, each busy with their own thoughts. Gen wondered how Will could even stand to be around her after the awful way she'd betrayed him. The thought that she'd once again so deeply hurt someone she loved tore at her even more than the grief over her job.

AS THEY WALKED, WILL glanced at her, concerned. The police had got a good outcome to the case, entirely thanks to her, but she seemed to be carrying the weight of the world on her shoulders. His own feelings were just as conflicted. The revelation of her true identity had shocked and hurt him, and his family's response even more so. He could see that Gen had just been doing her job, and John's ham-fisted attempt at framing him hadn't really come as a surprise either, but his parents' reaction was gutting. He found it hard to accept that they could believe he was the one who had tipped off the police. Did they really think so little of him? He was never going to be enough for them, he knew now, no matter what he did, and strangely there was peace in the thought of walking away.

But Gen—despite everything, Gen was the only person who saw him as he really was, beyond the cog tattoo and the ticking heart. She was the only one who, since he was twelve, had ever believed that he could be, and indeed was, more than anyone expected. There was a dull ache in his chest; never had his clockwork heart felt so heavy.

Gen's single-room basement flat was in a dingy building on the edge of the Old Town. She was glad it was dark so Will couldn't see her embarrassment. Her police wage was modest, and while it wasn't quite an Old Town slum, it wasn't far from it. But if Will was shocked, he showed no sign of it.

They paused at the top of the area stairs, a gas lamp fizzing above them. Gen's heart thundered in her ears. She found it hard to meet Will's eyes, but the thought of parting from him was equally unbearable.

"Would you like to come in for a cup of tea?"

Will looked at her for a long moment, and she began to regret her hasty words. "Are you sure you want me to?" he asked at last.

Gen nodded.

He smiled tentatively, as if he too was unsure whether it was a good idea. "All right."

Gen turned and led the way down the stairs, hiding a flush of relief.

On opening the door she was greeted by a rush of rather musty air, reminding her that the flat had been closed up for some time. The room was sparse but functional, with a bed, a wardrobe, a sink—with running water, no less—a small table, and a cupboard. She ushered Will to the single chair and hurriedly lit the lamps and the fire, disguising her discomfort with a burst of activity.

She filled the kettle and hung it over the fire, then went to the cupboard to get the cups and teapot. But her hands shook so much that the teacups rattled in their saucers and she feared she'd drop them. Then Will was at her side, gently taking them from her and setting them on the table, returning to clasp her trembling hands in his. His touch broke her and, unbidden, the tears began to fall. She swiped at them furiously, angry at her lack of self-control, but Will drew her to him and held her close, and she gave up and wept against his chest. Beneath his shirt she could hear his heart ticking. She wanted him to hold her like that forever, but a small voice in her head told her she had no right. Not anymore.

"I'm so sorry," she gasped, pulling away.

"What for?"

"For ... everything. For betraying you. You didn't deserve it. Can you ever forgive me?"

There was a long silence, which Gen took for a reply.

"I understand if you can't," she said. "I have a nasty habit of hurting those I love. If you never want to see me again, I understand. I just want you to know that you're the most extraordinary man I've ever met, and I'm so glad you were in my life, however briefly."

She went to move away, but Will caught her hand. "Wait," he said. "You haven't heard my answer yet."

She turned back, a small flame of hope flaring in her chest.

"I won't lie—I was devastated when I found out," he said. "But I can also see what happened. When you boarded my ship in Hong Kong you were a police officer and I was just a mark. You couldn't have known how things would turn out."

"I should have told you earlier. I shouldn't have let you find out the way you did."

Will shrugged. "Maybe. I know you tried to. But what's done is done." He took a deep breath. "I love you and I forgive you."

Gen gaped at him. "You ... love me?"

"Oh, Gen." He smiled. "How could I not, when you have such spirit? And you're the only person in nearly twenty years who's believed in me, who's seen me as something more than a filthy brasscore. Even my own family can't see beyond that." He tried to smile but turned his face away, unable to hide the pain.

Gen lifted his hand to her lips, brushing them gently against the blue cog tattoo on his wrist, just as she had on that first night in Aden. "You can't measure the strength of a man's heart by the way in which it beats," she said. "Anyone who thinks you can is a fool." She laid a hand against his cheek, and he raised his eyes to meet hers.

"I love you *because* of who you are, not in spite of it."

Suddenly the kettle began to sing loudly, breaking the moment. Will laughed, and Gen grinned back at him.

"Tea?" she said.

He perched on the edge of the bed and watched her as she moved around, filling the pot and setting out the cups. The weight that had been bowing her shoulders had lifted, and she stood tall and graceful. With the lamplight playing softly on her face and glinting in her dark hair, Will thought she was the most beautiful woman he'd ever seen.

She brought him a cup and sat beside him. For a while they sat close in companionable silence, sipping their tea. For the first time since he'd found out who she really was, Will felt like the storm in his mind had calmed.

"Can I tell you something?" Gen said eventually.

"Of course. You can tell me anything."

"I need you to know what happened to Becca. I mean, what really happened."

"Go on."

GEN SAT LISTENING TO the thud of raindrops on the roof of the steam wagon. The gloomy night was broken only by the hissing light of the gas lamps. They'd been parked outside the seedy coffee-house for nearly two hours now, and nothing had happened to capture their interest. She wondered how the place could stay in business with so few customers.

Next to her, Becca unwrapped a small parcel, sending delicious smells wafting through the carriage. Gen's mouth began to water.

"Want some?" Becca asked, handing it to her. Gen broke off a piece of the still-warm pie.

"I see Andy's been baking again. You've got a good one there."

Becca grinned sheepishly. "I do, don't I?" she said. "Want to come to dinner on Thursday? Unless you've got other plans?"

Gen chuckled. "I don't think that's likely. I'd love to." Sometimes it seemed like she spent more time at Becca and Andy's house than her own, but it was hard not to. Sitting in their warm kitchen with Andy bustling around the stove and Becca teasing him playfully felt like the closest thing to family she'd ever known. She and Becca had been catching up socially at least once a week since they'd first met at the police academy five years earlier. To Gen, Becca was like the best kind of sister, and she hoped the feeling was mutual.

"Actually, I have something to tell you," Becca said as they brushed away crumbs. She was habitually cheerful, but now she was positively glowing, and Gen noticed her hand go unconsciously to her belly.

"You're not ... ?" she gasped. Becca nodded, grinning. "Oh, I'm so happy for you!" Gen exclaimed, hugging her.

"Andy and I would like you to be godmother," Becca said. "Will you?"

"Of course! I'd be honoured." They embraced again, but pulled apart quickly as two men in dark coats crossed the street to the coffee-house, flat caps pulled down low over their eyes. Gen peered out through the spotted windscreen. She recognised Marcus Haverford, but the other man was unknown to her.

"This is it," she said. "Come on!"

They scrambled out of the carriage, trying to look nonchalant, although Gen could feel her heart pounding. She patted her jacket pocket, making sure her steam-revolver was still there. She missed the familiar weight of her utility belt, but this was plain-clothes work, so she'd have to make do.

They paused outside the door to the coffee-house.

"We need to see the deal going down," Gen reminded Becca. "Without that, we've got nothing. Once it's happened, we can arrest them."

Becca frowned. "The plan was surveillance only," she said. "Don't you think we should wait for backup? We don't know how many of them are in there. We don't want to walk into an ambush."

Gen's better judgement told her that Becca was right. But she'd been trying to bring down the Haverford crime syndicate for months, and this could be their only chance.

"I've got your back," she said. "Do you trust me?"

Becca nodded. "Of course," she said. "This is your op. We're in it together, as always." She smiled, and together they went into the coffee-house.

Afterwards, when investigators asked her exactly what went wrong, Gen couldn't really tell them. Everything had seemed fine when they first entered. There were four men sitting at a table in the corner—the two she'd seen in the street, and two others she recognised only from their police files. She and Becca took a table with a good line of sight but not too close, and pretended to study the menu. There were hardly any other patrons, and Gen felt more conspicuous than she liked.

Out of the corner of her eye, she saw a package change hands, followed by a large leather coin purse. Instinctively she rose to her feet, and that was when it all went wrong.

She had no idea how they guessed she was police. All she knew was that before she could even get near, let alone slap handcuffs on any of them, the man she didn't recognise had drawn a steam-revolver. It had escalated so fast that her memories left her with nothing but a blur and a feeling of terror.

She found out later that it was a team of her colleagues, Craig and Ellis, who had saved them. By sheer chance, they'd been conducting a routine patrol in the area, and when the shooting had started they'd been close enough to intervene quickly. But by then it was too late—Becca was dead.

Only one of the four criminals was arrested—the rest fled the scene. And he didn't talk; he was found hanging in his watch-house cell the next day.

The strongest memory Gen had of the whole night was the immediate aftermath, holding Becca's broken body close and keening like a wounded animal, until the medics prised her off. But the worst part was seeing Andy. She asked to be the one to tell him, because the pain of watching him realise that the love of his life was gone, along with all their dreams for the future, was the least she deserved. She'd asked Becca to trust her, and she had betrayed that trust in the very worst way possible. At that moment, Gen vowed that she would never ask anyone to do that again. Because it was very clear that she simply couldn't be trusted.

WILL SAID NOTHING, just let her talk. It had the air of a story she'd replayed many times in her head but had never spoken aloud, and he realised this was the first time she'd ever told anyone, apart from the official investigation. As she talked, it was clear to him that, although she'd made some errors of judgement, Becca had fundamentally been the victim of a tragic set of circumstances that no one could have foreseen. When, inevitably, the tears began to fall, he held her close, stroking her hair and letting her cry.

"It wasn't your fault," he said. "Your bosses didn't think so, and I don't either. And I suspect even Andy wouldn't blame you. He knew the risks she took."

"He wrote to me, you know. Afterwards."

"Did he? What did he say?"

"Almost exactly that. But I didn't...I couldn't believe him."

"Can you now?"

"Maybe."

Will smiled at her and gently wiped away her tears. There were dark shadows under her eyes; she looked exhausted. "It's late," he said, glancing at the clock on the mantelpiece. "I should let you get some sleep."

She looked up at him, longing in her eyes. "Will you stay with me? I...I don't want to be alone tonight."

Will felt his own longing surge within him. "Yes," he said without hesitation.

THERE WAS NO PASSIONATE, desperate lovemaking as there had been in Aden; they were both too emotionally raw for that. Instead, there was a slow, gentle exploration, as if they were meeting for the first time. Kissing her neck, along her collarbone and down to the gentle swell of her breasts, Will saw scars he hadn't noticed before. But rather than imperfections, they were lines in her story, part of what made her who she was. And when her fingers gently traced the long white slash running down his chest, he realised that his own were too.

"I want you," she breathed in his ear, pulling him down onto the bed. He had never wanted someone so much in his life. She lay back and drew him into her, and for a long moment they just held each other tightly, revelling in the depth of their closeness. Then desire overtook them, and they moved together until she arched against him in blissful release, calling out his name, her body pulsing against his as the wave broke over him too and their need was finally assuaged.

Afterwards, they curled together naked under the blankets, a bulwark against the night chill. He kissed the back of her neck and she murmured sleepily. "I love you."

"I love you too," he whispered as they drifted into sleep, their bodies entwined as if they'd never let go.

Epilogue

Gen glanced up at a knock on the door. It had been a long day and she was looking forward to getting home.

"Come in." Her shoulders sagged with relief as Will entered. "Oh, I'm glad to see you."

He walked over to the desk and kissed her. "Tough day?"

She shrugged. "Just winding up the Macgregor matter. But I've had worse. You?"

"Pretty good, actually. The Aerofleet just confirmed an order for thirty steering automatons—with likely more to come." He tried to say it nonchalantly, but he was glowing.

Gen jumped up and hugged him. "That's wonderful! I'm so proud of you! We should celebrate."

"I was hoping you'd say that. That's why I'm here—to take you out to dinner."

"Just let me get my things."

It hadn't been an easy year, Gen reflected as she packed away her files. Between starting her own private-detective agency and Will's new shop, things had often been less than certain. Six months after the tea-smuggling adventure, they'd married in a quiet ceremony and set up house in a small flat above Will's new brasswork shop. His parents hadn't exactly been enthusiastic about the match, but they'd come around eventually. Money had been tight for a while, but now she had some new clients—mostly adultery cases, but beggars couldn't be choosers—and Will's business was also on an upward trajectory. No, the year hadn't been easy—but it had been the happiest one of her life so far.

She was just packing her bag and tidying the desk when there was another knock at the door. Her heart sank, because as much as she loved her work, she really wanted to spend the evening with her own husband, not figuring out how to entrap someone else's philandering one.

"Come in," she called with little enthusiasm. But instead of some distraught wife, striding into her office came the last person she expected to see—Thomas Flint.

For a moment, Gen just stared at him, unsure what to say. "Uh...good evening, sir."

"Good evening, Genevieve." He looked around the room. "I heard you went into business. Very enterprising of you."

Gen frowned in puzzlement. "Thank you."

"In fact, that's why I'm here. Well...part of the reason. I'm glad to see you too, sir," he said to Will. "I need to tell you something. Can we sit down?"

"Of course." She ushered Flint and Will to the two visitors' chairs, then perched on the edge of the desk. "What can we do for you?"

Flint turned to Will. "You're aware, I presume, that your brother was sentenced last week?"

He nodded, and Gen squeezed his hand. John had been sentenced to hang for the murders of Matthias and Becca, but although they'd been expecting it—and in some ways it was no less than he deserved—it had still been difficult to hear.

Flint sighed. "I'm sorry to say that the Haverfords got to him before justice could be done. He was found in his cell this morning."

Gen glanced at Will—he'd gone very pale, but he didn't seem surprised. "I wondered when that would happen," he said. John had given the police enough information to take down most of the Haverford network; it was inevitable that they'd want him dead.

Flint rose. "I'm very sorry for your loss, sir." He turned to Gen. "We'll talk business another day."

"No," Will said. "It's fine. Say what you need to."

"Very well, if you're sure. As I mentioned, Genevieve, I heard you'd set yourself up as a private detective, and as it happens, I'm rather in need of one. We're still tracking smugglers, and we need a competent aeronaut to go undercover on a shipment for us. You'd be attached to the force as a consultant, and we'd pay you accordingly." He named a sum, and Gen almost fell off the desk.

"You don't have to give me an answer now," he said. "Take a few days to think it over and let me know. But it would be good to have you back." He tipped his hat to them. "Good evening to you both."

AFTER FLINT LEFT, WILL drew her into an embrace. They held each other in silence for a few moments; between John's death and the unexpected opportunity, there was a lot to take in.

"I'm sorry about John," Gen said at last.

"That's the nature of the business," Will said. "I'm only surprised they didn't get to him earlier."

"I know, but even if you did have your differences, he was still your brother."

"Only by blood," he said. "And I've learned it takes more than that to make someone family." He pulled back and looked at her. "What do you think about Flint's offer?"

"I'm not sure. It's tempting. Do you think I should do it?"

Will smiled and kissed her. "I think you'd make a brilliant undercover operative," he said. "Just don't go falling for any charming airship captains."

She grinned, pulling him towards the desk. "Oh, I think it's far too late for that."

FLYING HIGH
Chapter 1

"Have you got a minute, Millie?"

Millie Roberts paused in the doorway where she'd been chatting to her friend, Jean. The latest meeting of the Brasscore Political League had just adjourned, and they were eager to dissect developments.

"Of course," she said.

Jean squeezed her hand. "I'll see you tomorrow," she said, and Millie nodded. She turned to Will Eisman, the organisation's president.

"What can I do for you?" The hall was emptying out now, with just one or two clumps of people still in animated conversation.

"I wanted to talk to you about something," he said. "Specifically, the press."

"The press?" Millie's eyebrows shot up. "What about them?"

"Well, as you know, we've been discussing for some time now how the movement just isn't getting heard enough," Will said. "We need to have more of a public voice to let people know we exist, and what we stand for. So I've been contacting various newspapers to see if any of them would like to do a story on us—and one of them does."

Millie frowned. "Go on."

"You're the only person in the BPL who has any experience dealing with the press," he continued, "so I was hoping you could take the lead on this—look after the journalist, show him how things work around here, introduce him to people he can interview, and so on."

Millie sighed. As soon as Will had mentioned the press, she'd been afraid of something like this. True, she'd dealt with them a lot, once upon a time, but that had been a long time ago and it hadn't ended well. But it did mean she knew how the media worked—and she knew you couldn't trust journalists as far as you could throw them. She didn't really want this task, but better her than one of the other members, who might jeopardise the cause with some naive comment.

"All right," she said at last. "Which paper?"

"The *Daily Bugle*."

Millie gaped at him. "Please tell me you're joking."

Will shook his head.

"But surely you've seen some of the rubbish they publish? They *hate* brasscores. They're a lowest-common-denominator tabloid that thrives on spreading division."

"They're also the most widely read paper in the country," Will said with a shrug. "And Bruce Maddox is extremely influential politically. If we can change his opinion, we can sway the public to our cause. Giving one of his journalists the inside scoop is the best way to do that."

"Fine. Just as long as it's not that odious Nick Galbraith."

Will glanced away.

"Will! It's not, is it?"

"Actually ... I'm afraid it is," he said sheepishly. "I'm sorry—I had no control over who they sent."

"And you want me to babysit him, even after that article?" She didn't normally read the *Bugle*, but Jean had brought a copy to last week's meeting specifically to show her a gushing front-page headline: *Ten Years Since the Flight That Changed the World!* Jean and the others had been proud of the glowing retrospective of her famous flight, but she'd just been angry—the wretched scribbler hadn't even had the courtesy to tell her it was being published, let alone consult her. And now she was going to have to be his minder. She took a deep breath.

"Fine. When is he coming?"

"Tomorrow."

"Just for the day?"

"For a week. He'll probably attend the march too. Apparently it's going to be quite an in-depth piece."

Millie rolled her eyes. "I bet."

"Thank you," Will said. "I appreciate this isn't easy for you."

Millie felt a flush of shame; she knew how graceless she was being. "No, it's fine," she said. "After all, I don't have to like him in order to be professional."

"No," Will said. "You don't. Just take him out after the meeting and give him some background. We need him—and his readers—to see we're human, just like them."

"MR MADDOX WANTS TO see you, sir."

"Thanks," Nick Galbraith said to the copy boy, who ducked his head and hurried off on some other newsroom errand. As if on cue, the worries began flocking in. Even after a decade at the *Daily Bugle*, this sort of request from the newspaper's editor and publisher still increased Nick's heart rate. Maddox rarely summoned reporters in to praise them.

Nick finished the sentence he was typing then hurried across the newsroom to the editor's office. He knocked, waiting for the grunted "Enter!" before turning the handle and walking in.

Bruce looked up from the sheaf of papers he was editing. As always, a cigar drooped from the corner of his mouth. He was a beefy, red-faced man who always seemed like he was about to bust the buttons of his shirt, which invariably looked as though he'd slept in it.

"Ah, Nick, just the man I wanted to see," he said. "Sit down."

Nick sat obediently, wondering what he'd done.

"I've got a story for you."

This was the last thing he'd expected. "A story, sir?"

"Yes, a story. A proper one, not that city beat rubbish you usually write. Potentially front-page stuff, if you do it well."

Nick gaped at him. "What sort of story?"

"The brasscore rights movement."

Nick had thought he was beyond being surprised, but he realised he was wrong. "If you want me to write a takedown, I don't think I can do that ..."

"No, no," Bruce interrupted. "I'm talking about proper reportage. A week with the Brasscore Political League. Human interest, if we can call it that."

Nick took a deep breath, forcing down his anger at the jibe. Brasscores were people who, for various medical reasons, had had body parts replaced with sophisticated clockwork technology. Nick's own brother was one of Britain's most eminent surgeons, and he'd saved countless lives with his clockwork implants and prostheses. But many people still shared Maddox's view that brasscores were somehow less than human. They didn't even have the vote, despite incredible achievements in all sorts of areas. Hell, just the other week he'd published an article on Millie Roberts, one of the most famous brasscores of her generation, who, ten years earlier, had become the youngest person to pilot an airship around the world solo and unassisted, aged just fifteen. And yet the stigma persisted.

It was this thought more than anything that piqued his interest. He knew the BPL was the major force in the brasscore rights movement, and they'd had some notable successes. Now they were focused on getting the right to vote. There were definitely the makings of a good story there.

"Sounds interesting," he said. "When do you want it by?"

"It's all been arranged with their people," Bruce said. "You start with them tomorrow. Apparently there's some big protest next week, so they want you to be there in the lead-up to that. We'll publish the day after."

"Makes sense."

"There's just one more thing."

"Go on."

"I want you to keep me appraised of all the details. About their plans, I mean. Any issues within the group, that sort of thing."

Nick frowned. "May I ask why?"

"Let's just say I have a ... professional interest."

"What about off-the-record information?"

"That too."

"Forgive me, but that sounds an awful lot like you're asking me to spy on them."

"That's a strong word," Bruce said, steepling his fingers. He eyed Nick the way a shark might look at its prey. "But let's face it, Nick, you don't have much of a record with this sort of story. I'm giving you an opportunity here to get away from your regular beat and show me what you can do. It's natural that I'd want a bit more ... oversight."

Nick bit his lip. It was a bit of a sore point that, even after a decade in the business, he was still stuck doing boring day-to-day snippets of city news. He knew he was a good journalist—for even Bruce offered the odd word of praise now and again—but he'd never had the chance to get really stuck into a proper, meaty story. Even so, it still didn't feel quite right.

Bruce seemed to sense his reticence. "It's crunch time, my boy," he said, his eyes hardening. "Get this right and I'll make you a senior reporter. Get it wrong and ... well, I'm not sure the *Bugle* has room to carry a dead weight. And I don't know any other paper in this town that does either."

Nick swallowed. He knew Bruce was powerful enough that he could ensure Nick would never work again in

Edinburgh—or possibly even in the whole of Scotland. He didn't understand why Bruce was suddenly so interested in the BPL, but he really had no choice.

"All right," he said, his heart sinking.

"Good lad," Bruce said. He handed him a piece of paper. "Here's the address and time of their meeting tomorrow. They're allocating someone to look after you. Don't be late."

Nick knew a dismissal when he heard one. He took the paper and returned to his desk, but he felt like he'd somehow left a vital piece of himself behind.

Chapter 2

The next morning, Nick caught the air-tram down Princes Street to St George's Church, on the edge of the gardens. He'd been past the ornate neo-Gothic church countless times but had never really paid much attention to the parish hall beside it, which was a more modern addition and generally unremarkable. But it was here that Bruce's instructions had said to go, so he alighted from the air-tram at the Princes St Gardens stop and took the stairs down to street level.

As he approached, he began to wonder if he'd got the right place, for there was no sign of any meeting. Then he saw someone waiting on the hall steps, apparently looking out for him—his minder from the Brasscore Political League, he assumed. He wasn't sure what he'd been expecting, but it wasn't this—a woman just a few years younger than him. She wore a wine-red gown trimmed with black lace, and her blonde hair was coiled beneath a neat little black hat. As she noticed him arriving, she turned towards him and he had a second jolt of surprise, for he recognised her. Only a few weeks ago he'd thumbed through countless photos of her while researching his retrospective article. She was older now, of course, and dressed more like a lady than an aeronaut, but the resemblance was unmistakeable. He'd had no idea Millie Roberts was a brasscore activist, although it made all sorts of sense. He'd also had no idea that she'd grown up to be quite so beautiful.

She smiled when she saw him, although it looked a little forced.

"Sorry I'm late," he said.

"I was beginning to think you weren't coming," she said, by way of greeting. "I'm Millie Roberts. But I think you already know that, don't you, Mr Galbraith?" She held out her hand, encased in a fingerless black lace glove, and Nick shook it.

"I do," he said, slightly thrown by her brusqueness. "And please call me Nick. I didn't know you were a brasscore rights activist."

"You would have if you'd asked—for your article, for example."

Nick felt a flush creep up his cheeks. He wasn't normally given to confrontation, but he knew he'd have to address this immediately if he was to have any chance of writing a half-decent story. There was no point starting off on the wrong foot.

"I'm sorry about the story," he said. "I wanted to consult you and your family, but my editor insisted we go straight to press."

"That's convenient," she said icily. "Let's just say your little retrospective has done nothing to improve my opinion of your profession in general, or your paper in particular."

"Fair enough." He knew she was famously reclusive and media-shy, and who could blame her, after everything that had happened? "If you don't want to work with me, I understand," he said. "I can see if the paper can send someone else ..."

She shook her head. "No. There's no time. We've got our big march next week and we want you to see the preparations. And after all, being part of a movement like this sometimes means doing things you'd rather not, in the service of the greater good." She gave him an appraising look, her dark eyes flashing. "But if you try any underhanded tricks here, you'll have me to answer to. Do you understand?"

"Yes, ma'am." He gave her what he hoped was a winning smile. "Well, here I am. I'm all yours for the next week."

"Lucky me," she said wryly. "Don't worry, I'm sure we'll find plenty for you to do. Come inside and I'll introduce you to the others."

AS THEY ENTERED THE hall, Millie frowned to herself. Things really hadn't got off to the best start with Nick Galbraith, and she was now second-guessing whether she ought to have been quite so strident. He wasn't what she'd expected; he was much younger, for one thing, and much more handsome, for another. She also hadn't expected his apology—in her experience, journalists didn't care much about the facts or admit that they'd gone about something the wrong way. They just cared about what would sell papers. And she knew that, even ten years after her adventure, her name still had those papers flying off the shelves.

Still, rightly or wrongly, at least the confrontation had cleared the air. She knew that this was a big chance for the BPL to get their views across to a wide audience, but she wasn't really thinking about that. Even against her better judgement, Nick Galbraith intrigued her, and it had been a long time since anyone had done that, let alone a man. But he was still a journalist, and she'd have to watch him like a hawk.

She led him into the main hall, where a circle of chairs had been set up, along with a trestle table that was already covered with papers. A clump of men and women was milling around the table, while several others sat in small groups, chatting while they waited for the meeting to start. There was no sign of Will, so Millie marched up to the circle, trying to seem braver than she felt. At twenty-five she was one of the BPL's youngest members, and also one of the newest. She knew the only reason the leadership had entrusted her with seeking publicity was because she was the only one with any experience of the press, even if it was a long time ago and under less-than-ideal circumstances, and she had to prove she was worthy of the task. She took a deep breath.

"Ladies and gentlemen," she said, and they turned to face her. "I'd like to introduce Mr Nick Galbraith, a journalist with the *Daily Bugle*. He's going to be spending some time with us over the next week while he writes a story on the campaign." Every eye in the room turned to Nick, and Millie clenched her jaw; the stares weren't exactly hostile, but they weren't particularly welcoming either. The *Daily Bugle's* views on brasscores were well known.

"Not a hatchet job, I hope," Florence said. "I mean, really, Millie—of all the newspapers ..."

"Not at all, ma'am, I assure you," Nick said smoothly, before Millie could reply. "I'm just here to observe and write a fair account of what I see."

A door at the back of the hall opened and Will entered, much to Millie's relief.

"Nick, this is Will Eisman," she said as Will strode forward to shake the reporter's hand. "He leads the Brasscore Political League here in Edinburgh."

"For now," someone muttered, but nobody reacted, and Millie wasn't sure if they'd heard. She was well aware of the conflicts raging within the BPL, but she really hoped that they could keep Nick away from them. The last thing they needed was to give the impression of disunity.

"Do you support the cause, Mr Galbraith?" Will asked as they all sat down. Millie looked at him with respect; as always, Will had a knack for cutting to the chase.

"Well, as a reporter, sir, I have to keep my personal views out of it, I'm afraid," Nick said.

"Of course," he replied. "As a private citizen, then, what views do you hold? We're all familiar with your brother David's work, of course. In fact, many of us are his former patients."

Nick seemed to realise he was backed into a corner. "Like my brother, I believe that all people should have the right to life, hope, suffrage and political representation," he said. He smiled wryly.

"I imagine that doesn't make you very popular at the *Bugle*," Will said.

Nick just shrugged. "I've learned to keep my views to myself."

"In any case, thank you for your candour," Will continued. "You're welcome to attend our meetings and campaigns, and to speak to any member who consents to be interviewed. I look forward to reading your article." He turned back to the group at the table, and Millie breathed a sigh of relief. She ushered Nick to a seat, where he pulled out his notebook, and shortly thereafter Will called the meeting to order.

"I JUST DON'T THINK that will work," Florence said stubbornly. Nick tapped his foot restlessly; the meeting had been going for over two hours now, and progress seemed to have stalled. From what he could see, the group was divided along ideological lines: on the one side were the campaign veterans, like Will, who advocated peaceful protest, and on the other were the younger, newer activists, like Florence, who wanted more direct, militant action.

"We've been over this a hundred times before," Florence continued. "The ruling class will never voluntarily give up power; we have to take it from them by force. We can't just keep putting up our pretty little posters and hoping for scraps. We have to march in and overturn the table."

"But violence isn't the answer," said another woman, whose name Nick didn't know. "It solves nothing and just makes us look bad, plus it gives the police a reason to use force to suppress us."

"Can we please just get back to discussing the march?" someone else begged, but Florence scowled.

"I think the march on Holyrood should be the culmination of a campaign of direct action," she said. "Otherwise it's useless in and of itself."

"Aye," another woman said. "That way, they'll know we mean business."

Will sighed. "We're really not getting anywhere," he said. "Let's take some time to properly clarify our positions. It's no use going round and round in circles. We'll meet again on Friday afternoon and go from there. Meeting adjourned. Thank you all for coming."

Millie stood up and stretched. "And that's BPL politics for you," she said, turning to Nick as the hall began to empty. "Do you have any questions?"

"A few," he said. "Mostly background things."

"All right," Millie said, although she looked less than enthused. "There's a tea shop across the street. Let's go over there and I'll see if I can give you the information you need."

The tea shop was small and cosy, with frilly tablecloths and net curtains framing the windows. They chose a table and Millie ordered a pot of tea and scones with jam and cream.

"Let me make one thing clear," she said as Nick took out his notebook and pencil. "I'll answer whatever questions you like about the BPL, but there's to be no questions about my personal life or involvement. This is about the cause, not me." She looked at him fiercely. "Agreed?"

"Agreed. And for what it's worth, I really am sorry about the article. But out of interest, if I'd asked you to comment, would you have?"

She shrugged. "Probably not. But it would have been nice to have had the choice." The tea arrived and she busied herself pouring it. "And that's really what's at the heart of the movement," she said, handing a cup to Nick. "As brasscores, we currently don't have agency over our own lives. We lack the most basic choice—being able to choose who represents us, who makes decisions on our behalf. That's what we're fighting for. If there's one thing I'd like you and your readers to understand, it's that we're people just like them. We may have mechanical limbs or hearts or eyes, but in all other respects we're the same. We dream and plan and love just like them. And we hurt just like them too." She stared at him over the top of her cup, her cheeks flushed and eyes sparkling. Her passion dazzled him, and Nick looked hastily down at his notebook.

"Can I quote you on that?"

"No. You said this was background only, and if you start quoting me I'll become the story."

Nick nodded, because she was right. "Fair enough. Tell me about the BPL, then."

"It's been around in various forms for a long time," she said. "But it's only become really active in the last year or so, since Will came on board."

"I must say, I was surprised to see the scion of Edinburgh's most notorious crime family leading a political movement. What's he like as a leader?"

"Well, firstly, he's not involved with his family's dealings," Millie said defensively. "He's very much on the straight-and-narrow. His wife is a former police officer, for goodness' sake. So if you're planning to go down that road, I'd reconsider. And he's an excellent leader. He's very politically savvy and he can bring people from all walks of life along with him."

"Judging by the meeting, it seems that not everyone would agree with that assessment."

She shrugged. "Healthy debate occurs in any group," she said. "Differences of opinion can end up making us stronger. I have every faith in Will."

"Do you believe brasscores will have the vote in time for the next election?"

"I have to believe that," she said. She spread jam and cream on a scone, and for a few minutes there was silence as they ate.

"How did you end up in journalism?" she asked at last, wiping her lips.

Nick grinned. "I thought I was meant to be the one asking the questions."

"Humour me."

"Well, I always loved to write."

"So why not just be a writer?"

He chuckled, but it rang hollow. "In my family, one does *not* go into the arts," he said. "If you're good at science and mathematics, it's medicine or engineering. If you're not, it's law. Journalism at least pays a living wage, even if it is a trade. My father was less than pleased, but if I'd become a writer I probably would have been disowned."

She gave him a look he couldn't quite decipher. "And do you enjoy it?"

He shrugged. "It pays the bills. It's been a while since I've had the chance to work on a really meaningful story, though, which is why I'm so pleased to be doing this one."

"I assume meaningful stories are in short supply at the *Bugle*."

He couldn't help laughing at her audacity. "Ouch."

"Tell me I'm wrong."

"Much as I hate to admit it, you're not."

"So what keeps you there?"

Nick thought for a moment. "I don't really know," he said at last. "Comfort, probably." He swallowed, slightly discomfited by the intimate turn of the conversation. In the countless interviews he'd done over the years, none of them had ever ended up with him being interrogated by a beautiful, whip-smart woman. But then he'd also never met a woman quite like Millie.

She shrugged. "Fair enough."

Nick raised an eyebrow. "I thought you were going to tell me that comfort is overrated."

"Well, having spent a pretty large chunk of my life uncomfortable, there's a lot to be said for comfort," she said. "Complacency, though—that's a different story."

"You're saying I'm complacent?"

"I'm saying that having a moral compass and working for a paper like the *Bugle* would seem to me to be mutually exclusive," she said. "Either your values align, in which case I don't see why I should trust that you'll portray us in any remotely fair way, or they don't, in which case you're suppressing your own ethics for the sake of money. So which is it?"

If anyone else had spoken to him like that, he would have arced up immediately. And yet somehow with Millie he didn't feel defensive. He knew something of her history and, quite frankly, it was no wonder she despised the media. And so he found himself compelled to win her trust, not just for the sake of the story but for himself.

"Probably a little bit of the second," he said, knowing that she wouldn't accept anything less than radical honesty. "But also, at the start I hoped I could change things from the inside. And I did try to, in those early days. But I was young and naive, and I didn't understand the institutional might of a place like the *Bugle*. It has a momentum all its own, and a single young reporter doesn't stand a chance of changing things. So then I suppose I *did* become complacent. And now here we are."

She gave him an appraising look. "That's very frank of you to say."

Nick shrugged. "I know you don't trust journalists, and I can't say I blame you. But all I ask is that you give me a chance. I do think you've got an important story to share with the world, and I want to honour that."

Millie bit her lip. "All right," she said at last. "Is there anything else you want to know about the BPL?"

He shook his head. "You've given me a lot to think about. So the next meeting is at the hall on Friday—at what time?"

"Three o'clock. But things can change quite quickly around here. Should I just send a mecha-pigeon to the *Bugle* if they do, or is there another way I can contact you?"

Nick pulled out his calling card and scribbled his address on the back. It wasn't something he'd normally give an interviewee, and he was hard-pressed to explain why he was doing so now. He handed the card to Millie.

"This is my home address," he said. "You can reach me there if something happens after-hours." He paused. "I hope I'll see you soon."

She smiled at him enigmatically. "I'm sure you will."

Chapter 3

The doorman at the Edinburgh Club was a master of diplomacy. His domain was nothing special to look at—a discreet wooden door inlaid with brass, with the club's name etched in gold leaf into the stone lintel above. But only a very particular sort of person was allowed over the threshold: male, and of a certain level of wealth, class and political influence. And nobody with the mandatory blue cog tattoo marking them as a brasscore would ever get beyond the front steps.

Most ordinary city folk wouldn't look twice at the plain stone building, despite its prime location in the heart of the New Town, let alone dream of entering. Indeed, most of them had no idea of just how much their lives were controlled by the men who met within its walls. So the doorman had a special duty: keep out the riffraff and pay appropriate deference to members, while maintaining absolute discretion. This was the reason the Edinburgh Club was one of the last places in the city to still employ a human in this role, rather than a simple service automaton. Its members expected—and paid for—real service. Automatons were common as muck, and there was nothing like a human servant to reinforce the privilege of class.

Inside, the decor was discreetly opulent, with leather armchairs, fireplaces, and mahogany tables. The art on the walls was worth more money than most people would see in their lifetimes. Thick drapes at the windows and finely woven rugs on the floor insulated the club from the traffic noise outside. The maids were pretty and subservient, the butler deferential. It was everything a certain kind of man could wish for.

In a drawing room off the main hallway, five such men lounged in armchairs beside a roaring fire, crystal glasses of whisky at their elbows. The air was a fug of cigar smoke, and the decanter was regularly replenished. They jokingly called themselves the Gang of Five, and they comprised a Member of the Scottish Parliament, Sir Giles Pearson; Maxwell McPherson, a wealthy industrialist whose empire included textiles and steel; Robert MacIntyre, the chief of Edinburgh's police force; Jock Williamson, who had revolutionised the country's automaton industry; and Bruce Maddox.

Bruce Maddox was in many ways the odd one out. While he wasn't exactly self-made—he'd inherited much of his media empire from his father—unlike the others he was *new money*. But the *Daily Bugle* was the country's most popular newspaper, and Maddox was a smart player; he knew how to sway opinion. Not long after he'd taken over the business from his father, it had become apparent that those who wanted to get things done needed to have Maddox on side. And so the doors of the Edinburgh Club, and many other establishments of the rich and powerful, were suddenly opened to him.

"I see those damn clankers are at it again," Jock Williamson remarked, flicking open a copy of the *Scottish Times*. Maddox frowned; the broadsheet was one of his few competitors, and it was still the preferred paper of the establishment, much to his chagrin.

"They're gaining momentum," Pearson said. "The mood in the party is that we'll have to give way sooner or later."

"It's a slippery slope," McPherson grumbled. "Give them the vote and they'll want even more. It threatens the very foundations of a civilised society. What next—we'll have an automaton as prime minister?"

"Some would argue we already do," Williamson said, and the others guffawed.

"Plus they're a public nuisance," MacIntyre added. "My men get pulled away from important police work to deal with their vandalism and civil disobedience. They need to be clamped down on once and for all." He glared at Sir Giles. "You lot need to do what you're paid for and make some laws against it."

Sir Giles frowned. "You know I've been preparing a bill to declare the Brasscore Political League a criminal organisation," he said. "That would allow us to take some proper action. But I don't have the votes to pass it at the moment. The public mood just isn't that hard against them, and I don't see how that's going to change. And from what I hear, there's another big protest in the works sometime soon."

Bruce Maddox had been listening to this with interest. Now he stood up and walked over the cigar box. He unwrapped a cigar, clipped the end and placed it between his lips before lighting it. "I might just have a solution," he mumbled.

Four jowly faces turned towards him. "Oh?" Pearson said. "Do tell."

"One of my men has just been thrown a story going behind the scenes at the BPL," he said slowly. "*They* approached *me*, if you can believe it. My first inclination was to turn it down, but then I thought there might just be an opportunity here. He's going to spend a week with them, and presumably he'll be privy to all their plans. It might give us just the edge we need to disrupt the protest and turn the tide of public opinion against them."

"And he'll go along with it, this reporter?" MacIntyre said. "Heaven knows we could use the intelligence—it's the basis of effective policing, you know."

Maddox rolled his eyes. "He's a bit of a bleeding heart, I'm afraid," he said. "I haven't been able to bring him on board officially, but I've made it clear I want to know all the details. And I think that, if asked the right questions, he'll be quite forthcoming. After all, as his editor I'm naturally interested in how his story is progressing."

The other men chuckled, and Pearson clapped Maddox on the back. "Good show, old man," he said. "It might even work. Let's reconvene later in the week and see what your boy's got for us. Now, I don't know about you, but I could do with some grub. Ring the bell, would you, Jock?"

As Sir Giles harangued a pretty little maid about food, Bruce Maddox smiled to himself. If he could pull this off, then all these powerful men would be in his debt. And that would be a very useful place to have them.

Chapter 4

Nick spent the remainder of that day and all of the next back in the office, researching the brasscore rights movement and trying to make sense of what he'd seen at the meeting. But the words just weren't coming. Frustrated, he pulled the umpteenth draft out of his typewriter and scrunched it into a ball; the wastepaper basket was already overflowing.

The meeting with Millie had not gone as he'd expected; indeed, she hadn't been what he'd expected at all. He realised that all the research he'd done for the retrospective article had skewed his idea of her. After all, the photographs he'd seen of her had been from the time of her flight, when she'd been just fifteen—a tall, rather gangly girl standing awkwardly in front of her airship, the *Pride of Scotland*, or beside her father, the famous adventurer and explorer Sir James Roberts. And then there'd been her very public breakdown two years later, where she'd adamantly declared she would never fly again, and had subsequently vanished from view. Most people had assumed she'd ended up in an asylum, although the family had never confirmed it. And now here she was a decade later, savvy, articulate and passionate about her cause. He was honest enough with himself to admit that she'd knocked him for six.

"I'm heading home," he said to no one in particular as he packed his things, but nobody even looked up.

Normally he'd take the air-tram, but the summer evening was mild, the air golden and effervescent, so he decided to walk instead. As the air-tram rattled above him, he was glad not to be stuck in the sweaty box with everyone else who was finishing their workday. There was a pleasant rhythm to the walk, and he reflected that he spent far too much time dashing frantically from place to place, from story to story.

His thoughts drifted, alighting once again on Millie. It was hard to tell exactly where she stood with the activists; she'd been very quiet during most of the meeting the previous day, just watching and taking everything in. He got the impression that she was fiercely intelligent, but she played her cards very close to her chest, and he wasn't at all certain what her regard for him was. Certainly, his being a journalist was a mark against him, he knew, and he really couldn't blame her for that. But he hoped that he'd eventually be able to win her trust. If nothing else, it would be very difficult to get her cooperation with his story if she thought him a cad.

He arrived at his flat in the New Town just as the evening was deepening into twilight. His home was small but comfortable, although it could never be said to be luxurious. His cat, Mr Pickles, was at the door to meet him, as always. His family all saw keeping a pet as a hopeless extravagance, but Nick couldn't agree, and after Mr Pickles had turned up on the doorstep two years ago, it hadn't been long before he'd got the run of the place.

He'd just finished an early supper when there was a knock at the door. Surprised, he rose, wondering who could be calling at such an hour. But when he opened the door he found the last person he expected: Millie.

"Miss Roberts," he said in surprise. "Is everything all right?"

"I'm so sorry to call on you at home," she said, wringing her hands. "There's been an incident." Her cheeks were pale and her face was creased with worry.

"Come in," Nick said, shooing Mr Pickles out of the way. "Can I get you some refreshment? You don't look well."

She shook her head. "I'm fine, thank you. I've just had some distressing news."

"What's happened?" he asked, ushering her to a chair in the small parlour.

"Three of our members were arrested this afternoon," she said. "You might have met them yesterday—Florence, Bertha and Jean. They're part of the group that favours militant action over peaceful protest."

Nick nodded. "I remember."

"I don't know the specifics, but I believe they engaged in some sort of property damage," Millie continued. "Breaking windows and destroying a messenger mecha-pigeon roost, I believe. They're at the city watch-house even as we speak. And I know you're meant to be an impartial observer and so on, but I was hoping that, with your connections, you might know someone who can help them."

"Their solicitor should be able to get them bailed, I imagine."

"They don't have a solicitor. None of them is from the kind of family that could afford one. We're taking up a collection, but the bigger problem is access. Will and I approached a few law offices as soon as we got the news, and none of them were willing to represent us. They won't take brasscores for clients, even if we can pay."

She bit her lip; it seemed to be costing her a great deal to even ask him. "Do you know what the police do to the likes of us?" she asked. "They beat us. Brasscore activists who have protested in custody through hunger strikes have been force-fed. They *hate* us." She looked at him, her eyes bright. "Believe me, I wouldn't ask you if there was anyone else I could turn to."

"Your father doesn't have a lawyer who could help?"

Millie lowered her gaze. "My father and I don't speak."

Nick hadn't known that; he filed it away for future reference. They sat in silence for a moment as he contemplated the dilemma. He was meant to be writing an observational story—he shouldn't get involved. But he supported the activists' aims, and he'd heard before about some of the brutality they'd suffered. And then there was Millie herself, sitting in his house, begging him for help. He found his conscience wouldn't let him say no.

"All right," he said. "I may know someone who can assist. Come with me." Nick rose, pulling on his boots and jacket in the hallway, then ushering her out onto the street. He hailed a steam-cab and gave the driver an address.

"Posh," Millie said when she heard it. Nick shrugged. He wasn't really dressed to be making calls in that part of town, but he doubted Jerome would mind.

MILLIE SANK BACK INTO the cab's cushions with a sigh. It hadn't been an easy decision to call on Nick, but Will had come to her in desperation. Will's own family was very powerful, but they sat on the wrong side of the law—they pretty much controlled Edinburgh's criminal underworld—and she'd spent enough time with Will and his wife, Genevieve, to know that he was estranged from them. It was one of the many things they had in common. They'd be no use in the current situation, and nobody else in the BPL had the necessary money or connections. Nick was the only person she could think of who might be able to help. She glanced across at him surreptitiously, but his expression was unreadable. Did he now think her the worst kind of hysterical female, unable to solve her own problems? And, more to the point, why did she care what he thought?

She was still lost in her thoughts when the cab pulled up outside a stylish white stone residence. This part of the New Town was familiar to her—she'd grown up nearby—but she hadn't been back since she'd moved out of her parents' house five years earlier. Her own modest little terrace near the park would hardly rate a mention to the people who lived around here, but she infinitely preferred it.

Nick stepped down and helped her out. They walked up the broad stone steps together, and he rang the bell.

The door was opened by an elderly butler, who looked them up and down as if deciding whether they should be permitted entry. "Good evening, Mr Galbraith."

"Good evening, Thompson," Nick said. "I'd like to speak to my brother, if you please."

"The master and Mrs Galbraith are currently at dinner," the butler said. "Would you like to wait?"

"Yes, please."

"This way, sir, ma'am." He led them down the hallway and through a door into a library that reminded Millie strongly of the one in her father's house. Nick sat on a sofa beside the fire, but she was drawn to the floor-to-ceiling bookshelves that lined the walls. She glanced across and saw him watching her.

"Do you like to read?" he asked.

"Oh, yes," she said. "I always have done. You?"

"When I get the chance." He rose and joined her at the shelf. "I'm rather fond of poetry, actually."

"Really? You don't strike me as the type."

He grinned, his right cheek dimpling. "Why's that?"

Millie contemplated for a moment. "Actually, I don't really know." Their eyes met, and inexplicably she felt her heart beat faster. She quickly looked away.

At that moment, the library door opened, and a man entered. He was formally dressed for dinner, but he was otherwise so like Nick that there was no escaping the family connection. He strode over to them and clasped Nick's hand.

"Hello, old chap!" he exclaimed. "What a surprise! It's good to see you."

Nick returned the smile. "You too. It's been too long." He glanced at Millie. "Jerome, may I present Miss Millicent Roberts," he said. "Millie, this is my brother, Mr Jerome Galbraith."

"Pleased to meet you, sir."

"Likewise, Miss Roberts. Why don't we sit down and you two can tell me what brings you to our neck of the woods. Cathy is forever prevailing on this one to visit, without much success." He grinned, and Millie found herself smiling back, already warming to him.

"Actually, we need your help," Nick said as they took seats before the fire. "Millie is involved with the Brasscore Political League, and a couple of their members have got into a spot of bother with the police." He turned to Millie. "Jerome here is one of the city's best advocates. He'll make Queen's Council any day now."

"Hardly," Jerome said modestly. "But I might be able to help. Now, start at the beginning and tell me what happened."

AN HOUR LATER, JEROME was on his way to the city watch-house, and Millie and Nick were on their way home. It had all been something of a whirlwind, and Millie's head was still spinning. But she was confident that her friends were in safe hands, and Jerome had even assured her that he was willing to take on their case *pro bono*. She felt as if a weight had lifted from her shoulders.

They didn't speak much on the way, and before she knew it, the steam-cab was pulling up outside her house. Millie hesitated, unsure of what to say.

"I ... thank you for your help tonight," she said. "It really meant a lot." She cringed at how stiff the words sounded.

Nick smiled, and her awkwardness vanished. "You're welcome," he said. "Jerome's a good fellow. He'll take care of them."

"I hope I haven't made things difficult for you, getting you involved like this," she said. "I know maintaining your impartiality is important. I just ... I was so afraid for them." She glanced away, biting her lip in an attempt to fight back the mess of feelings that threatened to spill over.

"Millie, look at me," he said gently, and she did, her breath catching at the compassion in his eyes. "It's absolutely fine," he said. "I'm glad I was able to help. I don't think impartiality should extend to standing by while people get hurt if you're able to prevent it. Sometimes you have to observe, and sometimes you have to act."

She smiled in relief and opened the steam-cab door. "I'll see you at the meeting tomorrow?"

"I look forward to it."

As Millie went inside and readied herself for bed, she couldn't help feeling a flutter of anticipation at the thought of seeing him again. Perhaps this particular journalist wasn't so bad after all.

Chapter 5

The next morning, Nick returned to the office to finish typing up his notes and collect his messages. He'd hoped to be able to sneak in unobtrusively and work without interruption, but it wasn't to be—as soon as he set foot in the newsroom, Bruce Maddox caught sight of him.

"A word, Nick?"

Nick sighed inwardly and followed the editor into his office with the air of a prisoner going to the gallows.

"Take a seat," Bruce said, gesturing to the chair in front of the desk. Obediently, Nick sat.

"So," Bruce said, kicking his feet up onto the desk, "how's the story coming on?"

Nick shrugged. "Fine. It's early days."

"Of course. But you haven't had any problems getting access?"

Nick shook his head. "Not at all. They've been very accommodating. I think they want the publicity."

"Indeed. But this isn't an advertisement, you know. I'm expecting something hard-hitting. What have you got so far?"

"Well, I'm still putting it all together." Nick said, frowning a little. It had been many years since Bruce had been so hands-on with one of his stories, and he didn't like it. Despite his editor's denial, it still felt a lot like spying. "Is there a problem?"

"Oh no," Bruce said with a chuckle that sounded slightly forced. "I'm just interested in how it's going. I want to make sure it's on track, since I've taken you off everything else to cover this." He gave Nick a pointed look.

"Well, it's pretty much where I expected it to be at this point," Nick said. "I've been attending their meetings, getting to know them, learning about the organisation, and I'll go to their protest next week as well."

"Yes, about that," Bruce said. "What exactly are they planning?"

Nick was silent for a moment, but he felt himself wilting under Bruce's glare. "They still haven't finalised it," he said at last, hating himself even as the words left his mouth. "There's a bit of tension in the ranks between those who believe in peaceful protest and those who want more militant action. Three of the latter actually got arrested last night, in fact. So at the moment it looks like a march, but it could go either way at this point."

Bruce smiled in a way that sent chills down Nick's back. "Good lad," he said. "Now, I want you to keep me appraised of everything that goes on, do you understand? As soon as that plan is finalised, you tell me."

"Is that really necessary?" Nick asked. "I mean, you know I can write a good story."

"Of course. But this is potentially front-page stuff, and I want to make sure it stays on track. It could make your career, you know." *Or break it*, was what he left unsaid. "Now, when's their next meeting?"

Nick sighed. "This afternoon."

"Good. Report back to me tomorrow morning. I'll be here."

"But ... I'm not rostered on this weekend."

Bruce scowled, and Nick knew he'd overstepped. "Do I look like I care?" the editor thundered. "Be here tomorrow morning, or don't bother coming in Monday, do you understand?"

"Yes, sir."

"Good. You can go."

"Thank you, sir."

Nick returned to his desk, still discomfited by the meeting. He didn't understand Bruce's sudden interest—everyone knew he hated the brasscore rights activists—and it worried him in a way he couldn't quite explain. He sighed and went back to his notes, but he couldn't help thinking of Millie.

Chapter 6

At three o'clock that afternoon, Nick took the air-tram down to St George's. Millie was once again waiting for him on the steps of the hall, but she looked quite different—she was dressed like an aeronaut, in breeches, a voluminous white shirt, boots, and a many-pocketed waistcoat, on which a brass pocket-watch chain gleamed. Her sleeves were rolled to the elbow, revealing the blue cog tattoo on the inside of her right wrist that signified her brasscore status, and a thick, ropey scar on her right forearm that he'd never noticed before. Her hair was braided neatly down her back. She looked completely in her element, and Nick felt his heart beat faster.

"Been flying?" he asked as they greeted each other.

She flushed. "Oh ... sort of." She turned away. "Let's go in."

Nick followed her in, wondering what he was going to find. He hadn't had any update from Jerome, but that was hardly unexpected.

The ranks of the activists were thinner today, with several others missing besides the three who'd been arrested, and there was a palpable air of tension in the room. The buzz of chatter died down as Will called the meeting to order.

"First of all," he said when they'd all taken their seats, "I know you've all been appraised of yesterday's situation. I'm pleased to say that, thanks to the efforts of Advocate Jerome Galbraith, who has generously agreed to work *pro bono*, Florence, Bertha and Jean have now been released on bail." There was an enthusiastic murmur, and some people clapped.

Will ran a hand over his face. "I hope this can be a reminder of the importance of unity in our approach," he said. "I know there are some ideological differences within the group, but I hope we can focus instead on the things that unite us, and the greater cause we're all working for." A lot of the activists nodded in assent. "So I would ask you to work with me to put this behind us and continue our planning for our march next week. Remember, we're stronger together."

As the meeting continued, Nick watched, occasionally making notes or chatting to the various members. They seemed to have got used to his presence and were less hostile and more forthcoming than they had been previously. By the time things drew to a close two hours later, he was confident he had some good material for his story.

"That seemed to go well," he said to Millie as they stood on the steps afterwards.

She nodded. "Better than I expected, to be honest."

They lapsed into a friendly silence, watching as a service automaton loaded down with books and parcels crossed the busy street. Nick knew he should probably head home, but he didn't want to break the moment.

"Do you have any plans?" Millie asked suddenly.

"What, right now?"

"Yes."

"No, not really."

"Would you like to go to the markets over in the Gardens? We could have a look around and get some supper." She looked up at him, and as their eyes met, Nick felt the breath catch in his chest.

"That'd be lovely."

BACK WHEN MILLIE WAS young, the Princes Street Gardens had only hosted a market at Christmas. But somewhere along the line someone had realised there was money to be made, and now they were held monthly. Even though Millie lived nearby, it had been a long time since she'd visited, and the market seemed to have expanded; there were numerous stalls that she definitely hadn't seen before, and even a tethered-balloon ride. As they walked through the gardens towards the Ross Band Stand, she was acutely conscious of Nick at her side.

"Jerome seems like a nice man," she said at last.

"He is. He and Michael are the only brothers I'm really in touch with."

"Oh? How many have you got?"

"Four. I'm the youngest, and Jerome's next."

"I would have liked to have had siblings. I'm the only one."

Nick smiled ruefully. "It's not all it's cracked up to be. Don't get me wrong—I love my brothers—but the problem with being the youngest is you're always constantly compared to them. And I've never quite been able to measure up."

She frowned. "But you've done well for yourself."

"Ah, but you haven't met my family. David, who's the eldest, is a surgeon specialising in clockwork implants—I mean, you know that. He literally gives life to people who'd otherwise be dead. John is a senior Aerofleet officer and currently the commander of the base on Gibraltar. Michael is an engineer and inventor, who pioneered a more efficient way of mining thermocrystals. And as you saw, Jerome is on track to become the youngest Queen's Counsel in Edinburgh." He shrugged. "And then there's me—a beat reporter at a low-rent tabloid. I'm still not entirely sure what happened."

He stared straight ahead, his lips pressed together, and Millie felt her heart soften towards him. "But your work is worthwhile," she said. "And you're making a go of it, even if it doesn't seem that way. Look at what you're doing with us."

"Wasn't it just the other day you accused me of complacency and compromised ethics?" he asked wryly, but there was no malice in his tone.

Millie felt her cheeks begin to burn. "Perhaps I was too hasty," she said. "I *do* think that what you're doing is important, especially when your readers are unlikely to agree with what you write. You should be proud of yourself for sticking with it."

"I know. And I'm not unhappy. Journalism suits me—I could never do what my brothers do. But whenever we're together I also see that I can never live up to them." He sighed, and Millie suddenly wished she could smooth away the worries that were creasing his brow.

"If it helps, I know what it's like to disappoint your family," she said. She thought of her father and looked away across the park. It had been a long time, but she still felt the loss of their relationship keenly.

"See, *that* I don't understand," Nick said. "With all the amazing things that you've done, I'd have thought they'd be proud as punch."

"My mother is, I think," she said. "And that means a lot. But my father could never come to terms with the fact that I'm not the daughter he wanted me to be."

"Because of your leg?" It was common knowledge that Millie had been born without part of her left leg, and that it was clockwork from just below the knee. It had been mentioned in almost every press report about her flight, often with quotes about it from her own family.

She shrugged. "Not really. Because I'm not brave like him."

"Not *brave*? You flew around the world by yourself when you were just a child. I don't know how much braver you can get."

"And now I can't fly at all." She laughed mirthlessly. "I wasn't entirely truthful with you before. I didn't go flying this morning—I haven't flown in ten years. I really miss it, and I want to, and I have a friend who's offered to take me up in her airship, but whenever it comes down to it I just *can't*. So every now and again I get dressed up in my aeronaut clothes and go to the airfield, and I sit there and watch everything I'm missing." She felt the heat rush to her cheeks. "I don't even know why I'm telling you this. But if you want to talk about failure, then surely that takes the cake." She tried to grin, to cover the fact that she suddenly felt like crying.

Nick stopped and turned to face her, and she reluctantly met his eyes. The care in them was almost her undoing. "Did something happen on your flight?" he asked gently. "Something ... difficult?"

Millie felt like the wind had been knocked out of her. She opened her mouth, but quickly closed it again, unsure of what to say.

"How ... how did you know?"

"It was just a guess. Call it a sense for story."

She nodded. "Something did. But I don't want to talk about it now. I'll tell you one day."

"That's fine. I understand."

"Thank you."

They were approaching the edge of the market, and delicious smells wafted across from the food stalls. Millie's stomach rumbled audibly and Nick laughed, breaking the tension. "I think an early supper is in order."

She grinned. "I'll say."

NICK COULDN'T REMEMBER the last time he'd been to the Princes Street market, but he was sure he'd never enjoyed it as much as he did now, a fact that he put down to company. They bought skewers of barbecued meat and fried potatoes and sat on the grass to eat them, watching the world go by. The market was filled with a cross-section of city folk, from upper-class ladies in their frills and finery, to airmen on leave from the local Aerofleet base and working-class families enjoying an evening out. After they finished eating, they wandered among the stalls full of fascinating trinkets: tiny clockwork bumblebees that flew away and returned to your hand; thermocrystal lamps that changed colour when you blew on them; and delicate enamel hair clips in the shape of butterflies, with wings that really flapped. Nick watched Millie as she gazed at each new treasure, her eyes shining; she looked so beautiful it made his chest ache. She glanced up and saw him watching her, then gave him a little half-smile that blew every rational thought about the ethics of being attracted to an interview subject from his head.

Towards the edge of the market was a funfair, with a coconut shy, clockwork clowns, a carousel and, of course, the magnificent tethered-balloon ride. As they got closer, he could see that the balloon itself was actually in the shape of an airship, but it wasn't until they were almost underneath it that Millie gasped.

"What is it?" Nick asked in alarm.

"The balloon ... they've done it up like the *Pride of Scotland.*" She'd gone very pale, unable to take her eyes off it. Nick watched it descend with its load of merrymakers, and he could see that she was right; they'd even painted the name on the basket. He glanced across at the ticket booth and saw a sign above it: "Only 10p for your own world-changing adventure!"

"Are you all right?" he asked. He could only imagine what a shock it must be, seeing something so special being parodied for money.

She nodded, then turned to him. "I want to go up in it."

"Are you sure?"

She shrugged. "Not really. But ... I think I need to. Will you come with me?"

"Of course. Wait here and I'll get some tickets."

The ticket booth was manned by a matronly, middle-aged woman. "Two tickets, please," Nick said, passing over some coins.

"All right, love." She glanced across to where Millie was waiting. "Lovely evening for a night out with your lass, eh?" She gave him an enormous wink, then handed him his tickets and change before he could reply.

He rejoined Millie and together they walked over to the balloon. She was still pale, and Nick glanced at her, concerned. "You don't have to do this, you know," he said. "There's no shame in changing your mind."

She shook her head. "No. I want to." She raised her chin defiantly. "Let's go."

Nick handed the tickets to a man standing beside the large basket, who helped them up and then clambered in after them. "Looks like you've got it all to yourselves," he said. Nick was thankful that, if Millie was going to struggle, at least she wouldn't have to do it in front of a bunch of other people.

"Don't you get enough flying during the day, miss?" the man asked, glancing at Millie's aeronaut attire.

"Oh ..." she stammered, caught off-guard.

"Actually, this is for me," Nick interjected, and she smiled at him gratefully. "I've never flown before, you see, so she's indulging me."

"He don't know what he's missing, does he?" the airman guffawed. "Tell you what, I'll even give you a little bit longer, just so he can truly appreciate it."

"Thank you," Millie said weakly. Nick could see her hands trembling where they rested on the rim of the basket.

"Righto, hold on now," the airman called. "Up she goes!"

The thermocrystal jet flared with a deafening roar, and the basket lurched as the balloon left the ground. Millie involuntarily clutched Nick's hand, and he squeezed it reassuringly.

"It's all right," he murmured. "I've got you."

After that first moment, the balloon levelled out and rose smoothly into the sky. Soon they were up above the trees, the lights of the market glittering below them. There was a slight thud as the balloon reached the end of its tether, and they hung there, suspended in the sky, the city spread out around them like a thousand sparkling stars.

"Oh," Millie breathed. "I've missed this." Her eyes shone with wonder, and Nick was suddenly acutely aware that they were still holding hands. They stood in silence, looking out across the city. Then Millie turned to him and smiled, and Nick felt time stop. All he was conscious of was the space between them and the blood pounding in his ears. He could hardly breathe.

"All right then, down we go," the airman said, shattering the tension between them. But it was only when they landed that Millie let go of Nick's hand.

"Thank you," she said to the airman as they disembarked. "That was wonderful."

"My pleasure, miss." Then he glanced at her again. "I hope you don't mind me sayin', but you're the spitting image of Millicent Roberts, the young aeronaut." Nick tensed, but Millie just laughed self-consciously.

"You know, I get that all the time," she said.

The airman chuckled. "Must be the light," he said. "My, she was something, though, wasn't she? I was down at the airfield the day she came home, and I've never seen anything like it." He sighed. "Shame it all ended the way it did. Mind you, I don't think for a minute she was crazy like all the papers were sayin'. I think that father of hers just pushed her too hard. I know what some of these aeronaut types are like, and it's a lot of pressure for a young lass to bear. A cryin' shame, really." He looked wistful, then seemed to realise they were still there. "But anyways, here's me blatherin' on. Hope you enjoyed your first flight, sir, and best of luck to you." He tipped his hat, then turned to greet the next lot of passengers.

"Thank you," Millie said to Nick as they walked back through the market. "That meant the world to me. I don't think I could have done it on my own."

"You're welcome," Nick said. He glanced around at the stalls, many of which were closing for the night. "It's getting late. May I walk you home?"

She smiled. "Of course." Nick offered her his arm, and she took it as they left the glimmering lights of the market behind them.

Chapter 7

It seemed to Millie that they reached her little terrace house far too quickly; she would have been happy to walk with Nick in the park all night. She was still revelling in the exhilaration of finally going aloft again after all these years, but it was more than that. Nick had surprised her more than once with his vulnerability and his kindness, and she was very aware of his arm pressed against her side. His hand, when she'd held it in the balloon, had been warm and strong, and she couldn't help wondering what those hands would feel like running along her body. The thought made her catch her breath.

"Here we are," she said as they reached her garden gate. Her house was a narrow, double-storey terrace, with a red front door, two bedrooms and a tiny back garden—too big for her on her own, really, but the size of a postage stamp in her parents' eyes. Her mother had set her up here when it had become clear how badly relations had broken down with her father. It was unorthodox for an unmarried woman to live alone, to be sure, but it was by far the best solution and she was very happy. But she rarely entertained anyone at home; it was her sanctuary.

Nick opened the gate and walked her to the door, then waited as she found her key. "Thank you for a wonderful evening," he said. "I can't remember the last time I had so much fun."

She grinned. "Me neither." The silence stretched out between them, and Millie found she was unable to tear her gaze away from his deep blue eyes; she felt like she was falling into them.

"Well, goodnight," she said at last, reluctantly, stepping forward to kiss him on the cheek. She wasn't quite sure what possessed her to be so daring, to plant a kiss just above that charming dimple that captivated her every time he smiled, or to linger there just slightly longer than propriety allowed.

As she went to move away, Nick turned slightly so they were face-to-face. "Millie," he whispered, sending a thrill shooting down her spine.

"Yes?"

He reached up and tucked a strand of hair behind her ear, cupping her cheek in his palm. She closed her eyes and leaned into his touch. "May I kiss you?" he murmured.

"Oh, I wish you would."

Nick leaned in and kissed her gently on the mouth, so sensually that Millie felt her whole body tremble. She kissed him back, harder, desire throbbing between her legs.

"Would you like to come in?" she asked as they came up for air.

He nodded, giving her a little half-smile that showed the dimple in his right cheek, and her heart began to thunder in her ears. She turned, fumbling her key in the lock, then opened the door and led him into the hallway. As the door clicked shut behind them it was as if a pressure valve had been released, and suddenly they were in each other's arms. Nick kissed her passionately on the mouth, sending tongues of fire racing down her body to pool in her belly.

"Is this a breach of your journalistic ethics?" she gasped as she ran her hands through his hair.

"Screw journalistic ethics," he mumbled, kissing her neck until she moaned.

"Believe me, screwing journalistic ethics is all I've been thinking about all evening."

"Miss Roberts!" he said in mock-scandalised tones. He pulled back to look at her, his eyes dancing with laughter, and she grinned back. "I'll tell you a secret," he murmured, leaning forward until his lips brushed her ear. "Me too."

She pulled him towards her, finding his mouth with hers as they fumbled with clothes, gasping as he slipped his hands under her shirt and chemise to cup her breasts. His thumbs grazed her nipples, first one then the other, dashing every rational thought from her head. She reached down, stroking the length of his hardness through his trousers, drawing a groan of pleasure from him.

"Where's your bedroom?" Nick asked as they fumbled with the buttons and buckles of their remaining clothes.

"Too far," she murmured as his hands caressed her buttocks, pulling her against him. She kissed him deeply, then took his hand and led him into the small sitting room off the hallway. She lit the lamp and turned to find him watching her with an enigmatic half-smile.

"What?" she asked, a blush creeping up her cheeks.

"You're stunning," he said simply.

She crossed the room in two strides and pulled him to her, kissing along the stubbled edge of his jaw as she slowly unbuttoned his shirt and slipped it off his shoulders. His chest was broad and muscular, and she ran her hands down to the V of his hips, then gasped distractedly as he kissed her neck. Nick kissed her collarbone, then worked his way down, unbuttoning her shirt as he went. He caressed her nipples with his tongue through the silk of her chemise, then gently lifted the floaty material over her head. She tossed it to the floor and pressed herself against his chest, craving the touch of his skin on hers. He held her tightly, until her body ached with desire.

"Don't make me wait," she implored him, undoing his trousers and then her own. "I've taken precautions, so there's no worry in that regard."

"Millie," he murmured, stepping out of his clothes and standing before her. She let her own breeches fall to the ground, conscious that this was the first time he'd seen her clockwork leg, grafted into the flesh just below her left knee. Although she was generally confident in her body, she couldn't fully silence the niggling voice that wondered if he would be repulsed by this sudden, stark reminder that she was a brasscore.

But Nick was staring at her with an awestruck look on his face. "You're so beautiful," he said. He glanced down at her leg. "What works best for you? I want you to be comfortable."

Millie felt her worries melt away. "I can do most things," she said. "What did you have in mind?"

Nick guided her towards the sofa, settling down beside her and holding her close. "Show me where you like to be touched," he said.

Millie took his hand in hers, kissing his palm before guiding it along her body. "Here," she said, placing it on her breast. Nick leaned forward, taking her nipple in his mouth and flicking it with his tongue until she moaned, then doing the same with the other one.

"Where else?" he asked. Millie took his hand again, guiding it down her belly to the wetness between her legs.

"Here," she murmured, closing her eyes as he stroked her sex, spreading herself wider for him. "Oh, Nick," she gasped as he slipped a finger inside her, arching against his hand. She let him take her right to the brink of her climax, but it wasn't enough; she wanted to feel all of him.

"Stop," she murmured, groaning as he withdrew his fingers. She turned to look at him, the raw desire in his eyes making her catch her breath. "I want you inside me. Is that what you want too?"

"Yes," he said simply. Millie straddled him then reached down, feeling the wetness between her own legs, and guided him into her.

"*Millie*," he ground out as she settled over him. "Don't stop." She rocked her hips against him, gently at first, then more and more urgently. The world around them seemed to disappear; there was only their two bodies, locked together in desperate pleasure. She called out his name as her desire crested and fireworks exploded behind her eyes; a few seconds later she heard him moan and felt the warm surge of his release.

"Oh, Nick," she whispered, collapsing against him. "Nick ..." Reluctantly she eased herself off him, and they curled together naked on the sofa, holding each other tightly and basking in the afterglow.

"That was ... I don't know what to say," Nick said at last, grinning boyishly at her. He traced his fingers lightly along her shoulder, and Millie was surprised to feel a rush of desire returning. She leaned up and kissed him lingeringly.

"Shall I show you where the bedroom is?"

Chapter 8

When Millie woke, her first thought was that it had all been a lovely dream. Then she saw Nick asleep beside her and smiled to herself as she relived the night. It had been a long time since she'd woken up next to anyone, and if she'd told herself a week ago that her next lover would be a journalist, of all things, she would have laughed herself silly. Yet here they were, and she was a little surprised to find that she had no regrets.

She eased herself out of bed, careful not to wake Nick, then washed quietly and dressed in breeches and a shirt. She no longer felt like quite such a fraud in her aeronaut clothes—she was still a long way from piloting an airship alone, but going up in the fairground balloon had been a huge milestone, and she felt more like her old self than she had for some time. She tiptoed downstairs to the kitchen, where she lit the stove and set the kettle to boil. There were some rashers of bacon and half-a-dozen eggs in the larder, and she congratulated herself on being relatively organised for once. Setting the tea to steep, she pulled out a frying pan and began to cook breakfast.

The enticing smell of frying bacon must have woken Nick, because just as she was finishing the scrambled eggs, he came into the kitchen. He smiled when he saw her, and Millie felt her knees go weak; if possible, he was even more attractive than he'd seemed last night. But she suddenly worried that, in the cold light of day, things might look very different to him.

"Breakfast?" she asked, trying to sound nonchalant.

"That'd be lovely," he said. He came over to where she was standing beside the stove, put his hands on her waist, and kissed the nape of her neck. "It smells delicious." Millie turned to face him, and he kissed her deeply on the mouth. It was only the smell of burning that broke them apart.

"The eggs!" Millie gasped, laughing as she pulled the pan off the stove. "Blast," she said as she scraped them onto a plate; they were rather charred underneath.

"Doesn't matter," Nick said with a smile, taking the plates to the table. "It's a small price to pay."

"So what would you like to do today?" Millie asked as they finished their breakfast. "We could go out ... or stay in ..." She grinned at Nick wickedly, and he laughed.

"I wish I could," he said, "but I have to go to the office."

"Really?" Millie couldn't hide her disappointment.

"Afraid so. I've got a meeting with Bruce Maddox." He rolled his eyes.

"I didn't think esteemed editors worked weekends."

"Neither did I, but there you go." He took her hand and squeezed it. "I should only be a couple of hours. Then I'll take you out to lunch—how does that sound?"

Millie leaned over the table and kissed him. "That sounds wonderful. How long before you have to go?"

Nick glanced at the clock on the wall. "I could probably stretch to half an hour. Why, what did you have in mind?"

"Come back upstairs and I'll show you."

HALF AN HOUR LATER Nick kissed Millie goodbye on the front step. She was still pink-cheeked from their recent exertions, her blue eyes sparkling, and he found turning away down the street towards the *Bugle* offices disproportionately difficult. It was a beautiful, fresh morning, but he didn't care; he would have given anything to be back inside with Millie. But Bruce had made it clear that his job was on the line, so he reluctantly continued to the air-tram stop that would drop him at the newspaper's door.

When he entered the office, he found Bruce waiting for him. There were far fewer people in the newsroom than during the week—just a skeleton staff to keep on top of things.

"About time," Bruce said without preamble. "I was wondering when you were going to show up."

"You only said 'morning'," Nick said, but he tried to keep the defensiveness out of his voice. There was no point in antagonising his mercurial boss unnecessarily.

To his surprise, Bruce guffawed. "So I did," he said. "That'll teach me. Anyway, come in." He ushered Nick into his office. "So," he said when they were both seated, "fill me in on what's been happening with your clanker friends." Nick cringed at the term; he knew the slight was intentional. And he still couldn't shake the feeling that something wasn't quite right. Of course it made sense that Bruce wanted to keep track of a potentially big story, but Nick had never seen any of his colleagues managed so closely, even when they were working on much bigger things than this. The only conclusion that he could come to was that Bruce didn't trust him to do a good job—because why else would he be treating him like a naive cadet, rather than an experienced reporter of ten years' standing?

He sighed. "They pretty much finalised everything last night. The protest will take place next Tuesday morning—they're going to march down to Holyrood and stage a peaceful sit-in."

Bruce scowled. "Doesn't sound like there's much of a story in that. Why should I waste any more time and money sending you to cover this protest? They're just a bunch of jumped-up semi-automatons who need to learn their place."

Nick bristled, but kept his temper. "Well, like I said, there's some conflict between the peaceful and militant factions in the group," he said, trying to justify the story. "I talked to quite a few of them yesterday, and just between you and me, I got the feeling that things might boil over on Tuesday. I wouldn't be surprised if the more militant members decide to take things into their own hands. That's why I want to be there—to cover it as it happens." *And because it's worthwhile*, he thought, but didn't say it—that argument wouldn't sway his boss.

"All right," Bruce said at last. "You've convinced me. I want it on my desk by five o'clock Tuesday evening."

"Yes, sir."

Bruce lit a cigar. "Go on then," he mumbled around it. "Don't you have other places to be?"

Nick thought of Millie—he certainly did. "Yes, sir. Thank you."

The meeting had gone better than he'd thought it would, and it sounded like Bruce was seriously considering his story for the front page. But even so, as he waited for the air-tram back to Millie's house, Nick couldn't get rid of the feeling that he was missing something. He couldn't put his finger on it, but something was definitely off. He'd never much cared for Bruce's approach, but he'd set those feelings aside in order to pay the bills. But now—it was the way Bruce had referred to the activists that had done it. Maybe it was Millie's influence, but he hated hearing them disparaged like that, when their only crime was to want something more for themselves and their compatriots. He sighed. Maybe it was time to start looking for employment beyond the *Daily Bugle*—somewhere where he wouldn't have to compromise his values in order to do his job. He smiled to himself as he boarded the air-tram. Millie was clearly rubbing off on him.

Chapter 9

Sunday night at the Edinburgh Club meant a roast dinner and a string quartet, and consequently it was always popular. After the meal, the Gang of Five met in their usual side room for whisky and cigars. A young maid moved about the room, plying the decanter, as talk turned to the activists.

"Word on the street is they're planning to march on the Parliament," Maxwell McPherson said. "That'll make your day interesting, Giles."

Sir Giles Pearson rolled his eyes. "Honestly, we're just trying to do an honest day's work advancing this country, and we have to keep contending with riffraff," he spluttered. "I thought it was your job to contain all that, Robert."

"It's not illegal to protest," the police chief said. "At least, not if they're being peaceful. If they turn violent, that's another matter."

"We don't know that they *will* be peaceful, though, do we?" Sir Giles shot back. "Look at the arrests just last week." He scowled, turning to Bruce Maddox. "Didn't you say you've got a man on the inside? Any idea what they're planning?"

Maddox nodded to the maid, who refilled his glass; he didn't notice that she lingered within earshot. "As a matter of fact, I met with him just yesterday," he said. "He's got some good information. They *are* planning to march on Holyrood on Tuesday, but it sounds like there's some disagreement in the ranks. From what he said, there's significant tension between the ones who want to keep everything peaceful, and those who favour more militant forms of action."

"Interesting," Jock Williamson said. "Are you thinking what I'm thinking?"

"It's an ... opportunity," Maddox said. "If things turn violent, it will discredit the BPL. The public doesn't like anything that disrupts their daily lives. It might just sway the mood enough to get you the votes you need for your bill, Giles."

Robert MacIntyre frowned. "You're suggesting someone incite the activists to violence? I don't know about that, old boy."

"*Incite* is a strong word," Bruce said carefully. "Nobody wants to see police brutality, of course. But if there should be some other protesters there at the same time, for example ... well, it's possible the activists will pick a fight, if you know what I mean. And if police backup were to be slow to arrive, well, that can't be helped—after all, you were expecting a peaceful protest." He grinned wolfishly.

"And would the *Daily Bugle* be on board?"

"Well, the *Daily Bugle* reports the news, and this would certainly be that. And we obviously can't support violence, so it's likely there'd be a strongly worded editorial condemning any activist groups that engage in it. Hypothetically, of course."

"Of course."

Sir Giles chuckled. "That sounds like a rather neat solution," he said. "I hope you buy your man a drink for us, Bruce. Speaking of which, where's that damn girl with the Scotch?" He looked around, but the maid had disappeared—she'd heard enough.

Chapter 10

Monday morning, Millie decided, was cleaning day. She had a meeting in the afternoon to finalise the plans for the march on the Scottish Parliament at Holyrood, and she was feeling more jittery than she cared to admit. As she swept and mopped the floor, her mind drifted to the past few days she'd spent with Nick, and she smiled to herself. They'd finally parted company on Sunday night, and already she was aching to see him again. He was supposed to be coming to the meeting, and she hoped they'd continue on for dinner afterwards. She felt as if the sun had finally come out after a long, grey winter, and she was enjoying basking in its glow.

This rather pleasant train of thought was abruptly interrupted by a knock at the door. Millie propped the mop against the wall and wiped her hands on her apron. She didn't get many callers, and even though she knew Nick was at work, a small part of her hoped it might be him.

But standing on the step were a middle-aged, matronly woman, and a younger girl who looked barely twenty.

"Mrs Ferguson!" Millie exclaimed, smiling. "What on earth brings you here? Come in!" She ushered them inside without giving them a chance to reply. Mrs Ferguson was her parents' housekeeper, and Millie had known her since childhood; she looked up to her almost as a second mother. But since the falling-out with her father Millie hadn't been welcome at the big house, and it had been some time since they'd seen each other.

She led the two women into the parlour and bade them sit. "Tea?"

"Oh, no, thank you," Mrs Ferguson said. She fiddled with her gloves as if she was nervous, and Millie furrowed her brow in concern.

"Is everything all right?"

The old housekeeper smiled, but it seemed a bit forced. "Aye, everything's fine. Well, almost. But you must excuse my rudeness—let me introduce my niece, Miss Sarah Gilmore. Sarah, this is Miss Millie Roberts."

"Pleased to meet you, Miss Roberts."

"Likewise." Millie appraised her; she was a meek, pretty little thing, but she too seemed worried about something. "It's lovely to see you," Millie continued. "What do I have to thank for this visit?"

Mrs Ferguson sighed. "I wish it were on better terms, I really do," she said. "It's a bit...complicated."

"Go on—I'm in no hurry."

"Well, Sarah here is a maid at the Edinburgh Club," Mrs Ferguson began. "I don't suppose you've heard of it?"

Millie rolled her eyes. "Unfortunately I have," she said. "A bastion of stuffy conservatism. What of it?"

"Last night she was serving a meeting of a certain elite group of gentlemen," Mrs Ferguson said, "and she overheard ... well, I think it'd be best if she told you herself. Go on," she said, turning to Sarah, who stared at the floor. "Miss Roberts won't bite."

"There were five of them," Sarah said. "The chief of police, that awful MP Sir Giles Pearson, a couple of business types, and Bruce Maddox, who owns the *Daily Bugle*. And they started talking about the brasscore activists and how there's going to be some march tomorrow. And they talked about how there's divisions in the Brasscore Political League between the peaceful protesters and the militants. So they decided that if they can provoke some of the activists to violence, it will make people so upset with them that they'll support Sir Giles's new law to ban the BPL. And I remembered Aunt Mary mentioning that you were involved with the BPL, and I thought you might be going to the march tomorrow. So I wanted to warn you not to go, so that you don't get hurt."

Millie stared at her, stunned. It was hard to know what to consider first, but something Sarah had said niggled at her.

"How did they know there's division between those who want peaceful action and those who want militant action?" She wondered if Florence, Bertha or Jean had mentioned it in their police interviews, but she found that hard to believe. They were all tough as nails, and even though she didn't always agree with them, she knew they wouldn't turn on their fellows like that.

Sarah shrugged. "Bruce Maddox said he had a man inside the BPL who was updating him on what was going on."

"No ..." Millie felt as if all the breath had been knocked out of her. "Are you sure?"

Sarah nodded. "Quite sure. I'm sorry."

"I know it must be an awful shock," Mrs Ferguson said. "I wasn't sure at first if we should tell you, but when Sarah mentioned they were planning to provoke violence ... well, I couldn't face your mother if you got caught up in that and I hadn't tried to prevent it."

Millie nodded, biting her lip. "You did the right thing," she said. "Thank you for telling me. I'm just going to need some time to think it all through properly."

"Of course," Mrs Ferguson said, rising and pulling Sarah up with her. "We won't take up any more of your time."

Millie showed them out automatically, but as they turned to go she impulsively caught Mrs Ferguson's hand. "Thank you," she said again. "It's good to know I've got friends like you."

"Always," Mrs Ferguson said, laying a hand on her cheek with maternal tenderness. "It breaks my heart not to see you at the house anymore. You take care."

"You too."

Chapter 11

Millie arrived early for the meeting, still in a state of deep agitation. She didn't bother waiting for Nick outside as she usually did; she wasn't even sure she could bear to be in the same room with him at the moment. But the other members needed to know what was going on, and she had to take responsibility for bringing it all down on them—after all, she was supposed to have been keeping an eye on Nick. She was supposed to be the media-savvy one.

She tried to catch a moment alone with Will before the others arrived, but his attention was constantly in demand for one thing or another, and before Millie knew it, he was calling the meeting to order. There was still no sign of Nick, and Millie hoped that he wouldn't come. She took her seat, her legs jiggling with nerves. At last she could contain herself no longer, and just before Will launched into the first item of business, she rose. Everyone turned to look at her, but before she could speak, the door opened and Nick entered. *Sorry,* he mouthed, sitting down. Millie's heart sank, but it was too late now—she needed to tell them the truth.

"Yes, Millie?" Will said. "Do you wish to say something?" He peered at her more closely. "Is everything all right?"

"I ... yes ... I mean, no ..." Millie stammered. She took a deep breath and tried again. "I mean, I have something very important I need to say. It's about the march."

"Go on."

"I have some information from a reliable source that the police and the government know all about our plans," she said. "More importantly, they know about our ... ah ... disagreements. A small, powerful group among them has been meeting regularly at the Edinburgh Club. They intend to use force during the march to try to provoke us into violent retaliation, and thus weaken public support for our cause. They want to pass a law to criminalise the BPL." She paused, taking another breath; she felt sick to her stomach.

There was silence for a moment, then everyone began talking at once. Eventually Will clapped his hands and the chatter died down.

"Who is this group you speak of?"

Millie listed them as Sarah had told her.

"And how do they know about our plans and our weaknesses?"

This was the question she'd been dreading. "Because someone in this room told them."

There was a stunned silence.

"That's quite an accusation to level at your friends, Millie," Will said calmly.

Millie shook her head. "I'm not levelling it at my friends," she said. "My source ... well, she heard Bruce Maddox say he had a man inside the BPL." She turned to look at Nick. "That's you, Mr Galbraith." For a second, their eyes met, and the shock and hurt on his face briefly made her second-guess herself. But Sarah had been quite clear, and the connections were too obvious for it to be anyone else.

This time the uproar was instantaneous, and it took some time for Will to bring the room back under control. When things eventually quietened down, he turned to Nick, ice in his gaze.

"Is this true, Mr Galbraith?" he asked. "Did you give Bruce Maddox information about our plans and the ideological divisions in our ranks?"

Nick looked at him for a long moment, then he nodded. "But if I could just clarify ..." he began, but Will cut him off.

"No clarification will be necessary," he said. "Please leave."

"I didn't mean to," Nick said. "I support the cause, truly."

"Leave now, please, Mr Galbraith," Will repeated. "You're no longer welcome here."

Nick placed his notebook in his satchel and stood up. He looked as if he was going to say something else, then thought better of it. For a moment his gaze met Millie's, but she bit her lip and turned away. The sound of his footsteps echoed through the hall as he left, the door closing behind him with an ominous thud.

"Thank you for bringing this to our attention, Millie," Will said. "I know it can't have been easy."

Millie swallowed. "I take full responsibility," she said. "I know what journalists are like. I should have taken more care. I should have known better."

Will shrugged. "It was a strategy we agreed on as a group," he said. "We knew it was a gamble, bringing an outsider in, but I don't think any of us foresaw this. I'm just thankful that we've been able to address it in time. It's also once again shown up the great danger of division in our ranks. Of course we have differences, but we must be able to put those aside and work together. We mustn't lose sight of the greater cause." He paused. "And now we have to decide how we're going to move forward in light of this new information."

"Should we cancel the march?" Meredith suggested.

"No!" Florence said. "That way the bullies win, and we show we're easily cowed."

A storm of discussion erupted, but a plan occurred to Millie. She raised her hand.

"Yes, Millie?" Will said, then raised his voice. "Pipe down, you lot! One at a time!"

"You know I'm in the middle, philosophically speaking," Millie began. "I can see the arguments for both peaceful and more aggressive action. But I can't help thinking that this is a time for truly passive resistance."

"I'm not sure I follow," Will said.

"Bear with me," Millie said. "Now, the aim of this group of men is to try to goad us into violence, correct?" The others nodded. "So, presumably, they'll start by using some sort of minor force, even words, to try to provoke us, then escalate the situation. And the story will be that we're a group of violent, unhinged clankers who are a threat to society. It will ultimately serve their agenda, not ours. But we also need visibility. A nice petition or a few posters just isn't going to cut it. Everyone with me so far?"

There were more nods and affirmative murmurings.

"So what I'm proposing," Millie said, "is that we're completely passive. We march, and then we sit right in the middle of the street, and we refuse to move, speak, or otherwise engage. They can't provoke violence if we won't respond, but it will create enough of a scene to get people talking. It will take a lot of discipline, though. No matter what they say or do to us, we can't engage or fight back."

"You know," Florence said thoughtfully, "that just might work."

"Let's put it to a vote," Will said. "All those in favour, raise your hand."

Millie glanced around the room—everyone present had raised their hands. She smiled.

The rest of the meeting was spent finalising the last details of the plans, and by the end of it Millie felt both exhausted and exhilarated. Caught up in the wave of chatter as they spilled out into the early evening bustle of the city, she was unaware of her surroundings until Jean tapped her elbow and gestured with a nod of her head. Sitting on a park bench in the hall's small garden, looking utterly dejected, was Nick.

Millie sighed. "I suppose I should talk to him."

"Good luck," Jean murmured.

"Thanks," Millie said with a grimace. For a moment she contemplated ignoring him entirely and just going home, but she had questions that needed answering. And the memory of their time together was still so fresh that it amplified the sting of betrayal. She couldn't believe she'd let him use her like that. She walked over to the bench.

"Are you waiting for me?" she asked, standing in front of him.

Nick looked up. "Millie, I'm so sorry," he said. But the apology, far from mollifying her, just flared the coals of her anger back to life.

"How could you?" she spat. "I *trusted* you. I thought you cared about the cause. I even thought you cared about *me*. But you were just spying for Bruce Maddox the whole time."

"I wasn't spying," he said. "At least, not deliberately. Bruce called me in to ask how the story was progressing, and I told him. I mentioned the conflict between the peaceful and militant factions because I thought it added colour to the story. I had no idea that he was interested in that information for any reason other than selling papers. Please—you have to believe me."

She looked him up and down scornfully. "I don't *have* to do anything. I should have known better than to trust a *journalist*. Is it that you don't know right from wrong, or you just don't care?" She shrugged. "That's what I get for going against my instincts. Serves me right."

"Please, Millie—I don't want to lose you over this."

She stared at him for a long moment. "I don't think you understand," she said. "The cause is my whole life right now. These people are my family. The fact that you betrayed *them* hurts far more than you betraying me. I never want to see you again." She turned on her heel and hurried after Jean and the others, ignoring Nick calling her name. But despite her words, she couldn't stop the tears from falling.

Chapter 12

Nick was unsure how long he sat on the bench while the world passed him by; it didn't seem to matter anyway. All he could hear was Millie's parting words: *I never want to see you again.* The look in her eyes—contempt masking a deep hurt—was something he couldn't forget, and it was all the more painful knowing that he'd caused it.

There'd been other women in his life, but every time one of those relationships had ended all he'd felt was a profound sense of relief. This time was different. The thought of never seeing Millie again tore at his heart, and he realised with a shock that he loved her. He'd never felt this way about anyone before, and now it was too late. She was gone.

To try to distract himself, he turned his thoughts to Bruce Maddox, channelling his pain into a righteous anger. He kicked himself mentally; he was a patsy to have been played like that. Bruce had flattered his ego with all that rubbish about front-page material and had made him think he was *finally* going to make it. But it had all been a sham. Deep down he'd known it, but he'd chosen not to see. He'd cared more about keeping his job than the people he was hurting to do it.

Nick frowned to himself. If what Millie had said was true, what they were talking about was corruption at the highest level. *That* was a real story, but it would be hard to prove. But if he could ... exposing Bruce's clique would be the right thing to do by itself, but it would also hopefully help the BPL gain support for the brasscore rights movement. He didn't expect to win Millie back—he knew he'd forfeited all right to her affection—but maybe he could help right the wrong he'd inadvertently done to her and her compatriots. But first he needed to find her source.

JEROME'S CHAMBERS WERE in a luxurious, understated building in the heart of the city, and Nick knew he often worked late; it wasn't the first time he'd called on his brother there.

"Eleanora," he said, smiling at the secretary as he walked in. "It's been too long." Like most up-market businesses, Jerome's chambers still employed human receptionists and staff. Eleanora was an ash-blonde forty-something woman, and she and Nick had had a friendly flirtation for years, even though both of them knew he wasn't her type.

"Mr Galbraith," she said, raising an eyebrow and biting back a smile. "To what do we owe the pleasure?"

"Is he free?" Nick asked. "It's important."

"He's just finishing up with a client. Would you like to wait?"

"Of course." Nick bit his lip, chafing at the delay, but at that moment the door behind Eleanora's desk opened and

Jerome emerged, escorting an elderly lady bedecked in an array of black lace.

"Nick," Jerome said in surprise, catching sight of him. "Eleanora, would you mind showing Mrs Jacobs out?" He gestured to his brother. "Come in." Nick followed Jerome into the sumptuous office, which was all thick rugs and mahogany furniture.

"What brings you here?" Jerome asked, waving him to a chair. "Not more trouble with the activists, I hope?"

Nick frowned. "Sort of. You're a member of the Edinburgh Club, aren't you?"

"Well, yes ... not that I'm there that often these days," he said. "They got a bit too conservative for me. Why?"

"I need you to sneak me in."

Jerome's eyebrows shot up. "What's all this about?"

"I'm trying to track down a source—it's a long story."

"Well, you'd better fill me in."

AN HOUR LATER, NICK found himself standing in an alleyway outside the servants' entrance to the Edinburgh Club. Jerome—who, Nick was willing to admit, had approached the whole thing with a much cooler head than he had—was inside, discreetly asking questions. He'd persuaded Nick that bringing him in, even as a legitimate guest, would be a terrible idea, because it risked Bruce Maddox recognising him. Nick knew that Millie's source was a woman, so that meant she had to be one of the maids. It made sense; nobody ever noticed the people in the background who kept things running smoothly. Jerome was subtle, persuasive and skilled in the art of asking questions; Nick hoped fervently that he'd be able to winkle the information out of someone.

A cold breeze blew down the alley, and Nick huddled deeper into his coat. There was no one else around, and he hoped he didn't look too suspicious loitering in the half-dark. He began to think it was all a huge mistake. Even if he could find the girl, there was no guarantee she'd talk to him, or that her information would be worth anything. After all, who would believe the word of a young woman over that of five of the most powerful men in Scotland?

There was a noise at the entrance to the alley, and he turned to see a group of three—two young women and a young man—entering the lane. As they approached the servants' entrance, Nick decided to take a chance.

"Excuse me," he said, stepping into the pool of light that fell from the lamp above the door. "I was hoping you might be able to help me."

One of the women pressed a hand to her chest. "Mercy, you gave me a fright."

"What's the matter, then?" the young man asked. "Why are you hanging around here?" He frowned.

"I'm looking for someone," Nick said. "One of the maids at the club. I have a message from a friend of hers, Millie Roberts."

"What's her name, then?"

Nick swallowed; this was where his story came undone. "I don't actually remember, I'm afraid."

"You're passing on a message to someone but you don't know who?" the first woman said, raising her eyebrows. "That doesn't sound right to me."

Nick knew when he was beaten. "Don't worry about it," he said. "Sorry to bother you." They filed passed him through the door, but at the last moment the second young woman turned.

"Do you really know Millie Roberts?" she asked, pausing on the step. "Is she all right?"

"She's fine," Nick said. "The information was a big help."

"I don't know what you mean," the young woman said, but two bright spots appeared on her cheeks, and Nick could tell she was lying. He knew he needed to win her confidence, and the best way to do that was to be honest with her.

"My name is Nick Galbraith," he said. "I'm a journalist and a friend of Millie's. I was writing a story on the brasscore rights movement, and I've inadvertently caused them a lot of trouble. I want to make it right, but to do that I need to talk to the person who gave her the information in the first place."

The young woman backed away. "Sorry, sir, I don't know what you mean. I have to go to work."

"Listen," Nick said urgently, "I'm trying to put together a story that will expose the corruption and take those men down. I know you can't talk now, but my brother is in the club—he's a member. You'll recognise him; he looks a lot like me. Think about it, and if you want to talk, get a message to him about how I can contact you. That's all I'm asking."

She nodded once, then vanished into the club, closing the door behind her. Nick slumped back against the wall, feeling suddenly exhausted. That had been his best chance, and he could only hope he hadn't blown it.

IT FELT LIKE HOURS before he noticed someone else coming down the alley, and he realised with relief that it was Jerome. He got up from the discarded crate where he'd been uncomfortably perched.

"Took you long enough," he grumbled.

"You'll thank me for it later," Jerome said mildly. "Come on. There's a late-night coffee-house around the corner. We need to talk."

The coffee-house was warm and dim, filled with a fug of pipe smoke. Jerome chose a booth away from any other patrons, and Nick followed him in.

"Well?" he asked, unable to contain himself any longer. "What happened? Did you find the girl?"

"Yes and no," Jerome said. "It was always going to be difficult—the club has a lot of staff. But as it happens, I encountered your little conspiracy gang. And they invited me to join them."

"They *what*? Why?"

"Believe it or not, I'm rather respected in this town," Jerome said. "People like them want to cultivate my good opinion." He shrugged. "Plus I think Maddox in particular was taking a great deal of private delight in knowing that he's exploiting you while cosying up to me. Anyway, they clearly think I'm one of them."

"What makes you say that?"

Jerome shrugged. "They started telling me all about their little plan. You'd think they'd know better, given my position, but then I suppose the police commissioner's in it up to his neck, so ..." he trailed off, shaking his head in disbelief. "Also, one of the maids stopped me on the way out and asked me to give you this." He reached into his pocket and pulled out a folded piece of paper. "So you just might be in luck."

Nick unfolded the note and glanced at the scrawled writing within. *I finish work at 11. Meet me at the Aloft Coffee House. Sarah.*

"Looks like she wants to talk," he said. "But even with her account, it's not going to be enough."

Jerome smiled.

"What?" Nick asked, narrowing his eyes. "There's something you're not telling me."

Jerome reached into his pocket again and pulled out a small brass device. A tiny thermocrystal glowed blue through the filigreed case.

"What's that?" Nick asked, intrigued.

"Michael's latest invention," Jerome said. "Believe it or not, it records sounds. He gave it to me to test in client interviews—he's still ironing out some bugs. He tried to explain the technology to me but I'm afraid it went over my head. But it works surprisingly well. So well, in fact, that it can pick up conversation even when concealed in one's pocket."

Nick gaped at him. "You're saying you *recorded* them talking about the activists?"

Jerome shrugged enigmatically. "Might have done."

"And you'll let me use it? But they'll know the information came from you."

"There's an element of plausible deniability," Jerome said. "They've been overheard by the servants at least once—why not again?"

"Even so, I'm not sure I'd be able to protect you if it was printed."

Jerome's eyes hardened. "I don't need you to. What these men are doing is despicable. It undermines the very foundations of our democracy. They belong in gaol, and nothing would delight me more than to be the one who put them there."

"Are you sure?"

In answer, Jerome pressed the little brass device into Nick's hand. "Meet the girl," he said. "If this corroborates her story, then you're free to use it. Just promise me you'll publish it somewhere other than that God-awful *Bugle*."

Nick laughed. "I think that's a given," he said.

Chapter 13

The Aloft Coffee House was aptly named. Built from a decommissioned air cruiser, it floated above Princes Park, giving a commanding view of the city and Edinburgh Castle. Every half-hour it descended to allow patrons to embark and disembark, before rising into the night sky again.

Nick arrived at ten-thirty, just as the coffee-house landed and opened its doors. He went in and glanced around, but didn't see anyone he recognised. On the small stage, a fiddler and a piper were grinding out folk tunes. He took a table by the window and watched as the ground receded until the city was just pinpricks of gaslight.

Half an hour later the coffee house descended again, and when the doors opened Nick immediately recognised the young blonde woman from the alleyway. She glanced around nervously before catching sight of him and hurrying over. Nick rose.

"Good evening, Miss ..."

"Gilmore. Sarah Gilmore."

"Nick Galbraith."

"I know who you are. You're Bruce Maddox's spy."

Nick sighed. "I don't know what he's been saying, but I never spied for him—not consciously, anyway. I gave him an outline of the story like I'd give to any editor, but he played me for information. And like a fool, I trusted him, because I've worked for him for ten years and he'd never given me any reason not to."

Sarah said nothing, just looked at him shrewdly. "All right," she said at last. "I believe you."

"You do?"

"You don't seem to have very good judgement," she said, "but I know what Maddox is like. I've been serving him and the rest of them for years, and there's no better way to get the measure of a man. If it makes you feel any better, I doubt you're the first one to be taken in by him."

"Thank you."

"So you want to bring him down?"

"I just want to know what happened—what you heard—and yes, I want to expose any corruption that may have occurred."

"I could lose my job."

"I won't reveal your identity."

"Won't matter. The Edinburgh Club values discretion above everything."

"I have something else from a different source. If that evidence matches yours, no one will know it came from you."

"Is Miss Roberts in trouble?"

Nick shrugged. "I don't know. You spared the BPL from walking into a trap, that's for sure, but I don't know how the march will go tomorrow. These men are the kind who won't stop until they get what they want."

"I've always admired her, you know," Sarah said. "She's so brave, what with her flying and all. And brasscores *should* get the vote. I'm proud of her for fighting for them." She glanced out the window at the city below. "Very well," she said at last. "I'll tell you what happened. But you're not to reveal who I am."

"Of course."

Chapter 14

Early the next morning, Nick's alarm clock rattled in his ear. He hit out at it groggily, then remembered what he needed to do and sat up with a start. He'd spent over an hour interviewing Sarah the previous night—for the Aloft Coffee House was open all night—and by the time he'd got home, written up his notes and listened to Jerome's recording it had been half-past three before he'd got to bed. But by then he knew he had something explosive.

The activists' march would give him an excuse to be away from the office—Bruce didn't know about the falling-out he'd had with them, so he wouldn't be expected to be at work. Even so, it was best to be on the safe side.

He got up, washed, dressed and ate a quick breakfast and ventured out into the street. The air-tram would be quickest and cheapest, but he didn't want to be spotted, so he ended up taking a steam-cab in entirely the wrong direction before switching to another one back to where he needed to go. Glancing over his shoulder, he crossed the street and ducked into the offices of the *Scottish Times*.

As befitting the country's most-respected broadsheet newspaper, the *Times* still employed a human receptionist, rather than an automaton like he was used to seeing at the

Bugle. Nick tried not to tap his foot impatiently as the secretary pecked away at his typewriter without seeming to realise he was there.

"Uh, excuse me?"

The secretary held up one hand, then finished his line and looked up. "Yes?" he said.

"I'd like to see Mr Brown, if possible."

"Do you have an appointment?"

"No."

"He's busy, I'm afraid."

Nick dug his business card out of his pocket and handed it over. "My name's Nick Galbraith. I'm with the *Daily Bugle*. I need to see him about something serious and urgent."

The secretary raised an eyebrow.

Nick sighed. "Honestly," he said, "do you really think I'd be here, in the office of my employer's competitor, if it wasn't important?"

The secretary huffed sceptically. "All right," he said at last. "Go up to the eighth floor and tell Mrs March that Dominic said you could have five minutes."

Nick grinned. "Thank you. You won't regret it."

"I already do."

Nick took the paternoster lift up, then asked directions to the editor's office. Mrs March turned out to be a formidable older woman with steely grey eyes.

"So Dominic manages Mr Brown's calendar now, does he?" she grumbled when Nick did as he'd been told. "He's flat out today, I'm afraid. You'll have to come back tomorrow." But just at that moment, the door behind her opened and Mark Brown emerged.

"Who's this?" he asked.

"I'm Nick Galbraith, sir," Nick said, stepping forward before Mrs March could get a word in.

"From the *Bugle*?"

"I ... well, yes, sir." Nick was shocked to find out that the editor of a paper like the *Times* even knew his name.

"I read your retrospective on Millie Roberts. Good stuff—not that I'd ever tell Bruce Maddox that." He chuckled.

"Thank you, sir."

"Now, what can I do for you? Did Maddox send you for something?"

"Um ... not exactly. Can we talk in private?"

"This better be good."

"It is, sir. Trust me."

AN HOUR LATER, NICK emerged from Mark Brown's office. He felt like cheering. He'd been worried that Brown would either pooh-pooh his story completely or simply decide that it was too risky, but he did neither, especially after Nick played him Jerome's recording. His one concern was Nick's employment.

"I can't run this while you still work for the *Bugle*," he said. "But if you turn in your resignation today we can go from there. I'm not offering you a job, mind—just a freelance contract for this story."

Nick nodded. "I understand." He knew that when the story broke he'd probably be sacked anyway—better to quit first. The thought of leaving the safety of his predictable job was unnerving, but at the same time it felt liberating. He had some savings, so he had financial breathing space, and there was something enticing about the thought of new possibilities. And for the first time in a very long time, he felt like he was finally being true to himself.

"The other thing that's going to affect this is how the march goes this afternoon," Brown said. "I assume you're planning to attend?"

"Actually, I wasn't, sir," Nick said. "Things didn't go well when the activists found out about the conspiracy—they accused me of spying for Maddox. They won't tolerate me anywhere near them."

"Well, go as a normal reporter, then," Brown said. "Watch from the sidelines. I was going to send one of my men, but if you go then I won't have to. You need to be there to finalise the story."

"Yes, sir."

"Good. Have a draft on my desk by five. I'll see you in here at nine o'clock tomorrow morning."

"Yes, sir. And thank you."

Chapter 15

Nick knew the BPL's march was scheduled for twelve o'clock, when the lunchtime rush would give them maximum visibility, so he made sure to arrive at the Parliament in plenty of time. He noted with some apprehension that there was already a police presence.

On the way to the Parliament, he'd stopped by the *Bugle*'s offices and handed in his resignation letter. Maddox was out, and Nick was secretly glad to avoid what he knew would be a confrontation. For good measure, he'd cleared out his desk and left his things in the care of Max, the automaton receptionist.

He pulled out his notebook, jotting down a few impressions of the scene while he waited. He was just beginning to wonder if the BPL had decided to cancel after all when he heard chanting, and soon enough he saw them coming up the street. He immediately sought out Millie and was unsure whether to be pleased or concerned when he spotted her. She looked radiant in a long midnight-blue gown, the movement's red and gold ribbons streaming from her hat. Her cheeks were pink and she was yelling passionately.

It all seemed to be proceeding without incident, but suddenly Nick saw a scuffle towards the back of the group of marchers. He stood on tiptoe, trying to peer over the heads of the curious onlookers. It seemed like someone in the crowd had jostled one of the women, but the activists marched doggedly on.

Suddenly a projectile came flying, and another woman tripped and fell. Nick glanced around for Millie but couldn't see her, and he realised with a jolt of horror that she was the woman on the ground. It was all he could do not to rush into the throng, but he knew she'd never forgive him if he did. Her compatriots reached down to support her, and in a few moments she was back on her feet. Raw egg dripped down the side of her face, staining her gown, but her jaw was set and her eyes were blazing.

"Onward!" she yelled, raising her fist, and the rest of the activists—along with a fair number of people in the crowd—cheered.

More eggs began to fly, thrown by anonymous onlookers, along with rotten vegetables and other detritus. When the brasscores reached the steps of the Parliament they sat down, holding their placards and shielding their faces from the onslaught. The troublemakers, emboldened, pushed closer, and the police stood back and let them. Robert MacIntyre didn't have to instruct his forces to actually incite violence, Nick realised—they just had to look the other way. No doubt one of the other members of the Gang of Five had planted the goons who were making the trouble.

Over to Nick's left, a scuffle broke out in the crowd.

"Hey!" a man shouted. "Stop that—they've got as much right to protest as anyone!" A chorus of affirmative voices broke out around him, and Nick stared in surprise. He felt the mood of the crowd begin to turn—they were no longer simply neutral observers taking in the strange lunchtime spectacle. And most of them, he realised, seemed to be siding with the activists. There was something horrifying about seeing the group of people sitting quietly while being harassed, and it electrified the crowd. He wondered if it was Millie's idea; he would have bet any amount of money that it was.

MILLIE SHIELDED HER face as garbage rained down on the steps of the Parliament. There was a bump beginning to swell on her right cheek where the egg had hit her, but she felt no pain, only a strange exhilaration. Her fellow brasscores were conducting themselves magnificently; nobody had even tried to retaliate.

During a break in the rain of rubbish, she looked up. The crowd was beginning to surge, and it almost seemed like they were going after the main troublemakers.

"Oi!" someone yelled at the closest policeman. "You need to stop this! Protect them! Do your job!"

Eventually the police seemed to realise that they were about to have a riot on their hands, and they began moving through the growing crowd, breaking up melees and moving people on. Gradually the onlookers began to disperse, and Millie breathed a sigh of relief.

"All right, then," a burly policeman with a walrus moustache said, coming up to them. "You've made your point. Head off home now."

"And if we don't?" Will asked.

He rolled his eyes. "Don't make me arrest the lot of you."

"I'll tell you what," Will said, "if you and your officers look away, just like you did at the start, then we'll go in our own good time. You won't have any trouble from us. I give you my word. But we won't be bustled off home like children who are out past curfew."

The policeman sighed. "Fine," he said. "Between you and me, I think your cause has merit in any case. And arresting you all would mean an awful lot of paperwork."

"Good man," Will said, grinning.

They stayed sitting on the steps for three more hours, by which time the novelty seemed to have worn off for the public. "Come on, friends," Will said at last. "Let's go. I think we can all agree that today was a success."

"Could have been worse," Florence said with a shrug, which Millie thought was high praise indeed.

Will smiled at the policeman as they gathered their things. "Don't worry," he said, "you haven't seen the last of us."

"I don't doubt it, sir."

MILLIE WALKED WITH Jean back towards the air-tram stop, dodging the rotten fruit and other garbage that littered the ground. Now that the rush of activity was over, she felt very tired. She just wanted to go home and wash the foul-smelling egg out of her hair.

She was staring vacantly into space, waiting for the air-tram, when Jean gave an exclamation.

"Goodness, what's he doing here?"

Millie looked over to where she was pointing, only to lock eyes with Nick. He smiled and gave a little wave, and she felt the heat rise to her cheeks. She quickly looked away.

"Maybe he came to the march," she said.

"Do you really think he dropped us in it?" Jean said.

Millie shrugged. "It certainly looks that way. Why—what are you saying?"

"Only that things aren't always what they seem. He may not have done it deliberately."

"That's what he said."

"Why don't you believe him?"

"He's a journalist—they lie for a living."

"*Millie*." Jean rolled her eyes.

"What? They do. I've had a bit more experience with them than you have."

"You know what I think?"

"No, but I suspect you're going to tell me."

"I think you like this man—no, more than like him. I think there's something going on there that you haven't told any of us. And I think that the thought of falling for someone, especially a journalist, terrifies you, and this whole palaver is a convenient way of getting out of it, regardless of the truth." She grinned. "How am I doing so far?"

"Terribly. I don't *love* Nick Galbraith."

"Are you sure?"

"Look, here comes the tram. And as for the truth—well, I can only go on what I've been told. Unless something drastic happens to change my mind."

Chapter 16

Millie slept late the next morning, only waking when her bedside clock chimed nine. As she made a cup of tea in the kitchen, she heard the thunk of the front door letterbox. She went into the hallway, where she found two rather boring-looking letters—bills, probably—and the morning edition of the *Scottish Times* lying on the mat. Idly, she unfolded the paper, interested to see if there was any coverage of the march. The front-page headline startled her so much that she jumped, spilling her tea. She brushed absentmindedly at her blouse, unable to tear her eyes away from the paper. *Police chief, MP, newspaper magnate in corruption scandal*, the headline shouted, but even more compelling to her was the byline: Nick Galbraith.

The story took up most of the front page and continued onto page three, and everything was there: the secret meetings at the Edinburgh Club, and the conspiracy to discredit the BPL and gain support for Sir Giles Pearson's bill by provoking violence. It was all exactly as Sarah had told her, but there was more detail and things she didn't know—Nick must have had another source as well. He also didn't shy away from his own involvement, detailing how Bruce Maddox had jumped at his proposal for an in-depth profile of the BPL, and how he'd subsequently exploited Nick for information. It all made sense, and as the pieces fell into place, Millie realised that Jean had been right—she'd judged him without knowing all the facts, based on her own prejudice. And in doing so she'd let one of the best things in her life slip through her fingers.

The tears sprang to her eyes and she wondered if it would be possible to make it right—chances were he wouldn't even want to talk to her now, after the way she'd treated him. But she lifted her chin determinedly—she wasn't one to shy away from a challenge, and she had to at least try.

Mind made up, she hurriedly pulled on her boots, ignoring the tea stain on her blouse. She had no idea if he'd even be home, but she was prepared to wait all day if necessary, if he'd only hear her out.

She hurried towards the Princes Park air-tram stop, running through what she was going to say in her head. She was so distracted that she didn't notice anything around her until she cannoned into someone hurrying the other way.

"Oh, excuse me!" she exclaimed, trying to catch her breath.

"Millie?"

It was Nick.

Millie stood gaping at him; all the fine words she'd been rehearsing had vanished. He looked tousled, as if he'd raced out of the house as quickly as she had, but it gave him a boyish charm that made her heart beat faster. He was clutching a copy of the *Scottish Times*, and the sight of it reminded her why she was looking for him in the first place.

"I ... I was just coming to see you ..." she stammered. "I read your article this morning ..."

"You did?" he said, brightening. "I wasn't sure if you'd get the paper, so I was on my way to bring you a copy. I hope that's all right. I was just going to put it through the letterbox, because I didn't think you'd want to see me." He closed his mouth abruptly, as if worried he'd said too much, and a flush of pink crept into his cheeks.

"But I *do* want to see you," Millie said. "I'm so sorry for what I said. I should have believed you. I had no idea how deep this whole thing went." She bit her lip.

"No," Nick said, "I should be the one apologising. I caused so much trouble for you and the others—I never meant to, but I knew Bruce Maddox was off. I'd just got so used to what it was like working for him that I lacked the guts to challenge it. Can you forgive me?"

"Only if you can forgive me."

"Done."

"Done."

They smiled shyly at each other, both unsure how to proceed.

"Would you like to take a walk in the gardens?" Millie asked at last, in an attempt to break the tension.

"I'd love to." He offered her his arm, and she took it.

"So fill me in on what happened," she said as they walked. "You've clearly been busy since I last saw you."

As they wended their way through the park, Nick told her all about how he'd tracked down Sarah, and Jerome's secret recording.

"I've resigned from the *Bugle*," he said. "Maddox is going to be livid, but I don't care. I should have done it long ago." They walked on in silence for some minutes. "I saw how the BPL handled the march," Nick said at last. "It was a stroke of genius, the passive resistance. Your idea, I presume?"

Millie nodded, blushing. "Everyone executed it perfectly," she said. "It went better than we could have hoped." She stopped and looked around.

"What's wrong?" Nick asked.

"Nothing. I just want to show you something. Come with me."

She took his hand and led him off the path, across the grass. They were in a more secluded part of the park, where a grove of large boulders and trees pressed close against the shadow of the Mound. Being a weekday morning, there was hardly anyone around. They followed an improvised track between the trees until it opened onto a secluded clearing in between a tumble of massive boulders. It was completely invisible from the rest of the park.

"Where are we?" Nick asked, his eyebrows rising.

"One of my favourite places in the whole world," Millie said, smiling. "I discovered it when I was ten. I felt like an intrepid explorer. I still come here sometimes when I just want space to think. I've never brought anyone here before."

"I'm honoured." Their eyes met, and when he smiled at her it was like the rest of the world vanished. The tension that had been sparking between them suddenly burst into flame, and without even thinking Millie stepped forward and kissed him deeply. Nick pulled her into his arms, kissing her back with a desire that made her breath catch in her throat. His hands roamed down her back, and she ran her fingers through his hair.

"I want you," she whispered in his ear, and he grinned.

"What, here?"

She shrugged, pulling away to give him a cheeky smile. "Why not?"

He laughed, undoing his belt. "You'll get us both arrested."

"Nobody ever comes here. And I'm game if you are." She kissed him again, sliding her hands into the waistband of his trousers, and as he pulled her close she could feel how much he wanted her too.

"I thought you said nobody ever came here," he murmured sometime later, as they held each other, panting.

Millie laughed. "I guess I was wrong."

Chapter 17

"I've been thinking about something," Millie said as they walked back into the main park. "You'll probably think it's mad, though."

"What's that?"

"I'd like to stand for Parliament. Once the law gets changed, of course—which is going to happen sooner or later. Brasscores don't just need the vote—we need to be able to elect one of our own."

"I don't think that's mad at all," Nick said. "I think you'd make a brilliant politician. Plus people already know who you are, which is a huge asset in an election campaign."

"That's the other thing I was thinking about," she said. "For years now I've been keeping a low profile. I tried to forget all about my previous life. The other BPL members recognised me when I first joined, of course, but we've never talked about it and they never pressured me to appear more in public. But I feel like we've reached a point where coming out publicly in support of the cause could do some good. So I'd like to do an interview. With you, if possible."

Nick raised his eyebrows; it was the last thing he'd expected. "An exclusive interview?"

She nodded. "You know how I feel about the media in general. But I trust you not to twist my words or try to bend things to your own agenda. I'm prepared to talk about what really happened on my flight, and why I dropped out of the public eye so suddenly in the following years. I'll even talk about *that* press conference. What do you think?"

Nick mulled it over. He knew from how well his retrospective article had been received that there was still a big market for stories about Millie—and something like this, which would fill in all the mysterious blanks in her story, would possibly even be front-page material. He knew he'd have no trouble pitching it to Mark Brown.

"I'm happy to do it, as long as you're really sure it's what you want. You know you'll lose some control of things once it's out there."

"I know, but it is what I want. It's something I can do to help the cause, and I think I need to do it for me, too."

"All right. When would you like to do it?"

"Now, if possible."

THEY RETURNED TO MILLIE'S house and sat down at the little table in the tiny, walled back garden, the early afternoon sun warm on their faces. Nick pulled out his notebook.

"Are you really certain you want to do this?" he asked again.

Millie took a deep breath, then nodded. "I need people to know the full story. There were some things that happened that I never spoke about at the time. And I also want them to know about the cause—they can't hold me up as some sort of romantic heroine and then deny me and my friends our basic rights."

Nick smiled. "All right. Why don't we start with your flight, then?"

She swallowed, her hands fiddling with the edge of her skirt. Impulsively, Nick reached out and clasped them.

"Millie, look at me." She raised her eyes to meet his, and he saw the anxiety in them. "You don't have to tell me anything you don't want to," he said. "This isn't a hatchet job. And it's not about me getting an exclusive, although that's a bonus. This is your chance to set the record straight. You're in control and if you want to stop, we stop. All right?"

She nodded. "It's hard to know where to begin with the flight," she said. "So much has already been written about it."

"Why did you want to do it in the first place?"

"I think I said at the time that it was about the adventure," she said, "and about doing something no-one like me had done before. And it was, to a certain extent. But if I'm honest, I really wanted to please my father. Ever since I was little I'd flown with him and he'd talked about me being destined for something big. He'd done so many amazing things that it seemed natural that I should carry it on. So by the time I was old enough to go, I think I truly believed it was my dream too."

"It takes a lot of fortitude to keep going on a voyage like that, though," Nick said. "You must have had some sort of drive to do it?"

She shrugged. "Fear of failure can be a great motivator. Every time I thought about giving up, I pictured my father's face and what he'd say if I failed. That was worse than the thought of continuing."

"You had some mechanical issues along the way, didn't you? What was your biggest challenge?"

Millie took a shuddering breath, pushing her hair off her face. Nick saw that her hand was shaking.

"I was attacked by air pirates over the Gulf of Aden."

He gaped at her; this wasn't the answer he'd been expecting. "I never read anything about that when I was researching the retrospective."

She shook her head. "You wouldn't have. The only people who know are my parents and one or two trusted others. I couldn't bear to talk about it."

"Do you want to talk about it now?"

She nodded, biting her lip. "It was just after dawn; I'd barely woken up. They dropped down from above like some sort of predator hawk, and the next thing I knew there was a black ship pulling up alongside and a raiding party was boarding."

"What did they want?"

"Thermocrystals. You probably read in some of the newspaper reports about how I was carrying a full supply of thermocrystals so that I wouldn't have to stop to refuel. My hold was packed with them. This is why transcontinental merchant ships always stop en route—if they carried enough to go the whole way non-stop, they wouldn't have any room for cargo. Anyway, in hindsight, all the reporting about the thermocrystals, plus the constant public updates about my location and the obvious fact that I was alone, made me an attractive and easy target."

"What did they do?" Unconsciously, he leaned forward.

"There were three of them. They brought me up on deck and I think they were going to ransack the hold. I don't know what else they had planned, although you can probably guess." She rubbed a trembling hand across her face. "Then I shot the leader."

"You *what*?"

She stared out across the garden, seeing something far away. "It would have been madness to undertake a voyage like that unarmed. My father had taught me how to shoot when I was young, and I had a rifle and a steam pistol powered by a thermocrystal charge, so I didn't have to reload it until the chamber was empty. I didn't have time to grab the rifle, but when I heard the boarding party I shoved the pistol into my pocket. And when I got the chance I shot the leader in the shoulder. It didn't kill him—which I'm glad about, because I couldn't have had that on my conscience—but it incapacitated him."

"And they just gave up after that?"

She shook her head. "They roughed me up a bit. In hindsight, shooting him was a stupid thing to do—it badly escalated the situation and I was lucky I didn't end up dead. But I was fifteen—not an age that's known for making sensible decisions. I thought I was invincible. Anyway, I got a clear shot and hit another one in the thigh, and after that they apparently decided I was too much trouble and left."

"And you weren't injured? You just continued on after that?"

"Yes, I was, and yes, I did." She showed him the thick, twisted scar on her right forearm, which he'd wondered about. "One of them got me with a knife. But I bound it up and kept going, and when I radioed my parents I downplayed how serious it was."

"Why? You could have landed at Aden and got medical attention."

She sighed. "If I'd done that, I would have forfeited my shot at the record—it had to be solo, non-stop and unassisted. And at that point even the pain seemed better than failing and wasting all those years of preparation."

"But surely your father would have understood?"

"Maybe. But I doubt it. He's single-minded to a fault, although I didn't realise that then. When he gets his mind set on something, nothing else matters."

She paused, taking a sip of water. "In the end, going on was a foolhardy thing to do. The wound became infected, and by the time I got home I was lucky not to lose my arm.

"Anyway, when I got back, the record was all anyone could talk about. I told my parents the truth about what happened, and my father congratulated me for my 'bravery', and then we talked no more about it. He wanted to tell the press, but my mother convinced him not to. I guess that was one small mercy. But the media scrutiny was relentless, and it went on almost non-stop for two years. And on top of it all I was having nightmares every night about the pirates, and jumping at shadows when I was awake. Sometimes a noise or even a smell would trigger a flashback so intense I really thought I was there again. In every press conference and every interview I had to watch my words, paste on a smile and pretend everything was fine, until one day I just couldn't do it anymore."

"That was the day you were asked about your next flight?" He'd found numerous accounts of that press conference, and all of them painted Millie as an entitled little brat who didn't appreciate how lucky she was and who was showing contempt for the public by refusing to do what everyone wanted. But he remembered the words of Gilbert Clarke, a respected senior reporter and his mentor at the *Bugle* when he was just a young cadet: "Always look for the story *behind* the story." It was a habit he'd let slip of late, under the increasing pressure to please Bruce Maddox, and he regretted it. He wasn't the only one, he knew; none of those journalists at that infamous press conference had bothered to find out what was really going on. Perhaps conforming to the prevailing narrative was easier, or perhaps they just hadn't wanted to see, lest it compelled them to act.

She nodded. "I guess the record was becoming old news by then. You know better than anyone that you have to keep feeding the beast. And my father is nothing if not media-savvy. So when they asked about my next flight, he began telling them about how we were planning a solo, unassisted pole-to-pole flight that would make the circumnavigation look like a Sunday outing. But he'd never discussed that with me.

"I don't know what happened—something just snapped. I realised suddenly that none of these people really cared about who I was or how any of this affected me; they only cared about what I could achieve and how it looked. And I no longer wanted any part of it. So I said that, there and then, in front of the press from across Britain and around the world. And my father still hasn't forgiven me."

She shrugged. "After that, I told my mother just how much I'd been struggling. And to her credit, she shielded me from most of the fallout. She arranged for me to go away for a while. I know what the rumours were—that I went crazy and was sent down to Bedlam—but actually it was to a lovely place in the Highlands run by a doctor and his wife, who were friends of my mother. There was plenty of fresh air, good food and peace, and the support I needed to get back on my feet. I stayed for nearly a year, and while it wasn't easy working through it all, I'm not sure I'd be alive without that break.

"When I got home, things really weren't good with my father. He'd barely speak to me, and it was clear that it wasn't tenable for us to continue to live under the same roof. So my mother helped me get set up here—she has her own money from her mother's estate—and I started to live an ordinary life. I got a job at Jenners as a saleswoman, and that's where I met Jean. She recognised me and told me I was an inspiration to other brasscores like her. When I went along to a meeting with her, I realised I'd found my people. Suddenly I had something real to fight for, and I've never looked back."

"So what lies in store for you now?"

She shook her head. "I have no idea. But I'm going to continue to fight for brasscores. It boggles my mind that society can support me to fly around the world solo but not let me vote. We have brasscores serving in the Aerofleet and the police force who can't vote, for goodness' sake. We want this basic right extended to all brasscores over the age of majority. And we want brasscores to be allowed to sit in

Parliament, because we should be able to vote for someone who will represent our interests. There's a general election in just over a year—there's no reason why these two things can't be achieved by then. All it takes is some willpower and some moral fortitude, and we won't stop fighting until those in power show some."

She sat back with a sigh; she looked like a weight had lifted off her shoulders. "I think that's all I have to say, really. Is that enough?"

Nick smiled. "That's more than enough." He reached out and took her hand. "You're incredible, you know?"

She rolled her eyes. "Because of everything I've done?"

"No," he said, "because of who you've become as a result. You're strong, and brave, and resilient, and even if you never did another damn thing for the rest of your life, you'd still be all those things. And that's why I love you. You've taught me how much more there is to life than just ticking things off a list."

"Wait ... you love me?"

"Is that so strange?"

"No...I guess I'm just not used to being ... well ... seen." She took his face in her hands and kissed him. "And that's why I love *you*, Nick Galbraith. I know you don't believe it, but you're one of a kind."

Epilogue

"Excuse me." Nick pushed past the rows of finely dressed gentlemen to the front row, where a group of people—the Brasscore Political League—held prime position. Jean smiled at him as she removed her bag from a saved seat.

"We thought you weren't going to make it," she said.

Nick shook his head and sat down. "I wouldn't miss this for the world."

It was the opening of the new session of the Scottish Parliament, which ordinarily would have gone unremarked-upon by all except the most ardent followers of politics. But this time was different. In the recent general election, the vote had been extended to all brasscores for the first time, regardless of class or status, and it had also seen three brasscore candidates standing. And, in a result that had shocked the old guard but had surprised no one else, one of them had been elected.

Nick looked down into the chamber to where Millie was seated, reading calmly through her notes. In just a few minutes she'd make her maiden speech—the first speech of her political career—and both the public and the press galleries were crammed with people wanting to mark the historic day. Nick felt suddenly nervous for her; he took a deep breath and wiped his sweaty palms discreetly on his trousers, but nothing escaped Jean.

"She'll be fine," she said, giving him a reassuring smile.

"I know."

It was a short speech—only ten minutes—but Nick felt like he was holding his breath for the whole thing. When the first heckler yelled out, he tensed, but Millie just raised an eyebrow archly and kept going. Two more hecklers were subsequently ejected from the chamber, but she didn't bat an eye. As she laid out her vision and agenda for her time in Parliament, Nick knew she'd have her work cut out for her. As the *Scottish Times*'s chief political correspondent, he'd become intimately familiar with the byzantine workings of the Parliament. But he also knew that she could handle it.

As Millie concluded her speech, the brasscore activists scrambled to their feet, clapping and cheering. The Speaker banged his gavel and tried to restore order, but others in the public gallery joined them. Nick turned to the man next to him.

"That's my wife!" he exclaimed proudly.

After the speech many of the public patrons filed out, but Nick stayed. The rest of the session was dull by comparison, but he didn't want to miss it. The past eighteen months had been a whirlwind—the BPL's march on Holyrood and his corruption exposé had catalysed things, but Millie's exclusive interview had been what had kept the momentum going. He'd been worried that the swirl of publicity that ensued would be difficult for her, but she'd handled it with aplomb, and it had only strengthened her resolve to stand for election. Eventually the politicians had had no choice but to change the law. He'd proposed to Millie the same day.

As the session closed, Nick took the stairs from the public gallery down to the foyer. He could tell that Millie was emerging by the sudden buzz of reporters near the doors to the chamber; on any ordinary day he would have been among them. He watched from a distance as she stopped and patiently answered questions for what seemed like forever, until the journalists apparently ran out of things to ask. It was an unusual tactic and Nick smiled to himself. She was going to be just fine.

THE MEDIA THRONG BEGAN to disperse, and Millie looked around, searching for Nick. Now that the thrill of the moment was beginning to wear off, she felt suddenly exhausted. Her eyes alighted on him standing near the stairs, leaning casually against a pillar; he saw her and gave her the grin that, even after nearly a year of marriage, still made her heart flutter. She hurried over and he caught her up in an embrace, heedless of onlookers.

"You were magnificent!" he said, kissing her. "How does it feel?"

She thought for a moment, then laughed. "It feels like flying."

HIDDEN DEPTHS

Chapter 1

"Excuse me, ma'am? Mr Mackenzie said he wants to see you before you leave."

"Thank you." Astoria Penrose smiled at the lad, who looked terrified. He couldn't have been more than fifteen—the age she'd been when she'd first started working at the thermocrystal mine, over half her lifetime ago. She supposed she'd been in awe of her shift supervisor back then too, although she couldn't really remember it. Sometimes it still felt odd to find herself in such a senior position.

The boy bobbed his head and darted away, and Astoria checked her watch. The whistle that signalled the shift change would be blowing any minute now, and she was itching to get out. Most of the time, a summons to Bertie Mackenzie's office didn't bode well, but she knew what it would be about. They'd finally made a decision about the job. *Her* job.

She took a deep breath, trying to tamp down the flutter of excitement in her chest. *Mine supervisor.* Bertie's second-in-command, and a role that would finally catapult her away from the crystal-face and into management. And that transition would most likely be the difference between a long, healthy life and dying of lung solidification in her fifties, like her father. She'd been the only real candidate from within the mine hierarchy—the other shift supervisor who'd applied was young and green, although he clearly had ambition. She'd known the moment she'd finished the interview that the job was as good as hers.

The whistle finally shrilled, and it was all Astoria could do not to race down the hill from the mine to the administration block. But she had duties, and she couldn't leave until the last person on her shift was accounted for. Thankfully, they all seemed just as keen to get out as she was, so she finished the sign-off quickly and handed over to her night-shift counterpart, an older man called Harry Murdoch. She changed out of her uniform in the ablutions room, stuffing it into a canvas haversack to take home and wash, then scrubbed the glistening crystal dust off her hands and face at the water barrel. Her auburn hair was still matted with it, but there was nothing to be done about that now. And Bertie wouldn't mind.

Feeling marginally cleaner, she grabbed her haversack and followed the stream of other miners down the hill to the mining camp and, beyond that, the village. Single miners tended to live in the camp, where they could bunk for free, while those with families had houses in the village. The administration block was the first building she came to. The other miners passed it by on their way home, but Astoria turned off. She took a deep breath as she climbed the steps to the outer office. She wasn't usually the nervous type—you didn't last long in a thermocrystal mine if you were—but she felt a twinge of butterflies in her stomach as she pushed open the office door.

Miss Beaumont looked up automatically as she entered. Bertie's longtime secretary was well into her sixties, making her just about the oldest worker at the mine. But nothing got past her, and she guarded Bertie like an attack dog.

"Good evening, Miss Beaumont," Astoria said politely, wanting to keep her on side. "I was told Bertie—I mean, Mr Mackenzie—wanted to see me?"

The secretary sniffed, her expression betraying nothing of her thoughts. "You can go in," she said. Astoria smiled and thanked her. She was never quite sure whether Miss Beaumont liked her or not.

She gave Bertie's door a cursory knock, then entered at his call. Her boss was seated, as always, behind a cheap wooden desk piled high with seemingly endless paperwork. A lit cigar rested in a brass ashtray beside the heap, and she worried briefly about fire. The man himself looked perpetually rumpled; his suit jacket had been tossed across a nearby chair, and his shirtsleeves were rolled to the elbow. His waistcoat stretched taught across a belly that spoke of a good many years out of the pit. But his face was as open and welcoming as always. He grinned when he saw her and sprang to his feet.

"Storie!" he said, coming around the desk to kiss her warmly on both cheeks. "Good to see you!"

"Hello, Bertie," Astoria said, unable to stop herself grinning back. She'd known Bertie Mackenzie since she was a child—he'd been a great friend of her father's—and she looked up to him almost as another parent. When she'd first started rising up the ranks there had been unkind whispers that this connection was the reason, but years of hard work had finally quashed them. Now, nobody questioned her right to be there.

Bertie ushered her to a chair and reseated himself behind the desk. "I suppose you're wondering why you're here," he said.

Astoria shrugged. "It's about the job, isn't it?" She tried to sound nonchalant, but the butterflies, which had temporarily stilled, fluttered back to life.

"Well ... yes." Bertie's affable manner suddenly dimmed, and he frowned to himself, as if trying to figure out what to say.

Astoria swallowed. "Go on then," she said with a brightness she didn't entirely feel. "Give me the bad news." She'd been joking, but when she caught the look on Bertie's face she realised she'd inadvertently hit on the truth. Her jaw dropped. "You mean I didn't get it?"

"I'm so sorry, Storie," Bertie said, sorrow clouding his features. "It was taken out of my hands. I still believe you're the best person for the job, and if it had been up to me you would have got it in a heartbeat. But head office wants to parachute someone in from Edinburgh."

Astoria's stomach felt like it had plummeted to her toes. She took a deep breath and bit her lip, not wanting to show how upset she was.

"But why? Is the mine in trouble?" It would make sense, she supposed, if head office wanted to oversee operations more closely. From everything she could tell, Bertie was an excellent manager—but then she wasn't privilege to all the details.

"Not at all." He sighed. "Just between us, they've got a political problem. They need to find an out-of-the-way position for someone, and apparently we're it. And as a result, you, my dear, got royally shafted."

In spite of everything, Astoria bit back a smile at his rough language. You could take a miner out of the mine, but some things stuck.

"So who is it, then? Some upstart manager who's overstepped the mark?"

Bertie shook his head. "An engineer. Not much management experience at all, as far as I know."

Astoria rolled her eyes. "Of course," she said cynically. "And I suppose he cocked up in some spectacular way and now they're trying to hush it up? What's his name, then? I assume it's a 'he'," she added.

Bertie nodded. "Michael Galbraith," he said.

This time Astoria didn't even try to hide her shock. Anger burned like a hot coal in her chest. She'd long ago accepted that life was unfair, especially to someone like her—a woman in a man's industry, in a man's world—but this was beyond the pale. She had worked so hard for this job. She'd spent years studying at nights, learning all the intricacies of thermocrystal mining that she'd need to understand in order to one day manage a site. She'd learned accounting and politics and how to manage people, with all their foibles. She understood where their little mine fitted in the company's overall plan; she'd spent countless hours in this very room with Bertie learning about the international strategy of it all. She'd even done what she could to improve her social graces so as to be able to interact better with the big bosses from Edinburgh when the time came. And now, just as all her hard work was set to pay off, she was being cast aside in favour of some trumped-up city engineer with no experience at the crystal-face or with the people who worked it, and who by all accounts was barely even competent at the job he was trained for. She very rarely cried, but right now she wanted nothing more than to throw herself down and weep with frustration at the injustice of it all. She took a deep breath and looked Bertie in the eye, but she didn't trust herself to speak.

"There is a silver lining," Bertie said.

Astoria said nothing, just waited for him to continue.

"I convinced the powers-that-be that they need to take you seriously if they want to retain you," he said. "I told them I'd only accept Galbraith as mine supervisor if they also created a position for you. You'll be the shift superintendent."

"What does that even mean?" She could barely keep the disgust out of her voice. She didn't want scraps and she didn't want pity.

"It's a promotion," Bertie said. "And a management position. You'll be in charge of the shift supervisors and making sure everything continues to run smoothly with our people. It'll mean you're at the same level as Galbraith—you'll both report directly to me. His role will be more ... technical. Think of it as a division of responsibility. He deals with the engineering, you deal with the workforce, and everyone stays happy. And when he moves on, which he will, you'll be able to pick up the other side quite easily."

"I still don't understand why they have to send him here at all. Why not just sack him after what he did?"

Bertie sighed. "The investigation was inconclusive. I imagine it was just easier to shunt him sideways and avoid a long and presumably very public battle over it."

Astoria scowled. "Will I have to work closely with him?"

"Well, yes. But probably not for too long."

He looked at her hopefully, and Astoria felt some of her ire cool. He was telling her to be patient. If Galbraith was as hopeless as he sounded, it wouldn't be long before Bertie had a reason to send him packing back to Edinburgh, and then the mine supervisor job would be hers. She just had to wait for him to trip over. She sighed.

"All right. When does he arrive?"

"The airship is due this time tomorrow. And thank you, Storie. You won't regret it, I promise."

I wouldn't be so sure about that, she thought.

Chapter 2

At eight o'clock the next morning Astoria clocked on for her shift as always, but she couldn't deny it felt different. It was hard to believe that this was her last stint at the crystal-face, hopefully forever. As much as she'd been longing to get away, now that the moment was here it was bittersweet. She'd made many friends, and a few enemies, toiling together in the mine. Over the years she'd lost some as well, either to accidents or to the dreaded lung solidification. She'd still be around, of course, but now she'd be Management, and she knew that would erect a subtle but important barrier between her and her compatriots.

The shift was mostly uneventful, and she toiled through it mechanically. The one small excitement was when one of the automatons that moved the heaviest loads broke down, but that was such a regular thing now that hardly anyone stopped what they were doing. The automatons were old and creaky, and often buckled under the strain. By necessity, Astoria had become something of a de facto mechanic. She opened the door on the automaton's brass back and tinkered with its innards until it slowly groaned back to life. Slamming the door shut, she wondered who would take over that duty once she moved on. No doubt somebody would—no one was indispensable in a thermocrystal mine.

She was so absorbed in the work that she didn't have much time to think about Michael Galbraith's imminent arrival, for which she was thankful. But as soon as the end-of-shift whistle blew everything came rushing back. She'd had less than twenty-four hours to get used to the idea, and now she'd have to meet him in the flesh, this person whose incompetence had undone all her hard work.

As she got changed in the ablutions room, she wondered what he'd be like. She didn't know anything about him apart from the little she'd read in the papers, and none of that was flattering. She pictured him as somewhere around Bertie's age, probably red-faced, balding and blustery, with an excuse for everything. He probably wouldn't take kindly to having to work alongside a woman—that type usually didn't. He'd probably expect her to do everything he wanted. But that was nothing she hadn't seen before. And he'd learn pretty quickly that it was wise to keep his opinions, and his hands, to himself.

She took longer than usual scrubbing her face, as if she could somehow delay the inevitable. When she finally emerged at the tail-end of a gaggle of miners, she found the late-afternoon sun reflecting off the red-and-gold envelope of a large Braithwaite Corporation airship that was just landing at the field beyond the administration block. She swore and began running down the hill, ignoring the friendly jibes from the other miners. She'd hoped to be able to go back to her room and change before Galbraith arrived, but that wouldn't be possible now; Bertie had wanted her there to meet the airship, and she was cutting it fine enough as it was.

She made it to the airfield just as the airship's passengers disembarked. Bertie was already greeting them when she hurried up, still gasping for breath. She could feel her hair sticking out like wire, matted with crystal dust. She knew she must look frightful, but she squared her shoulders and walked over to the small group.

Bertie was talking to two other men, both of whom were immaculately dressed. The older one was exactly as she'd pictured—red-faced, beefy, bullish. That must be Michael Galbraith. She had no idea who the other man was. Bertie noticed her and waved her over.

"As I was saying," he said as she approached, "this is Miss Astoria Penrose, our current day-shift supervisor, who will be moving into the position of shift superintendent alongside Mr Galbraith." He smiled at her reassuringly and she felt a little of her tension ease. "Storie, this is Mr Donald Braithwaite, the chairman of the Braithwaite Mining Corporation." He indicated the older, beefy man.

"Pleased to meet you, sir," Astoria said, trying to hide her surprise. She wondered why such a company bigwig was visiting their remote little mine.

"And this is Mr Michael Galbraith, our new mine supervisor."

For the first time, Astoria got a proper look at the younger man. He was in his late-thirties, she guessed, with a shock of dark hair that had resisted his attempts to tame it. There were the beginnings of smile lines around his brown eyes, although he wasn't smiling now. He had a square jaw and a lean, muscular physique that was only accentuated by his well-cut suit. He was nothing like she'd expected.

"Lovely to meet you, Miss Penrose," he said, holding out his hand.

"Likewise." She shook it, wincing inwardly as the calluses on her palm scraped his smooth, unblemished one. She had never felt so rough.

"Storie, would you mind showing Mr Galbraith to his quarters? I need to discuss some figures with Mr Braithwaite. I'll see you both in my office first thing tomorrow morning." There was something in the way Bertie looked at her, and then she realised—he hadn't known Braithwaite was coming. Exactly what that boded she couldn't tell.

"Of course, sir." She turned to Michael Galbraith. "Do you have a trunk?"

"They're just unloading it now."

"Don't worry about that," Bertie interjected. "I'll ask Miss Beaumont to send an automaton for it."

"Thank you, sir." She gestured to Michael. "Follow me, please."

MICHAEL LOOKED AVIDLY around him as he followed the red-haired woman down the hill towards what looked like a village. The scenery was beautiful, tucked in among the mountains, but the infrastructure was rough and utilitarian. The road down to the village was unpaved and pitted with rivulets; he assumed they were caused by water running down the hill whenever it rained—which, in the Highlands, was most of the time.

Miss Penrose walked quickly, with long, purposeful strides, and he hurried to keep up with her. He noticed she wore sturdy black boots, very different from his smooth-soled leather shoes. He'd have to get a pair if he could.

When Donald Braithwaite had told him he'd be sharing his role with a long-time mine employee, Michael had been relieved. He knew that being parachuted into a management position from outside wasn't going to win him a lot of friends. He'd made assumptions about his new colleague—a grizzled miner, old before his time, who wasn't that knowledgeable about new technologies and liked to do things the old-fashioned way. He certainly hadn't expected a thirty-something woman with fiercely intelligent eyes and a handshake that told him she meant business.

About halfway between the mine and the village, a series of low, barracks-like buildings rose up. Miss Penrose turned off the main track and onto a smaller path that led between them.

"These are the workers' dormitories," she said. "The single miners can live here for free. Married ones usually take houses in the village."

"How many to a room?"

"Four for anyone who's been on the job less than five years. Two for the rest. And the two shift supervisors each get our own room, although we share a bathroom.

"But you're in luck," she continued, leading him behind the dorms to a small cottage set back from the main buildings. "This is the mine supervisor's cottage. You even get your own bathroom and a small kitchen, in case you don't want to eat at the mess with the rest of us minions." She arched an eyebrow sardonically.

"Where's your cottage?" Michael asked, looking around.

Miss Penrose gave a bark of laughter. "My *job* didn't even exist until yesterday," she said. "I'll be staying in the shift supervisors' dorm. And consequently the poor bugger who takes my old role will lose his privileges too."

"Oh," Michael said with a flash of understanding. Braithwaite had told him the role was to be shared, but he hadn't mentioned that he was taking someone else's job. He realised Miss Penrose had ended up with a consolation prize that was decidedly second-rate. No wonder she was being so cold to him.

The cottage was worn but clean. It was very different from what he was used to back in Edinburgh, but Michael minded it less than he'd thought he would.

"We even have running water," Miss Penrose said, opening the door to the tiny bathroom, which was little more than a shower-head and a basin. "But you'll need to boil it before you drink it. It gets piped up from a bore below the village by a thermocrystal-powered pump. Mind you, the pump often breaks. Most things do around here."

The 'kitchen' was really just a small thermocrystal stove and a bench set in a corner of the large main room. There was also a settee in front of the fireplace, and a double bed that was separated from the rest of the room by a movable paper screen. A chest of drawers and a small wardrobe stood beside it.

"Is there anything else you need?" Astoria asked. "The mess is the next building over. Meals are at 6 am and 6 pm. They also leave out a spread during the day so you can make yourself a sandwich between-times. Have you eaten?"

"Not really. Just something small on the airship."

"All right. I'm going to clean up and then I'll come and get you for dinner."

"Thank you. Miss Penrose?"

"Mm?"

"I'm sorry for taking your job. I had no idea."

She shrugged, but didn't smile. "Call me Astoria. And it's fine. Just don't screw it up."

But as she turned on her heel and left, Michael knew that it was anything but fine.

Chapter 3

"This way, if you please, sir," Miss Beaumont said, ushering Donald Braithwaite into Bertie's office. Bertie followed, feeling a momentary pang as his boss glanced at the untidy desk with obvious disdain.

"Bring some tea, please, Euphemia," he said to Miss Beaumont, and the secretary nodded then discreetly departed.

"Please, have a seat," Bertie said, gesturing to a chair. "Cigar?"

Braithwaite glanced at the cigars, clearly decided they were of inferior quality, and fished one of his own out of his jacket pocket. Bertie passed him the clippers and matches. When they were both puffing away he sat back in his chair, trying to force himself to relax. The last thing he wanted to do was show the chairman how discombobulated he was. But Donald Braithwaite seemed content to keep him hanging, and at last Bertie could stand it no longer.

"To what do we owe this unexpected visit, sir? We weren't expecting you for another two months."

Braithwaite shrugged. "Sometimes it's good to drop in unannounced. Before things have a chance to be ... tidied up, don't you know?"

Personally, Bertie thought just 'dropping in' was unaccountably rude, but he held his tongue.

"Well, of course you're welcome here at any time," he said.

"I should think so," Braithwaite said. "After all, it is *my* mine."

Bertie frowned.

"Production is down—again," Braithwaite said, cutting to the chase. "That makes the third consecutive quarter. Care to explain what's going on?"

Bertie sighed. He'd wondered when this conversation would come, and here it was.

"I know it is," he said, "but as I'm sure you've seen in my reports, we are working under rather trying conditions. Some of our automatons are nearly as old as I am. The fleet as a whole is in dire need of replacement. My people spend half their time fixing them. That's one of the main factors affecting production."

Braithwaite rolled his eyes. "I doubt that very much," he said. "None of the other mines have complained of such an issue."

"With all due respect, sir, the other mines have seen significantly more investment than we have," Bertie said, trying to keep the edge out of his voice.

"Yes, well, you've always liked to go your own way, haven't you?"

"I beg your pardon, sir?"

"I've given you considerable leeway with your free clothing and various other programs," Braithwaite said. "You assured me that those conditions would have a pay-off. Well, I'm yet to see it."

"It *has* paid off," Bertie said. "We have the lowest accident rate in the whole company, and the highest retention rate. Our people *want* to work here. Morale is generally good. But not investing in the technology that will allow them to do their jobs properly is starting to undermine that."

Braithwaite took a long draw on his cigar, rolled the smoke around in his mouth and then blew it back into Bertie's face. "You know what I think the real problem is?" he said. "Your people are coddled. They've become soft. They wouldn't know hard work if it bit them on the backside. I was prepared to try your schemes, but I always thought it would end up like this. You offer people too many free things and they become entitled."

"Basic safety *is* an entitlement," Bertie said. He clenched his jaw to stop himself from saying anything further he might regret.

"All right," Braithwaite said, removing the cigar and leaning forward to make his point. Even with the desk between them, Bertie had to fight the urge to lean away from him. "Here's the deal. I'm finished with throwing good money after bad. You have three months to turn things around. If production isn't up by the end of the next quarter, I'm pulling the pin."

"You're going to close us down?" Bertie felt a lurch of horror.

"Of course nobody wants that," Braithwaite said. "But the company can't continue to carry dead wood. And I suspect it will be a great motivator for your people."

"And I take it that means you won't be investing in new automatons?"

"Why would I plough money into something that may not exist in three months, my lad?" Braithwaite chuckled, and Bertie felt sick.

"Because sooner or later there's going to be an accident," he said. "Those things are becoming a safety issue."

"Get production up, and then we'll talk," Braithwaite said, rising to his feet as the door opened and Miss Beaumont entered with the tea. "Now, walk me back to the ship, if you please. The last thing I want is to be stranded here overnight." He gave a booming laugh, but Bertie couldn't join him. They left the secretary standing bewildered, clutching the tea tray, and walked back up the hill in silence.

"See you in three months," Braithwaite said, turning and walking up the gangway. Bertie wished heartily that the damn airship would crash on the way back to Edinburgh. The violence of his feelings surprised him. He was furious at Braithwaite, and equally furious at himself for not being able to get his point across better. If only the Board could see what a parlous state things were really in. For although Donald Braithwaite was the chairman and majority owner, there were other board members who might be more sympathetic. If something happened and he could prove Braithwaite knew about the risk, they would surely act. And Bertie had no doubt those old rustbucket automatons were going to cause an accident one of these days. It was only a matter of time.

Chapter 4

Astoria stood under the hot shower, scrubbing the crystal dust from her hair and skin. As basic as the dorms were, she was thankful as always for the luxury of plumbed hot water. There were plenty of other mines, she knew, where they weren't so fortunate.

She could have happily stayed there all night, letting the warmth soothe away the stress of the afternoon, but she was mindful that she'd said she'd take Michael Galbraith to the mess. As resentful as she felt, it still didn't seem quite right to leave him to face his new colleagues alone. She remembered how intimidating she'd found the mess on her first visit, and that was despite having grown up with most of them.

Reluctantly, she turned off the water and got out of the shower, hurriedly towelling herself dry—for even though it was summer, the breeze coming in through the window had a bite to it. She dressed in clean breeches and a shirt, and fought her damp hair back into a braid. Sometimes she thought she should just cut her hair short and be done with it, but she could never quite bring herself to do it—it was, she reflected, her one vanity. She appraised herself in the mirror a little longer than normal, then caught herself doing it and raised an eyebrow. Why should she care what she looked like? It was only Michael Galbraith, and his opinion didn't matter. Apart from anything else, she'd only known him for all of ten minutes.

Even so, she couldn't help noticing a slight flutter of nerves when, a few minutes later, she knocked on the door of the mine supervisor's cottage. It opened immediately, as if he'd been waiting for her. He was still wearing his fancy suit with the unsuitable shoes, she noticed—she'd really have to find him a pair of boots first thing tomorrow—and she couldn't deny he wore it well. But she wasn't yet sure if Michael Galbraith could be trusted, and experience had taught her that it was the handsome ones you really had to watch out for.

"Astoria," he said with a smile.

"Michael." He hadn't said she could call him by his given name, but she didn't care about silly formalities—if he was going to call her Astoria, she'd be damned if she was going to address him as Mr Galbraith. Not when they were supposedly equals.

"Are you ready?" she asked.

"Absolutely. Lead on." He shut the door behind him and they set off across the camp, Astoria pointing out the various buildings as they went.

"It reminds me a bit of an Aerofleet barracks," Michael said as they crossed behind the ablutions block.

"Did you serve?" Astoria asked, surprised. He didn't strike her as a military man.

He shook his head. "No. My brother did, though—still does, in fact. He's the fleet commander on Gibraltar at the moment. So I've been to the odd base event with him over the years."

"Right." Astoria watched him out of the corner of her eye as they walked. What different lives they'd led. He was trying to relate to her as best he could, she supposed, but he was clearly out of his depth. She felt a twinge of apprehension as the mess loomed up before them. They were going to eat him alive in there. And she wasn't quite sure whether to let them.

MICHAEL TOOK A DEEP breath as Astoria pushed open the heavy door. He felt like he was walking into a lion's den. He'd been on mine sites before, of course, but then he'd always been dealing with managers and the odd senior supervisor. He wasn't even sure what his expectations were any more—Astoria had totally upended everything he thought he knew about the industry and the people who ran it. All he knew was that he wasn't really wanted here.

As the door opened, the noise of the mess broke over him—voices chattering, plates and cutlery clinking. The building was a typical dining hall, filled with long communal tables and a servery at the far end, which presumably opened onto the kitchen. The tables were packed with men, and the occasional woman, wolfing down plates of what appeared to be some sort of stew.

"Come on," Astoria said, leading him down the main aisle between the tables. Michael could feel the miners' eyes boring into his back, and the conversations seemed to still as he passed by.

At the servery window they collected plates of delicious-smelling stew and mash from a kitchen automaton.

"Looks great," Michael said.

Astoria raised a sardonic eyebrow. "Tell me that in a few weeks' time," she said. "They do a *lot* of stew here."

"Do you get bored with it?"

She shrugged. "Sometimes. But it is what it is. If I really want a home-cooked meal, I go down to the village and have dinner with my mum."

Michael opened his mouth to ask her more about her family, but she'd already turned away and he had no option but to follow.

The long tables were mostly full, but as a group of three got up and left Astoria made a dash for the vacated space. Michael hurried after her.

"Hey, Storie!" a miner down the table called as they sat down. "Who's the toff? Don't tell me you've finally found yourself a fella?" Several of his friends guffawed, but Astoria just rolled her eyes. She seemed to be biting back a grin.

"You might want to pull your head in, Jock," she said. "This is your new boss."

The man called Jock, who had just taken a sip of something from an enamel mug, choked and spluttered. One of his mates thumped him on the back, laughing.

"Good one, son!"

"Put your foot right in it, didn't you?"

Astoria laughed along with them, and Michael's heart sank. He'd begun to think of her as something of an ally in this strange new world, but of course she'd spent years toiling at the crystal-face with these men. This was where her loyalties lay. There was no way he'd ever be able to break into that. 'Toff,' they'd called him, and he knew they were right—he was suddenly conscious of his suit, and how different he looked and even sounded to these men in their rough breeches and stained shirts. He remembered how Astoria's hand had felt when they'd shaken, with the calluses of hard work on palm and fingers, and how miserably soft his own were. He didn't belong here. But he couldn't let them see that, or he'd lose any chance he had at winning their respect.

"Boss, you say?" One of the men was saying to Astoria. "And here I was thinking that was going to be you, Storie."

Astoria shrugged nonchalantly, although Michael noticed her frown slightly to herself, as if something bothered her. "The company decided it was better to share the load," she said. "I'll be looking after personnel, and Mr Galbraith here will be dealing with the technical side."

The miner frowned. "Galbraith ... I know that name ..."

"As in 'Galbraith inverter'?" Jock asked, narrowing his eyes. Michael took a deep breath.

"That's right," he said. He'd known he'd have to confront this eventually, but he'd hoped it wouldn't be quite so soon.

There was a whisper among the miners further down the table. Jock folded his arms across his chest, lifted his chin and stared at Michael.

"So, how does it feel to have blood on your hands?"

"Jock!" Astoria interjected.

"What? Tell me I'm wrong. His wonderful invention kills men at two separate sites, and they put him in charge?" He shook his head in disbelief.

"The investigation was inconclusive," Astoria said. "You don't have to like it, but at the very least you can speak respectfully. And if you really have a problem, you can come and see me and we'll deal with it through the appropriate channels."

Jock stood up. "I've heard enough of this," he said. "You've changed, Storie. And here I was thinking you were still one of us."

"Jock, come on ..."

But the miner just picked up his plate and left without a backward glance. Several of his friends followed, leaving Michael and Astoria sitting on their own.

"Who knew I could clear a room so quickly?" Michael said, trying to break the tension. "Thanks for defending me."

Astoria just stared at him stonily. "Of course," she said. "A united front is basic professionalism." She took a bite of stew and swallowed. "But they were right, weren't they?"

Michael felt like he'd been slapped, but he looked her in the eye. "Yes," he said.

She nodded, and they finished their meal in silence. He could hardly taste it.

Chapter 5

The next morning Astoria woke early but couldn't get back to sleep. She lay in bed, weighed down by thoughts of the previous evening. She was still disconcerted by how badly things had gone at the mess. She'd anticipated some sort of reaction, of course, but she hadn't realised that Bertie hadn't yet told the workforce about the changes at the top. She knew it had all happened quickly, but even so, she'd expected he would ease the way, given it was such a contentious appointment. Dropping her and Michael into the thick of it like that was unprofessional. It was almost like Bertie wanted him to fail.

She knew that standing up for Michael had been the right thing to do, but it still stung. She'd lost some of her credibility with Jock and the others, who were not only her friends but one of the most influential groups on the whole site. It would be very hard to win them back. And then there was Michael himself. He clearly had no idea what he was getting into, and to be honest, she wondered about his competence. Of course, if he did a terrible job, that would clear her way to becoming mine supervisor that much faster. But she wouldn't want that at the expense of her fellow workers' safety, or the security of their jobs.

She glanced at the clock on her nightstand and sighed. Bertie wanted to see them first thing, and she'd have to get up if she wanted breakfast before that. She briefly thought about calling for Michael but decided against it. He could find his own way up the hill.

When Astoria arrived at the administration block, there was no sign of Michael. Following Miss Beaumont's instructions, she waited in the outer office until her colleague arrived, breathless, one minute after their meeting was due to begin. The secretary frowned at him and glanced at the clock. He gave her an apologetic grin, which quickly withered under her stony gaze.

"You can go in now," she said icily.

Bertie rose from behind his desk as they entered, coming forward to shake their hands.

"Welcome, officially," he said to Michael. "We didn't get much chance to speak yesterday, but I'm glad you're here. I think you and Astoria will make a good team. How are you settling in?"

"Fine, sir, thank you," Michael said, giving no hint of the unpleasantness that had taken place the night before. It would have been so easy for him to drop Jock and the others in it, Astoria reflected, and it was a mark in his favour that he didn't.

"Well, of course it's going to take you some time to get to know the lay of the land," Bertie said, sitting down at the desk and waving them to chairs. He seemed to be trying to be his jovial, affable self, but there was a tightness around his mouth that hadn't been there yesterday. Astoria wondered if he was ill.

"We don't want to throw you in the deep end too quickly," Bertie continued. He turned to Astoria. "I think it'd be best if you spent today giving Michael a tour of the site. Take him up the hill and into the pit, introduce him to the lads. Show him how the whole operation hangs together. Then we can really get stuck in tomorrow. What do you say?"

"Of course, sir," Astoria said, sighing inwardly. She'd almost rather be back at the crystal-face than spend a whole day babysitting Michael Galbraith. Almost.

"Excellent," Bertie said. He pulled some papers across in front of him. "I'll see you both tomorrow, then. Enjoy."

Astoria rose at the clear dismissal and Michael followed. They trooped through the outer office, where Miss Beaumont glared at them, and out into the road.

"Right," Astoria said, turning to him. "First thing we need to do is get you some decent boots."

MICHAEL FOLLOWED ASTORIA to another low, squat building further up the hill, towards the mine. He wasn't sorry to be spending the day on a tour with her. She clearly knew everything he needed to know about the mine and its workers, and he would have to learn as much as he could as quickly as possible. But more than that, he also wanted to learn more about her. He appreciated the way she'd defended him at the mess the previous evening, against friends whose opinions she shared, no less. She was clearly well-respected, and he was already beginning to think highly of her. He hoped that one day she might just be able to revise her opinion of him too.

The building turned out to be an equipment storehouse, packed to the gills with neatly organised shelves of clothes, shoes, helmets, goggles and other paraphernalia. A bell over the door dinged as they entered, bringing, a small, rotund man scurrying out from behind the shelves like an oversized mouse.

"Storie!" he exclaimed, catching sight of them. "What can I do for you?"

"Hello, Bob," Astoria said, smiling. "I'm after a pair of boots for my new colleague here."

The little man looked Michael up and down.

"Size ten?" he asked.

Michael gaped at him. "How did you know?"

Bob tapped the side of his nose. "I've been in this game a long time, son. You get a knack for these things. I'll be right back."

He disappeared back into the maze of shelves and they could hear him rummaging around. Then, surprisingly quickly, he reappeared holding a cardboard box.

"They're not quite new, I'm afraid," he said. "But only one prior owner, and he didn't need them long." Astoria glanced at him sharply, and he shrugged. "Waste not, want not, my dear," he said. "You know how it is around here."

He handed the boots to Michael to try on. They fitted perfectly, and seemed to be already broken in.

"You can leave your shoes here and pick them up when you're finished for the day," Bob said.

"Assuming Bob doesn't give them away first," Astoria interjected, arching an eyebrow.

"Thank you," Michael said, placing his shoes on the counter. "How much do I owe you?"

"No charge."

"No, really, I insist."

Bob glanced helplessly at Astoria.

"That's not the way things work around here," she said. "People don't have to pay to work here. Uniforms and safety equipment are free. Speaking of which, if you're going into the pit you'll need a helmet, goggles and gloves. You can change into overalls up there."

"That's all down to this one, you know," Bob said, nodding at Astoria as he lifted down equipment.

"What is?"

"The free gear. For many years we had to buy our own. It was an unofficial part of the contract that your first two pays went towards your gear. Bit rough if you had a missus and kids to support, but there it was." He shrugged. "Then Storie here came along and had the gumption to call it out, and the lads got behind her. She convinced management, and for the last four years we've been the only crystal mine in the country that doesn't make its workers pay for the privilege of working there."

"Stop it, Bob," Astoria said, her cheeks flaming. "You make it sound so much bigger than it was."

Bob looked at her gravely. "It was a big thing for those of us with wee ones to feed," he said quietly. He glanced at Michael. "Don't you be fooled by her modesty. This lass'll be running the mine within the next five years, and the company another five after that, you mark my words."

"We should be getting on," Astoria said, still blushing. "Thanks again, Bob."

"Pleasure," he said. "Hope you have a better time than the last fella who wore them boots."

"What did he mean by that?" Michael asked as they left the stores.

Astoria sighed. "A few years ago there was an accident, and three lads died. Those boots belonged to one of them."

"Oh. I'm sorry."

She shrugged. "It's a dangerous industry. And it's made worse here by the lack of investment from the company. This place is falling apart. Things keep breaking down, and although the workers try to stay as safe as they can, accidents happen. But management down in Edinburgh doesn't care about that. We're expendable. All they want is more efficient ways of getting crystals out of the ground and saving pennies. No matter the human cost."

She turned away and began walking up the track.

"We'll go up the hill first," she called over her shoulder. "It'll give you a view of the whole site. Hope you don't mind a bit of a walk."

'A bit of a walk' was a gross understatement, Michael reflected as he toiled up the rough track that ascended the hill above the mine site. He considered himself reasonably fit, but the climb was testing him. In contrast, Astoria seemed to have the strength and stamina of a mountain goat; she was hardly even out of breath.

"Don't worry," she said as they crested the final ridge. "It'll be worth it."

Michael clambered up behind her and stood, gasping, at the summit. She was right—it was absolutely worth it. The mine valley stretched out below them, and beyond it were other ridges of blue-grey hills and the silvery glint of a loch. Clouds chased each other across the sky, throwing patches of shadow on the vista below.

"It's beautiful," Michael said as soon as he got his breath back.

Astoria nodded. "Whenever things get a bit hard down there, I come up here. It helps me see more clearly."

Michael glanced across at her, but she was gazing out it the view, a wistful expression on her face. He wondered what she was thinking.

"Here," she said, digging in her pocket. She handed him a chunk of foil-wrapped chocolate. "I swiped it from the mess this morning."

"Thanks."

They perched side-by-side on a conveniently placed boulder, munching the chocolate.

"So this whole valley is owned by Braithwaite?" Michael asked, peering down. He could see the road that led into the mine in the hill below their feet, then beyond that the administration block and workers' dormitories. And farther down still were the grey-roofed houses of the village.

Astoria nodded. "Everything except the village. It was here long before the mine was. But in reality they all but own that too."

"You grew up there?"

She nodded again.

"What was it like?"

Astoria shrugged. "I don't really know anything different. It was ... small ... but in a cosy way. We didn't have much money, but we were happy."

"When did you join the mine?"

She glanced at him. "Why the interrogation?"

"Sorry." Michael felt his cheeks burning. "Just my rather ham-fisted attempt at getting to know you. I'll stop now." He scuffed his boot in the dirt, annoyed at his own haplessness. He couldn't seem to do anything right these days.

But, unexpectedly, Astoria smiled at him.

"It's fine," she said. "I started working in the mine when I was fifteen, after my father got sick. At first it was just covering some of his shifts, but then I started taking on more and more as he got worse, and eventually I had to leave school. He died when I was eighteen and my sister Jenny was only seven. My mother was taking in washing, but it wasn't enough on its own. Someone had to provide for the family, so I did." She shrugged, then raised her chin proudly. "My wage meant that Jenny was able to stay at school. She just graduated from the grammar school in town at the top of her class. She's been accepted into the University of Edinburgh."

"That's wonderful!"

Her face clouded. "It is. But I was counting on my promotion to be able to send her, and I don't think that will be possible now."

"I'm not sure I understand," Michael said. "I mean, you've still been promoted, haven't you?"

"In title, yes," Astoria said. "But you've been around this industry a while—you must know that splitting a job between two people doesn't mean paying double the wages."

"You mean … they've split the salary between us? We're getting half each?"

She gave him a withering glance. "I'm a woman—they were never going to pay me the same as a man. So I'd guess the split is more like sixty-forty. To you."

Michael's eyebrows shot up. He couldn't quite believe what he was hearing. "How much do you get paid?"

She told him, and he did some quick sums in his head. "You're right," he said. "It's sixty-forty. I can't believe it."

"It must be nice to have the privilege of being that naive," Astoria said.

"I'm so sorry. I really had no idea."

She shrugged. "It is what it is. But I don't want Jenny paying the price for it. Part of the reason I live in the camp rather than in the village with them is so the money goes further. This way, I get my room and meals for free, and I can give as much as possible to my mother." She frowned to herself. "I can't believe I told you all that. Anyway, that's more than enough about me. It's your turn."

"What do you want to know?" He felt his stomach flutter in trepidation.

"How did *you* end up in the mines?"

"In general? I always loved tinkering with things and finding out how they worked, so engineering seemed like the natural choice. And I was good at it."

"And how did you end up here?"

Michael pressed his lips together. The recollection was still painful. "Turns out I wasn't as good at it as I thought."

"You mean the inverter?"

"Yes." When his device had first come out, he'd been hailed as a genius. Rather than hammering away at the rock, the inverter turned the process around and sucked the crystals down. It was faster, cheaper, and more efficient, and the mining companies couldn't get enough of it. Almost overnight, Michael had found himself rich and with invitations to all the best society functions in Edinburgh. And then it had all come crashing down.

"I wasn't surprised, you know," Astoria said, bringing him back to the present. "About the accidents, I mean."

"Why is that?" Surprisingly, Michael realised he felt curious rather than defensive. What had he missed?

"They brought one in to try here, so I saw it first-hand. It creates so much more dust than the regular methods. An accident was inevitable."

"I'm not sure I follow."

She stared at him in disbelief. "Thermocrystal dust is explosive." She spoke slowly, as if explaining something obvious to a child.

He took a deep breath. "There's no evidence of that."

"Only because they haven't yet been able to replicate the necessary conditions in a laboratory. But you ask anyone who has worked at the crystal-face and they'll be able to give you plenty of examples of near misses. In fact, the Gibbons article in the most recent issue of *Thermocrystal Quarterly* advocates doing just that. If I remember rightly, he says that although such anecdotal evidence can't prove causation, a correlation of such strength warrants further investigation. If you ask me, not talking to the workers comes down to sheer snobbishness, or laziness, or both."

Michael stared at her, gobsmacked.

"What?" she said. "I read the same things you do. Bertie gets all the industry journals, and he passes them on to me when he's finished with them."

"You said you never finished school."

She shrugged. "I didn't. But that doesn't mean I stopped learning or being interested in the world around me. And this is the problem," she continued, more forcefully. "By your standards, and the standards of anyone in head office, I'm uneducated. They never bother to consult those of us on the front line because they think we're too stupid to understand. And that's the fatal flaw. I could have told you that, sooner or later, the inverter was going to cause an explosion, because I've seen smaller dust pockets combust before my very eyes. Just like I can tell you there's going to be an increase in lung solidification deaths over the next few years in mines where the inverter was used, for the same reason—the dust. In fact, that was the reason we campaigned so strongly against it here. And Bertie backed us, thankfully. He stands by his workers, because unlike the bigwigs in Edinburgh, he started as one of us."

"Unlike me."

She shrugged. "It's not just you. But you can start to make amends. Come down the pit with me and meet the lads and lasses who pay your wages."

He nodded. "Lead on."

Chapter 6

Michael followed Astoria back down the hill to where the mine entrance gaped like a yawing mouth. It was similar to all the other thermocrystal mines he'd visited. Unlike other minerals, which were found deep underground and required fleets of complicated steam elevating machines and automatons to recover them, thermocrystals grew under hills, so the mines were relatively shallow. A typical cold-climate thermocrystal mine consisted of a long tunnel dug into the hillside, which opened out into caverns beyond. In many of the older mines, like this one, the entire hill was practically hollow, it was so honeycombed with tunnels.

Michael had been in mines plenty of times, of course, but usually as part of a much bigger team on an official visit. It felt strange to just wander in like this. He followed Astoria to a rough stone building around the corner from the mine entrance, which he guessed was the ablutions block. She stopped at a cupboard in the entryway and pulled out a pair of overalls, holding them up as if judging the size.

"Here," she said, tossing them to him. "They might be a bit big, but they'll do."

"Thanks."

"You can get changed in there," she added, gesturing to a door marked 'Gentlemen'. "You'll see a locker in there with 'extra' written on the door—there'll be a helmet and a pair of gloves in there that you can use. You can put your clothes in there too. I'll meet you back here when you're ready."

Michael nodded and went into the changing room. Three walls were covered with small wooden cupboards, each with a number painted on the door. He assumed it was easier than writing names, given the turnover of miners. Along the fourth wall were three sinks with taps, presumably so the miners could wash after work. Lines of wooden benches ran under the rows of lockers.

He stripped down to his vest and underpants, then pulled the coveralls on. He felt strangely naked underneath, but he knew it would be so hot in the mine that he wouldn't want many layers. The overalls were slightly too long in the arms and legs, but it was nothing a few judicious folds at wrist and ankle couldn't fix. He found the locker marked 'extra' and, as Astoria had said, it contained a helmet and a pair of gloves. He removed them, replacing them with his folded clothes, and tried them on for size. Both were a reasonable fit. He pulled on his boots and then went to meet Astoria, feeling a jangle of nerves in his belly.

ASTORIA TAPPED HER toe impatiently on the rough floor, resisting the urge to look at the clock. She wasn't sure why she was so on edge about taking Michael into the pit; it certainly wasn't the first time she'd done a tour. But this wasn't just leading some manager around and hoping he didn't get too dirty—this was a new colleague, and she wasn't quite sure what result she was hoping for. The faster he failed, the faster her own career could advance. But it had been awful watching the reception Jock and the others had given him in the mess. She couldn't abide bullies—she'd been on the other end too often—and if that was the way it was going to go, she knew she'd have to step in. And it wouldn't do her reputation any favours if she had to keep coming to the aid of an incompetent engineer who'd been parachuted in to get him out of the way of the main game. Like almost all the miners, Astoria had no time for incompetence. Incompetence got people killed. And what was the Galbraith inverter if not a supreme act of incompetence?

After what seemed like an age, but was probably only a few minutes, Michael emerged, looking much less like a city engineer and much more like a miner, albeit far too clean. *We'll soon fix that*, she thought.

"This way," she said.

At the mine entrance was a booth with a lone guard, and a board with neat rows of hooks. From each hook hung a little metal circle engraved with a name and number. Astoria pulled a chain out from under her shirt and unclipped an identical tag. On one side it bore her name, and on the other the number 617. She hung it on the board beside the others.

"I need to sign in a visitor," she said to the man in the booth. He grunted and opened a massive ledger. "Write your name and other details here," she said to Michael. He did so, and the guard handed him a token. Without being instructed, he hung it on the board next to hers. Not his first time down a pit, then. At least that was something.

"We'll get your own token made in the next couple of days," Astoria said. "Then you'll be able to come down by yourself if you need to."

"Thanks." He smiled, but she detected a hint of nerves behind it.

Behind the guard's booth were a stack of oil-wick cap lamps. Astoria lit two and handed one to Michael. He took it, looking slightly surprised as he fastened it onto his helmet.

"You don't use thermocrystal lamps?"

Astoria raised an eyebrow. "You think we're made of money?"

"No ... I just thought the company ..." He trailed off, seeming to come to a realisation. "Forget it. I was being naive again."

"The ones who hold the purse strings aren't the ones who have to breathe in the soot," she said. "It makes no difference to them whether we're clean or not. And since nobody high up believes thermocrystal dust is combustible, working with ignition sources isn't an issue. So why would they waste precious thermocrystals on us when they could sell them for an extraordinary profit?"

"Have you always been this cynical?"

"There's a difference between cynicism and realism," she snapped. "If you hang around here long enough you might even learn it. Now let's go." She took a deep breath, trying to calm the anger flaring in her chest. She hated to admit it, but he'd touched a nerve. Michael wisely said nothing further, just followed her into the yawing mouth of the pit.

THE TUNNEL WAS BROADER than Michael had expected, with narrow-gauge rails running down the centre so the automatons could push trucks from the deep caves to the surface. The ground beside the rails had been worn by the passage of many feet until it resembled a path. The way was lined periodically with oil-wick hand lamps that gave off a sputtering, smoky yellow light. He tried to recall the other mine tours he'd been on—he was sure they'd had thermocrystal lamps, which were much brighter and far cleaner, since the crystals produced their own internal light and glowed without burning. Then something clicked and he realised that maybe they'd been provided just for their visit. After all, the mine administration would have wanted everything to look slick for upper management. He shook his head, astounded that he hadn't seen it before. But then maybe he hadn't wanted to see it. It had been easier just to pretend that everything was fine and all the miners were safe and happy. He hurried after Astoria, who was striding ahead with sure, purposeful steps.

Soon they came to a place where the tunnel split into three, with directions painted on the walls in whitewash. Michael noticed that there were more timber reinforcing beams as they got further into the hill and, as always, he began to feel the weight of the earth above them. He wasn't exactly afraid of being underground—he was in the wrong industry for that—but he was always conscious of the precariousness of the situation. He wondered how long it took to get used to the idea that at any minute one could be crushed by tons of earth and rock.

Astoria, for her part, seemed unbothered. She walked confidently past the crossroads, further down the main tunnel. From one of the side tunnels Michael heard the clank and crash of machinery.

He began to lose track of how long they'd been walking—time did odd things in the dark—but eventually the tunnel opened out into a large cavern. There were yellow spurts of light from the lamps hung on the walls and on the miners' helmets, but the cave itself also gave off a blue-white glow. Michael could tell just from looking at it that the place was riddled with thermocrystals.

All around the cavern walls miners were chipping away at the rock by hand, excavating around the crystals until they were loose enough to be pried out. Nobody wanted to be the person who broke a crystal—the bigger they were, the more energy they produced and the more value they had. He remembered the first time he'd seen thermocrystal miners at work, and how painstaking the job was; it had got him thinking that there had to be a better way. That train of thought had eventually led to the development of the inverter, which latched onto a protrusion of thermocrystal and then sheared away a thin layer between it and the rock, essentially 'sucking' the crystal out. There was a small loss of crystal mass, but this was compensated for by efficiency. It was so much quicker than chipping them out by hand. But he'd never thought too much about the dust that was created from shaving off that layer. He'd read the research, of course, but it always played down the risk.

When the first explosion had happened, he and everyone else had written it off as coincidence; after all, mines were inherently dangerous places. But when the second one had occurred just a few months later it had been harder to dismiss. Those two mines were the only ones using inverters for all their operations. The subsequent investigation had found a strong correlation but couldn't go so far as to establish a causal link although, after speaking to Astoria, Michael had no doubt. He'd been allowed to remain with the company, but he could never forget that he had the blood of two men on his hands. This was the first time he'd been back into a mine since the accident and, looking around at the miners, he had to suppress a shiver. The men who'd died had been just like them—they'd come to work trusting that they'd be going home again safely at the end of their shift, and they hadn't. Thanks to him.

He squared his shoulders and hurried after Astoria, who was crossing the cavern. Miners looked up as they passed, then turned back to their work. As they lifted the crystals down, they handed them to one of an army of brass automatons to load into the trucks. The automatons were a model that was at least thirty years old, by Michael's estimation; probably older. They would have been some of the first humanoid industrial automatons built at scale. Battered and dented, they rattled and clanked as they went about their work, lumbering awkwardly between the miners and the trucks. Each automaton sported a small boiler in its chest cavity, where a tiny thermocrystal glowed blue. The thermocrystal heated water, which created steam to power the automaton. The thermocrystal power was probably retrofitted; in their original design they likely would have been powered by some sort of combustible fuel like wood or oil. It was a miracle of engineering that they were still going, given that they were in use around the clock, but it wouldn't be sustainable for too much longer. If he was going to be in charge of managing the engineering and technological side of the mine, the first thing he'd have to do would be to convince company management that they needed to invest in new, modern automatons. He suspected he'd have his work cut out for him.

Astoria led him over to where a young man Michael took for a supervisor was in discussion with a couple of miners. The three of them were standing around the prone body of an automaton, which was wheezing as though it had run a marathon. This model didn't have anything beyond a basic sentience that allowed it to follow simple orders, such as moving trucks from one place to another, but there was still something disconcertingly human in the way the brass eyelids flickered as it lay there.

"Hello, Tom," Astoria said. "How's your first day going?"

The supervisor grimaced. He was a few years younger than Astoria, Michael guessed. This was probably his first management role.

"I've had better." He shrugged. "Had worse, too."

"I wanted to introduce Michael Galbraith," Astoria said. "He's the new mine superintendent in charge of engineering. He's the one to talk to about anything technical. Michael, this is Tom Jenkins, the newly promoted day-shift supervisor." She smiled. Michael extended his hand, and Tom shook it.

"So you're a technical whiz, are you?"

"Well ... " Michael wasn't quite sure how to answer that. "What's the problem?"

Tom jabbed the automaton with the toe of his boot. "It's this hunk of junk. Not a day goes by without at least one of them keeling over on us, and we don't have enough to begin with. We patch them up as best we can, but this one isn't responding to our usual tricks. Any ideas you have would be welcome."

"All right," Michael said, kneeling down beside the prone automaton. "Let's have a look." He could feel Astoria watching him. There was an open tool box on the ground and they'd already unhinged the cover of the automaton's chest cavity; blue thermocrystal light washed over the scene, giving it an eerie glow.

As soon as he focused on the automaton's workings, Michael began to relax. Not because it was an easy fix, but because this was where he felt at home. He'd grown up tinkering with automatons alongside his brothers, and although he'd later moved on to more complex engineering systems, they were still his first love. Automatons, especially once they'd started being mass-produced and the cost had come down, made a real difference to people's lives. Suddenly, menial tasks could be completed much more efficiently. The technology had even made its way into other industries, like medicine; his older brother David was a doctor who had pioneered brasscore technology, giving people who had lost organs or limbs clockwork alternatives.

David was now even working on developing thermocrystal-powered prostheses. The possibilities were endless.

He smiled to himself as he bent over the automaton, probing the intricate clockwork within. As he'd suspected, the thermocrystal power system was a retrofit, but what he hadn't reckoned on was that these automatons had originally been pure clockwork; they would have had to be wound frequently, and hadn't had a power source beyond that. He understood why the boiler had been added—constantly winding an army of automatons would have been no joke—but it had destroyed the elegance of the machine. It was no wonder its function was impaired. But it was nothing that couldn't be fixed, at least for the short term. He really would have to talk to Bertie about replacing the entire fleet. He nodded to himself and settled down to work.

Chapter 7

Astoria watched as Michael peered into the automaton's innards. She could tell from the way he handled the tools that he knew what he was doing. In spite of the dark and the noise, and the people watching him, he seemed oblivious to anything except the problem before him. His only words were an occasional request to Tom for a particular tool, like a surgeon asking for a scalpel, and he operated on the automaton with the same efficient precision. Astoria hated to admit it, but she was impressed.

It wasn't long before Michael was screwing the automaton's chest cover back into place and hauling it to its feet. Tom gaped at him. The automaton stood, awaiting orders.

"Where does it need to go?" Michael prompted, and Tom came back to himself.

"Go to truck number seven," he said to the automaton. "Load it until it's full and then take it to the outside depot." The automaton clanked off, and Tom turned to Michael.

"We've been tinkering with that beast for at least an hour," he said. "What did you do?"

Michael shrugged. "These older retrofitted models sometimes get loose connections around the back of the thermocrystal mount," he said. "Basically, they stop receiving power, so the boiler goes out and they essentially revert back to clockwork. It's not always easy to see the problem, and it tends to get mistaken for other things. But if you get into the habit of checking the connections as the first thing when an automaton goes down, that should help. And failing that, you can always wind them up."

"Wind them up?"

"They were clockwork originally. They'll still work that way if all else fails. It's tedious, but it'll keep them functioning."

Tom's eyebrows rose. "I never knew that. Thanks."

"My pleasure. Anything else I can help you with?"

"You don't have a shiny new fleet gathering dust in a storeroom somewhere, do you?" Tom asked wryly.

"Not yet," Michael said. "But I'm going to do my best to get one for you."

"Really?"

"I can't make any promises, of course, but I'll try."

"I hope you heard that," Tom said to Astoria, grinning.

"I did," she said. She knew that, even if Bertie agreed, getting it past upper management in Edinburgh would be a challenge. But Michael seemed sincere in his promise to try, and she couldn't help but admire him for it.

"Well, we'd better keep going," she said. "I'm giving Michael a tour of the whole operation."

"Lucky you," Tom said dryly. "Nice to meet you, Mr Galbraith."

"Call me Michael, please," Michael said, shaking the supervisor's hand. "And please let me know if there's anything you need."

"Careful," Tom said. "You'll be wanting to see the back of me before the week is out." He grinned, and Michael grinned back.

"Catch you later, Tom," Astoria said, and the young miner nodded absently. His mind was clearly already on other things.

"I didn't know they taught rustbucket mechanics at engineering college," Astoria said as they made their way back out of the mine.

Michael smiled. "They don't—well, not really. Automatons are my hobby, not my profession."

"Well, you certainly seem to know your way round them."

He shrugged. "I've been tinkering with them since I was a lad. It's been a long time since I've seen one of that vintage, though. Some of the newer technology is quite astounding. There's a man in Edinburgh called Will Eisman who is building navigation and steering automatons for airships that are almost fully sentient. It means a captain can go to sleep and leave the automaton to fly the airship, trusting that it'll be able to make decisions—up to a point, of course. They're no substitute for a human, but they're revolutionising industries. Their potential is almost limitless."

Astoria was surprised at the animation in his voice. Even in the half-dark, it was obvious how passionate he was about the topic.

"I just don't understand," he continued, "why old clankers like these are still in service, when there are so many better alternatives."

"Don't you?" Astoria asked, quirking an eyebrow. Daylight from the entrance was beginning to trickle into the tunnel.

"Well, of course I do," Michael said. "I'm not stupid. But it's such a false economy. The new automatons are expensive, of course, but they save so much in the long run through increased efficiency."

"And through not having to pay human wages," Astoria said. "Nobody likes the rustbuckets, it's true. But no miner wants to be replaced by a newfangled bag of bolts either."

"I don't think it would come to that," Michael said as they emerged out into the light, extinguishing their lanterns. "Automatons are a tool. They're not meant to replace people, just to make their lives easier."

"Huh." His faith was rather touching, she thought, if misguided. "That's not how upper management works. If a machine can do it cheaper than a human, then the human goes. If your inverter had worked out, that probably would have replaced people eventually too."

"No," Michael said. "That's not what I ever intended to happen. It was just meant to help them."

Astoria shrugged. "Ultimately, once it was taken out of your hands, your intentions became irrelevant," she said. "Trust me, that's what would have happened. I've seen it before, and I dare say I'll live to see it again."

Michael frowned to himself, and Astoria softened.

"Can I give you some advice?" she asked, as they stopped at the door to the ablutions block.

"Please do."

"Braithwaite didn't move you here to shake things up. He moved you here to get you out of the way. If you want to resuscitate your career, you'll keep your head down and not rock the boat. I'm not saying you shouldn't ask Bertie for new automatons—you promised Tom you would, and I strongly believe in keeping one's word. But don't go looking too hard for 'improvements', at least not straight away. Take your time to learn how the place works. Otherwise you'll get bitten by the law of unintended consequences. Trust me."

She thought about Donald Braithwaite's unexpected arrival, and Bertie's shock—almost horror—at it. "There's things going on here that even I don't fully understand," she said. "And if we're serious about looking out for the lads and lasses who work that pit, then we have a responsibility not to go blundering around making things worse."

She realised as she said it that she'd used *we*. Was she actually starting to see Michael as a teammate already? She shrugged mentally. It was entirely pragmatic; it wouldn't do her reputation any good to go acting like a spoiled child who hadn't got the toy she'd been coveting. She supposed that made them a team of sorts, for now, anyway. She was counting on the fact that, like pretty much all the men she knew, he'd be arrogant enough to not only utterly disregard her warning, but to take it as blueprint for what he should do, just to prove he knew better. She knew she was right, but these men always wanted to put their stamp on things, like dogs pissing on lampposts. They couldn't help it. He'd rub the wrong people up the wrong way, without a doubt, and then he'd be out and she'd be free to get on with things.

"Thank you," he said without rancour, and she tried to hide her surprise.

"Pardon?"

"Thank you for the advice. You know everything I need to know about how things work here, and you're right—I shouldn't go blundering around in places I don't understand. I'm glad you can be frank enough to tell me when I've overstepped."

Well, I'll be damned, she thought. *Who would have expected humility from the fancy Edinburgh engineer?* Or maybe he was just a very good actor, and she was the one being played. It wouldn't be the first time. She decided to reserve judgement.

"After we get changed I'll show you the rest of the operation," she said, taking refuge in the ablutions block. She was feeling discombobulated; just when she thought she'd got Michael Galbraith figured out, he surprised her. She was going to have to watch herself.

Chapter 8

By the end of the day Michael was so tired that all he could think about was a hot shower and bed. It had been a long time since he'd done so much walking. After they'd left the pit, Astoria had taken him all over the rest of the site, following the rails down to the airfield, carved out of the hillside, where the trucks were taken to load their precious cargo into the large commercial airships that landed around-the-clock. Michael had seen one out the window of the Braithwaite airship as they'd come in to land; it had dwarfed the corporate vessel, even though the Braithwaite airship was by no means small. The mining airships were giant grey leviathans, rusted and creaking, the workhorses of the aviation world. Their crew quarters were minimal—all the available space was taken up by cargo bays. They were built for volume, not speed, but were impressive nonetheless. Astoria had told him they departed twice a day, at midday and midnight, and they wouldn't fly without a full load. It amazed him that the mine was productive enough to fill two airships a day, but Astoria had simply shrugged and told him that was nothing; in the bigger mines the airships departed hourly.

Finally, he was able to return to his cottage to shower and change, then he walked down to the mess for dinner. Astoria had offered to escort him again, but he knew she had some paperwork to do, so he declined. He realised he'd have to stand on his own two feet sooner or later—might as well get it over with.

This time fewer heads turned as he walked in, for which he was grateful. He collected his meal from the servery and looked around for an empty seat. He didn't expect anyone to offer themselves as a dining companion—the best he was hoping for was that they didn't vacate when they saw him coming—so he was surprised when Tom Jenkins waved him over.

"Evening, sir," Tom said. "Hope I'm not being presumptuous, but I figured you probably still don't know many people here yet." Michael smiled gratefully and took the offered seat. Tom gestured to his companion.

"This is Harry Murdoch, the night-shift supervisor," he said. "We usually grab a bite together before he heads off to work. Harry, this is Michael Galbraith, the new technical superintendent."

"Pleased to meet you," Harry said with a nod. "I hear you've got a handy way with our old rustbuckets."

Michael shrugged. "I just like to tinker."

"Well, be careful," Harry said ruefully, "with the rate them things break down around here you won't have time for anything else."

Michael laughed. He liked these two wry, taciturn miners. Even though they were technically his subordinates, they didn't stand on ceremony, which he appreciated. The hierarchy at the mine seemed much looser than he'd seen in other places, even within the company management. It meant there might sometimes be a juggle between balancing friendships and professional relationships, but he preferred that to the isolating, uptight stuffiness he'd experienced elsewhere.

They kept chatting about the automatons until the door opened and Astoria walked in. For the first time, Michael realised how much her presence commanded a room. It wasn't that people were afraid or in awe of her; on the contrary, it seemed like everyone wanted to talk to her. As she walked towards the servery, she kept getting greeted or pulled aside by people who wanted a chat. It must have been exhausting if that happened at every meal, Michael thought.

Tom noticed him watching her. "She's pretty popular round here," he said. "Poor lass can hardly stir outside her door without somebody wanting something."

"It's because they know she'll get things done," Harry said. "It weren't always that way, but now they trust her much more than they trust either of us." He nodded in Astoria's general direction. "That's what respect looks like," he said. "She makes it look easy, but by God she's earned it."

Michael opened his mouth to ask more, but Astoria had seen them and was making her way over with her dinner tray. She collapsed into her seat with a sigh of relief.

"I see you're getting to know everyone," she said to Michael.

"We've just been picking his brain about automatons," Tom said. "There's not much he doesn't know. I'm thinking of drafting him in as a full-time mechanic."

"Oh, are you now?" Astoria said, as Michael felt his cheeks redden. Somewhere above them, a bell rang out.

"That's me out, then," Harry said, standing up. "I'll see you later." All around them, night-shift miners were rising to their feet.

"I'm surprised they let the shifts cross over for meals like that," Michael said, watching them leave. "I would have thought they'd just open the mess for longer so the shifts could swap straight over and there wouldn't be a pause at the pit. It would be more efficient."

Astoria shrugged. "It would," she said. "But Bertie's a big believer in teamwork. He says he doesn't want to be running essentially two separate mining camps. He wants people from the opposing shifts to get to know each other. That way, if people need to swap roles, or if there's a crisis, they come together more easily. He says it's good for morale."

Tom snorted. "I'm not sure Donald Braithwaite would agree."

"Depends if you prioritise profit or people."

"I think we know which side Braithwaite falls on."

"Careful, Tom," Astoria said, a warning note in her voice. "I'm not saying I disagree, but you're a shift supervisor now. People look up to you, and they'll follow your lead. Sometimes you'll need to be a bit more ... circumspect ... with your opinions."

Tom nodded, chastised. "Anyway," he said, "I'd best be off. Enjoy your evening." He cleared his plate and left.

Astoria sighed. "I hope I didn't upset him."

"He's a smart lad, but he's still quite young," Michael said. "He needs guidance. He'll learn. And better he learn from you than the hard way."

"I suppose so." She took another bite of her dinner. "You don't have to wait for me, you know."

"I know. But I don't have anywhere else to be. Unless you'd rather not have company ...?"

She smiled. "Of course not. It's nice of you to stay."

"I appreciated the tour today. I've got a lot to learn."

"The good thing is this place thrives on routine. You'll get the hang of it soon enough."

To Michael's surprise, Astoria turned out to be right. The next day was spent in his new office in the administration block, learning the operations side of things with Bertie. As the days and then the weeks passed, the pieces began slotting into place and he began to develop a rhythm to his days. Before he knew it, he was coming up to his one-month anniversary. He wasn't quite sure how it had happened. People no longer stared at him when he entered the mess, and some had even started saying hello when he passed them on site. He made it a point to get down the pit at least once a week for both day and night shift, just to talk to people and get to know them. And almost every visit down the mine involved fixing at least one of the automatons. While he enjoyed tinkering with them, he knew it was indicative of a bigger problem. As the end of his first month approached, he felt it was time to take his concerns to Bertie, just as he'd promised Tom on that first day. He dutifully booked a time with Miss Beaumont—for nobody got in to see Bertie without an appointment, even if they worked next door—feeling his anxiety rise even as he did so. This would be his first big test.

"So, one month tomorrow," Astoria said as they walked back to the dormitories in the evening. "How does it feel?"

"Good, I think," Michael said. "It's gone fast." He bit his lip, distracted by thoughts of his meeting the next day.

"Are you all right?" Astoria asked.

Michael took a deep breath, then nodded. "I'm fine. I'm just seeing Bertie tomorrow to talk about the automatons."

Her eyebrows rose. "You're really going to push him to replace the fleet?"

He shrugged. "I'm going to try."

"Well, you've got guts, I'll give you that."

"I promised Tom I would."

She gave him a look that he couldn't quite decipher. "I know you did." There seemed to be something left unsaid; perhaps she didn't really think he'd intended to follow through? He hoped she'd have a better opinion of his integrity, but after the inverter debacle, who could really blame her?

They walked on in silence for a few minutes.

"Would you like me to help you prepare?" Astoria offered unexpectedly.

"I ... well, yes, please."

"Bring your things to the mess. We can talk in the lounge after dinner."

IT WAS STRANGE, ASTORIA thought as she settled herself into a threadbare armchair in the lounge that adjoined the dining hall. She'd never really expected Michael to actually address the automaton issue with Bertie. Managers made grand promises all the time, but she'd not known many who actually kept their word. Something—usually money—always came up. It was something she'd tried very hard to avoid doing in her own career: she would never promise what she couldn't deliver. And maybe Michael *wouldn't* be able to deliver, but at least he'd be able to hold his head high and say he'd tried. The lads and lasses would respect him for that. Hell, *she'd* respect him for that. It wasn't what she'd thought when he'd got off the airship a month ago. But maybe, just maybe, this trumped-up Edinburgh engineer wasn't so bad after all.

"All right," she said, as Michael sat down opposite her and pulled a leather-bound notebook out of his pocket. "Some things you need to know about Bertie. One, he likes logic. Make a convincing argument with facts, figures, cost savings and so on. I'm sure that'll be right up your alley." Michael nodded, scribbling notes. "Two—and this is what people don't generally know—he's actually a bit of a softy. He cares about his people. So if it's something that affects safety or wellbeing, he'll generally try to act on it. Put those two things together and I think you'll have a good shot at winning him over."

"Thanks."

"Well, go on then."

"Pardon?"

"Take fifteen minutes to develop your argument, then convince me."

Michael took a deep breath. "You're a hard task-master."

"You bet. But you won't have a hope in hell of convincing Bertie if you can't get it past me first, I assure you."

"All right."

Astoria made herself a cup of tea while he gathered his thoughts. She had no doubt he'd be able to mount a convincing logical argument—he was an engineer, after all. But how would he go with the people side of things?

After a quarter of an hour, she returned to her seat, looking expectantly at Michael. He took a deep breath, glanced at his notes, and began.

"Not bad," she said when he was done. "I think you can lose some of the really technical detail, but it's actually sounding pretty good."

"If you were Bertie, would you replace the fleet?"

She shrugged. "If I were Bertie, I'd probably try." In truth, she was surprised at how strong a case Michael had made, even down to the safety aspects. He'd clearly picked up a lot more in his month on the job than she'd given him credit for. She was torn; on the one hand, she almost hoped he'd perform badly. A couple of poor appearances and his job would be as good as hers. And yet ... they really needed new automatons. If he was prepared to fight for them, she didn't think she could undermine that and still hold her head high. Like it or not, for the good of the mine they had to work as a team on this.

He smiled. "That's good enough."

"Do you want me to come to the meeting with you? You know, for moral support?"

He mulled this over, gnawing his lip. "No," he said at last. "It's a kind offer, but I think I need to do this myself. I need to show him I can stand on my own two feet."

She nodded. "I understand. Good luck."

Chapter 9

When Michael woke the next morning, his stomach immediately began to flutter with nerves. He took a deep breath and thought back to his preparation the previous night. He felt confident in what he had to say, thanks in no small part to Astoria's feedback. But would it be enough to convince Bertie? There was only one way to find out.

He moved through his morning routine automatically, his mind already racing ahead. He hadn't expected Astoria to help him so much; he still sometimes got the feeling she didn't like him very much, or at the very least was reserving her judgement. But he didn't think she really wanted him to fail either. She was still an enigma to him, but he was grateful nonetheless.

Thankfully, his appointment was first thing, so he was spared the agony of waiting half the day for the meeting. He put his things in his office, picked up his notebook, then, at Miss Beaumont's signal, knocked on Bertie's door.

"Come in."

Michael entered. He and Astoria had weekly catch-ups with their boss, but this was the first time he'd formally met with him on his own. As usual, Bertie was seated behind his desk, surrounded by paperwork, a cigar perched precariously on the edge of the ashtray that sat on top of a pile.

"What can I do for you?" he asked, waving Michael to a chair. Michael shifted a pile of papers from the chair to the floor beside it, and sat down.

"Good morning, sir," he said. "I'd like to talk about the automaton fleet."

Bertie raised an eyebrow. "Yes? What about it?"

"Well, as you know, the fleet is really getting beyond the end of its useful life," Michael began. "Breakdowns are increasingly common." He consulted his notes. "According to the shift supervisors, they're dealing with two automaton breakdowns on average per shift. Sometimes these are easy to fix, but often the automaton in question will be out of action for the whole shift, plus the person or people needed to fix it."

Bertie said nothing, just steepled his fingers together. Michael swallowed and continued.

"The models are clockwork retrofits that are fundamentally unstable," he said. "There's no way to prevent further breakdowns; in fact, they'll continue to get worse as the automatons age. I know replacing the fleet would come at a significant cost, but I think we also need to examine the cost of *not* replacing it." He unfolded a sheet of figures from his notebook and passed it to Bertie. "This charts the expected replacement cost versus the continuing costs of maintenance and the opportunity cost of continued breakdowns," he said. "The new technology is so much more efficient that, although new automatons would be expensive, we wouldn't need to buy as many. It wouldn't be a one-for-one replacement program. More like one-for-two."

Bertie took the paper and glanced at it. "Anything else?" he asked.

"Well, yes, sir. I strongly believe the old fleet poses an increasing safety risk. As I mentioned, these are clockwork models retrofitted with thermocrystal power packs. The connections are unstable and are becoming worse as they wear. In the best-case scenario, a broken connection just stops the automaton working, but in the worst case it could short the power pack and cause a fire or explosion. I'm personally not comfortable sending people in to work with such dangerous machinery, and I'm sure Astoria would agree."

Bertie sighed. "Thank you, Michael," he said. "Please understand that I'd replace the fleet tomorrow if I could. But my hands are tied, financially speaking. The truth is, we just don't have the ready cash, and I doubt head office would authorise such an expense right now, what with the price of thermocrystals being so low. I appreciate you bringing this to my attention, but acting on your request is impossible right now."

"But sir, the safety implications ..."

Bertie's jaw tensed. "Mining is an inherently dangerous business, son," he said, his voice hardening. "The men and women who work here know that, and they willingly accept those risks because they need the job. Things are ... well, without going into too much detail, they're not good for the company right now. So, unfortunately, if our people want to retain their jobs, this is a risk they'll have to continue to bear."

"Is ... is the mine in trouble?" Even as he said it, Michael wondered if he'd gone too far.

"Not if I can help it. I'll do *everything* in my power to keep this place going."

"Yes, sir," Michael said, slightly taken aback by his vehemence.

"Anything else?" Bertie asked, clearly itching to dismiss him.

"No, sir. Thank you." Michael stood up, suppressing a sigh. He'd really thought he had a chance at convincing Bertie, especially after all Astoria's talk about how reasonable and safety-conscious their boss was. Maybe it was just because she'd known Bertie far longer than he had, but to Michael he seemed like every other senior manager he'd ever encountered—worried about money above all else. Even if that wasn't entirely true in a general sense—and he was fair-minded enough to acknowledge that it may not be—it was certainly true in this case. And he hadn't realised how much he'd hung his own reputation on getting the automatons replaced. In his mind, he'd already jumped ahead to the conversation with Tom and Harry where he got to tell them that he'd solved one of their biggest problems. It would have given him the credibility boost he needed if he was going to make a go of this long-term. But now here he was, right back where he started.

"Would you like me to collect the morning-tea things?" he asked Miss Beaumont as he passed her desk. No boring old biscuits for Bertie; Miss Beaumont had arranged with the mess to have morning tea made fresh every day. She was usually the one who trooped down the hill to get it, but Michael needed a walk, and it never hurt to get on Miss Beaumont's good side. Through the open door to his office, he could see Astoria watching him.

"Thank you," Miss Beaumont said, sounding slightly harried. "That would be most helpful."

Michael left, glad to be out in the fresh air. He needed to shake off the gloom that had descended following the meeting.

He wasn't that surprised when he soon heard hurried footsteps behind him.

"What happened?" Astoria asked, puffing slightly from her rush to catch up with him.

Michael shook his head. "No go, I'm afraid."

"*Really*? Why?" She sounded genuinely shocked.

"The usual reason. Not enough money."

"No, surely not. Bertie has always found the money before, especially for safety issues."

"Well, not this time. He told me straight up that the workers understand the risks, and if they want to keep their jobs then they'll have to continue to bear those risks."

Astoria was silent for so long that Michael wondered if she'd heard him.

"Astoria?"

"Yes, I heard ... I just can't quite believe it. That doesn't sound like Bertie at all. Are you *sure* that's what he said?"

"Afraid so."

"And that was it?"

"Well ... he intimated the mine is in trouble. I asked him straight up about it, and he said he'd do everything in his power to keep the mine going. Then he dismissed me."

"So that's why Donald Braithwaite was here," Astoria mused. "Do you think they'll shut us down?"

How would I know? Michael wanted to snap. *You know this place far better than I do.*

"I don't know," he said. "All I know is that Braithwaite is ruthless when he's chasing a pound."

"If this place gets shut down, it will throw the entire village into poverty," Astoria said, her face flushing. "It's not just the miners who'll suffer—it's all our families, and the people who run the village shops and things as well. We can't let them close it."

"If Braithwaite wants to close the mine, there won't be a lot we can do," Michael warned, trying to inject some realism into the conversation. "I've seen this happen before."

"So, what, you'll just roll over and let him?" Astoria demanded, stopping and facing him. Her cheeks were red and her eyes flashed.

"No, I didn't say that."

"Listen, Michael, in these sorts of situations you're either with us or against us."

Michael took a deep breath, feeling his own anger rising. He normally had a long fuse, but the pressures of the past month had been taking a toll.

"No, *you* listen, Astoria. Being a manager is more complicated than that. Sometimes it means making decisions you don't want to make, for the greater good. And sometimes it means taking into account interests you'd rather not consider. You no longer have the luxury of the black-and-white perspective of the person on the ground. And if you're not able to handle that, then I wonder that Bertie was so keen to promote you." He turned and walked away, before he said anything more he'd regret, but she followed him.

"Oh, so now you're saying I only got promoted because Bertie likes me?" She sounded hurt, and Michael realised he'd hit a nerve. He frowned; there was something else going on here, but he had neither the energy nor the inclination right now to find out what it was.

"Of course I'm not saying that. I'm saying that he clearly thought you could be a manager, so now it's time to start thinking and acting like one. If you really want to save the mine, you've got to stop being so black-and-white about everything and start playing the game."

"Like you do?" she said sarcastically.

"No. Do you think I'd be here if I was any good at playing the game? I hate it and I'm terrible at it. I just want to be an engineer. But you're smart and you know this place backwards. You'll be better at it than I am." They'd reached the door of the mess. Michael went inside to collect Miss Beaumont's tea things, but Astoria hung back. By the time he came out again, she was gone.

Chapter 10

Astoria studiously avoided Michael for the rest of the day. She wasn't quite sure what she felt in the aftermath of their fight, if that was what it was. She'd initially thought him spineless for not pushing harder for the automatons or demanding more information about the possible closure. But she also couldn't get his words out of her head, and the more she mulled them over, the more she had to admit he was right. She needed to learn how to play the political game. She was good at everything else, but she'd been sheltered under Bertie's coat-tails in that regard for a long time. Bertie was a master of politics. She'd never needed to handle it because he had, and they'd always been on the same side. But now, if she was completely honest, she wasn't even sure they still were. And as for Michael ... she had no idea how to feel about him. He still confounded her, and she couldn't say for sure if he was an asset or a liability. She didn't know which she wanted him to be.

Given that they shared an office, it made for an awkward afternoon. Astoria left as soon as propriety would allow, feeling like a weight was lifting as she stepped out into the fresh evening twilight. She ate her dinner quickly, not seeing Michael at the mess. She wondered idly why he was so late, but reasoned he was probably avoiding her too. Wanting to get out of her own head, she adjourned to the lounge, joining a card game that Jock and some of the others had rustled up. There was still no sign of Michael.

Her heart wasn't really in the game, and the money was all but flowing out of her pocket. She was just about to call it a night when the wail of a klaxon cut through the air.

"Shit," Jock said, glancing up, the colour draining from his cheeks. Nobody needed any further elaboration. Chairs were overturned as they were hurriedly pushed back. Miners streamed out of the mess and dormitories and started running up the hill towards the pit. They all knew what the siren meant: there'd been an accident.

Astoria caught up to Tom Jenkins just as they reached the mine. She'd only ever seen one awful accident—the one that had claimed the previous owner of Michael's boots—and it had been chaos. This scene was much calmer. Harry Murdoch was standing at the centre of a crowd of night-shift miners, marking names off a roll. She did a quick headcount; as far as she could tell, they were all there. She hurried over.

"What happened?" she asked. Harry handed the roll to his deputy and drew her aside.

"A near-miss," he said. "Everyone's out safe, no harm done."

"Thank goodness." She waved Tom over. "Stand everyone down," she said. "There's no rescue required." Tom nodded, looking relieved, and the day-shift miners began to trickle slowly back down the hill. Astoria pulled a notebook and pencil out of her pocket.

"Give me the details," she said. "There'll obviously be an investigation, but I want the bones of it before you forget."

"It was one of the automatons," Harry said. "One that Mr Galbraith fixed for us. It must have shorted or something. All I know was suddenly the bloody thing caught fire. The lads nearby said there was a spark just before it went up. Luckily it was right near the sand bucket and we were able to put it out quickly, but it was a close call. I wasn't taking any chances with it, which is why I told them all to get out. And I won't be letting them back in until we're sure it's safe." He glowered, as if expecting her to challenge him.

Astoria swallowed. A fire in a thermocrystal pit, with so much explosive dust around, was every miner's worst nightmare. "Of course," she said. "There'll be a proper investigation, don't worry." She frowned to herself. "You said it was an automaton that Michael had fixed?"

Harry nodded. "Just this afternoon, in fact," he said. "It had conked out as usual, and he's such a dab hand with them that I sent a lad down to get him. Caught him just before he knocked off for the day. He did something to the power pack and got it going again. And then, bang."

"Thanks," Astoria said as Bertie joined them. "I'll probably need to talk to you again, but you've given me a good deal to be getting on with."

Harry nodded again, turning to their boss. Astoria glanced across the clearing and saw Michael, looking like he wasn't sure where to be. She closed her eyes briefly, but she knew she'd have to deal with him sooner or later. He spotted her and came over.

"What happened?" he asked.

"An exploding automaton, apparently," she said. His eyebrows shot up.

"A *what*?"

"Harry said it was the one you worked on this evening. Apparently it just spontaneously caught fire."

Michael ran a hand through his hair. "Oh, God. Was anyone hurt?"

"No, although that seems to have been good luck more than anything."

"There'll be an investigation, I assume?"

She nodded. "Of course. I'll probably be the one doing it, especially given your involvement with the automaton."

"You don't think I had anything to do with it ...?"

"I don't think anything yet," she interjected. Because a nasty thought had occurred to her, and she didn't want to talk about it. Not with him.

Astoria returned to the dormitories shortly afterwards; there was nothing more to be done at the mine that evening. She went to bed early but found it hard to sleep. There was something about the accident that didn't feel right. On the one hand, it could be a straightforward explanation—the automatons were old and creaky, and Michael had said himself that they were unsafe. Such an incident had probably only been a matter of time. And yet it did seem to be a strange coincidence that an accident should happen now, right after Bertie had refused Michael's request to upgrade the fleet. She didn't want to go too far down that line of thought, though. It would never do to pre-empt the investigation findings.

She eventually slept, but it was broken and fitful, and in the morning she woke feeling groggy and despondent. She ate a quick breakfast and hurried up the hill to the office. She wouldn't be able to speak to Harry and the other miners until late in the afternoon, before their shift, and there were things she had to do first.

Bertie was already there when she arrived, despite the early hour, and she barged right into his office over Miss Beaumont's protestations.

"Good morning, Storie," Bertie said, looking up. He didn't seem that surprised to see her.

"Shall we talk about the accident?" she asked, sitting down without waiting for an invitation.

"By all means," Bertie said. "There'll have to be an investigation, of course."

"Who's going to conduct it?"

"I was thinking Jock could do it."

Astoria gaped at him. "Surely not."

Bertie looked at her, apparently unflappable. "Why not? He's very experienced and the workers trust him."

"Don't get me wrong," Astoria said. "Jock's a good fellow. But he's not ... well, he's not very thorough. He doesn't pay attention to details. I just don't think he's a good choice for this."

"I disagree."

Astoria clenched her jaw. "*I* want to do it," she said.

"No," Bertie said. "There's plenty of other work for you to be getting on with."

"Nothing urgent," Astoria shot back. She wasn't sure why Bertie was being so reticent, but she had no doubt that her stubbornness could outweigh his. "You put me in charge of looking after our people, didn't you? Now something has happened that directly affects their safety, and I'm going to find out what exactly went on."

"And what if I, as your boss, forbid you to?"

Astoria stared at him levelly. It wasn't like Bertie to pull rank, but she wasn't intimidated. She'd known him far too long for that. "What usually happens when people tell me not to do something?"

Bertie considered this for a long moment. "Fine," he said at last. "Talk to those involved. Tell them I said they're to help you in whatever way you need. And I expect you to keep me abreast of developments."

"Will do." She stood up. "It *was* just an accident, wasn't it?"

Bertie shrugged. "Of course it was."

Chapter 11

Astoria left the office before Michael arrived and walked up towards the mine. The automaton had been brought out and placed in the shift supervisors' changing room. It lay under a canvas tarpaulin, its humanoid shape giving it the eerie appearance of a corpse. Astoria pulled back the covering and looked at it. She knew her way around an automaton well enough, but while she could fix one in a pinch, she wasn't confident diagnosing a fault under these sorts of circumstances. But she couldn't ask Michael to do it either, not when he'd been directly involved in the incident and she was going to have to interview him as a witness. She wracked her brains for a moment, then had an idea.

She went out to the guard's booth, where the numbered tags of the day shift were hanging on their board.

"Morning, Mack," she said to the guard. "Is Annis Macleod down the pit?"

Mack looked at the number board. He didn't even need to consult his book; he seemed to know everyone's number by heart. "Aye," he said.

"Could you send someone in to fetch her? I need her help with something."

Mack nodded. "Herbert!" he bellowed. There was a clanking noise and an ancient automaton creaked into view behind him. Mack passed a scrap of paper and a pencil to Astoria, and she scribbled a quick note: *Annis Macleod to meet Astoria Penrose, shift supervisors' room, ASAP.* She folded it and handed it to Herbert.

"Give this to the shift supervisor," she said. Herbert blinked at her and clanked off towards the mine entrance. Astoria thanked Mack and returned to the shift supervisors' room to wait.

Quicker than she'd expected, there was a knock at the door.

"Come in," she called.

The door opened and Annis Macleod peeked shyly round it. She was a young woman, probably in her early twenties, Astoria guessed, who had already shown herself to be one of the brightest minds on site. In the two years she'd been going down the pit, she'd developed a keen interest in and skill with the automatons. Until Michael had come along, nobody had known more about them than her.

"You wanted to see me, ma'am?" she asked.

"Come in, Annis," Astoria said, waving her over. She had been the girl's shift supervisor and held her in high esteem. "I need your help."

"What with, ma'am?"

"I need to know what went wrong with this automaton," she said. "I know finding that out won't necessarily be easy. You can take all the time you need—the whole day, or more, if necessary."

Annis knelt down beside the automaton and uncovered it. "I'll need to open it up," she said.

"Of course," Astoria said. "There's a tool bag here, and a lamp too, in case you need more light."

Annis lit the lamp and laid out the tools methodically. Then she unscrewed the automaton's chest plate and began poking around inside, frowning to herself.

"Help me roll it over," she said, her frown deepening. Astoria did as she asked, biting back her questions.

Annis pulled off the automaton's back plate, exposing its thermocrystal power pack. She held the lamp close to it, as if to confirm something. Then she sat back on her haunches.

"Well, it's not going to take the whole day," she said. "It's pretty clear what happened." She looked shaken.

"What is it?" Astoria asked, kneeling down beside her and peering into tangle of the automaton's innards. The thermocrystal glowed a faint pearly white, so different from the vibrant blue it should have been.

"See this?" Annis said, pulling a wire to the surface with a pair of pliers. "It's been severed. That would have shorted the power pack and caused a spark. The only thing that saved them was that this thermocrystal is practically dead. A new, high-energy one would have blown the place to bits." She shuddered.

"Could it have broken through wear-and-tear?" Astoria asked. "Maybe it was rubbing against something." But Annis shook her head.

"I doubt it," she said. "Look at it. It's been cut clean through—there's no ragged edges. Someone has snipped it."

Astoria peered closely at the wire and saw she was right. "Could they have cut it by accident?"

Annis shrugged. "I suppose so," she said dubiously, "if they didn't know what they were doing. But Harry knows his way around an automaton. And I heard Mr Galbraith was fixing it. There's no way he'd cut it by accident. He knows much more about them than even I do."

"And how long would it have taken between the wire getting cut and the explosion?"

The young woman thought for a moment. "I'd say it'd have been pretty much instant," she said. "It's not like it was on a timer or anything. Whoever did it would have had to get out of the way pretty quickly. It was a huge risk. If the rustbucket had been in better condition, they'd be dead."

"Thank you, Annis," Astoria said, jotting down notes. "That's all I need for now. Please keep this matter confidential. I'm sure you understand that we don't want to jeopardise the investigation through loose talk."

"Of course, ma'am." The young miner stood up, packed away her tools with brisk efficiency, and left. Astoria sat with the automaton for several minutes more, biting her lip and thinking. It was clear this wasn't any old accident; this was sabotage. But the big question was, *who*? And as much as she hated to admit it, the evidence seemed to be pointing to Michael.

When she returned to the office Michael wasn't there, but the presence of some documents on his desk indicated he'd been and gone while she was out.

"Where's Michael?" she asked Miss Beaumont.

"He's over at the stores," she said. "Something about auditing safety equipment." Astoria nodded; she remembered him talking about it. "And Mr Mackenzie wants to see you," Miss Beaumont added. "Right now."

Astoria sighed. She was beginning to feel like more and more weight kept being loaded onto her shoulders. She knocked at Bertie's door and entered at his call.

"Ah, good," Bertie said as she sat down. "How's it going?"

"Fine."

"You've been up at the mine, I take it?"

She nodded.

"And?"

Astoria shrugged. "There's not much to say, yet," she said. "I still need to talk to some people."

"But you must have some idea of what happened?"

"I'd really rather not discuss it until the investigation is finished."

Bertie steepled his hands. "This is about safety, Storie," he said. "I need to know if our people are in danger. But I assume it was just a one-off accident."

"I ... well, I'm not so sure about that."

"What do you mean? I know the fleet is old. To be honest, I'm surprised this is the first serious trouble we've had. There was bound to be an accident sooner or later. I tried to tell Mr Braithwaite that myself when he visited. I'm sorry to have been proved right."

"That's the thing. I don't think it *was* an accident."

Bertie looked taken aback. If Astoria didn't know better, she'd have almost said he was afraid. "I beg your pardon?"

"Well …" She paused, unsure how to start. "I had Annis Macleod look over the automaton. A wire was cut, and she's sure that's what caused the spark. She said it had to have been deliberate. There's no way it could have been an accident."

Bertie frowned, biting his lip as if he were thinking hard.

"You're saying someone sabotaged the automaton?"

Astoria swallowed. It seemed such an awful thing to say aloud, but there was no getting around it. "That's what it looks like, yes."

"And … who do you think did it?"

"I don't have enough evidence to point the finger at anyone yet."

"But you must have some idea."

"I'd really rather not say."

"Astoria, if there's someone you suspect, I want to make sure they're not going anywhere near that pit. So tell me what you know so far."

Astoria twisted the hem of her shirt, unable to meet her boss's eyes. "Well, it seems like Michael was working on it right before the accident."

A line appeared between Bertie's eyebrows.

"That doesn't mean he did it," Astoria said hurriedly. "Like I said, I've still got people to talk to. I'm just telling you the basic circumstances as they currently stand."

"Hmm," Bertie said. "It sounds pretty incriminating to me. And he had a motive."

"Oh? What would that be?"

"Why, the fact that I'd just denied his request to replace the automaton fleet, of course," Bertie said, raising an eyebrow.

"That's ridiculous."

"Is it?

"He would never do something like that, no matter how much he disagreed with you."

"And you know that for a fact, do you?

"I ..."

"How well do you really know Mr Galbraith, Storie?"

Astoria raised her chin. "Well enough." But secretly she couldn't help but wonder. Maybe there *was* a side to Michael she knew nothing about.

"Think about it, Storie," Bertie continued. "He's shoved unceremoniously into this backwater to get him out of the way, and then he's not even given the autonomy here that he so desperately wants. If you were in his shoes, wouldn't you resent the company for everything that had happened? Wouldn't you want to see Donald Braithwaite brought to his knees?"

"I ... I don't know," Astoria said. On the face of it, Bertie's logic made sense. But it still didn't sit right with her. It didn't fit with the Michael she knew—the one who was still so upset about the toll his invention had taken on those unlucky miners, and his role in it. She couldn't see him having such a wilful disregard for life that he would deliberately do something that had the potential to kill or injure dozens of people. But on the other hand, there was always the possibility that she didn't know him anywhere near as well as she thought she did. Maybe he was an exceptionally good actor who had successfully hidden his real motives all this time. Maybe she was being taken for a fool.

"I have to finish the investigation," she said at last. "I haven't even talked to Michael yet. I'm reserving judgement until I have."

Bertie nodded. "Very well," he said. "Just remember that people aren't always what they seem."

Astoria nodded, rose and saw herself out. She left the office and stood outside for a few minutes, taking deep breaths of the fresh air. Her mind was racing and she felt shaken and discomfited. She glanced up and saw Michael coming down the hill. She cursed inwardly, but there was nothing for it. It was time to talk to him.

Chapter 12

Astoria waited for Michael to reach her, dread roiling in the pit of her stomach. It was made that much worse by the way his face lit up when he saw her. Try as she might, she couldn't return his smile.

"Is everything all right?" he asked as he approached.

"We need to talk," she said. She didn't have the emotional energy for small talk. "I need you to tell me what happened in the mine."

Michael's grin faded and he nodded. "Where?" he said. "In the office?"

Astoria shook her head. For reasons she couldn't explain, she didn't want to be somewhere they could be overheard, even if it was just Bertie and Miss Beaumont. Something about this whole thing was troubling her, although she couldn't quite put her finger on what it was.

"Walk with me."

They set off up the hill, both staring fixedly ahead. "Tell me what happened," Astoria said. "Start from the beginning."

Michael took a deep breath. "Well," he said, "I was just finishing up and about to go home when a runner came down from the mine saying they were having a problem with one of the automatons and could I please come and help. So I packed up my things and went up there."

"And what did you find when you arrived?"

"It was one of the rustbuckets they've been having a lot of issues with. Harry and Tom have been nursing it through, but really it should have been replaced years ago. So I wasn't that hopeful I could fix it."

"And could you?"

"I opened it up and had a look around, but it was pretty clear the power pack was on the blink. Basically it had got to the point where the only way to extract more life out of it was to replace the thermocrystal. And I could guess what Bertie would say about that."

"You didn't think he'd agree to it?"

Michael stopped and turned to her. "Look, I know Bertie is your friend as well as our boss," he said, "but he's not as safety-conscious as you seem to think he is. He's made it clear that he doesn't want to spend any money on the fleet. Replacing the thermocrystal would be expensive, and it would only be a temporary fix anyway. We'd be lucky to get six months out of it, if that. The whole unit needed replacing, and if you're going to do one then you might as well do them all—it's cheaper in the long run, and they're all in similar shape. But you know how that suggestion was received."

"You seem quite upset," Astoria said.

"I'm frustrated, I won't lie," Michael said. "It's such a false economy. And, more to the point, it's putting lives at risk. This accident won't be the last one. Sooner or later, somebody is going to get killed. It's as simple as that."

Astoria felt a chill go down her spine.

"So what did you do after you diagnosed the automaton's fault as terminal?"

"I went and talked to Harry to try to figure out what we should do about it. I was still talking to him when the thing went bang, and then we were just scrambling to get everyone out safely."

"And you're sure it exploded while you were talking to him, not before?"

"Yes."

"Is there any way you could have accidentally cut something while you were poking around—something that might have caused the explosion?"

Michael stared at her, realisation dawning on his face.

"You think *I* did it," he said slowly.

"I don't think anything, yet," Astoria said. "The investigation is ongoing." She looked away, unable to deal with the hurt in his eyes.

"I would *never* ..." he said. "People could have died. *I* could have died. You can't possibly believe I'd do such a thing."

"I know you and Bertie have your differences over the automaton fleet," Astoria said, trying for tact but conscious she was failing miserably. "And he doesn't get into the pit often these days. Maybe you just wanted to show him how dangerous they really are?"

Michael gaped at her. "By sabotaging one of them? You can't be serious."

"I have to investigate all possibilities."

"Huh. It sounds to me like you've already made up your mind."

"I *haven't*. I still have to talk to Harry."

"Of course," Michael said. He took a deep breath. "Is there anything else?"

Astoria shook her head. He gave her a long look, full of pain and disappointment. Then without another word he turned and headed back down the hill. She watched him until he rounded a bend and vanished from view.

Astoria went to the mess early, just before it opened for dinner service. Harry was already there, waiting for her.

"I assumed you'd be wanting to talk to me," he said as she greeted him.

"Thanks," Astoria said. "Shall we sit down?"

They sat in armchairs in a corner of the lounge, which was deserted. Astoria pulled out her notebook and pencil.

"Tell me what happened again," she said. "I know we spoke earlier, but I want to confirm the details."

Harry frowned in thought. "Well, I guess it started with the rustbucket breaking down. We've had a lot of trouble with that particular automaton, so it wasn't exactly a surprise. Normally we can get it up and running again pretty quickly, but this time none of our usual tricks worked."

"And you didn't want to leave it?"

Harry shrugged. "We could have, I suppose, but it would have slowed things down a lot. We already had one out of commission. With a second one down there's no way we could have met our quota."

Astoria nodded, understanding the difficult position he was in. Every shift had a weight quota of thermocrystals they were meant to extract. Missing it once or even twice wasn't the end of the world, but more than that and management would start asking questions. And then Harry's job could be on the line.

"So you asked Michael to come and fix it?"

"Yes. I know it's not technically his role, but he really is the most knowledgeable automaton technician we've got. And I figured if he couldn't fix it, he'd at least be able to support us if we missed the quota."

"So he came and looked at it?" Astoria said, lowering her voice slightly as a group of young miners came in and sat down to wait for the dining hall to open.

"Aye. He tinkered around with it for quite a while; I'm not sure how long. But he didn't seem to be making much progress. He came over to talk to me about it, and that's when the thing went bang. After that we were just focused on getting everyone out in case the roof came down. There was a small fire but a couple of the lads nearby managed to put it out. It's still not clear to me what actually happened."

"That's what I'm trying to find out. And you're sure Michael was talking to you when it exploded? Where were you?"

"Aye, I'm sure, because we both jumped a mile. We were standing over by the wall. I'd been helping some of the lads over there figure out the best way to leverage out a crystal, and he left the automaton and came over to me."

"Annis Macleod told me the explosion was caused by a spark from a cut wire. Do you think Michael could have cut it?"

Harry frowned. "Well now, I don't really know. He wasn't talking to me for more than thirty seconds before it went off, so I suppose it's possible. I guess it depends whether the spark was caused as soon as the wire was cut, or if there was a delay, and I don't know enough about them to be able to say that."

"Annis said it would have been instant."

"Well then, I suppose that answers your question."

The young miners stood and started to move into the dining hall. Harry glanced at the clock, and Astoria got the hint.

"Thanks for your help," she said. "I think that's all for now. I'll let you know if I need to follow up on anything."

"My pleasure," Harry said. "I hope you get to the bottom of it." He rose and they shook hands. After he left, Astoria sat down again, biting the end of her pencil and thinking.

"Excuse me, ma'am?" said a voice. She looked up and saw one of the young miners standing before her, looking nervous. She smiled in what she hoped was a reassuring way.

"What can I do for you?"

"I'm sorry to intrude, ma'am, but I couldn't help overhearing you talking to Mr Murdoch."

Astoria kicked herself mentally; they should have gone somewhere more private. "Oh?"

"It's just ... well, I was helping Mr Galbraith with that automaton. The one that exploded."

"Were you, now?" Astoria was intrigued. Harry had clearly forgotten to mention it. She racked her brains for the lad's name. He couldn't have been more than seventeen, and she knew he'd only just begun working on the site. "It's Thomas, isn't it?"

"Yes, ma'am. Simon Thomas."

"Well, Mr Thomas, why don't you sit down and tell me what happened."

The lad sat, hunched over his knees as if trying to suppress a churning in his stomach. "Well, after the automaton broke and Mr Galbraith came, Mr Murdoch asked me to assist him—pass him tools and that sort of thing. I think he wants to train me in automaton maintenance and he thought it would be good experience for me."

"And did you see Mr Galbraith cut anything?"

"No, ma'am. He poked around in there for a while, looking at things. He tightened a few connections with a wrench. Then he got up and went to talk to Mr Murdoch."

"And did you cut anything?"

"Absolutely not, ma'am."

"So what did you do while he was talking to Mr Murdoch?"

"I went to help some of the other lads lift a crystal down. I didn't want to sit around doing nothing, you know? But as we were loading it onto the truck I saw something. Someone else was looking at the automaton and he seemed to be poking around in it. For a second I thought it was Mr Galbraith and I thought I should go back to help him, but then I saw him still talking to Mr Murdoch. So I just sort of assumed this was someone else they'd asked to help. Then there was a bang and it was all chaos. I saw the automaton on fire, so I grabbed a sand bucket and a couple of the other lads did too. We poured them over and managed to put it out. Then we all got out."

"That was very brave, fighting the fire like that," Astoria said, and Simon blushed. "Now, this other man who was working on the rustbucket—did you recognise him?"

"No, ma'am. But I still don't know many people yet. I've only been here two weeks."

"Would you know him if you saw him again?"

"Maybe. The light wasn't good, but I might be able to tell."

"Thank you, Simon. You've been most helpful."

"You're welcome, ma'am."

"I think that's all I need for now. Go and enjoy your dinner."

"Yes, ma'am. Thank you."

Astoria watched him go, biting her lip. It was starting to sound like Michael couldn't have done it, and the apparent existence of this mysterious saboteur threw further doubt on his guilt. She didn't think the young lad was lying. But could he have been mistaken? Maybe he did in fact see Michael come back to the automaton. But no—Harry had been adamant Michael had been talking to him the whole time. The facts pointed only one way. Someone else had been there and had sabotaged the automaton for reasons of their own. And they must have chosen their target carefully; as Annis had said, a high-powered automaton would have blown them all to smithereens, including the saboteur. So they were very familiar with the mine and its workings.

Astoria shivered. That meant that it was an inside job. She'd known all along that it was possible, even likely, but to see it confirmed was chilling. The miners were like a big, slightly dysfunctional family. The thought of one of their own putting everyone at risk shook her to the core. Why would they do that? And why would they so clearly try to frame Michael? She supposed he was an obvious target, given his history and his relatively new arrival. But it still struck her as an unspeakably cruel thing to do. And it had very nearly worked. For a second there, even she had entertained the thought that perhaps he *could* have done it. If someone else had been conducting the investigation—someone not so thorough, perhaps, or more biased against him—he would probably be on an airship back to Edinburgh at this very moment, to face who knew what sort of consequences. Maybe the saboteur had been betting that she had enough resentment towards Michael for doing her out of her hard-won job that she'd want to see him go down. She raised her chin, feeling defiance surge through her. If that was the case, they'd be wrong. Granted, she hadn't always liked Michael. Indeed, she'd wanted to dislike him much more than she did. But he'd shown himself to be a man of integrity, and she respected that. And she'd be damned if she was going to let some shadowy figure destroy his life, or the lives of any of her colleagues. She was going to have to find the saboteur herself, before they struck again. And she suspected she'd need Michael's help to do it.

Chapter 13

Astoria left the mess and hurried up the hill, back towards the office. It was still light, and she knew Michael would probably still be working. But when she got to the administration block, although Bertie's office door was closed and Miss Beaumont was still in residence, her own office was empty.

"Have you seen Michael?" she asked the secretary.

Miss Beaumont shrugged. "He left maybe ten minutes ago." She turned back to the document she was reading, in a gesture that discouraged further questions.

"Thanks," Astoria said. She left the administration block and stood in the road, thinking. She hadn't seen Michael in the mess or on the road down to the camp, and given the timing, she probably would have run into him if he'd gone that way. He wouldn't go into the mine unless he had business there, which, as far as she knew, he didn't. Perhaps he'd gone for a walk. She glanced up the road towards the mine and glimpsed a figure climbing the hillside. There weren't many private thinking spots on site; it made sense he'd borrow hers.

She hurried up the hill after him, mentally running through what she was going to say. When she reached the top she saw him sitting on a rock, staring out across the valley to where the faint dots of airships taking off could just be seen. He looked pensive and sad, and her heart suddenly ached for him, a feeling which surprised her. She should be rejoicing in his downfall, not empathising with him.

"Michael," she said softly, not wanting to startle him.

He jumped and turned, his shoulders slumping when he saw her. "Astoria," he said with a deep sigh. "What can I do for you? I suppose you've come to fetch me back so Bertie can dismiss me?"

"No," Astoria said. "I've come to apologise."

He stared at her. "For what?"

"I should never have accused you like that without proof," she said. "It was wrong of me to leap to such conclusions before I'd finished the investigation. Because I now know you couldn't have done it."

Michael's eyebrows rose. "You do?"

"The young fellow who was assisting you swears he saw someone else tamper with the automaton, although he didn't recognise them," Astoria said. "And Harry said you were talking to him when the automaton caught fire. There's no way you could have done it, and I'm sorry for doubting you."

"In the absence of this other mysterious person, though, people are still going to assume it was me, aren't they?"

Astoria bit her lip. She couldn't lie to him. "Probably."

"Then maybe I should just tell them it was," Michael said.

Astoria gaped at him. "But it wasn't!" she said.

Michael put his head in his hands. "It might as well have been."

Astoria opened her mouth to argue with him, then shut it again. "Is this about the inverter?" she asked at last.

Michael nodded.

Astoria looked at him for a long moment. "Tell me," she said gently, "do you blame the person who invented the hammer every time somebody gets their head bashed in with one?"

Michael said nothing.

"Of course you don't," Astoria said, "because that would be ridiculous." She sighed. "If you take responsibility for this, all that will happen is you'll be sacked. Then they'll probably bring in the police. You could even wind up in gaol. I know you made mistakes with the inverter, but is that really what you want?"

"Maybe it's what I deserve," he said. Astoria was torn between compassion for his pain and wanting to shake some sense into him.

"May I speak frankly?" she asked at last.

He smiled ruefully. "When do you not?"

"Self-destruction is not the same as atonement. If you really want to make up for what happened with the inverter, the solution isn't to martyr yourself over something you didn't do through some misguided sense of duty, or self-pity, or whatever this is. It's to stay here and help me make the mine safer—right here and now. Because if we don't find out who the real saboteur is, not only will they get away with it, they'll probably keep on doing it. And that puts all our lives at risk. So are you going to continue to wallow, or are you going to step up and work for the people whose lives you can still change for the better?"

There was a long pause, and for a moment she wondered if she'd gone too far. Perhaps he'd be defensive, or worse, hurt. But then he took a deep breath and looked her in the eye.

"You're right," he said slowly.

"I am?"

"Sometimes I get too stuck in my own head. And it's been a long time since I've had anyone to provide the required boot to the backside. So thank you."

"We all need that sometimes," Astoria said. "I'm counting on you to return the favour one of these days."

"Any time."

They sat for a moment, looking out at the view.

"Since we're speaking frankly," Michael said, "may I ask you something?"

"Of course."

"Do you resent me for taking your job?"

Astoria thought about it for a while.

"Yes," she said at last. "Sometimes. But ... well, much as I hate to admit it, I think we make a pretty good team. So even though I want to hate you, I can't. Although I still reserve the right to."

Michael chuckled.

"What?" Astoria said, biting back her own smile. "You asked me to be honest."

"I did," he said, grinning. "One of these days I'll learn."

"You're coming to the ceilidh in the village tomorrow night, I assume?" Astoria asked, changing the subject.

"Well, yes, I suppose so. Bertie indicated it's expected."

"You might even enjoy yourself. Everyone from the mine and the village will be there. I'm not exaggerating when I say it's the social event of the year. We all look forward to it."

"In that case, how could I miss it?"

"I'll walk down with you, if you like," Astoria said, not looking at him. "I mean, so you don't get lost."

Michael smiled at this. "Thanks," he said. "I wouldn't want to get lost."

She glanced at him. "Are you making fun of me?"

"Maybe just a little. But in all seriousness, that would be lovely. I'm looking forward to it."

The sun was beginning to sink into the west, the shadows lengthening.

"We should be getting back, I suppose," Astoria said.

"Thanks for the chat," Michael said. "I really appreciate it."

Astoria shrugged. "That's what friends are for."

"So we're friends now?" he asked as they stood up.

"Do you want to be?"

He nodded. "I'd like that very much."

"Well then," Astoria said, "I'll race you down the hill. Go!" She took off like a hare, laughing, and Michael dashed after her, as if they were ten years old rather than supposedly sensible adults. He caught up to her just as she reached the bottom, and they both doubled over, laughing and gasping for breath. And as they walked home in the twilight, Astoria couldn't remember the last time she'd had someone to laugh like that with.

Chapter 14

The ceilidh was all people had been able to talk about for weeks—as Astoria had said, it was the social event of the year. From all accounts, it was likely to be a most enjoyable night, but Michael couldn't help but feel a flutter of apprehension. The miners had just to begun trust him, and now this sabotage business was going to set things back again. Plus the real saboteur was still out there, and heaven only knew what they were planning. His one comfort—and it was a substantial one— was that Astoria believed in him. It was surprising how much her friendship made life bearable in this place where he didn't know whom he could trust.

The day passed uneventfully, and everyone was permitted to leave work early to get ready. The night shift was cancelled; this was the one day of the year, apart from Christmas, when the mine operations shut down completely.

Michael washed and dressed in his kilt and jacket. Astoria had told him that Highland dress was expected, and he was glad he'd brought it with him, for he'd never really thought he'd have an occasion to wear it. His shoes were polished until he could see his face in them, and when he looked in the mirror he was quite pleased with what he saw. He wondered idly if Astoria would be too, then caught himself. Why did he care if she thought he looked nice? It was a question he wasn't sure he wanted to know the answer to. He valued Astoria's hard-won friendship dearly; the last thing he wanted to do was jeopardise it with more-complicated feelings.

They had arranged to meet at the crossroads at edge of the camp, where the road led down to the village. He made sure to arrive a few minutes early, but she wasn't far behind. At first, he hardly recognised her out of her usual shirt and breeches. She was wearing a long green tartan skirt, a white blouse and a tartan sash that crossed from her right shoulder and was pinned with a brooch at her left hip. Her auburn hair hung loose about her shoulders, with just the front pinned out of her face. Michael's breath caught in his chest. He'd known she was beautiful—for even the roughness and grime of the mine couldn't hide that—but he'd never seen her like this.

"Good evening, Miss Penrose," he said, giving a slight bow.

She laughed. "Are we going all formal now?"

Michael flushed. "I'm sorry. It's ... these clothes. Force of habit." It was true—years of Edinburgh society functions had made the courtesies second-nature to him.

Astoria smiled. "Don't be sorry," she said. "I actually rather like it."

Michael offered her his arm and she took it. He tried not to think about how close they were.

"You look lovely," he said as they walked down the hill, other miners strung out in couples and groups before them.

"Thank you," Astoria said, a blush creeping up her cheeks. "You clean up rather well yourself."

"So tell me about the ceilidh," Michael said. "What can I expect? Why do you love it?"

She smiled. "Well, everyone from the mine and the village will be there. They have dances and things in the village, of course, but this is the only one I get to go to with my family. It's a chance for the young folks to court and the older ones to catch up. Like any good ceilidh, there'll be dancing and singing and recitation. It's just an all-round enjoyable night." She laughed. "I hope I haven't talked it up too much."

"Not at all."

The ceilidh was being held in the village hall, which was decked out in garlands and hung with coloured-glass thermocrystal lamps. In the twilight it glowed like a jewel. Michael took a deep breath as they entered, fearing a repeat of the reception he'd received on his first visit to the mess. But perhaps people hadn't been as quick to blame him for the accident as he'd thought, or perhaps Astoria's nonchalance had forestalled any issues. Either way, nobody seemed to pay him much mind, which was exactly as he liked it.

Astoria glanced around the room, then lit up at the sight of someone over by the far wall.

"Come on," she said to Michael, leading him across the room. "Come and meet my family."

Michael followed her, surprised and gratified that she wanted to introduce him to the most important people in her life.

An older woman and a younger one were standing near the musicians, deep in conversation with another lady. Upon seeing Astoria, the third lady smiled and excused herself. The older woman turned, saw them, and drew Astoria into an embrace. She was plump and jolly-looking, with rosy cheeks and brown hair streaked with grey. Astoria kissed her on both cheeks.

"Mother, allow me to present my new colleague, Mr Michael Galbraith. Michael, this is my mother, Mrs Mary Penrose, and my sister, Miss Jennifer Penrose."

"Pleased to meet you, ma'am, Miss Penrose," Michael said, bowing to them with genuine enthusiasm. Jenny Penrose was around eighteen, with blonde hair elegantly styled, and sparkling blue eyes. Although she initially seemed to bear little resemblance to her sister, Michael could see it in her ready smile and the determined set of her jaw.

"It's very nice to meet you too, Mr Galbraith," Mary Penrose said. "Astoria speaks very highly of you." Michael glanced at Astoria, who flushed.

At that moment the musicians finished their tuning up and broke into a reel. Michael turned to Astoria to ask her to dance, but he wasn't quick enough; Jock was already at her side.

"May I have this dance, Storie?" he asked.

"Of course," she said, glancing apologetically at Michael. He smiled at her, wondering why he suddenly wished Jock would disappear.

"Storie tells me you're from Edinburgh," Mary said as Astoria joined Jock and Jenny left to dance with a tow-haired young man.

"That's right," Michael said.

"It's quite different here from the big city, I'll warrant."

"It certainly is. But it's not without its pleasures. The ... scenery ... is beautiful." Out on the dance floor, Astoria threw back her head and laughed at something Jock said.

"I wouldn't worry about him," Mary said unexpectedly, following Michael's gaze.

"I'm sorry?"

"I've known Jock since he were a lad. He's a nice enough fellow, but he's no match for our Storie. She runs rings around him. She needs someone who'll challenge her."

"I ... uh ..." Michael wasn't quite sure how to respond, so he changed the subject.

"Astoria was telling me Jenny will soon be starting university in Edinburgh. You must be very proud."

"Aye, we are that," Mary said. "Couldn't be prouder. She's worked hard for it, as has Storie. She was determined Jenny should get through school and have every opportunity."

"She loves her sister very much. It's admirable."

Mary Penrose smiled wistfully. "Aye, she does. Jenny was just a wee bairn when my dear husband died, and I went half-mad with grief. I didn't step up like I ought to have, and Astoria took on more than any young lass should have to. She became like a second mother to Jenny, and then she took it upon herself to become the main provider as well."

"She's nothing if not determined. I've seen it myself."

"Aye, but always for others, never for herself. And I worry about what that will do to her in the long run. She's clever enough to have gone to university too, but she never got the chance. More than anything, I want her to get out and see the world, not be trapped here like her father and I were."

"You wouldn't miss her if she went away?"

"Of course, every day. But it would break my heart to see her waste away here. I've already seen so much of the light go out of her smile." She laughed self-consciously. "There now, here's me rabbiting on when we've only just been introduced. Forgive me for being so over-familiar. I don't often encounter strangers these days."

"There's nothing to forgive, ma'am," Michael said, and he meant it. He liked Mary Penrose and her frank, honest manner—the same quality he admired so much in her daughter. "To tell the truth, it's a relief to be met with openness. Not everyone says what they mean."

She looked at him shrewdly, and Michael got the impression she saw more than she was letting on.

"It can't be easy, I imagine, coming into a place like this," she said. "I still struggle to keep up with the politics of it all, and I've been here half my life. But the way Storie talks about you, I can tell she respects you. And there aren't many people who can win her respect. You're doing just fine, lad."

She smiled at him in such a kind, motherly way that Michael suddenly felt a strange lump in his throat.

"SO ARE YOU HERE WITH Galbraith?" Jock asked Astoria as they danced. She frowned.

"We walked down the hill together, if that's what you mean."

Jock raised an eyebrow, and Astoria felt her hackles rise.

"There's nothing going on, Jock. And even if there were, I don't have to justify myself to you."

"Of course not. I just worry about you, Storie. I mean, how much do any of us really know him? He was working on that automaton right before it caught fire. He could have killed that new lad, what's his name, Thompson?"

"Thomas," Astoria said, frowning. "Simon Thomas. And how do you know he was assisting Michael?" Jock was a day-shift man; he should have been in the mess at the time of the accident.

Jock looked discomfited for a moment, then his composure returned.

"I was there. Alistair Grimbald wanted to swap a shift—he wanted to be home for his wife's birthday dinner, I think it was. So I offered to fill in for him."

"And you saw Michael and Simon working on the automaton. Did you see anything else?"

Jock shrugged. "Not really. It went bang shortly after and then we were just busy trying to get everyone out. But my point is, I don't think you can trust him."

"I understand your point perfectly, thank you."

"Now then, no need to get snippy."

"I'm not. But I came here to have fun, not to talk about work." She was very glad when the dance sent them wheeling away from each other. Something in what Jock had said niggled at her, but she couldn't quite put her finger on it. She knew Michael couldn't have sabotaged the automaton, so why was Jock trying so hard to convince her that he had? Someone was certainly untrustworthy, but she didn't think it was Michael.

The dance ended shortly afterwards, and Jock took her arm and escorted her from the floor.

"No hard feelings, I hope, Storie?" he said. "I'm not trying to make things difficult for you. I'd just hate to see you get into another... situation, like last time."

Astoria took a deep breath, trying to calm her anger. She pasted a smile on her face.

"No hard feelings," she said. "And you don't need to worry about me. I can look after myself. Now, I'm going to get some punch." She hurried away to the drinks table to collect two glasses of punch, making sure she lost Jock in the crowd. She'd just poured them when she turned around and almost cannoned into Emma Grimbald, Alastair's wife.

"Hello, Emma," Astoria said with a smile. "Many happy returns for last week."

"Why, thank you," Emma said, looking puzzled. "But my birthday's not for another three months."

"Oh." Astoria frowned, confused. "Sorry, I must have got the wrong end of the stick. I could have sworn Jock said he swapped a shift with Al last week so he could attend your birthday dinner."

"I think you must be getting me mixed up with somebody else," Emma said. "Al said Jock begged him to swap that shift, although he wasn't quite clear why. But he was happy to do it. It was nice to have him home in the evening for a change."

"Sorry, you're right," Astoria said, thinking quickly. "It was someone else. It can be hard keeping all the shift changes straight sometimes."

"I meant to congratulate you on your promotion," Emma said. "You deserve it. And it's nice to finally see a woman in one of the top jobs."

"Thanks."

"You must come to tea one day. It's been a while since we caught up."

"I'd like that." She gestured with her glass. "I'd better get this punch to my mother. It was good to see you."

Emma smiled. "You too."

Astoria returned to her family and Michael, her head spinning. Jock was one of her oldest friends—why would he lie to her?

Seeing Michael chatting with her mother as if they'd known each other for years, however, pushed Jock out of her head. All through the dance she'd worried about leaving him at the mercy of Mary's insatiable curiosity, but they seemed to be getting on fabulously.

"Enjoying yourself?" she asked him as she handed a glass to her mother.

"Very much so," he said. "Mrs Penrose has been filling me in on all the latest gossip. And telling me stories about you, of course."

"Mother!"

Mary Penrose laughed. "They're all very flattering, my dear, don't worry. But don't let me keep you two young folk from dancing."

"That's the first time in many years I've been called young," Michael said with a grin. "But a dance would be lovely." He turned to Astoria and offered his hand. "May I?"

She smiled and drained her punch, then set the glass on a nearby table. "I thought you'd never ask."

Chapter 15

Michael found it difficult afterwards to remember much about the dance itself. He was just conscious the whole time of being so near to Astoria, their hands touching, connecting then moving away as the steps dictated. When they moved together, their closeness made him catch his breath. He knew himself well enough to realise the rush of desire for what it was, and it worried him. He would never do anything to upset the good working relationship he'd finally built with Astoria, and she deserved better than having her colleague drooling over her. No doubt she'd had to deal with such things before, in this world of men, and he wouldn't want to put her through such discomfort again. Without some definitive encouragement from her, the deepest desires of his heart would have to remain just that: buried deep. But when the dance brought them together again, their eyes met and it felt like the whole world stopped. Astoria gave him a small smile, a flush creeping up her cheeks. Neither of them broke away until the dance ended and everyone applauded the musicians. Astoria was breathing hard, and he wondered that she should be so taxed by dancing when he'd seen her lift pounds of thermocrystals without breaking a sweat.

Supper was served shortly afterwards, and Michael sat down to eat with Astoria and her family. As the plates were cleared away, people began moving their chairs to the dance floor.

"Singing?" Michael guessed.

Astoria nodded. "Singing, music, poetry, whatever you like," she said. "The musicians will have a break, and then there'll be more dancing later."

"Are you going to perform something?"

She shrugged. "Maybe. You?"

"I ... hadn't thought about it." He was a confident singer, but among friends, not in such a group as this.

Bertie, as the official host, stood up and called forth anyone who had something to offer. There was an initial reluctance, until a girl of around fifteen stood up and sang 'Wild Mountain Thyme' in a clear, sweet voice that raised hairs on the back of Michael's neck. He saw Harry Murdoch looking proud as punch and guessed she was his daughter.

After that, people seemed to lose their inhibitions. As Astoria had said, some people sang, others recited, and others brought out fiddles or flutes. Michael was astounded at the talent in the room.

"Well, ladies and gents," Bertie said sometime later, coming to the front. "That just about concludes this portion of the evening. I think, yes, we've got time for one more. Who will it be?"

Michael swallowed, trying to quell a sudden rush of nerves. Then he took a deep breath and rose to his feet.

"Mr Galbraith," Bertie said, his eyebrows rising. "Welcome to your first ceilidh. Let's make him welcome, everyone." People clapped, although not as enthusiastically as they had for Astoria. Michael looked out across the sea of faces. Then he met Astoria's eyes, and suddenly his nerves vanished. With no introduction, he broke into song.

ASTORIA HAD ASSUMED Michael wasn't the musical type, although she couldn't say where she'd got the impression. But it was clear from the first note that he had a stunning baritone voice. Her heart began to beat faster as she recognised 'Loch Lomond'.

At the chorus, the whole room spontaneously joined in, sending shivers down Astoria's spine. She couldn't tear her eyes away from Michael, even as the people around her stood and swayed to the music. There was a joy in his face that she'd never seen before, as if the music was illuminating him from within. And suddenly she found herself wishing that she knew how to bring that look to his face every day. It wasn't to be, of course; they were colleagues, hopefully even friends now, but they could never be anything more. There were too many obstacles in the way, even if she wanted it, which ... she wasn't sure she was ready to be completely honest with herself about what exactly she wanted with Michael. It was too complicated. The risk of getting hurt was simply too great for both of them. Friends would have to be enough. But as the song drew to a close and he smiled at her as if they were the only two people in the room, she found that her body didn't give a fig about her resolutions. She wiped her sweaty palms discreetly on her skirt, then joined in as the hall erupted in applause. People thumped Michael on the back as he returned to his seat, grinning.

"Well!" said Mary. "You've certainly made an impression, Mr Galbraith!"

"Please call me Michael," he said, blushing. "I just love to sing. I'm glad people enjoyed it."

"You're a dark horse," Astoria said. "I had no idea you were musical."

He shrugged. "Most of my family is. My mother insisted on it."

"Well, it was lovely."

"Thank you."

Astoria was growing tired and she was glad the night would soon be drawing to a close. The musicians launched into their final set and people once again took to the floor. Others stopped by to chat, drinks in hand, and to congratulate Michael on his performance, and so they passed the final pleasant hour.

At last the band played their final song and people began to trickle out of the hall into the night, tired but happy.

"It was so nice to meet you, Michael," Mary gushed as they said their goodbyes. "It's Astoria's day off tomorrow so she's coming down to have dinner with us. You'd be most welcome to join us."

Astoria shot her mother a look, but Mary was oblivious—deliberately so, Astoria suspected.

"It was lovely to meet you too, Mrs Penrose," Michael said. "And thank you for the invitation. I'd love to come."

"Well," Astoria said, "we'd best be going. See you tomorrow, Mum." She kissed her mother and Jenny, and Michael bowed.

"Until tomorrow," he said. He offered Astoria his arm, and they set off up the hill.

Chapter 16

"Did you enjoy yourself?" Astoria asked as they walked. The full moon cast a brilliant silver sheen over the valley, giving them enough light to see by. Other miners were strung out in small groups along the path as they all made their way back to the camp.

"I did," Michael said with a smile. "It's a long time since I've been to a ceilidh—too long. I didn't realise how much I missed it. You?"

"Oh yes. It's pretty much the highlight of my year," Astoria said.

"I suppose there's not much chance for a break in this industry."

"Not really. The only 'holiday' I've ever had was when I went to Edinburgh, and that was for a company conference."

"How did you like the big city?"

She sighed wistfully. "It was wonderful. I'd love to travel properly someday, and have real adventures. There's a big wide world out there, and I just ... can't get to it."

Michael heard the frustration and longing in her voice, and wished he could say something that would help. He thought of all the travel he'd done, first as a boy with his family, then later with his work, or even just for fun. He'd taken so many things for granted. And he realised that, if he could, he'd whisk Astoria away from here and take her all around the world, if she wished it. The strength of his feelings surprised him.

"You will," he said with conviction. "Someday."

"Maybe. And I can't imagine you want to be stuck here for the rest of your days either?"

"Well, no. But it has more compensations than I thought it would."

She glanced at him, and their eyes met for a long moment. "Well, I never thought I'd say this, but I quite like having you around."

"Now that's high praise indeed," he said, laughing.

She grinned. "Consider yourself fortunate. I'm not this nice to everyone."

"I don't doubt it."

"Did you just insult me, Mr Galbraith?"

"I believe I may have, Miss Penrose."

"You're a brave man."

"What can I say? I like to live dangerously."

She laughed, and Michael's stomach fluttered. He loved that he could make her laugh.

They reached the intersection at the top of the hill. To the left lay the dormitories and mess hall, while a path to the right led round the back of the camp to Michael's cottage.

"May I do the gentlemanly thing and walk you to your door?" Michael asked, a little surprised at his own daring.

Astoria glanced at him, her cheeks flushed. Then she bit her lip and looked away, shaking her head.

"I don't think that's a good idea. I'm sorry."

Michael's heart sank, but he forced a smile. "Nothing to be sorry for. I didn't mean to overstep."

"No," Astoria said. "It's not ... I mean, if circumstances were different ... but there's too many people about. If someone were to see and rumours started, it would undermine both of us."

A tiny hope flickered in Michael's chest. "I understand."

She smiled. "Thank you."

"Would it be better if I didn't come to dinner tomorrow?"

"No! I mean ... my mother invited you. It's not like we'll be unchaperoned."

"Of course. As long as you still want me to come?"

"I do. I'll meet you here at six tomorrow. But I think it's best if we say goodnight now." She held out her hand, slightly awkwardly. Michael took it.

"May I?" he asked. She blushed, then nodded. Michael pressed the back of her hand gently to his lips. Their eyes locked, and he felt a sudden rush of desire. Astoria took a deep breath, and he wondered if she felt it too. He released her hand.

"Goodnight, Miss Penrose."

"Goodnight, Mr Galbraith."

ASTORIA WALKED DOWN the moonlit path towards the dormitories, forcing herself not to look back. How had Michael managed to make a simple courtesy so intimate? Her body still tingled when she thought of it, setting off an unaccustomed ache of desire between her legs. She had despised Michael before she met him, and she was a little shocked to discover just how much her feelings had changed. Not that her feelings mattered one whit; being with him was impossible. She reminded herself of all the sound, logical reasons why, but her body was having none of it. The memory of the way he'd smiled at her in the moonlight made her catch her breath. Remembering how his arm had felt, tucked into her side, was enough to set her throbbing.

When she reached her room, she undressed hurriedly and climbed into bed. The bed was cold, but even the chilliness of the sheets didn't help. Astoria lay on her back, staring at a sliver of moonlight splashed across the ceiling. Her mind wandered back to the ceilidh and landed, inevitably, on Michael. She smiled in the dark as she recalled dancing with him, the warmth and wittiness of his conversation, and how their bodies had felt pressed together.

She tossed her head against the pillow in frustration—such thoughts weren't conducive to sleep. Slowly, tentatively, she slipped her hands beneath her nightgown, running them gently up her inner thighs. She was already wet. With one fingertip she slowly circled her clitoris, breathing deeply with pleasure, while with her other hand she slipped a finger inside herself, feeling for the place that, she knew from experience, would soon tip her over the edge. She closed her eyes, imagining that it was Michael's hands caressing her, that it was Michael inside her. Her nipples hardened, pressing against the fabric of her nightgown, as she envisioned Michael's lips on her mouth, her neck, her breasts. That it could never happen in reality didn't matter at this moment. She increased the pressure of her fingers as her body responded, then clenched her teeth to keep from crying out as the world exploded and she felt herself pulsating on a wave of pleasure. Blessedly released, she rolled over and drifted into sleep.

Chapter 17

Astoria spent most of the next morning agonising over the approaching dinner. Maybe it wasn't such a good idea after all. At the very least, she owed Michael an explanation for her odd behaviour the previous night. And what if she'd completely misread the situation? What if his offer to walk her home had been just that—a kind, gentlemanly gesture—and she'd instead interpreted it as something else?

In any case, remaining simply colleagues was by far the safest and most sensible decision. She hadn't worked so hard for so long to blow it all on a silly flirtation, if indeed that was what this was. Her mother and Jenny still needed her. Nothing was worth risking her job over.

In the end, she decided to go for a walk, to spend at least part of her day off in a semi-productive manner and hopefully clear her head. Almost without intending to, she found herself climbing the hill above the mine. She loved it up there. Looking out over the mountains, she could pretend she was the only person in the world. And if she turned the other way, she could see the faint dots of the airships taking off from the town some twenty miles away, their balloons glinting in the afternoon light. The airships reminded her that there was a whole world out there. One day, she vowed, she'd see it.

As the afternoon sun began to slant down the mountainside, bathing everything in gold, she scrambled to her feet and began to walk slowly down the hill. She'd always enjoyed visiting home, and it seemed like she could never stay long enough. But tonight was different. She wondered if her mother had some sort of ulterior motive in inviting Michael. She almost wished she'd taken him up on his offer to stay away.

She returned to her room, where she washed quickly and dressed. She didn't normally put in any special effort to go home, but tonight she chose one of her nicest pairs of breeches and one of her few shirts that wasn't threadbare. She briefly contemplated wearing her only skirt, but she thought that might be taking it a bit too far. Her attempt to impress would be obvious, and her mother and Jenny would never let her forget it.

At the last minute, she pulled a packet of powdered herbs from the drawer of her nightstand. It was a preparation for preventing pregnancy, which her mother had given to her when she first moved into the dormitories. While, in theory, the conservative village families expected girls to save themselves for marriage, in practice the mothers knew all too well what went on at the mine site, and instructed their daughters in the anatomical realities well before their wedding nights.

Using a small wooden scoop, Astoria tipped a quantity of the herbs into a glass, then filled it with water from her flask. She stirred it and drank the preparation down, pulling a face at the bitter taste. She wasn't quite sure what possessed her to take it; after all, she wasn't going to be *doing* anything with Michael. Of course she wasn't. But better safe than sorry, and it wouldn't do her any harm.

The shadows were growing longer by the time she walked across the camp to meet Michael at the crossroads where they had parted the night before. Walking there, Astoria felt her stomach fluttering in anticipation. It was hard to forget the previous night, the touch of his lips on her skin. She bit her lip, trying to reason with herself. This dinner invitation was a simple kindness, something that her mother would have extended to any newcomer. It meant nothing. But all her protestations vanished when she saw him standing there in the golden light of evening. The sun burnished his dark hair, and he was gazing off into the distance, looking pensive. She wondered what he was thinking about. She doubted it was about her.

He heard her coming and turned, a grin breaking across his face. She couldn't help smiling in return.

"It's good to see you," he said. Astoria breathed a sigh of relief. She'd worried they'd be awkward, but his manner was free and easy. If he'd been as discomfited as she had by their parting the previous evening, he wasn't showing it.

"I'm glad you could come," she said.

"Are you really?"

"Of course. And my mother seems quite taken with you."

"Should I be worried?"

Astoria laughed. "I would be."

Michael offered her his arm, and she took it as they set off down the hill towards the village. Even though they were walking at an easy pace, she suddenly found it hard to catch her breath.

"How was your shift?" she asked to distract herself from the feeling of his arm pressed against her side.

"It was fine. Quiet."

"That's always good. A busy shift usually means there's something to worry about."

"What about you? What did you do with your day off?"

"Not much. I went for a walk up the hill. I like to watch the airships taking off."

"Do you?" he grinned. "I'd never have taken you for a balloon-spotter."

She shrugged. "I just like to imagine where they're going."

"Do you wish you were on one?"

"Sometimes. I haven't had much chance for adventure."

"My younger brother Nick's wife is an aeronaut. Well, she used to be. She even broke a world record when she was just a lass. Youngest person to circumnavigate the globe solo and unassisted."

"Not Millie Roberts, the brasscore politician?"

Michael nodded. "That's right. Do you know her?"

"I know *of* her, of course. She's doing some incredible work. It's very inspiring."

"I'll introduce you to her one day, if you like. I think you two would get on."

"I'd like that."

Michael grinned ruefully.

"What?" Astoria asked.

"Nothing. I was just thinking about Nick and Millie. Nick and I were always the confirmed bachelors of the family. I think everyone had just about given up on both of us. I would never have expected him to end up with a woman like Millie, but they're so good together. So now it's just me."

"You don't want to marry?" Astoria asked, feeling her heart jump inexplicably into her throat.

"It's not that," Michael said. "I just never met the right woman. The girls in my parents' circle ... well, they're bred to be society wives. All style and no substance, most of them. I never encountered someone I could envisage as a true partner in life." He shrugged. "Maybe my expectations of what marriage should be are just too high."

"I don't think so," Astoria said. "Forever is a long time. It has to be spent with the right person."

"And you?" Michael asked.

Astoria laughed. "Have you seen the men here?"

Michael grinned. "Fair enough."

"No," Astoria said, "I suppose I'm just the same as you. I don't want to settle for good enough. I want someone who sees me as—well, as a partner, like you said. Not just as someone to cook his meals and clean his house and bear his children."

Michael gave her a searching look. "And, I imagine, you want someone who can keep up with you," he said.

"I want someone who's not intimidated by me," she said, then felt the blood rush to her cheeks. She closed her eyes briefly, cursing her mouth for running away with her.

"Fools are scared of trailblazers," Michael said vehemently. "They're particularly scared of clever women, because you threaten their mediocrity. And men like that don't deserve you."

"Thanks," Astoria said, her face burning. The conversation had taken a far more intimate turn than she'd intended, and she was suddenly acutely aware of every place their bodies touched.

ASTORIA LED MICHAEL to a small, unassuming cottage towards the far end of the village. There wasn't much to differentiate it from its neighbours except the small patch of garden, which was packed with flowers and clearly lovingly tended. The front step had been scrubbed within an inch of its life, and the net curtains at the windows were crisp and gleaming white.

Jenny must have been looking out for them, because the front door opened as they were walking down the garden path. She grinned at them in welcome.

"Ma!" she called over her shoulder. "They're here!"

Mary Penrose came bustling out to greet them, pulling Astoria into an embrace and kissing her on both cheeks. Michael was a little startled when she did the same to him.

"Well, that's quite a welcome," Astoria said, her eyebrows raised.

"We're just glad to see you," Jenny said, with a meaningful look at Michael. As her mother and sister turned to go back inside, Astoria glanced at him and rolled her eyes, and he had to bite his lip to keep from laughing. It was quite clear that her family thought—or hoped, at least—they were a couple. And, to his surprise, he found that he didn't mind the idea at all.

The cottage was small, but neat and spotlessly clean. Mary went to show them into the small parlour, but Astoria protested.

"Stop it, Mum," she said. "It's a family dinner. We can help you in the kitchen like always."

"We have a *guest*, Storie," Mary said pointedly.

"I don't mind," Michael interjected before Astoria could reply. "A family dinner sounds lovely. It's been a very long time since I had one of those." Mary looked at him for a long minute, then nodded, and he was rewarded by Astoria's grateful glance.

"If you're sure," Mary said, still sounding doubtful. "I'd hate for you to think us inhospitable or lacking in manners."

"I could never think that, I assure you," Michael said with perfect sincerity.

"Very well," she said, and led them into the kitchen, which took up the entire back of the cottage. There was an enormous stove down one end, and a scrubbed wooden table in the middle of the room. It was clear that this was the heart of the house.

Mary ushered Michael to a seat at the table and downright refused his help with the meal; a guest helping to prepare dinner was apparently a bridge too far. There were enticing smells emanating from the oven, and soon a veritable feast was brought forth: roast beef, roast potatoes, green peas, Yorkshire pudding, and, of course, an enormous jug of gravy. Michael's stomach rumbled audibly, and he blushed. Astoria laughed.

"Sounds like we need to get you fed up," she said. "Believe me, it'll be hard to go back to the mess after this."

"I don't doubt it," Michael said as the dishes were brought to the table.

"Would you do us the honour of carving?" Mary asked, holding the knife out to him.

"Of course," he said, standing and taking it from her, before turning his attention to the joint of beef.

There wasn't much awkwardness to begin with, and any remaining was soon dismissed by good food and the genuine pleasure they all took in each other's company. It was about as different from the family dinners of Michael's experience as it was possible to get.

"Do you have a big family, Michael?" Mary asked, as if reading his mind.

"Yes, ma'am," he said. "I'm the third of five boys, so mealtimes were always rather raucous, as I'm sure you can imagine. And now, of course, they all have their own families too. Not that we're together very often any more."

"Are they all in Edinburgh?"

"Three of them. My second-eldest brother, John, is an Aerofleet officer on Gibraltar, but the rest are in Edinburgh. The eldest, David, is a surgeon who works with brasscores, and then the younger ones, Jerome and Nick, are a lawyer and a journalist respectively."

"Nick is married to Millie Roberts," Astoria interjected.

"Really? The politician and aeronaut? She must be very interesting."

Michael smiled. He was used to people quizzing him about his high-flying brothers, so much so that he no longer really resented it, but it was a welcome change to see them passed over for his famous sister-in-law. He knew Nick would be proud as punch—his brother had no compunction about standing in his wife's shadow.

"She is," he said. "Astoria reminds me a lot of her, actually. I hope I'm able to introduce you all to her someday."

"There now, wouldn't that be grand?" Mary said. The conversation lulled as they all contemplated this.

"You have a beautiful garden," Michael said at last.

"Why, thank you," Mary said. "Are you a keen gardener yourself?"

"More ... aspirational," Michael said with a grin. "The will is there but the skill leaves something to be desired. I do like to admire the work of those who know what they're doing, though."

"Why don't you show Michael the garden, Mum?" Jenny suggested. "It's still light enough, and Astoria and I can take care of the pudding."

"MICHAEL SEEMS LIKE a nice man," Jenny said as they served up the bread-and-butter pudding. Astoria wondered how long it would take for her sister to say what was really on her mind, but she wasn't going to make it easy for her.

"He is."

"And he seems to like you a lot."

Astoria glanced at her younger sister. "What's your point?"

"Only that you could do a lot worse."

"Jenny!"

"What? Do you like him?"

"As a colleague and a friend, of course."

Jenny rolled her eyes. "That's not what I meant, and you know it. If you like him, you should do something about it. And if you don't, you should put the poor lad out of his misery. So *do* you like him?"

Astoria thunked a plate down with more force than she'd intended.

"Whether I like him or not is irrelevant, Jen. We work together. I can't risk my job by fraternising with a colleague. I *won't*. It's the only thing keeping the family afloat."

"I know, Storie, but just listen to me ..."

"Will you stop nagging me if I do?"

"Promise."

"Fine. What is it?"

"I've won a scholarship to the university."

Astoria turned to her sister, her frustration forgotten.

"Jen, that's wonderful! I'm so proud of you!" She swept Jenny into an embrace. "I'm not surprised, you know. You've always been the smartest of us all."

Jenny smiled, her cheeks flushed with pleasure. "Thanks. But anyway, that will pay my tuition fees. You don't have to support me any more."

Astoria frowned. "But you'll still need money to live on, presumably?"

"I'm going to work for it."

Astoria felt her stomach lurch with sudden anxiety. "You are *not* going down that pit," she said firmly. "I haven't worked all these years to keep you out of it just for you to do it now."

Jenny rolled her eyes. "Of course I'm not," she said. "I'm talking about a secretarial job in Edinburgh. Bertie has already arranged it with one of his contacts."

"Oh, has he?" Astoria said, hurt that he hadn't told her.

"Please don't be upset, Storie," Jenny said. "I'll never forget what you've done for me and everything you've sacrificed. And now it's my turn. I'll be able to support myself, and whatever is left over I can send to Ma. You won't have to work so hard, unless you want to. You could even leave the mine if you like and try something new. I know what they're going to pay me, and I've done the sums. I'll be able to afford it. You don't need to let fear for your job hold you back from following your heart."

Astoria smiled at her youthful exuberance, suddenly feeling every year of their age difference.

"That's very sweet, Jen. We'll see."

Jenny gave a satisfied smile and went back to serving up pudding.

Chapter 18

"Thanks again for having me, Mrs Penrose," Michael said as they finally made it to the door. After the pudding had come tea and biscuits, and Mary had even broken out the port. "She must *really* like you," Astoria had whispered.

Mary Penrose smiled and kissed him on both cheeks.

"My pleasure, my dear. I hope we'll see you again soon." She gave Astoria a pointed look.

"Goodnight, Mum," Astoria said, just as pointedly ignoring it. "I'll pop down in a couple of days." She kissed her mother and waved to Jenny, then set off up the hill with Michael. She hoped her family would at least wait until they were out of earshot before they began dissecting the visit.

"Your mother is wonderful," Michael said as they walked. "Jenny, too. Thank you for allowing me to meet them."

Astoria chuckled. "It wasn't a matter of *allowing*. I would never have heard the end of it until I'd properly presented you. Mum is a bit of a force of nature."

"So that's where you get it from."

"Apparently."

"Well, regardless, it was a most enjoyable evening."

"It certainly was."

They walked on in companionable silence.

"Penny for your thoughts?" Michael said at last, as they neared the crossroads at the top of the hill.

"Oh, nothing much. I was just thinking about something Jenny said to me."

"Oh?"

"It's nothing. Just about figuring out what's important in life." She smiled. "Well, here we are."

Unlike the previous night, the camp was quiet; there wasn't another soul to be seen. The rhythm of daily life, which had been broken by the ceilidh, had returned, and everyone was either working or sleeping.

"I suppose this is goodnight," Michael said, turning to face her. Their eyes met, and Astoria felt her heart begin to race. Suddenly, standing at the crossroads felt much more literal. She thought about what Jenny had said: *You don't have to let fear get in the way of following your heart.* It would be so easy to simply part ways now and go back to her room alone. It would undoubtedly be the sensible thing to do. But she also realised, with a certainty that surprised her, that if she did so she'd regret it—and she didn't want to spend the rest of her days wondering what might have been. She smiled.

"Perhaps. Or may I do the ladylike thing and walk you to your door?"

Michael's eyebrows rose in surprise, then he smiled back. "Of course."

They walked the short distance to Michael's cottage in silence. Astoria was suddenly full of doubt. Heaven knew it wouldn't be the first time she'd got the wrong end of the stick about something like this—she'd always found feelings, especially other people's, difficult to navigate. Maybe he was just being polite. And yet, there'd been something in the way he'd looked at her ...

"Here we are," Michael said, breaking her train of thought. Without her even realising it, they'd reached the cottage. "Would you like to come in?" She was surprised to see the depth of longing in his eyes, along with something else ... uncertainty? Could it be that he was just as nervous as she was? Astoria was used to being propositioned by men who were absolutely cocksure about what they wanted and were prepared to wear a woman down until she gave in. In her limited experience, the result hadn't exactly been mutually satisfying—but then those sorts of men never intended it to be. Michael was different, she realised. He actually cared about whether she wanted him as much as he wanted her. And, by God, she did.

She nodded.

MICHAEL UNLOCKED THE door, then stepped back and ushered her in before him. The interior of the cottage was dark, apart from the faint light of the fire, which had been banked and was burned down to glowing coals, and the sheen of moonlight through the windows. He hastily lit a lamp and warm golden light spilled across the room. He stoked the fire, adding logs from a basket beside the hearth.

"Tea?" he asked. "Or something stronger?" He indicated a bottle of scotch on the mantelpiece. Back in Edinburgh he wouldn't have dreamed of offering whisky to a lady. His mother and sisters-in-law would have been appalled—well, except for Millie. But here it was different. Astoria didn't give a fig about that sort of stuffy, performative propriety, so why should he?

"Aye, I'll have a wee dram," she said with a grin, and he found himself smiling back. He poured two glasses, and turned back to see her sitting down on the settee before the fire. He flushed; he hadn't even realised he'd left her standing.

"I'm so sorry," he said. "I should have offered you a chair. You must think I've no manners at all."

She thinks you're fussing about like a mother hen, muttered an unhelpful voice in his head, but Astoria just patted the settee next to her. "Come and sit with me," she said. Michael did as she asked, handing her the drink. "Cheers," she said, raising her glass to his.

"Can I ask you something?" he said as their glasses clinked. He couldn't help noticing how the firelight glinted in her hair, burnishing it with gold.

"Of course."

"What's changed? Last night you were worried about being seen if I simply walked you home, and yet now ... well, here we are. I don't quite understand."

Astoria looked at him. "I'm sorry," she said. "I didn't mean to make things so confusing." She took a sip of whisky, her brow furrowing. Then she sighed. "It's a bit ... complicated," she said at last.

Michael smiled in what he hoped was a reassuring way. "I'm not afraid of complicated."

"All right." She took another drink. "Don't say I didn't warn you." She sighed.

"As you probably know, one of the big rules the Braithwaite Corporation has is no fraternising on site. It's a sackable offence. I guess it's because they want everyone to keep their minds on the job." She shrugged. "Anyway, a few years ago, I ... got involved with someone—another miner. I was young and stupid and still believed in fairytales, which made it easy for him to tell me what I wanted to hear in order to get what he wanted. I fell for him hard, but my career was also on the rise, and when I got promoted above him he couldn't handle it. He broke things off, and shortly afterwards, it somehow got around that I'd been fraternising with someone, even though we'd been extremely discreet." She shook her head. Michael raised his eyebrows.

"Next thing I know, I'm hauled into Bertie's office. He asked me straight up if it was true, and because I've known him all my life and he's like a second father to me, I couldn't lie to him. I still remember how disappointed he looked. He asked me for the man's name, but I wouldn't tell him—I still have some pride. So, bless him, he said that although he was obligated to read me the riot act, he'd be damned if he'd sack me for an offence that obviously required two people while letting the other party get off scot-free. I promised I wouldn't do it again, and he warned me that if I did, he'd have no choice but to enforce company policy." She sipped her drink.

"Bertie even let me keep my promotion. I hoped that would be the end of the matter. But then the rumours began."

"What kind of rumours?" Michael asked, although he could take an educated guess.

She shrugged. "The kind you'd expect. The kind that women in places like this always have to put up with—that I'd go with anyone, that I'd slept my way to a promotion, even that I was Bertie's mistress." Her mouth twisted in disgust. "Men would even bang on my door late at night, wanting ... well, you know what they were wanting. It went on for months. I knew who'd started it, of course, but there was nothing I could do, so I just tried to ignore it."

Michael stared at her, gobsmacked. He'd seen how much the other miners respected Astoria, but it was shocking to realise what she'd had to endure to earn it. "Then what happened?" he asked.

She smiled. "It turns out I'm not entirely friendless here. One night, the man in question had a bit of an accident. Nothing major—he ... tripped and fell. Landed on his face and got a broken nose and a black eye out of it. It was a bit of a night for clumsiness, actually. Jock hurt his hand too. Funny how these sorts of things all happen at once."

Michael grinned. "It certainly is."

"Anyway, after a few more little accidents, the rumours stopped. Eventually, the man in question left. And over time I earned the respect of the lads, and when I became shift supervisor they all knew I'd got it fair and square. But I've also had to conduct myself unimpeachably. I've never even looked at another man—because another on-site romance would have been too risky. Never mind that the lads are off sowing their wild oats all over the place and nobody thinks twice. It's so different for men.

"So last night, I worried that if someone saw you walk me home and got the wrong idea, it would start all over again. I'm not sure even Bertie could protect me a second time, and he'd probably have to sack you too. It wouldn't be fair on you, and it would devastate my mother."

Michael watched her face keenly. There was the echo of remembered pain in her eyes, and he realised that, as dispassionately as she'd tried to tell it, what had happened hadn't just been a few vicious rumours: it had been a sustained campaign of persecution. She must have been terrified. His heart ached for her.

Astoria drained her glass and set it on a low side table. "As for what's changed," she said, "well, tonight I discovered that, while I haven't been looking, my sister has grown into a brilliant, wise, responsible young woman. She said something to me about not living my life in fear. And I realised she's absolutely right. For the first time ever, I'm starting to see a life beyond the mine. And it would be such a shame if I gave up the chance to get to know you better simply because I was afraid of what people might think. But I should have told you about all this before, because it affects you too. So if you want me to go now, I will. Nobody will know, and I'll make sure we avoid any appearance of impropriety in the future. Everything will be strictly above board."

Michael smiled ruefully. "I doubt anyone here could think worse of me than they already do. So you don't need to worry on my account." He shrugged, hoping he sounded nonchalant. In truth, the wounds of his spectacular fall from grace were still raw.

Astoria gave him a shrewd look, and he knew she hadn't been fooled. "That's only because they don't know you," she said. "You improve on closer acquaintance."

"Oh, really?" He couldn't help grinning. Astoria was unlike any woman he'd ever met. He knew that a major reason he'd never had much truck with the girls in his mother's set was his refusal to play the mystifying games that apparently constituted courtship. He was an engineer: he liked clear operating parameters. Astoria's frankness was refreshing. He loved knowing that he could ask her something and she'd give him a truthful answer, even if it was unvarnished.

"And you want to get to know me better?" he asked.

"Is that so odd?"

"After I stole your job? A little."

She shrugged. "Sometimes, missing out on the thing you think you want turns out to be the best thing that can happen to you," she said. "I'm now considering possibilities I'd never thought of before. There's a big world out there. So I suppose I should really thank you for that. And I know you didn't ask to be dropped into this job. Although I won't deny that I thought you were a bit of a stuck-up prig to begin with."

Michael laughed, and she seemed to realise what she'd said.

"Sorry," she said, blushing. "That was rude of me. My mother's always telling me I should think before I speak." She grimaced.

Impulsively, Michael reached out and took her hand. She looked up at him, and their eyes met.

"Don't change," he said softly, and she smiled. Michael's heart thundered in his ears. Gently, he tucked a lock of her hair behind her ear. She leaned in to his touch. Then she moved forward and kissed him slowly, sensuously on the mouth. Michael felt a rush of desire so powerful it teetered between pleasure and pain. It was as if an invisible wall between them had come crashing down. He pulled her to him and kissed her passionately.

After a few minutes they broke apart, gasping. Michael stroked her hair. She was so beautiful, and he wanted to explore every inch of her, to hear her call out his name in pleasure. But he also couldn't forget the haunted look in her eyes when she'd talked about her last, disastrous venture into courtship.

"Are you sure this is what you want?" he asked, cupping her face in his hands. "We can just leave it here, or take things slowly. I will *never* ask you to do anything you don't want to do."

Astoria smiled. Then she leaned in, her cheek pressing against his. "I want you," she whispered in his ear. "All of you. I want you inside me and on top of me and wrapped all around me. I want you here, and I want you now."

She sat back and looked at him. "Is that what you want too?"

"Oh God, yes." He was so hard he ached with desire. He pulled her close and kissed her, his hands slipping under her shirt. She gasped as he cupped her breasts, her nipples hardening beneath his fingers. He kissed the pale arch of her neck, moving down towards the gentle swell of her breasts, slowly undoing buttons as he went. Her fingers tangled in his hair. He undid the last button and slipped the shirt over her shoulders, admiring the way her thin undershirt clung to the curves of her body. Years of hard work had made her strong and supple, the muscles in her arms and back sculpturally defined. She left him breathless, and yet Michael noticed a flush in her cheeks, and the way she cast her gaze down, as if she were self-conscious.

"You don't like me looking at you?" he asked gently.

She raised her chin, meeting his eyes briefly before looking away again. "It's not that," she said. "It's just ... I know I don't look like other girls, all thin and willowy."

"I wouldn't want you to." But she didn't seem reassured, and he suddenly had an inkling why. "Oh, my darling," he said, "what did he say to you?"

Astoria folded her arms across her chest, biting her lip. "He said ... I'm so muscled, it was like making love to a man."

Michael was beginning to hate this man. He was very glad Jock had taught the bastard a lesson.

"Then he's an idiot," he said vehemently. "You're strong—" he kissed her collarbone, "and smart—" he kissed her neck, "and — stunning." He kissed her mouth and felt her smile.

"Thank you," she said.

"I mean it. You take my breath away."

"You're not so bad yourself," she said, kissing his jaw. She took his hand and pulled him to his feet. She kissed him again as her hands slipped beneath his shirt, fumbling at the waistband of his trousers. One hand slid lower, grasping his length through the fabric in a way that made him groan.

"Too many clothes," she whispered, unbuttoning his shirt. Michael tugged it off as she fumbled with his belt buckle, her fingers made clumsy by need. He found the buttons on her breeches and they fell to the floor. She finally succeeded with the buckle, and as he stood before her in his nakedness, she smiled in a way that told him she liked what she saw. She kissed him deeply, then slowly, teasingly, lifted the undershirt over her head. Michael bent to kiss her small, perfect breasts. His tongue flicked her nipple and she moaned. She pulled him up into an embrace, kissing him again. The touch of her skin on his made him tremble as they sank down onto the sheepskin rug before the fire.

Astoria lay back, inviting him towards her. "Take me," she said. Michael breathed deeply. She was mesmerising, and he wanted nothing more than to thrust himself inside her, for their bodies to move together in bliss, for that ultimate closeness. But there was a look in her eyes that gave him pause, as if she was bracing herself for pain. He realised then that a man who had tried to destroy her over a silly promotion would hardly have been a man who cared about her satisfaction. Had she ever really known pleasure with a man? Suddenly, he was resolved that before the night was out, she would.

He leaned over her and kissed her. "Not yet," he whispered. Their eyes met. "What do you like?"

"I ... I don't really know."

"Would you like to find out?"

She gave him a smile, then nodded. "Yes."

Slowly, he slid lower, planting soft kisses on her neck, her shoulders, her breasts. He took her right nipple into his mouth, caressing it with his tongue, smiling as he heard her breath catch, then did the same with the left. Then slowly downwards to the curves of her belly and hips, and the neat triangle of dark red curls below. He sat back, running his hands along her legs, gently caressing her inner thighs, the skin smooth and soft. Then he bent and kissed the same spot, feeling her tremble in response.

"May I kiss you here?" he asked. She propped herself up on her elbows and looked at him, her breath coming fast.

"Yes," she breathed, opening herself to him. He dropped his head again, finding her already slick with arousal. His own desire throbbed. He caressed her gently with tongue and fingers, finding all the places that made her sigh with pleasure. She arched her back with a sharp intake of breath as he brought her close to the edge.

"I want you inside me," she begged, tugging him up towards her.

"Are you sure?" he asked. "I don't want to get you into trouble ... of any sort."

She nodded. "There's a medicine that the village women use. I've taken it. There won't be any babies." She reached up and kissed him passionately. "Please."

He leaned over her, and she stroked him, before guiding him into the warmth between her legs. She wrapped her legs around him as he thrust deep, and for a long moment they held each other tight. Then desire overcame them and they moved together with desperate urgency. "Oh, Michael!" she cried as she threw her head back and he felt her pulsate around him. "Michael!" And as she called his name, his own body shuddered with release, banishing all other thoughts.

Chapter 19

Astoria was woken by the first rays of dawn light slanting in through the window. She blinked, wondering for a moment where she was, then smiled as the memories of the night came flooding back. After their exquisite tumble on the rug before the fire, she'd reluctantly prised herself out of Michael's arms, knowing she ought to return to her own room before somebody noticed her absence. But his goodnight kiss had been all it had taken to undo her resolve. At least that time they'd made it to the bed.

Michael was still sleeping peacefully beside her, a faint smile on his lips, as if he was having a lovely dream. Astoria lay there watching him, a little surprised at the tenderness of her own feelings. It was hard to believe she'd ever disliked him or thought him arrogant. It wasn't just the way he'd transported her into realms of physical ecstasy she'd never known existed, but how much he clearly cared about her pleasure, her comfort, and her safety. She'd thought the protective shell she'd built around herself was impenetrable, and yet he'd dismantled it so easily. The thought was both exhilarating and a little terrifying. She wasn't used to being so vulnerable.

And what now? A little doubt bubbled up, but she quashed it. She just wanted to enjoy the moment; she didn't want to think about what came next.

As if her gaze had woken him, Michael rolled over and slowly opened his eyes. He saw her watching him, and smiled.

"Morning," Astoria said, fighting down the urge to kiss him.

"You're a wonderful sight to wake up to," he said, pulling her to him.

It was some minutes before she got hold of herself enough to break gently away. "I should go," she said. "Before everyone else gets up, you know."

"Storie?" Michael asked, looking suddenly serious.

"Mm?"

"Do you regret what happened last night?"

She stared at him, startled. "Regret it? No, of course I don't. It was wonderful." She smiled at the memory, then sobered. "Why, do you?"

"No, not at all. I just ... I know you're worried about mixing work and, well, whatever this is."

"Pleasure?"

"It's certainly that." He grinned. "But I'm serious. I don't want to make things difficult for you. If you want to just leave it as one night of happy memories and go back to being colleagues, well, I understand."

Astoria's heart lurched painfully at the thought. "Is that what you want?"

"Me?" he said softly, as if the question surprised him. "No, it isn't."

"Me neither," she said, and he visibly relaxed. "I know it's risky, but I want to get to know you better. Not just like this—" she gestured vaguely at their nakedness—"although I won't deny last night was incredible, but as a person. I want to spend time with you, even if that means carving out little pockets in secret."

"So work is work, and then once we're off the clock ..."

"... What we do is nobody's business but ours," she concluded. She had a feeling it might not be quite that easy, but she stamped it down. They'd just have to find a way to make it work.

"All right," he said with a smile. He leaned over and kissed her deeply. "You should go. I promise things won't be odd at work. But can I see you tonight?"

"I was counting on it." She kissed him again then rolled reluctantly out of bed, searching for her various garments that had been strewn across the room in the previous night's throes of passion. She turned and saw Michael watching her, a smile on his lips.

"What?" she asked playfully.

"Nothing. You're beautiful."

"Stop it," she said, flushing. "Any more talk like that and we'll definitely be late for work."

"We wouldn't want that," he said, trying to look chastened and failing. Astoria laughed.

"You're incorrigible," she said, pulling on her clothes then returning to him for one final kiss.

"I know," he said. "What *are* you going to do with me?"

"Well," she whispered in his ear, "you'll just have to wait till tonight to find out, won't you?"

"Storie," he groaned. "That's just cruel."

She grinned. "I really have to go." She kissed him passionately, then pried herself away. At the door she turned, gave him one final smile, and stepped out into the camp.

Astoria was worried she'd left it too late, but although she spotted a few early risers from a distance, most people were still abed. She was almost to her door when she heard someone call her name. She turned, her heart sinking.

"You're up early," Jock said.

"I've just been for a walk," she said, although she was aware that her rumpled clothes and messy hair hanging loose around her shoulders told a different story.

Jock gave her a look that said he wasn't fooled. "Nice morning for it," he said.

"You're up early yourself," she said.

He shrugged. "Not really. I'm usually up at this time. I like to get some exercise before breakfast."

"Fair enough." She glanced down, hating the sudden awkwardness but unsure how to break it.

"Anyway," he said, "we'd best be getting on. You'll be wanting a shower after your ... walk."

"Yes," Astoria said, grabbing gratefully at the exit. "I'll see you later."

"He's bad news, Storie," Jock said suddenly.

"What?"

"Michael Galbraith. I just don't want you to get hurt."

"I don't know what you mean. I have to go."

She hurried inside and shut the door, then leaned against it, trying to catch her breath. For a moment she tried to tell herself it was just a coincidence, but it was no good—it was clear that Jock knew what was going on. She could only wonder what he'd do with the information, and hope that he was a good enough friend to maintain discretion.

By the time she'd had a shower and got changed she was feeling better. She'd made a choice, even knowing the likely outcome should the relationship be revealed, and she'd just have to live with it. She wasn't going to give Jock the power of hanging around in her thoughts. She'd much rather focus on something more agreeable, like Michael.

She rushed to the mess and managed to grab a quick breakfast just before it closed, then got to the office with a couple of minutes to spare. Michael was already there, clean-shaven and without a hair out of place. He greeted her as he did every morning, and it was all so normal that, for a moment, Astoria wondered whether the events of the previous night had all been a dream. But then, when Miss Beaumont wasn't looking, he glanced at her and gave her a knowing smile that somehow managed to be both cheeky and tender, and her knees suddenly felt like they were going to give way. Then Miss Beaumont called, "Mr Galbraith," and the moment was lost as Michael rose and went out to see what she wanted.

Michael had promised he wouldn't let things get odd at work, and he held fast to it. But Astoria hadn't counted on how difficult it would be for her. It was excruciating being in the same room and unable to touch him, or to even look at him too long lest she forget herself. When they went down to the mess for lunch, they walked close enough that the backs of their hands brushed occasionally in exquisite torture.

The day seemed interminable, but at last their shift came to an end. Astoria left first; she didn't think it wise for them to turn up to dinner together. She was certain she'd betray herself in some small way, and she knew Jock would be watching. She wolfed down her meal then hurried back to her room, listening to the noises of the camp as people went about their business. She picked up a book, but found she was reading the same sentence over and over again. Gradually the shadows lengthened and the sounds outside began to settle down. She knew most people would now either be at work, in the mess lounge, or in their own dorms. Sure enough, when she opened the door and peered out there wasn't a soul to be seen, and she dashed the short distance to Michael's cottage without encountering another person.

He opened the door on the first knock, as if he'd been waiting for her. He'd removed his waistcoat and cravat, and the neck of his shirt was unbuttoned, the sleeves rolled to the elbow. Astoria took a deep breath, but then he smiled at her and she was completely undone. She barely managed to get the door closed before they fell into each other's arms.

"Oh," she gasped as he kissed her neck, "you don't know how much I've been longing for this all day."

"Don't I?" he asked, fumbling at the buttons on her shirt. "It's been killing me too."

"Well," she said, pulling him towards the bed, "I did promise it'd be worth waiting for, didn't I?"

MUCH, MUCH LATER, THEY lay tangled together, their need finally exhausted. Michael stroked Astoria's hair as she dozed, her head pillowed on his shoulder. He still couldn't quite believe she was here with him. And she'd certainly kept her word; even now, the thought of some of the ways she'd pleasured him made his heart race.

He knew she was taking an awful risk, getting involved with him, and the thought that she cared enough to do so warmed his heart. Of course, it was a risk for him too, but much less of one—he had enough savings that losing his job would pose no particular hardship. Indeed, he could have retired after the drama with the inverter and still lived quite comfortably for the rest of his days, but his pride wouldn't allow it. He'd needed to take this job, not for the money but for the chance to prove himself. And yet he'd give it up quite happily if it meant having Astoria in his life. But he also knew she had no such safety net. If they both got sacked for fraternisation he'd support her, of course, but he had the feeling she wouldn't want that. So they'd just need to make sure they didn't get caught.

He gently kissed the top of her head, and she smiled, stirring in her sleep. Michael was a little taken aback by the depth of his feelings. It wasn't even about the sex. He'd been in lust plenty of times before, but he'd never really been in love. And yet he knew that, if things continued this way, he was on track to fall very much in love with Astoria. He wasn't sure if the thought excited or scared him, because he had no idea if she felt the same. After her past experience, he knew she'd be reluctant to make her heart so vulnerable again. But he was willing to wait. They had all the time in the world.

Chapter 20

It was several weeks before Astoria and Michael could be in the same room together without wanting to rip each other's clothes off, but gradually the relationship began to settle into something Astoria found she was enjoying even more—a comfortable intimacy she'd hitherto never experienced. There was something akin to deep friendship in it, although Michael was much more than a friend, of course. She found she loved spending time with him, not just because of the intense physical attraction between them, but because she found him fascinating as a person. Getting to know him was like slowly peeling back the layers of an onion, and she doubted she'd ever tire of it.

But even amidst the bliss of her personal life, there was still a niggling worry about the investigation. She knew Michael couldn't have been involved in the near-miss, but she'd hit a dead end as far as finding out what had actually happened. And now, with their relationship progressing the way it was, she wasn't sure she could ethically continue to investigate. It didn't help that Bertie appeared to be stonewalling her every time she tried to raise the issue.

Astoria knew she needed to talk to Bertie again. As much as she hated to admit it, she realised she wasn't impartial enough to be able to carry out a proper investigation. It wasn't just her relationship with Michael, although that was part of it. It was her own experience at the crystal-face. She didn't trust her empathy with the miners not to colour her search for evidence regarding the automatons. Bertie would have to bring someone in from outside the mine to investigate—preferably even someone from outside the company. There were just too many vested interests otherwise. But hopefully she'd be telling him what he already knew.

Walking to work alone in the morning, she resolved that she would discuss the issue with Bertie. She wasn't sure if she could manage it without telling him about her and Michael, and that was undoubtedly a risk, but she couldn't see an alternative that would let her maintain her integrity. She took a deep breath and pushed open the door of the administration block. Miss Beaumont looked up as she entered.

"Good morning, Miss Penrose," she said.

"Morning," Astoria said. "Is Bertie in?"

Miss Beaumont shook her head. "I believe he's on his way to a pit inspection."

"Bugger."

Miss Beaumont pursed her lips at the profanity, but didn't comment on it. "Is there something I can help you with?"

Astoria ran her hand through her hair, feeling her courage starting to waver. "No. Yes. Maybe. I don't know."

"Sit down," Miss Beaumont said, gesturing to one of the chairs against the wall. She lifted a teacup and saucer down from a shelf, and poured a cup from the steaming teapot on her desk, adding milk from a small jug. "Here," she said, handing it to Astoria.

"Thank you," Astoria said. Suddenly she found her hands were shaking, setting the cup and saucer rattling. She took a sip and tried to calm her nerves. Miss Beaumont just waited with her hands folded in her lap, saying nothing.

"I need to tell him I can't conduct the accident investigation," Astoria said at last, once she'd collected herself. "I'm just not objective enough."

"Because of your ... involvement ... with Mr Galbraith?" Miss Beaumont asked, as if discussing the weather.

Astoria gaped at her. "How did you know?"

Miss Beaumont smiled, something Astoria had hardly ever seen. "With all due respect, Miss Penrose, I have eyes and ears and work barely fifty feet from you."

Astoria felt a flush creeping up her cheeks. All this time they'd thought they'd been *so* discreet, and Miss Beaumont had known all along.

"Does Bertie know?"

At that, Miss Beaumont laughed, a sound so startling Astoria jumped. "Of course not," she said. "He's completely oblivious to things like that. And I certainly haven't told him."

Astoria closed her eyes briefly. "Thank you."

"Just between you and me," Miss Beaumont said, "I think the fraternisation rule is ridiculous. We're all adults, and people are here to do a job, not take a vow of celibacy. But here we are. Your relationship didn't seem to be affecting your work, so I wasn't going to be the one to drop you in it."

"I don't know what to do," Astoria said, second thoughts flocking in like a murder of crows. "If I tell Bertie about the investigation I'll have to explain why. I'll lose my job. Michael will too. But if I don't, I could be accused of bias and sanctioned anyway."

"Maybe," Miss Beaumont said. "But maybe not. Tell me what you've found so far."

Astoria sighed. "It's complicated," she said. "Everything just feels ... *off*, somehow. On the face of it, it was just a straightforward accident. Except I'm really not sure it was."

"You suspect sabotage?"

"I don't know. The automaton had a wire cut, so it certainly seems like it. And there's all this pressure from people like Jock to conclude that it was Michael, but so many things don't add up, and I honestly don't think it was him. But now I've compromised myself, and who's going to believe me when I say I think someone is trying to frame him?"

"Why would they want to frame Michael?"

Astoria shrugged. "Maybe because he's an easy target?" she said. "That's as good a reason as any. He's already got a history of high-profile accidents, and nobody here knows him or will defend him. If someone else has an agenda and wants a scapegoat, framing him is a good solution." She put her head in her hands. "I'm well aware that this sounds crazy."

"Actually, it doesn't," Miss Beaumont said. "Maybe they wanted everyone to think it was an accident. But just in case someone—like you—started to suspect it wasn't, Michael was set up to take the fall."

"But I have no proof of any of it."

They sat in silence, each thinking hard.

"Tell Bertie that you can't continue the investigation," Miss Beaumont said at last. "At this point, I'm not sure he'll care about your relationship. He's got far too many other things to worry about. Everything is in flux at the moment, but I'm confident it'll work itself out in the end. You're an asset to the company and he'd be a fool to get rid of you."

"Thank you, Miss Beaumont. That means a lot."

"Please call me Euphemia."

"Thank you, Euphemia." Astoria drained her cup and stood up. "I suppose I should face the music," she said.

"Don't forget where you've come from," Miss Beaumont said. "They can't take that away from you."

Astoria nodded, then walked into Bertie's office and sat down to wait.

Around half an hour later the door to the administration block opened and Bertie strode through to his office without so much as glancing at Miss Beaumont. He looked tired and drawn, as if he'd aged decades in the past two days.

"Storie," he said tiredly when he saw her. "How can I help you?"

"How did the pit visit go?" Astoria asked.

Bertie rubbed his hand across his face. "About as well as could be expected," he said. "Tom is pushing for the results of your investigation. But I have some concerns about that."

Astoria blinked at him, taken aback. "What concerns?"

"Well, not to put too fine a point on it, your ... *boyfriend* ... was the last person working on the automaton before it exploded." He said the word as if it left a bad taste in his mouth.

Astoria felt like she'd been punched in the stomach. Bertie *knew* about her and Michael? She had no idea what to say.

"How long has it been going on?"

She closed her eyes briefly; there seemed to be no point in denying it. "About six weeks. Since just after the ceilidh."

Bertie groaned. "Bloody hell, Astoria! After everything I went through for you last time—this is how you repay me?"

"I didn't exactly plan it, Bertie. It just happened."

"Well, you sure know how to pick 'em, don't you?"

"And what's that supposed to mean?"

"The man is a liability! Trouble follows everywhere he goes! Why would you voluntary hitch yourself to that?"

"That's bullshit and you know it," Astoria said, her gaze hardening. "He had nothing to do with what happened. Somebody is trying to use him as a scapegoat."

"Oh, now I've heard everything. And I was right—your judgement *is* compromised." He sighed, running a hand through his thinning hair. "You know," he said, "I promised your father I'd look after you and Jenny, and I've tried to. Most of the time it's been easy—you're so bright and so driven that I've hardly had to do anything, with the exception of that one time. But lately, something has changed. I feel like I don't know you any more."

He looked at her then with a mixture of anger and something else, almost sadness. "Do you know Braithwaite wants to close the mine down?" he asked.

Astoria gaped at him. "It's true, then?"

"Of course it's true. When he visited, he gave us three months to get our production targets up or we're done."

"Three months," she said. "That's ridiculous. How are we supposed to do that if the automatons keep breaking down?

Bertie sighed. "I tried to tell him that, but he wouldn't listen. You know what these corporate types are like. And now it looks like we're going to close—the three months is up in a couple of weeks, and Braithwaite is coming back to check on us. I hoped the accident might bring it to his attention a bit more, show him that we really do need the upgrade, but it hasn't. I suppose a near-miss isn't serious enough for the company to take action. And now with my two senior managers breaking the fraternisation rule, how am I ever going to be able to justify keeping this place open? They'll just use that as an excuse to shut us down."

"I had no idea," said Astoria. "Why didn't you tell me?"

"I don't know," Bertie said, rubbing his eyes. "I suppose I wanted to protect you."

"If you're going to have me as a manager, you have to trust me."

"I know," Bertie said. "But sometimes I still can't help picturing you as a little girl."

"Bertie, I'm thirty-three," Astoria said. "I have to start living my life before it passes me by."

"The mine *is* your life," Bertie said, "just like it's mine. I'm nothing without this place, you know that. And that's why this thing with Galbraith, whatever it is, needs to stop. Don't see him again. I'm sorry, Astoria, but unless you break it off with Galbraith I'm not going to be able to sort out that job for Jenny in Edinburgh. And I'll just have to call my contact at the university and ask about her scholarship, too."

"Are you ... *threatening* me?"

"That's not what this is. I just want what's best for you. And for everyone here. Your actions don't just affect you, you know. And the fact is, you knowingly flouted one of the company's most important rules with a full understanding of the consequences."

"You're asking me to choose between Michael and the security of my family? Bertie, please ..."

Bertie shrugged. "Being a leader means making choices—sometimes very difficult ones. Do you think I haven't given up everything for this place? I will *always* fight for it. And I'm asking you to fight for it too."

"I've heard enough," Astoria said, standing up. Her throat was beginning to ache with suppressed tears.

"This isn't over," Bertie said. "You're going to have to choose, just like I did."

Astoria turned on her heel and walked out of his office without another word, before she lost control completely.

"I thought you said he didn't know," she said to Miss Beaumont as she passed her in the outer office.

"I'm so sorry," Miss Beaumont said, but Astoria had already gone.

Chapter 21

For the rest of the day, Astoria avoided Michael as much as she could, Bertie's warning still ringing in her ears. But she knew she owed him an explanation for her odd behaviour, and it would have to be done sooner rather than later if she was to protect Jenny.

"Will I see you tonight?" Michael asked softly as they left the administration block at the end of their shift. Astoria swallowed the sudden lump in her throat, then nodded.

"I'll come by after dinner," she said. Michael smiled, setting butterflies fluttering in her stomach and adding to her mental anguish.

"I look forward to it," he said. Astoria gave a watery smile and fled, dread weighing down every step.

She ate hardly anything at dinner, her appetite completely gone. Leaving the dining hall, she walked to Michael's cottage as if she were approaching the gallows.

She knocked at the door and Michael opened it immediately, smiling and drawing her into an embrace.

"Astoria, what's wrong?" he asked, sensing her discomfort and pulling away.

"Nothing," she said, but he gave her a look and she knew that she owed it to him to be honest. She sighed.

"Bertie threatened me."

Michael gaped at her. "He did *what*? Why?"

"He said that if we don't stop seeing each other, he'll cancel Jenny's scholarship. And it goes without saying that we'll both be sacked. He thinks that we're a liability for breaking the fraternisation rule ... or at least that's what he's saying, anyway."

Michael scowled, taking her hand and leading her to the sofa. "I don't even know what to say. I didn't think he had it in him."

"The mine is his whole life," Astoria said, sitting down. "He never had a family of his own—all he does is work. And now Braithwaite is threatening to take that away. I can understand why he feels desperate."

"Hold on a minute—what's this about Braithwaite?"

Astoria sighed and relayed what Bertie had told her about the production targets.

"I see," Michael said at last. He took a deep breath. "I know I've put you in an impossible position," he said, "and I'm so sorry. Maybe it would actually be for the best if we took a break for a while. Just until he calms down."

Astoria closed her eyes briefly, biting her lip to keep the tears from falling. She nodded.

"Just so we're clear," she said, "if I had a choice, that's not what I want. I want to be with you more than anything."

"I know," Michael said, drawing her close until their foreheads were touching. "But I know how hard you've worked to give Jenny the opportunities you never had. And I won't do anything to jeopardise that—no matter how much it goes against my own feelings. It wouldn't be fair on either of you."

"I'm so sorry."

"Oh, Storie," Michael said, pulling her into his arms. "It's not your fault. None of this is our fault. And when it's all over, I'll still be here."

Astoria kissed him. "I really don't deserve you."

"Rubbish. Don't ever let anyone tell you you're unworthy of being loved."

Astoria felt a sudden lump in her throat, but she couldn't bear the thought of crying in front of him. "I have to go," she whispered.

He nodded. "So this is goodnight?"

"Yes. But not goodbye. I promise."

Chapter 22

Astoria felt discombobulated and out of sorts all the next day. She'd cried herself to sleep the previous night, worried that she'd somehow ruined the best thing in her life. But she also knew she'd been honest with Michael—she couldn't give up Jenny's future for her own desires. For his part, Michael had been friendly but slightly distant, and he seemed to be out of the office more than usual, as if he was deliberately trying to give her space. She both appreciated his solicitude while also feeling his absence like a physical pain.

She leaned back in her chair, stretching her arms above her head. She still wasn't used to spending all day at a desk; it made her body tense up and ache in ways she'd never experienced, despite a lifetime of manual labour. Michael had gone down the pit for his weekly technical inspection of the equipment, and she almost envied him. She wondered if Bertie would mind if she took a short walk.

She was just getting up to ask him when a klaxon rang out, piercing the still air. Astoria's heart began to pound, increasing with each warning blast until it was thundering in her ears. She dashed out of her office just as Bertie's door was flung open and he emerged, cursing the air blue. Not bothering to wait for him, Astoria ran out of the administration block and pounded up the hill, grateful that she hadn't lost all her fitness in her move to a desk job. She knew what that dreadful sound portended. And Michael was down there.

All around her, off-duty night-shift miners were streaming up the hillside. Many looked bleary, having been wrenched from sleep by the siren. But they'd trained for this, and they knew time was critical. For some of the older ones, this wasn't the first time they'd had to do it for real.

By the time Astoria reached the mine entrance, there was already a small gaggle of people there, with more arriving every minute. Some of the miners were pulling on overalls and protective gear. Bertie hadn't yet arrived, but Astoria saw that Harry Murdoch, as night-shift supervisor, was directing operations.

Relief dawned on his face as he caught sight of her, and he hurried over.

"What happened?" Astoria asked, pushing down thoughts of Michael and fighting to stay calm. The best thing she could do for him now was to get the job done.

"Some sort of explosion, I think," Harry said. "I only got here a few minutes before you did, but that's what the lads who got out are saying."

He nodded towards a small group of miners, all covered in crystal dust and with varying degrees of injury, who were being helped by their fellows. Astoria swallowed.

"All right," she said. "You take charge of the survivors and coordinate the medics. Get a medical area cordoned off and start sorting people out. Get the worst ones to the infirmary. Anyone who comes out of that pit goes directly to you to be crossed off the roll. I need to know how many we've still got down there. You know how it goes."

Harry nodded wordlessly. Astoria knew this wasn't his first rescue; he'd been there at the last one, four years ago, and he knew what needed to be done. He'd already started marshalling the rescue teams. She ran over to where they were standing, trying to appear more confident than she felt. Many of them looked relieved to see someone in a position of authority, and she wondered briefly where Bertie was. But she couldn't think about that now.

"Right," she said as they crowded around her, "who volunteers to go in?" Other mine managers might force their people down the pit in situations like this, but it was one of Bertie's central tenets that nobody went into a dangerous environment without consenting to it, and she wasn't about to break that now.

Every miner in the team raised their hand, and Astoria felt a lump in her throat. Not a single one of them would leave their fellows to die in there without at least trying to do something about it.

"Kirk, McGuinness, Jacobs, Brown," she said, pointing to them. "You're the scout party. Go in as far as you safely can—no further, mind—and report back on what we're dealing with. You six—" she gestured at another group—"are the extraction team. Go and help those who are coming out under their own steam. Take the stretchers; we'll probably need them soon for those we have to bring out ourselves. The rest of you, get your gear on and get ready to go. We'll move as soon as we know how bad it is." All of them nodded and went about their duties with calm efficiency. Astoria took a deep breath and headed over to the medical area. There were more miners there than she'd expected. She did a quick headcount and realised that most of the shift was there. Medics were patching up cuts and scratches, but only a few of the miners seemed to be more seriously injured—mostly broken bones and head wounds, from what she could tell. She searched the crowd for Michael but couldn't find him. But caked in sparkling thermocrystal dust they all looked the same; it didn't mean he wasn't there, she reasoned, trying to tamp down a rising panic.

"Who are we missing?" she asked Harry, who was studying his list.

"Only three," he said. "Tom Jenkins, poor lad."

Astoria felt sick, recalling how excited Tom had been when he'd learned of his promotion to day-shift supervisor. "Who else?"

"Jock Adams." *No*, Astoria thought. Harry looked at her steadily. "And ... Michael Galbraith."

Astoria felt the world lurch. Harry must have sensed her shock, because he glanced at her with concern. "Are you all right?"

Astoria swallowed and raised her chin. "I'm fine. The scouts are going in as we speak; we'll know more shortly."

"We'll bring them home, Storie," Harry said gently. "One way or another."

She nodded. *One way or another.*

Suddenly there was a shout of "Scout!" from the mine entrance. Astoria ran across just as McGuinness emerged. There was no sign of the other three.

"Report," Astoria said. McGuinness gasped as she caught her breath.

"There's a chunk of ceiling come down in the tunnel at the entrance to the main pit," she said. "We couldn't tell how deep the blockage is, but it goes right the way across the tunnel. But we found two survivors. The others are bringing them out now."

"Good work," Astoria said, patting the girl's shoulder. She wanted to ask more questions, but a commotion at the entrance diverted her attention. There were people appearing from within the cloud of dust. As it cleared, she could see Jock, hopping on his right leg, with his arm braced around Kirk's shoulders. She peered into the gloom. Where was the other survivor? And who was still down there? Then she saw Jacobs and Brown, carrying a body between them. A team of medics hurried over with a stretcher, and as they laid the man on it Astoria saw his face. *Michael.*

She gasped, her hand over her mouth. She wanted to run to him, to check his pulse with her own hands, to reassure herself that he lived. She wanted to kiss him back to life like a fairytale prince. But she couldn't, not while there was work left undone.

"What about Tom Jenkins?" she asked Kirk as he helped Jock sit down in the medical area.

Kirk shook his head. "No sign of him, I'm afraid."

"He's still in there," Jock said, wincing as a medic cut the laces on his boot. "We were working on an automaton with Galbraith when something went bang and the roof started to crumble." He licked his lips, and the medic handed Astoria a flask of water. She held it out to Jock.

"But everyone else got out?" she asked as he drank.

Jock nodded. "He and Galbraith between them got everyone out. But just before they got out themselves, the tunnel started to come down." He coughed. "It caught Jenkins's leg. Galbraith started trying to dig him out with his bare hands. I've never seen anything like it, and I've seen a few things in my time." Astoria started, realising that tears were welling in Jock's eyes. "He might have even managed it too, but another chunk came down. It buried Jenkins, and Galbraith was caught in the head by debris. I don't know how he wasn't buried too. I tried to pull him out as best I could, but he was unconscious by then and he's a big bloke. And then I tripped on a chunk of rock. My bloody leg gave way and I couldn't get up again."

"That's how we found them," Kirk said. "Lying in the tunnel, just this side of the cave-in."

"You did well, Jock," Astoria said, smiling at him. "I have to go, but I'll be back soon, all right?" She tried not to look across at where Michael lay, medics swarming around him.

"Right," she said as she rejoined the rescue team. "We're looking for Tom Jenkins. Apparently he was buried under the rockfall. We'll treat this as a rescue operation for now, but ... I think we all know it's more likely to be a recovery."

The miners nodded silently and began hefting their gear.

Chapter 23

The next few hours passed in something of a blur. Even after Bertie turned up, Astoria remained the de facto leader of the rescue operation. She wondered where he'd been, but didn't have time to dwell on it. Three teams of miners took it in turns to carefully excavate and shore up the collapsed tunnel. It was slow going; the last thing anybody wanted was for more rubble to fall in on them.

Shortly after midnight, a cry went up, and an hour later a team emerged, carrying Tom Jenkins's body on a stretcher. It was clear he'd been killed instantly. As they passed, miners removed their helmets in an impromptu guard of honour. Many wept openly on each other's shoulders. Tom had been affable and well-liked. Astoria, awash with a complicated mix of grief for Tom and worry about Michael, wished she could join them, but she bit her lip and held fast. She had to stay strong for her team.

"Storie," Bertie said, appearing at her side, "go home." Astoria glanced at him. He looked haggard, as if he'd aged a decade in the space of a single night. She caught a whiff of alcohol on his breath and frowned. Had Bertie been *drinking?* Surely not. She shook her head, distrustful of his sudden compassion.

"I insist," Bertie said. "I'll handle things here. You've done more than enough for today. We'll just secure the site and then I'll send the rest of them home too. Now that we've found Jenkins, everything else can wait. Get some sleep."

Astoria looked at him for a long moment, then she nodded. She set off down the hill with some of the others from the search team. Nobody spoke, but as she turned off towards the infirmary a couple of them thumped her on the back in a wordless gesture of solidarity.

The infirmary was dimly lit and quiet. Peering through the ward door, Astoria was rather relieved to find only five beds occupied. The rest of the wounded had clearly been well enough to be patched up and sent home. Jock was there, his left leg swathed in white and elevated in a sling, but when she looked for Michael she couldn't see him. Her heart began to pound.

"Astoria?"

She turned and saw Matron coming down the corridor, a tired smile on her face.

"Hello, Louisa." The two of them had grown up in the village together; Louisa had started as a trainee nurse at the hospital the same year Astoria had first gone down the pit.

"How are things at the site?" Louisa asked.

Astoria sighed and shook her head. "They're packing up for the night. It's going to take a week or so to clear it, I think."

"And how are you?"

It was impossible to lie to Louisa; many years of caring for people at their most vulnerable had given her an incredible depth of insight. Astoria bit her lip, suddenly feeling perilously close to tears.

"I ... I don't know."

Louisa squeezed her hand. "You should get some rest. But I assume you're not here to chitchat with me."

"I was hoping to see Michael Galbraith."

"Ah, yes. We've put him in the private room so he doesn't disturb the other patients."

"What do you mean?"

"He regained consciousness and he's doing well, but he was in a lot of pain so we've given him a sleeping draught. But it can cause hallucinations. They often get a bit loud when they start coming out of it."

"Can I see him?"

"It's late, Storie. It'd be better for both of you if you get some sleep and come back in the morning."

At this final rebuff, Astoria felt her control break. The tears began to run unchecked down her cheeks. She knew Michael was in good hands, but the thought of not being able to see for herself that he was all right was too much for her. And who knew what could change overnight?

The matron took her elbow and gently steered her into the hallway, away from the other patients.

"Want to tell me what's going on?"

"Please, Louisa," Astoria begged, fighting back a sob. "He's ... he's like family to me." As the words echoed round the hall, she realised they were true.

Louisa gave her a shrewd look, clearly getting the measure of the situation. "All right," she said at last. She led Astoria down the hallway to an open door. "Don't wake him," she said. "He needs to rest. I'll be back in half an hour to check on him."

Impulsively, Astoria grasped her hand. "Thank you."

Louisa smiled. "He's lucky to have you," she said. "And you know you can rely on my discretion. I remember what happened last time."

"Nobody else knows," Astoria said, although she remembered her encounter with Jock and wondered if that was true.

"And we'll keep it that way," Louisa replied, closing the door behind her.

Chapter 24

In the dim light of a single thermocrystal lamp, Astoria could see Michael lying on his back in a narrow bed. He had a bandage around his head and there were cuts and scrapes all along his arms and on his face, but his breathing was deep and steady. She pulled a hard wooden chair over to the bedside and sat down, gently taking his hand in hers. He stirred, and she held her breath. Mindful of not waking him, she didn't say anything, just sat. And in the dark and quiet, the tears she'd been fighting back for hours finally began to flow. She wept silently until there was nothing left, then laid her head on the bed, listening to Michael's breathing. She felt hollowed out and numb. She wasn't sure if she'd ever be able to feel anything again.

She was woken by the early-morning sun streaming in at the window. The muscles in her neck and back protested sharply as she sat up. Someone—Louisa, probably—had draped a blanket around her shoulders. Astoria shook it off and stood up, stretching to ease her stiff neck. She felt groggy and exhausted, and for a moment she wondered if the events of the previous day had just been a bad dream. But no; Tom Jenkins was dead, and here was Michael, having barely dodged death himself. Astoria felt as if every nerve in her body had been scraped red-raw. She walked over to the window, looking out at the gold-drenched hillside. She knew there were things she needed to do, but it was still very early; no one would begrudge her another hour here.

A sound from the bed made her turn. Michael's eyes were still closed, but he was tossing his head on the pillow and mumbling something unintelligible. Then he began to whimper, the sound of a terrified child. Astoria hurried back to her chair and took his hand.

"Michael," she said softly. "It's all right, my love. I'm here." She was momentarily surprised at hearing herself use such an endearment; after last time, she'd convinced herself she'd never fall in love again. And yet she *did* love Michael, she realised. Losing him would be like cutting out a piece of her heart.

He let out an agonised yell, and Astoria jumped. She squeezed his hand in what she hoped was a reassuring manner. The door opened and one of the medics came in, followed closely by Louisa. The matron smiled encouragingly.

"It's all right," she said. "It's just the sedative wearing off. He'll be awake soon." She placed her fingers on his wrist to check his pulse, then opened his eyelids and flashed a small thermocrystal torch into his eyes. "He's doing fine," she said. "Come and get me when he wakes. He'll probably be a bit disoriented to start with."

Astoria nodded, taking a deep breath. This waiting was agonising. Michael continued to toss and turn, but as she watched, his eyes fluttered open. He blinked, as if unsure where he was, then looked around him, terror dawning on his face. Astoria squeezed his hand.

"Hello there," she said with a smile, standing up so she was in his line of sight. "Welcome back."

"Storie?" he said hoarsely. He lifted his hand to her cheek, running his fingers over her face as if to confirm she was real. "Am I ... dead?"

"No, my love," she said, kissing his palm. "You're very much alive. You're in the infirmary. You've had a bump on the head." She poured a glass of water from the jug on the nightstand and held it to his lips. "Drink."

Michael sipped, and some of the terror left his eyes. "I ... saw you ..." he said. "You were trapped under the rock, and I tried to dig you out, but ... I couldn't ..."

"It wasn't me," she reassured him. "The medics gave you something to help you sleep. You were dreaming. That's all." She'd wait until he was stronger to tell him about Tom, she thought.

"You're alive?"

"Yes, my love. We're both alive and kicking. Now, I need to tell them you're awake. Will you be all right on your own for a few minutes?"

He nodded, and Astoria left to find Louisa. The matron was in the main ward with Jock, who was sitting up in bed and looking much more like his old self.

"Come to see if I'm still alive?" Jock said with a grin.

Astoria smiled distractedly. "Nah," she said. "It'd take more than a little cave-in to kill you."

Louisa glanced up from her inspection of Jock's broken leg. "Is he awake?"

Astoria nodded.

"All right. I'll be right there."

"Won't you stay awhile and keep a fellow amused, Storie?" Jock asked, almost pleadingly.

Astoria bit her lip. "I'm sorry, Jock, I really can't right now," she said, glancing back over her shoulder towards Michael's room. "I'll pop by later, I promise."

Jock's face fell. "Ah," he said. "I see." But Astoria, distracted by a sound from down the hall, barely heard him. She turned and hurried back towards Michael's room.

When she entered, she found one of the young medics there, propping up pillows and helping Michael to sit up. Already he'd regained some colour in his cheeks, although there were dark shadows under his eyes. Louisa came in, checked him over thoroughly, and seemed pleased with what she saw.

"Another day in here and you'll be right as rain," she said. "As long as you rest, mind. If I think you're overdoing it, I'll have to bar visitors." She gave them both a pointed look.

"Yes, ma'am," Astoria said, biting back a smile, and the matron left, taking the young medic with her.

"Do you remember what happened?" Astoria asked, resuming her seat by the bedside.

Michael frowned to himself. "Bits and pieces," he said. "There was a bang, and the ceiling fell in, and then ..." He looked at her, a look of creeping horror on his face. "Oh, God," he said. "I remember now. It wasn't you under that rubble—it was Tom Jenkins. Is he all right?"

Astoria closed her eyes briefly, taking a deep breath. She couldn't lie to him. "I'm so sorry," she said. "Tom didn't make it."

"No ..." he said, putting his head in his hands.

Astoria sat on the edge of the bed and wrapped her arms around him. "You did everything you could," she said softly, holding him close as he wept. "And Jock told me how you got the others out. You saved many lives yesterday."

"But not Tom."

"Nobody could have saved Tom," she said, remembering the awful crush injuries she'd seen. "It was instant. He didn't suffer." Tears sprang to her own eyes, and for a long time they just held each other.

When they pulled away, Michael looked exhausted. "Why don't you get some more sleep?" Astoria suggested.

He nodded, lying back against the pillows. "Will you ... stay with me?" he murmured drowsily.

Astoria smiled, touching his cheek. "Of course."

He leaned into her hand. "Storie?"

"Mm?"

"I love you."

Her heart swelled with happiness. "I love you too, my darling. Sleep well." She kissed his cheek as his eyelids fluttered closed.

Chapter 25

Astoria waited until she was sure Michael was sleeping soundly before tiptoeing out of the room. She felt physically exhausted and emotionally wrung out, but the day was just beginning and she knew she had too much work to do. Rest would have to wait. But Michael was conscious and Louisa seemed to think he'd make a full recovery. That knowledge lifted a weight from her shoulders. And he loved her. She wrapped the memory of his words around herself like a shield against whatever was to come.

As she passed the doorway to the general ward, she heard someone calling her name. She poked her head around the door and saw Jock sitting up in bed, looking for her. She fought down an irrational surge of frustration. Jock was one of her oldest friends and he'd been there for her during some tough times. It wasn't fair to resent him for wanting her company when he'd just been through something terrible himself.

"How're you feeling?" she asked, walking over to his bed. She noticed with relief that there was now only one other bed occupied, which meant that all the other injured men were well enough to have been discharged. She glanced over and realised with a jolt that the other patient was Simon

Thomas, the young lad she'd interviewed about the previous incident. He had a bandage wrapped around his head and was still looking slightly dazed. She smiled and gave him a little wave.

Jock shrugged. "Fine," he said. "They're sending me home this morning. Is Galbraith awake?"

Astoria nodded. She couldn't bring herself to say more—her feelings were still too raw.

"Listen, Storie," Jock said, leaning forward and lowering his voice, "there's something you should know about him."

Astoria frowned but said nothing.

"He was working on an automaton right before the roof came down," Jock said. "Jenkins and I were nearby. There was a flash or a spark or something from the automaton, and then the explosion. And then the roof caved in."

"What are you saying?"

"Well ... just that it's the second incident in as many months involving Galbraith and an automaton. Once can be an accident, but twice ...?"

"You're saying he deliberately sabotaged the equipment? That's quite an accusation."

"I'm not *accusing* anybody," Jock said, sitting up straighter. "I'm just saying that it's an odd coincidence. I know it's probably not what you want to hear."

"There'll be an investigation. You know that."

"And who will be doing it? You?"

Astoria sighed. "I don't know. Possibly."

"Is that a good idea? I mean, you're not exactly impartial, are you?"

Astoria felt what was left of her self-control snap. "For God's sake, Jock, the dust hasn't even settled yet! I don't know who will be doing the investigation, but if you have a problem with it you can take it up with Bertie."

"Storie ..."

"I have to go. There's a lot to do."

"Wait ..."

"Goodbye, Jock."

Astoria was still seething as she left the infirmary and climbed the hill towards the mine. She knew that Jock had every right to question whether Michael was involved in the accident, but his implication that she wasn't objective enough to do her job still rankled. She sighed, rubbing her eyes. Maybe he was right. She wasn't thinking clearly. She pushed all thoughts of Michael and Jock aside and focused on the crunch of her boots on the rough road. One thing at a time.

When she reached the entrance to the mine she was surprised to see how quiet it was. She'd expected a hive of activity as workers cleared the rockfall, but instead there was only a small team working in the tunnel near the entrance, with Harry Murdoch supervising.

"Morning, Harry," she said, walking up beside him.

Harry glanced at her. "Morning, Storie," he said. "How's Michael?"

"On the mend," Astoria said. She didn't trust herself to elaborate without breaking down. "What's going on?" she asked, to steer the conversation into more comfortable territory.

Harry sighed. "We're just checking the reinforcements from yesterday." He turned to look at her. "Then we're downing tools, I'm afraid."

Astoria's eyebrows rose. "You're going on strike?"

Harry nodded. "Nobody wanted it to come to this. But nothing changed after that near-miss, despite our warnings, and now Tom's dead." He stopped and swallowed. "There's no way I'd ask anyone to go into that pit until we know for sure that it's safe. Even if they were willing to go, which they aren't. We put it to the vote this morning."

Astoria said nothing. In her heart she was on the side of the miners and always would be. But an industrial dispute probably wouldn't be in any of their long-term interests either.

"What are your demands?" she asked.

"We want a thorough investigation," Harry said. "That means understanding exactly what happened and how to prevent it happening again. More than that, we want it acted on, not just meaningless words. And we want the entire automaton fleet replaced. We've been telling you the things are death traps for years but nothing has been done about it. It's not good enough."

"And what has Bertie said to this?"

"We're meeting with him shortly," Harry said. "So I guess we'll see. Excuse me." He strode over to where one of the miners was examining a wooden beam, leaving Astoria standing speechless in his wake.

Walking back down the hill, Astoria was so physically and emotionally exhausted she could barely see straight. She wanted to see Michael, was aching to see him, but she knew she'd be no good to him in her current state. She needed to eat and sleep, but more than anything what she wanted was a good cry.

As she opened the door to the administration block Miss Beaumont looked up sharply, taking in her dishevelled appearance and the shadows under her eyes.

"Go home, Astoria," she said in a voice that brooked no opposition.

"But I've got work to do ..."

"And it won't get done in your current state. Go home, and I don't want to see you back here today, understand?"

"Yes, ma'am." She nodded gratefully, too tired to argue.

She was walking through the accommodation block, thinking longingly of her bed, when she heard somebody calling out her name.

"Storie!"

She turned and saw Jock, levering himself along on crutches, his leg sporting a white plaster cast. He must have just been discharged from the infirmary. She sighed, but stopped and waited for him to catch her up.

"They let you out—congratulations," she said, forcing a smile.

"Thanks. Listen, I just wanted to apologise ... about before. I don't want to fight with you."

Astoria nodded wearily. "It's fine. I'm fine." But she couldn't stop her lip from trembling.

"Come on," Jock said, hopping over to a nearby bench. He sat down with a groan and patted the place next to him. Astoria followed, a little reluctantly.

"Are you sure you're fine?" Jock asked as she sat down beside him.

"Of course. I'm just tired."

"Is this about Galbraith? Louisa seems to think he's on the mend."

"You asked her about him?"

"Just out of professional interest."

Astoria sighed. Suddenly, the burden felt too much to bear alone. "Bertie knows about us," she said. "Me and Michael."

"Ah. And?"

"He threatened to cancel Jenny's scholarship if we don't stop seeing each other."

Jock whistled. "I'm sorry, Storie. That's rough."

"I just don't know what to do, Jock." The admission seemed to open a floodgate, and suddenly she couldn't stop the tears from falling. She buried her face in her hands and wept. Then she felt an arm about her shoulders and Jock pulled her against his side.

"It's all right, sweetheart," he said. "Everything is going to be fine."

The term of endearment startled her, slowing her sobs to a hiccupping cough. She looked up at Jock and saw a depth of feeling in his eyes that she'd never noticed before.

"I should go," she said, slipping out of his embrace.

"Storie, wait," Jock said. "It doesn't have to be this hard, you know."

"What doesn't?"

"Life. You've got everything you could ever want right here. A great job, your family, a community of people who look up to you. Me. Don't let big ideas from Edinburgh blind you to what's really important."

"If by 'big ideas' you mean Michael, then I assure you I'm not. And I don't have to explain myself to you."

"Is he worth it, Storie? Is a fling of a few weeks really worth compromising your family's future? Think of Jenny."

"Leave my sister out of this."

Jock held up his hands in reconciliation. "All I'm saying is it doesn't have to be this way. There are people here who've known you forever and who love you. Haven't I been a good friend to you? I picked up the pieces from last time and I stuck by you when nobody else would. I just hoped that one day you'd see that, not pass me over for some pretty-boy engineer from the big city who needs help tying his own shoelaces."

Astoria frowned, anger burning away her fatigue. "So you've been my 'friend' all these years just because you wanted to sleep with me?"

"Of course not. I've loved you since our school days—I only hoped that one day you might grow to feel the same."

She sighed. "You're right—you *have* been a good friend to me. But I always assumed that was enough in its own right. I've never seen you as anything more; you must have known that. I would never want to hurt you, but I can also never be more than your friend, Jock."

"He doesn't deserve you, you know. Is it any wonder accidents follow wherever he goes? Quite the coincidence, don't you think?"

Astoria didn't even dignify that with a response. Without another word she turned and headed for her room, leaving Jock staring after her.

Chapter 26

Astoria returned to her room intending only to splash some water on her face before going to see Michael. But she made the mistake of lying down on the bed—just for a few minutes, she told herself. When she woke, the late afternoon light was slanting through her window and someone was banging on her door. She must have slept for at least three hours, she realised, blinking groggily. The conversation with Jock came trickling back, and her heart sank. She hoped it wasn't him at the door, and considered just lying quietly and pretending she wasn't home.

"Astoria, pumpkin, are you in there? It's Mother."

Astoria sprang up in surprise. Her mother never visited the camp, and she'd sent a message in the aftermath of the accident to let her family know she was fine. What on earth could have brought Mary to her door?

"Mum!" she exclaimed, opening the door. "What are you doing here?"

"Hello, darling," Mary said, pulling her into an embrace, and Astoria had to swallow hard to tamp down the feelings that suddenly threatened to spill over. "Can I come in?"

"Of course." She ushered her mother to the only chair and perched on the end of the bed.

"I'll not mess about," she said. "But I heard … something … about Bertie. I heard he's pressuring you to make some decisions you perhaps don't want to make?"

"Who told you that?"

"Euphemia Beaumont came to see me this morning. She's worried about you. And so am I."

Despite her best efforts, Astoria felt the tears beginning to trickle down her cheeks. She'd cried more in the last twenty-four hours than she had in the preceding twelve months. "I don't know what to do, Mum," she said. "I love Michael, I do. But I can't jeopardise the family like that—everything Jenny's worked for. Everything *we've* worked for."

Mary sat beside Astoria on the bed and wrapped her arms around her. "I know I wasn't there for you when your father died, sweetheart," she said. "I wasn't there in the way I should have been, to stop your sacrificing yourself like you did. But I'm here now. And we'll find a way, even if Bertie makes good on his threat."

"How?"

"We'll figure it out. Penrose women are built tough." She took out her handkerchief and wiped Astoria's tears away. "It's time to stop letting other people run your life, Storie. If you really love Michael and he loves you, then he's your family too now. You don't have to choose. You just have to do what you know to be right."

After saying goodbye to her mother, Astoria had dinner at the mess and then went to see Michael. She was initially a bit nervous about what would happen if Bertie found out, but as her mother had said, she couldn't give in to fear. She had to live her life, regardless, and so she squared her shoulders and set off down towards the infirmary.

There were very few people around and nobody seemed to notice her. When she got to the hospital, there was only one person in the bed on the ward: Simon Thomas.

"Miss Penrose," he called as she passed. Astoria paused and then stepped into the ward.

"Hello, Simon," she said. "How are you feeling?"

"Much better, thank you," he said. "They're saying I might be able to go home tomorrow."

"I'm very glad to hear that," Astoria said. "It must be lonely being the only one left here."

Simon shrugged. "It's fine," he said with a smile. Then his face creased with worry. "Actually, I've been hoping you'd stop by," he said. "There's something I need to talk to you about."

"Is everything all right?"

The lad's hands twisted in the blanket. "Do you remember when we spoke after the first accident, and I told you I saw someone working on the automaton but I didn't know his name?"

"Of course," Astoria said. "You said you'd probably know him if you saw him again, though."

Simon nodded, anxiety clouding his features. "That's just it," he said. "I *have* seen him. He was here."

"You mean a visitor?"

Simon shook his head. "No, a patient. He went home this morning. He was in that bed over there and he had a broken leg." He pointed across the room to the bed where Jock had been.

Astoria's stomach swooped as if the floor had suddenly dropped out from under her. "You're sure that was the man you saw? It couldn't have been someone else?"

"I'm positive," Simon said. "When I heard him speaking, I recognised his voice."

Astoria closed her eyes briefly. "Thank you," she said. "That's a huge help. Really."

"I'm glad," Simon said, looking as if a weight had fallen from his shoulders. "I know you're here to see Mr Galbraith, so I won't keep you. I just thought you should know."

"Thank you." Astoria smiled. "I hope you get to go home soon."

"Me too. Goodnight, Miss Penrose."

"Goodnight, Simon."

Still reeling, Astoria walked down the hall to Michael's room. He was sitting up in bed eating his dinner and he looked much, much better.

His face lit up when he saw her walk in. "Storie!" he exclaimed when he saw her.

"How are you feeling?" She asked, bending down to kiss him. "You're looking well."

"Much better," he said. "It's been a good day. In fact, Louisa said they're discharging me tomorrow."

"That's great news!" Astoria exclaimed.

"Are you sure you should be here?" Michael asked, worry clouding his face. "I mean, what if Bertie finds out?"

Astoria took a deep breath and raised her chin. "You know what," she said, "I've been thinking about it, and I'm done bending my life out of shape for this company and its stupid rules. I'm not an automaton—neither of us are. We're human and we should be allowed to have our own lives. Just because Bertie has made the company his life doesn't mean I have to, and it certainly doesn't mean you have to."

"Are you sure? You know we're probably going to get sacked."

"I know," she said. "But I think it's time to move on anyway. Mum came to see me today. She refuses to let Bertie hold her and Jenny hostage like that. And with them behind me I know I can do anything."

Michel squeezed her hand. "I know how hard it is for you to do this," he said. "And I think you're incredibly brave. And wherever you want to go, I'll be there."

"I know," said Astoria, smiling. "I think it'll be for the best, you know. It'll be scary leaving here, but eventually you have to step out of your comfort zone if you're going to grow. I think that time has come."

"And what about the investigation?" Michael asked.

Astoria shrugged. "There isn't an investigation at the moment."

"What?"

"Bertie thinks I'm compromised, so he's used that as an excuse to put it on hold. And he's probably right. But the miners are striking because they want a full investigation, among other things. Honestly, I don't understand anymore. And Braithwaite arrives tomorrow."

"It doesn't make any sense," Michael said. "I would have thought an investigation would help Bertie's case. He wants new automatons, doesn't he? I thought he wanted to show Braithwaite just how unsafe the conditions are.

"Unless he's afraid of what it'll find."

"You mean sabotage?"

"Well, we already know the previous accident probably wasn't an accident," Astoria said. "And I'm worried that Bertie's going to try and blame it on you, particularly because you were in there again this time around."

"I wasn't even working on the automaton this time," Michael said. "Not the one that exploded, anyway. There was a second one that had broken down—that was the one I was dealing with."

"Oh. That's very strange. So who was working on the other one?"

Michael looked at her. "Jock was," he said.

Chapter 27

"I have to go," Astoria said, scrambling to her feet. "There's something I need to do."

"Storie, wait."

"I'm sorry," she said. "It's not you, I promise, but it's very important." She kissed him and left the room. On the way out of the infirmary, she stuck her head into Louisa's office. Luckily, the matron was there.

"Can you make sure that Michael gets to the Braithwaite meeting tomorrow?" She asked with no preamble.

"Well, yes, of course," Louisa said. "He's doing really well. I was planning to discharge him tomorrow morning."

"It's vital that he's there," Astoria said.

"Storie, what's going on?" Louisa asked.

"I can't explain right now, but can you just make sure it happens?"

"Of course."

"Thank you."

Astoria left the infirmary and walked up the hill to the dormitories. She paused for a moment outside Jock's door, took a deep breath, and knocked.

"Storie," Jock said in surprise as he opened the door. "What are you doing here?" He looked shaken to see her, probably still reflecting on the events of the morning, she guessed.

"We need to talk," Astoria said, trying and failing to keep the cold out of her voice.

"Of course. Why don't you come in? Neil's out at the moment, so it's just me."

Astoria stepped inside, still wondering whether this was really a good idea.

"How can I help you?" Jock asked as they stood awkwardly just inside the door.

Astoria sighed. "I know you were involved in those accidents," she said.

"What do you mean?"

"Come on, Jock. I've got evidence the first automaton was tampered with, and witnesses in each case who saw you working on the automatons just before they exploded. I know they weren't accidents. Why did you do it, Jock?"

"I don't know what you're talking about."

"Bullshit."

Jock raised an eyebrow. "Do you have any proof?"

"Like I said, I have witnesses."

"That's circumstantial," Jock said.

"Maybe," Astoria said. "But I just need to understand. You're a company man—you always have been. You love this place. Why would you risk the safety of your friends and your own life like that? It just doesn't make sense to me."

Jock was silent for a long moment. "I heard Braithwaite wanted to close the mine," he said eventually. "I thought that maybe if they saw that there was a risk to safety, they'd put a bit more money into the automatons. I meant it to look like an accident."

Something about that explanation niggled at Astoria; she felt like she'd heard it before, and recently, but she couldn't remember where. She pushed it aside.

"But you tried to frame Michael. Why?"

Jock scowled. "Why do you think, Astoria?" he snapped. "He took your job. And from the moment he arrived, I saw the way he looked at you. I thought that if it looked like he was involved, Bertie would have a good excuse to ship him back to Edinburgh."

Astoria took a deep breath and bit back her first reaction. There was no point re-litigating her relationship with Michael—it would get them nowhere, and she had more important things to do.

"Were you the only one involved?"

Jock looked shifty and wouldn't answer.

Astoria pursed her lips. "Jock, do you remember what they called me when I was on the crusade for better safety gear?"

Jock nodded. "They called you the Terrier."

"Yes, because I never give up, and you should know me well enough to know that I won't stop now. So I suggest you tell me the truth. You've made a run of bad decisions lately, but you've got a final chance to make things right. Tell me who you're working with."

Jock was silent for a long moment, as if weighing up his options. "All right," he said at last. "You'd better sit down."

Chapter 28

As soon as Astoria opened her eyes the next morning her mind started racing, sending her stomach fluttering with butterflies.

She'd stayed up late the night before, going over everything Jock had told her and formulating a plan. She knew it was crazy and she knew that it would almost certainly lead to her and Michael's sacking, but she couldn't see another way out. She lay in bed, going over and over it in her mind until her alarm clock rang and she decided it was best to get up and get on with the day.

She went to the mess out of habit, although her stomach was churning too much for her to eat any substantial breakfast. As she was leaving, she ran into Harry. He tipped his cap to her and held the door open to let her pass.

"Thanks," Astoria said with a tight smile. Then, on impulse, she added, "Do you know Braithwaite's coming today?"

Harry paused, then stepped outside with her, letting the door thud shut behind him. "I'd heard something about that," he said.

"Are you going to be there?"

"Maybe."

"Are you going to bring the lads?"

He gave her a shrewd look. "Maybe," he said again. "Why?"

Astoria shrugged. "No reason. I just think you should, that's all."

"Oh, really? What aren't you telling me?"

Astoria stared straight ahead, wondering how much to say. "It's to do with the accident," she said. "I just ... well, I could use your support."

"That's very cryptic," Harry said. "But you haven't led us wrong yet. So I suppose I'll see you there."

"Thank you," Astoria said, feeling a rush of relief that at least she wouldn't have to face it alone.

Donald Braithwaite wasn't due until nine o'clock, and the morning crept on interminably. Rather than go to the office and risk having to face Bertie, Astoria headed up the hill to her thinking spot. It was comforting to see the wide expanse of the world laid out before her feet, to remember that there was life outside the mine and that she would find it, one way or another.

As she watched, the red-gold Braithwaite airship came into view. She scrambled up and hurried down the hill. It was time for the reckoning.

As she raced towards the airfield, Astoria couldn't help but remember the last time, all those months ago, when she'd dashed to meet the Braithwaite airship. It was hard to believe how much had happened since then. She'd had no idea just how much that day would change her life. And now, here she was again: another airship and another momentous day, for better or for worse.

Bertie and Miss Beaumont were already standing at the mooring mast as the airship glided its way in. Astoria took a deep breath and walked slowly to join them, hoping she looked more composed than she felt. There was no sign yet of Michael, Harry or the miners. She felt anxiety begin to gnaw at her belly. This plan of hers suddenly seemed much more risky than even she had anticipated.

The airship took a while to come to a complete stop and tie up at the mooring mast. The gangway was lowered and passengers began to disembark. First came a couple of hangers-on whom Astoria didn't recognise. And then, there he was: Donald Braithwaite. He looked just as she remembered: thick, beefy and blustery, his red nose speaking to regular indulgence. But his small grey eyes were sharp, and Astoria began to realise exactly what she was up against.

"Mackenzie," he said to Bertie, disregarding any courtesy.

"Mr Braithwaite," Bertie said, reaching out his hand in greeting. Braithwaite shook it, but there was no friendliness between them.

"Will you come to my office?" Bertie asked.

"I'm not sure that's necessary," Braithwaite said. "This won't take long."

Astoria clenched her hands into fists. And then she heard a sound of footsteps coming up the hill. She turned and saw Harry at the head of a group of miners. And there was Michael walking beside him, with Louisa at his elbow.

She bit her lip. One way or another, they would now know the truth. There was no going back now.

"What's all this?" Braithwaite said, catching sight of the group.

"I guess they heard about your visit," Bertie said.

"Is this your doing?" Braithwaite asked.

"They deserve to hear about their fate directly from you, sir," Bertie said. He glanced Astoria questioningly. She just shrugged; it was easier to pretend to know nothing about it.

"Hmm," Braithwaite said. "Are you sure that's really how you want to do this?"

"I'm sure," Bertie said.

"Very well," Braithwaite said. "Have it your own way. And on your own head be it."

Three other men descended from the airship and walked over to where Braithwaite was standing. Astoria gasped as she realised they were policemen. Two of them were in uniform, while the other was in plain clothes.

Everybody else had noticed them too.

"Bertie, what are the police doing here?" Harry asked, frowning. Bertie silenced him with a look.

"I'd like to know the same thing actually," Braithwaite said, scowling. "It's been a damned expense and bother bringing them all the way up here, and you wouldn't even tell me why."

"It's about those accidents," Bertie said, "the ones that have caused us to miss our production targets. I have reason to believe they weren't accidents at all."

Astoria bit her lip, her heart thundering in anticipation.

"What do you mean?" Braithwaite said.

"Our preliminary investigations have shown that they were an act of sabotage," Bertie said, "by our new technical supervisor, Michael Galbraith."

Every head in the place turned towards Michael.

"No!" Astoria cried. "No, you're wrong!"

"Wrong?" Braithwaite said. "Miss Parker, isn't it? You think Mr Mackenzie is wrong?"

"Penrose," Astoria said, trying not to roll her eyes. "And yes, he's wrong. Not about the sabotage, but about the person. It wasn't Michael."

"What do you mean?" Braithwaite asked, looking unsettled.

"I'm afraid Astoria's judgment is clouded," Bertie interjected. "She and Mr Galbraith have been, shall we say, fraternising ... against company policy."

"That's got nothing to do with it," Astoria snapped. She took a deep breath, knowing she couldn't afford to lose control. "I know for a fact that it couldn't have been Michael. There are multiple circumstances, verified by multiple witnesses, that make it impossible. And, furthermore, I not only know that Michael wasn't the saboteur—I know who was."

"Rubbish," Bertie said. "You haven't spoken to me about any of this."

"No," Astoria said, "because it was *you*, Bertie."

A hush descended over the assembled company, as if everyone present was holding their breath.

"Me?" Bertie said, his laughter echoing hollowly across the airfield before dying away. "Storie, I don't know what you're talking about. It couldn't possibly have been me."

"You didn't do it yourself, of course," Astoria said. "But you ordered it, and I know who you got to do it for you."

"Poppycock," Bertie said. "You're just trying to protect your lover." He turned to Braithwaite. "I'm sorry, sir. We've made some questionable hiring decisions in the last six months, it seems, for which I naturally take full responsibility. My recommendation is that these good officers of the law take Mr Galbraith into custody until this is all sorted out. And Miss Penrose could be charged as an accomplice if she's not careful," he added, looking pointedly at Astoria, his lip curling.

It was like a knife to the heart, seeing the man she'd once regarded as a second father looking at her with such contempt. But she knew the truth, and she knew she had to uphold it, whatever the cost.

"It was you, Bertie," she said again.

Bertie raised an eyebrow. "But you have no proof, my dear," he said. "This is all just fanciful lies."

"No, it's not," said a voice from the crowd. Astoria jumped, her mouth dropping open as Jock strode forward.

"She's right," he said. "It was you, Bertie. I know it was you."

Bertie blanched.

"Now, enough of that," Braithwaite said, trying to wrest back control of the situation. "How do you know?"

Jock looked the company chairman dead in the eye. "Because he asked me to do it for him." He reached into his jacket and pulled out a notebook. "And I wrote everything down. Every single order, everything he asked me to do. He wanted to be able to pin it on Galbraith, just in case anybody suspected it wasn't an accident."

"But why?" Michael said, speaking for the first time. "What have I ever done to either of you?"

Jock shrugged. "You were just an easy target, mate," he said. "You're not from around here, and with your history … You just got caught in the crossfire."

Michael shook his head in disbelief.

Astoria felt sick. Her hands were shaking. Even though she'd known the truth, it was still awful to see it so publicly exposed in this way.

Bertie looked like a balloon that had had all the air let out of it; he suddenly seemed much older and smaller. "I was just trying to save this place," he said to Braithwaite. "You wouldn't listen, so I had to make you see. This mine has been my entire life, and you were going to take that away from me."

The police inspector stepped forward. "I think you'd better come with us, sir," he said. Bertie nodded, his shoulders slumping.

"And you too," the constable said to Jock.

"I'm so sorry," Jock said to Astoria as he passed. "I'm so sorry, Storie."

"I know," Astoria said, biting her lip.

Bertie looked her dead in the eye as the policemen led him up the gangway and onto the airship, but he said nothing. Astoria felt the look twisting like a knife in her belly. She balled her hands into fists in an attempt to stop them trembling.

"Now," Braithwaite said, "what's all this about fraternisation?"

Astoria lifted her chin. "With all due respect, sir, your rule is ridiculous."

"Oh, is it now?" Braithwaite asked, his voice dangerously soft.

"Yes. We're people, not automatons. You can't expect us to go through life devoid of any feeling, devoted only to your production targets. Bertie did, and look where that got him."

"Be very careful, Miss Penrose."

Astoria raised her chin. "Not to worry, sir. I'll save you the trouble of sacking me. I hereby resign, and I'll have it to you in writing before you go."

Braithwaite looked at her and shrugged. "Fine," he said. "It doesn't matter to me how you go. But I want you out by the end of the day, do you understand?" He turned to Michael. "You too."

Astoria swallowed, but there was no going back now. "Yes, sir," she said. "I understand." Michael also nodded his assent. The miners were all staring at her and she felt herself wilting under their gaze. She stared up at the airship's red-and-gold envelope, wishing she could fly away.

Braithwaite turned to Miss Beaumont. "Take me to the office, if you please," he demanded. "I need to look through Mackenzie's records and see exactly how much of a shambles this operation has become."

"Of course, sir," Miss Beaumont said. "Right this way." She gave Astoria a tight smile, then led the way down the hill, Braithwaite following.

As soon as he was out of sight, Astoria's control broke. Her ears ached with suppressed tears, and she wasn't sure how much longer she could hold them back. And then suddenly Michael was there beside her and she was turning to him, burying her face in his shoulder and sobbing as though her heart would break. Everyone was staring, but she no longer cared who saw. There were no secrets anymore.

Chapter 29

Astoria clung to Michael as if she were drowning. He held her close, worried she would shatter into pieces if he let her go. He was still reeling from the revelations about Bertie and Jock. And not only had Astoria figured out what they were doing, she'd sacrificed herself rather than let them bring him down too.

For a moment, he found himself wracked with guilt. If only he'd never come to the mine, none of this would have happened. She wouldn't have had to risk everything to defend him, and at such great cost. It felt just like how it had after the inverter disaster.

Yet, somehow, things were also different. He'd made plenty of mistakes in his life, to be sure, and he had paid for them over and over again. The inverter had been a disaster, the design flawed from the start, and yet it had been put into production and use because it had given the mining companies something that they desperately wanted—a quicker way to make money, with fewer people involved. He'd been too naive, too caught up in the thrill of the new technology, to understand what was happening, and anyone who had tried to ask the hard questions—people like Astoria—had been ignored. He still blamed himself to a certain extent for everything that had happened, but now he no longer *solely* blamed himself. And he realised he had Astoria to thank for that. She'd given him a perspective that he hadn't had before, had picked him up when he was at his lowest and given him a reason to keep going. Thanks to her, he now knew that starting over was survivable.

Michael clenched his jaw in determination. Whatever happened next was going to be hard, but it wasn't going to be impossible. They would both be fine—he'd see to that—but he also knew that it would take her a long time to believe it; after all, she'd just lost everything she'd ever known.

He pulled her closer, planting a kiss against her hair. Over the top of her head, he saw Harry Murdoch approaching. The other miners were all milling around, and he could hear the gossip flowing freely. This event would be talked about for years; it would go down in village lore as the day that changed everything.

Harry laid a gentle hand on Astoria's shoulder and she looked up, tears streaked down her face.

"I'll take it from here, Storie," he said, his voice warm. "You go and do what you need to do." Astoria nodded, her lip trembling.

"I'm sorry," she whispered. Michael took her hand and squeezed it.

"It'll work out," Harry said with a wry grin. "One way or another. We've all been through worse, and we'll all come out of it. This place was due for a shake-up anyway."

Astoria nodded again, and Harry turned back to the group of miners, beginning to corral them into something a bit more organised. Michael took a deep breath, feeling some of the tension loosen from his shoulders. He squeezed Astoria's hand again.

"Let's go home," he said.

They didn't return to the dorm; instead, they went down the hill to the village, to Mary's house. Michael had barely knocked on the door before it flew open and Astoria's mother tumbled out, pulling her daughter into an embrace.

"Oh, love," she said. "I heard what happened. It's going to be all right. You're so brave for doing what you did. Jenny and I are so proud of you, and we always will be."

Astoria nodded, tears springing to her eyes again.

"Thanks, Mum," she murmured.

Mary ushered her into the house, then turned to Michael.

"And I'm proud of you too," she said. "I know it may not be my place to say it, but you've done well."

"I'm not so sure about that," Michael said. "Everything was running smoothly before I got here, and now ... well ..."

"It would have come out sooner or later," Mary said with a shrug. "I never would have expected such a thing of Bertie. He's one of our oldest friends, and my darling Dan would be spinning in his grave to see what's become of him. But sooner or later the truth will out, and other people may have died before it did. He'd lost all sense of reason and he needed to be stopped. And you and Astoria did that."

Michael shook his head. "It wasn't me," he said. "It was all her. She's the one who figured it out."

"And who do you think gave her the courage to do it?" Mary asked, looking at him shrewdly. "So often we get our strength from those who are standing behind us."

"Thank you," Michael said, a lump coming into his throat. "I'll always look after her."

"I know," Mary said. "And I know she'll do the same for you. That's always been my dream, that she would find someone who loved her the way her father loved me. It's pretty rare, you know, but with you I think she might have."

Michael felt the colour rise to his cheeks; he didn't know what to say.

"Anyway, let's not stand here on the step all day," Mary said. "Come into the house and we'll have a cup of tea."

Astoria and Jenny had already set the kettle to boil, and after tea and biscuits Astoria began to look a bit more like her old self, much to Michael's relief. The rest of the day was spent in the kind of gentle family time he had no real recollection of ever experiencing, even as a child—eating, talking, playing cards and pottering in the garden. Occasionally he wondered what was happening up at the mine, but he didn't bring it up. He could tell by her face that Astoria needed this moment with her dearest ones; she'd been under such enormous strain for so long, and this was a balm to her soul.

They ate supper outside in the little garden, under the trees, and as the shadows began to lengthen talk turned to the future.

"So what will you do now?" Jenny asked.

"I don't know," Astoria said. "What would you have me do?"

Jenny glanced at her mother.

"Whatever you want," Mary said with steely resolve. "The two of us will be absolutely fine. You've looked after us so well for so long—now it's your turn. Go off and see the world."

MARY INVITED THEM TO stay the night, but there wasn't much room in the little cottage, and Astoria felt like she needed to spend one last night up at the camp. She knew that in the morning it would be time to pack her things; Braithwaite would have her escorted off the premises whether she was ready to go or not.

So after dinner she and Michael said their goodbyes and walked back up the hill to his cottage. There was no question about whether she'd come in—they both knew they couldn't bear to spend the night alone.

They said little as they got ready for bed, both overwhelmed with the events of the day. Snuggling under the covers, Astoria cuddled up to Michael, loving how her head fit neatly in the crook of his shoulder, how safe she felt wrapped in his arms.

"So what happens now?" she whispered.

"Well, you know those airships you always watch?" Michael said, and she could hear the smile in his voice through the darkness.

"Mm?"

"How about we get on one and see where it takes us?"

She took a big breath, simultaneously excited and terrified at the thought of it. "And then what?"

"Well, who knows?" Michael said. "Someone once told me there's a big wide world out there. Why don't we go and see some of it?"

Astoria laughed. "Why not?" she said. "There's nothing keeping me here anymore."

"Storie?" Michael said.

"Yes?"

"I hope you know how proud I am of you. Of everything that you've done for the mine—and for me. And I hope you know how much I love you."

Astoria smiled through the tears springing suddenly to her eyes. "I love you too," she said. She propped herself up on an elbow and looked at him. The moon shone through the window, lighting up his features, and she saw his answering smile. She bent down and kissed him deeply. "In fact, let me show you exactly how I feel."

Epilogue

My darling Astoria,

By the time this letter reaches you you'll be in London and, I must say, I'm missing you already. As you know, Jenny left for Edinburgh last week, and a mecha-pigeon arrived yesterday with a message assuring me she's settled in and is happy and well. The house feels rather empty without you both, but rest assured I've got plenty to be getting on with. Edith Murdoch and I have started a village improvement society, and my do we have our work cut out for us!

I know that, before you left, Harry told you of his plan to form a workers' cooperative to purchase the mine from the Braithwaite Corporation. While the process isn't yet complete, it turned out to be more straightforward than we'd hoped; after Mr Braithwaite reviewed the accounts, it seems he concluded that production was not high enough, and had no prospect of being high enough, to keep the mine as a going concern in the company's eyes. But Harry and the others in his team disagreed, mostly because their purposes are different. They're not looking to develop an international mining conglomerate, after all; they just want to build something that will make the village prosper, and they believe it's more than capable of that. They gave the workers the choice to stay and join the cooperative or leave, and almost all have chosen to stay. Harry is a fair and sensible leader, and I have every faith that both the mine and the village will thrive under him. He also says to remind you that there are jobs here for both you and Michael should you want them. And he's done away with the no-fraternisation rule!

All my love,
Mother

P.S. Write to your sister when you get the chance. I'm sure she'd love to hear from you. —M

DEAREST JENNY,

I'm sorry for not writing to you sooner; I'd intended to send you an account of our journey to London, but all was in such a whirlwind after we arrived that we almost missed our airship across the Channel! Thankfully we caught it just in time, and the flight to France was uneventful. We arrived in Paris two days ago, and oh, Jenny, what a magnificent city it is! It truly is the jewel of the Continent, and so romantic. Although on that score, perhaps, my opinion is not to be entirely trusted, for anywhere Michael is would be the most romantic place on Earth to me.

Yesterday we visited the site of the great Paris Exposition of 1889. I wish I could have seen it, for by all reports it was magnificent. Its grand centrepiece, of course, still stands—the Eiffel Tower, and the pictures do not do it justice. It truly is a feat of engineering. We ascended it, along with what seemed like half the city, and at the top, gazing out across the City of Light, Michael asked to make an honest woman of me (although, naturally, he phrased it far more eloquently, and I'm blushing even as I write this). I never, never expected to experience such happiness in a hundred lifetimes! And of course I said yes!

Tomorrow we board the Orient Express for our journey to Constantinople. I am very much looking forward to seeing some of the world's greatest cities: Munich, Vienna, Budapest, and of course Constantinople itself. I will write again once we arrive. From there we will make our way back across the Continent and return to Edinburgh to plan our wedding, at which I hope you will serve as my maid of honour. And after that, who knows? There's a big, wide world out here, Jenny, with so many grand adventures to be had. I hope you get to see it one day.

Your ever-loving sister,
Astoria